DR DECEMBER

BY

SANNE AMPTON

SNOWBOUND
WITH THE SURGEON

BY

ANNIE CLAYDON

MILLS & BOON

Married to the man she met at eighteen, **Susanne Hampton** is the mother of two adult daughters—one a musician and the other an artist.

The family also extends to a slightly irritable Maltese shih-tzu, a neurotic poodle, three elderly ducks and four hens that only very occasionally bother to lay eggs. Susanne loves everything romantic and pretty, so her home is brimming with romance novels, movies and shoes.

With an interest in all things medical, her career has been in the dental field and the medical world in different roles, and now Susanne has taken that love into writing Mills & Boon® Medical Romance™.

Cursed from an early age with a poor sense of direction and a propensity to read, **Annie Claydon** spent much of her childhood lost in books. After completing her degree in English Literature she indulged her love of romantic fiction and spent a long, hot summer writing a book of her own. It was duly rejected and life took over. A series of U-turns led in the unlikely direction of a career in computing and information technology, but the lure of the printed page proved too much to bear, and she now has the perfect outlet for the stories which have always run through her head, writing Medical Romance™ for Mills & Boon®. Living in London—a city where getting lost can be a joy—she has no regrets for having taken her time in working her way back to the place that she started from.

FALLING FOR
DR DECEMBER

BY
SUSANNE HAMPTON

Published in Great Britain 2014
by Mills & Boon, an imprint of Harlequin (UK) Limited,
Eton House, 18-24 Paradise Road, Richmond, Surrey, TW9 1SR

© 2014 Susanne Panagaris

ISBN: 978-0-263-90809-1

Harlequin (UK) Limited's policy is to use papers that are natural,
renewable and recyclable products and made from wood grown in
sustainable forests. The logging and manufacturing processes conform
to the legal environmental regulations of the country of origin.

Printed and bound in Spain
by Blackprint CPI, Barcelona

Dear Reader

In my third book, FALLING FOR DR DECEMBER, I am thrilled to introduce you to the New England town of Uralla, located three hundred miles north of Sydney. The name originates from a local Aboriginal word *'oorala'*, meaning 'a camp' or 'a place where people come together', and it is where my brother and his family live.

Late last year, the wedding of my very handsome nephew Myles to his gorgeous fiancée, Anne, gave me the opportunity to travel to Uralla and experience a true country wedding. Myles—along with my other equally handsome nephews, and his groomsmen Ben and Eric—would be more than suited to the role of my hero, the tall, dark and handsome Dr Pierce Beaumont!

The wedding reception was held in a farm building on the Samaurez Homestead property and it was one of the loveliest I have ever attended. Dancing on a cobblestone floor, open paddocks surrounding the celebrations, and gingham-trimmed jam keepsakes were just a part of an unforgettable evening.

The town inspired me to write FALLING FOR DR DECEMBER as I wanted to capture the wonderful feeling of a close-knit, caring community like Uralla. It is a town where you literally do not have to lock your front door because everyone in the street is either family or friend.

I hope you fall in love with the town and the people as you read the heart-warming story of Laine Phillips and Dr Pierce Beaumont.

Warmest wishes

Susanne

Dedication

To my wonderful family who call the town
of Uralla home—Greg, Tracy, Myles, Anne,
Ben, Eric, Emma, Poppy and Bob.

To their friends in Uralla and Armidale
for being so warm and friendly,
just as you imagine country people to be.

You live in a beautiful part of Australia
and I hope I have done the town justice.

Recent titles by Susanne Hampton:

BACK IN HER HUSBAND'S ARMS
UNLOCKING THE DOCTOR'S HEART

**These books are also available in eBook format
from www.millsandboon.co.uk**

**Praise for
Susanne Hampton:**

'From the first turbulent beginning until the final
climactic ending, an entire range of emotions has been
used to write a story of two people travelling the
rocky road to love…an excellent story. I would
recommend this story to all romance-readers.'
—*Contemporary Romance Reviews* on
UNLOCKING THE DOCTOR'S HEART

'I recommend this read for all fans of medical romance.
It's the perfect balance: spunky, emotional, heartfelt, a
very sweet and tender romance with a great message!'
—*Contemporary Romance Reviews* on
UNLOCKING THE DOCTOR'S HEART

CHAPTER ONE

'JUST ONE MORE step and I'll shoot!' Laine waited for some reaction, but there was nothing.

The man before her appeared unmoved by her words. He stood in silence, shaking his head, his dark, deeply set eyes staring back coldly. The clenched muscles of his jaw made his face appear even more angular and harsh. Laine was painfully aware that he had no intention of taking her seriously. *But why would he?* Her willowy stature would pose no threat to his potent six-foot frame now stripped bare to the waist. He wasn't about to listen to her plea.

The afternoon sun slipped through the curtain breaks and she watched the curves of his broad chest and powerful arms etched by the light. Slowly he ran his fingers over his open belt buckle. She felt the need to swallow as his fingers moved to the top stud of his jeans. Her eyes closed for the briefest moment but opened just as quickly. She hoped it was not more than a blink. Showing any sign of intimidation she was feeling would give him the upper hand. She had learned that over the years.

'I promise, take another step and it'll be your last,' Laine called aloud, while silently she chided herself for having been talked into coming back here in the first place. *Why had she done it?* She should have known no good would come from returning to this town. The lump in her throat that had formed when she'd driven her hire car down the New England Highway and into Uralla that morning showed no sign of being swallowed. It was lodged firmly and going nowhere. It was a sign she should not be here. She had left the town twelve years ago for good reason.

She waited for his response in action or words but there was nothing. He showed no emotion. She couldn't read his face. Instead she felt the weight of his gaze as it roamed her body, slowly, painstakingly, making her feel uneasy with every lingering moment, until it came to rest on her mouth. Running his hand through his short black hair, he appeared distracted as he stared at her in silence. Then abruptly his husky voice made her stiffen as he asked brazenly, 'You really know how to use that?'

Only able to catch his unshaven profile, she could see his mouth curve into a smirk. She fought his intimidation with all her strength. She refused to let him know he was close to succeeding in his desire to unnerve her. She had to maintain the upper hand and stay in control and that meant staying calm.

'Take that step and you'll soon find out how accurate I can be.' Her tone was mild and steady, even though inside she wavered. Laine hoped her newfound composure, albeit at odds with her true feelings, might prove more successful. She knew this was the last time she could issue her ultimatum without it echoing as an empty threat. She would not get what she'd come for and all of this would have been for nothing. No one was going to get the better of her. Not here and not now.

She held her ground and prayed this time he'd take her seriously. And he did. Grudgingly, and with a level of hesitation Laine didn't fully understand, he set his dusty boots up another rung of the ladder and eased his long leg over the top to sit astride it.

'At last,' she muttered to herself as she tucked some stray wisps of her long brown hair behind her ear and reached for another lens from the table behind her. With her camera focused, and maintaining eye contact with her handsome but obstinate subject, Laine moved behind the ladder prop and began a photographic shoot with the confidence and expertise that only someone with her ability and experience could execute.

A cold sweat rushed over Pierce but he swallowed hard and kept his eyes from looking down. His heart was pounding roughly in his chest as he struggled to push unwanted images from his mind. Memories were rising to the surface and no matter how logic reasoned with his fear, fear was close to taking hold. Despite the fact that he wasn't that twelve-year-old boy balancing precariously on a balcony ledge, he suddenly found himself feeling equally vulnerable. His knuckles clenched whitely and he willed the shoot to be over. Nervously he rubbed his brow. He had to stay on task, remind himself it was just a ladder in an unused consulting room of his practice in order to maintain any remnant of composure. He knew it wouldn't be easy when he took the first step, but he hadn't expected it to be so overwhelming all these years later. Some memories were clearly hard, if not impossible, to forget.

'You can come down now but seriously, Dr. Beaumont, was that so terribly difficult?' she asked with exaggerated politeness, as she removed the lens and packed the camera body back into its case. 'If you'd gone up another rung without the dramatics, we could have wrapped up twenty minutes ago,' she complained as she began to dismantle the lighting umbrella. She was tempted to comment further on his bad attitude but didn't want to cause any more animosity. Better to keep her opinion to herself, she mused as she began packing the tripod in the longest of her waterproof equipment bags.

Pierce Beaumont couldn't answer her. He climbed down from the ladder in silence. With both feet on solid ground, anxiety morphed to anger. 'What was so damned important about going up one more step?'

'It's about framing the picture. I won't compromise when it comes to my work. And please don't be late tomorrow. I'm hoping to get the sunrise over the McKenzies' property,' she replied flatly, as she glared back at the man who had made the last hour very difficult. 'I've already photographed eleven other GPs across Australia and you have been without doubt the most uncooperative. Why on earth agree in the first place if you don't want to see yourself in a calendar? I saw the contract, it was clearly your name and signature on it.'

'That's just it,' he snapped back. 'I didn't agree to any of this. My former partner, Gregory Majors, forged the paperwork before he retired. He did it as a prank. Thought I'd see the humour in it. Clearly, I didn't.'

Laine knew the name instantly. Dr Majors, the town's general practitioner. It was a name that brought memories rushing back at lightning speed. It was something he would do. The man had an impish side to him. Laine had been his patient many times when she'd lived in Uralla. The first time when she'd come down with tonsillitis, then there had been her broken arm from a fall during a high-school netball game and a few other teenage scrapes. He had been the local doctor since he'd finished medical school when, like so many of the townspeople, he'd come back to nest.

But not Laine. She had left and vowed never to return. She took a deep breath. The time that she had called Uralla her home was over and she could never think of it that way again. She had planned it would be her forever home but that dream had ended and taken with it her belief in the words 'for ever'.

'When I tried to back out of it, the organisers told me that they'd booked your flights and the budget wouldn't allow them to reschedule,' Pierce continued, bringing Laine back from her reverie. 'I offered to pay for new flights for you to wherever they could find another mug who'd agree to take my place but apparently they couldn't find anyone. They explained that the entire timeline would have blown out and they wouldn't have met the deadline. No calendar meant there'd be no fundraising for next year. They played the guilt card very well.'

There was more to it than that. Pierce hadn't been able to walk away after he had read the charity prospectus and realised what a worthwhile cause he would be assisting. He had been torn. Posing for the calendar irked him beyond belief but he couldn't them down. Building a facility in each capital city to assist those foster-children who had turned eighteen and were aging out of the system was so needed and such a huge task. Although it went against his better judgement to bring attention to himself, he'd decided that he needed to put the charity first. He would deal with repercussions, if any arose, later.

'How noble of you to go ahead, then.' Laine rolled her eyes, unaware of his knowledge and belief in the charity. She was not impressed. She took both her work and the cause seriously and she was annoyed with his apparent lack of respect towards her and the project. This charity meant the world to her. She would give, and do, whatever she could to help make a difference to the lives of foster-children. Someone had to.

It was tough being in foster-care sometimes but it was even tougher when the stay came to an end. Laine knew that firsthand. She wanted to provide assistance for the children before the system scarred them and also to assist those transitioning into adulthood. She had been involved with the charity for a number of years, and each year she took on a greater workload. Some days when the loneliness of the life she had chosen was almost untenable, she thought of all the foster-children enduring a swinging-door childhood and knew there had to be a way to improve their lives. Any assistance she could provide from her connections and her work she would give without reservation.

Carefully, and in silence, she continued to pack away her equipment, cleaning the front and rear elements of her lenses before storing them. She was fastidious about the tools of her trade and valued everything she owned. She used the best, she could afford it, but it hadn't always been that way and having scrimped and saved when starting out for even the basic photographic equipment ensured she never took any of her belongings for granted now.

'I might have to do this shoot but I sure as hell don't have to climb up a ladder again. In fact, I'm calling the shots tomorrow. My way or *no* way,' Pierce said, not masking his disdain for the entire situation.

Laine looked at the man who would be her subject for the next two days and knew it could easily become one of the most frustrating and difficult assignments of her almost ten year career. Frustrating because of the subject, difficult because of the location. Dr Pierce Beaumont was ridiculously uncooperative and Uralla held memories she wanted to forget.

When she'd left the small town, almost three hundred miles north of Sydney, all those years before, she had never expected to return. A part of her past, it bore no relevance to the life she had forged in New York. Laine knew she had never been happier than when she'd lived in Uralla but she also knew she wasn't that girl any more and she could never fit into this town again.

She was a citizen of the world, a woman for whom her career was her entire life. There was no room and no need for anyone else in it—and particularly not the people of this town. They were warm and welcoming but she didn't want that level of sentiment in her life. It didn't fit with her any more. Those years living in a small town had allowed her to finally understand what it felt like to be a part of a family. Someone had actually cared how she'd felt and had wanted her to be safe and protected. For the very first time she had stopped feeling abandoned. She had stopped expecting that all promises would eventually be broken.

The perfect picture she'd painted of a life with one loving family—a life she had only dreamt of when she'd constantly moved homes, meeting new foster-families and being bullied by foster-siblings—had actually come true. It had been a home where she'd learned the true meaning of unconditional love, and one that had provided the answer to the question she had asked all her life: *Where did she belong?* It was right there.

But after four wonderful years it had all come to a

terrible, tragic end. Her adoptive parents had died in a car accident. They were gone, and never coming back— and she had been alone once again.

So Laine had used the scars to give her strength. She'd turned her back on the security of the small town and chosen a new life, far away from Uralla. It had taken years to finally become successful but she'd known she could do it. Eventually, her determination to take control of her life, to make the most of every day and to rely on absolutely no one had driven her to the top.

Travelling the world, working with models and managing their demands, and those of the clients, at fashion shoots and waking up in a different hotel every day had finally become way of life for Laine. It was a mad schedule but being frantically busy allowed her to keep her thoughts of the past at bay. There were lonely times but it was the price she paid for the life she led and she never complained. Even the demands of models didn't unnerve her. They all had a job to do and at the end of the assignment they all had great shots in their portfolios. If they played the thorny card, Laine was at a level in her career when she could refuse to work with them again, and generally bad attitudes meant their careers were short-lived.

Laine loved what she did. It was that simple. She was a well-respected photographer and she never needed to look for work. Her name was synonymous with work in high-end magazines representing the finest fashion houses and most expensive jewellery lines, and recently she had completed an assignment on the Italian Riviera for an iconic sports-car company. Her portfolio was eclectic, with the most beautiful, timeless and cutting-edge photographs of any living photographer.

She had worked hard for everything she had achieved and no doctor from New South Wales with little or no knowledge of her profession was going to try and tell her what to do.

She was not little Melanie Phillips of Uralla. That young girl no longer existed. She was Laine Phillips, international photographer. She wasn't about to be pushed around by any man, however handsome or crucial to her shoot.

'So you're styling the shoot tomorrow? Interesting premise.' Laine took a deep breath and sat down cross-legged near the last of the bags she was packing. There was absolutely no way he would be making any decisions about tomorrow, other than his choice of cologne. She would dictate everything else about the shoot. It was her name and reputation on these photographs and that meant she was the one in control. Just as she had been about everything in her life for the last twelve years. No one took control from her hands. *Ever.*

'If you think you can waltz into our town and lay down the law, you can think again.' Pierce was not impressed with her desire to order him about. He wouldn't tolerate it and he could make her stay increasingly difficult if she kept it up. She could take her arrogant, big-city outlook and hop straight back on a plane. 'Don't bring your condescending attitude here. I'm doing you a favour.'

'Me a favour? You're helping a charity, not me personally. And not doing a lot except taking off your clothes. Hardly a huge ask. So contrary to your suggestion about running things tomorrow I have bad news for you. The shoot will be done *Laine's way.*'

Pierce eyed the stunning brunette who had just given him a serving. She certainly wasn't a shrinking violet.

She was a tiny dictator of sorts. A very beautiful dictator. He wondered for a moment why she wasn't on the other side of the camera. Her flawless figure was evident in a tight white singlet top and faded blue jeans. She was a natural beauty with little, if any, make-up, yet she didn't seem to fuss about her appearance. But he needed to forget how attractive she was and remember that she was telling him what to do—and he didn't take kindly to that.

'I can sit on a tractor on the McKenzies' farm. No great planning needed. Country doctor, on a farm, on a tractor. Shoot done. Photo taken. *It's a wrap*—isn't that what they say?'

Laine rolled her eyes. She couldn't believe how little he valued or understood her craft. In his eyes, her livelihood was quickly and simply reduced to plonking a doctor on a tractor and taking a snap.

'Perhaps you could just take a selfie with your phone and send it to me?' Laine was not about to try and explain the process she undertook in planning and delivering a quality shoot to a man who had no idea. She continued zipping up the last of her bags.

'I still don't agree with the calendar idea,' he remarked, choosing to ignore her sarcasm.

'It's a proven formula,' she replied matter-of-factly. 'Eligible shirtless men, with a bit of tweaking, become every woman's fantasy.'

'Tweaking?' he asked, with a frown knitting his dark brows. 'You are on a roll, aren't you? Do you insult all of your subjects so matter-of-factly?'

Laine stopped what she was doing for a moment and looking at Pierce with a stoic expression replied, 'It wasn't an insult. It's a fact. I edit photos to bring out the best and hide the flaws. Photography is often pure fantasy. I make the subject irresistible. Whether it's a string of pearls, a leather handbag or an automobile that only two per cent of the population could actually afford to buy. I make it the most desirable possession. Something the consumer cannot live without. I make it shinier than it really is, more beautiful than it might be and in doing so turn it into the stuff of dreams.'

'So it's all smoke and mirrors?' Pierce remarked. 'No real shots for you. Nothing of any depth. Doesn't really surprise me. It's just about selling a product, full stop.'

'And what gives you the right to say that? You know nothing about me,' she retorted, getting back to her feet and facing him. 'I love my gritty real shots, like photographing older people. I don't remove a single line or make any changes. The character in faces that have seen hardship and joy in equal amounts are priceless. But if I'm contracted to make a product sell, then I will tweak until I can't tweak any more!'

Laine knew well enough that none of Pierce's shots would need any editing on her behalf. He had a kind of refined magnetism that would stir any female and she wouldn't tamper with *that*.

The last hour in Pierce's presence had been professionally frustrating but that was the least of her problems. There was something about this man and this situation that was making Laine feel ill at ease. Whether it was Pierce's very real and very natural sensuality or just being back in Uralla wasn't clear to her, but something was making her feel uncomfortable.

She was accustomed to models and their ability to turn it on and turn it off, but Pierce didn't seem to have a switch. He was genuinely this sexy, twenty-four seven. It was innate and palpable and he had an inner strength that shone though. And for some inexplicable reason he was unnerving her.

'Were you being difficult for the sake of it or was it another reason why you didn't want to take the step up the ladder?' she asked, trying to bring the conversation back to business. 'You really did seem to overreact to my request.'

'I told you that I didn't want to be involved. Let's leave it at that. You won't convince me that there's not a better or easier way to raise funds to support your charity.'

Laine turned away again and wound up the cords draped across the floor. She suspected there was more to his reticence in taking that step than just arrogance but she thought better of pursuing the matter. She just wanted to finish the shoot on time and get away from him. With the cords packed up, she closed her laptop, slipped it into her backpack and turned towards him.

'They did their market research and decided on a calendar. It worked for the firemen last year so the charity chose twelve of Australia's most eligible general practitioners. And you, Dr Beaumont, have the dubious honour of being the last for the year. You're Dr December,' she announced as she zipped up the last of her bags.

'Call me Pierce, Dr Beaumont is way too formal and correct me if I'm wrong, as I'm sure you will, but I can't see anything around here that looks at all festive.' Pierce rubbed his chin and added dryly, 'What about I remove what's left of my clothing and you strategically place a Christmas tree in front of me?'

Pierce would never normally have spoken this way to a woman he barely knew. His behaviour was always beyond reproach. *Always.* But with his feet securely on the ground and his anger subsiding, Laine's behaviour was bringing out a different, irreverent side of him and he suspected with her New York attitude Laine could take it. And give it back. She clearly wasn't the shy type.

'Strategically positioned Christmas tree?' she muttered as she returned her gaze to him. Suddenly her heart began to race. She had to push the visual from her mind. He was leaning on the desk with his arms folded across the ripples of his tanned chest. She had captured photos of some incredibly good-looking men over the last three weeks, but he was clearly the most handsome. Hands down. She swallowed and tried to think of him as just another subject but he was different from the other doctors. They had been helpful and a little flattered to be asked and two had even very politely invited her out to dinner, which she had equally politely refused, but Pierce Beaumont had an attitude that both annoyed and intrigued her.

She wasn't sure that he knew just how good looking he was, but she suspected he knew women would not run away from his advances. He wasn't overly close but there was electricity in the air she had to cut. It made her feel uncomfortable that he was stirring up feelings she didn't want to feel. She had another two days' shooting with him and she couldn't let him get under her skin.

Laine hated to admit it but the sight of his toned body so close to her did make her breathing a little shallow. She bit her lip. This was crazy. She had filmed ludicrously handsome male models for an underwear shoot in a New York subway a month ago and they had left her cold. It had always been a job. But now this country doctor with his defiance and an aversion to ladders was making her feel very self-conscious.

She had to push him away. She preferred being alone. No one to depend on. No one who could leave and make her feel as if her heart had broken in two, wondering whether she could go on. No, Laine Phillips was alone in this world and she liked it that way.

'Perhaps mistletoe would suffice,' she replied, as she scooped up her bag and walked towards the door.

Pierce smirked at her remark. He was right, she could dish it up, and do it well. Perhaps another couple of days with this gorgeous brunette, despite the circumstances, would be less traumatic than he imagined. She had spirit. He crossed the room, picked up the heavier bag containing the grip and lighting equipment and walked to the door with it. Reaching for the handle, he opened the door for Laine with his free hand.

'Mistletoe will definitely *not* suffice,' he said as she squeezed past him, the narrowness of the doorway causing her bare shoulder to inadvertently brush lightly across his chest. 'Not even close.'

CHAPTER TWO

LAINE WAS AMUSED and a little taken aback by Pierce's comment. This country doctor definitely had an edge to him. He was actually a little more *city* than she had first imagined. She smiled to herself then decided to delete the mental image that had crept into her mind. Edge or no edge, this trip to Uralla needed to stay professional. The thought of Pierce as anything more than a photo shoot couldn't happen. Not even a fling. Her flings were very separate from her work.

Gossip spread quickly in the circles in which she travelled and she wasn't about to become the photographer who overstepped the mark and fell into bed with her models. No matter how tempting it could be at times. It risked a shift in power. It also complicated life and she had never allowed herself to become fodder for rumours. It was one of her rules.

Along with another, which prevented her flings developing into relationships. Her heart was safely tucked away behind a stone wall that was carved with her rules. Her own invisible armour, it kept her safe from ever becoming attached to another person. From ever needing someone, only to find they had gone. From ever feeling secure, only to find she was alone again.

Laine Phillips was a one-woman show. And nothing would ever change that. Definitely not a three-day stop-over in Uralla.

'You can put your shirt on now,' she told him, without looking again at his stunning physique. 'The shoot is over.'

Her professional demeanour was in full throttle now, he thought. Perhaps it had been his remark about the mistletoe, he mused. His intention had been to lighten the mood, but clearly that wasn't about to happen in the near future. She had shut him down and any light-hearted banter was over. Apparently Laine Phillips was all business.

Drawing breath, he looked at her very pretty face. It was devoid of emotion. He wondered what her story was—what made this very attractive woman so defensive. So aloof and untouchable. Her walls were so high that Pierce wondered if it was more than big-city conceit. This seemed more personal.

Laine Phillips seemed to be a gorgeous island that perhaps no one had ever discovered.

He found it odd that he was making sweeping statements in his own head about a woman he barely knew. He had never summed up a woman so quickly. He had never *wanted* to before. But she was such an enigma.

'So shall I meet you at the McKenzies' property to-morrow morning around four-thirty?'

'Four-thirty in the morning?' he questioned her, as he did up the last of his shirt buttons. 'Are we milking the cows?'

Her eyes smiled. She didn't give her mouth permission to do the same. 'It's the perfect lighting then. Nothing to do with cows. I want to capture you in the wide-open paddock just as the sun rises, with a single eucalyptus tree on the horizon. Single man, single tree. Blatant symbolism.'

'Single eucalyptus tree?' he asked with a quizzical frown dividing his dark brows. 'Have you actually seen the McKenzies' property or are you just hoping to find a backdrop like that?'

Laine shifted the heavy bag a little on her shoulder. She didn't want to admit she knew the property like the back of her hand. That she had spent time there when she'd been growing up. She had hoped to avoid questions like this but realised that it was nearly impossible. When she had discovered that Dr Pierce Beaumont, her final shoot in the calendar, was the resident general practitioner in Uralla she had been filled with dread. When the bus had pulled out of the town all those years ago, its final destination Sydney, she had begun to barricade her emotions—one brick at a time. Each signpost she had passed had laid another piece of rock around her heart.

For a few years Sydney had become her home and then New York. She chose cities that prevented her from forming lasting relationships. Cities as cold and detached as the person she needed to become. She wasn't strong enough to remain in a town as kind as Uralla. She didn't have any more tears, or anything left inside to save her again. There could never be another heartache, for the next one would most definitely be the end of her. So Melanie Phillips had taken matters into her own hands. She had changed her name just enough to feel like a different person and she'd moved on, successfully burying herself in a busy and demanding life. A life without love and all the risks and sadness it brought.

When she had agreed to the calendar assignment, Laine had had no inkling that she would be spending time in this familiar little town in country New South Wales. She'd assumed it would be capital cities or large beachside towns. Not a town so small it didn't really factor into most people's knowledge of Australian geography. It was as pretty as a picture but famous for nothing more than being not too far from the centre of country music in Australia and for having a major highway as a main street. It was a town where you could leave your front door unlocked and know nothing would be taken because the locals were either family or friends.

She had once loved living there and now she assumed Pierce felt the same.

'I was out at the McKenzies' this morning. I drove there to check the setting was suitable after my plane touched down in Armidale.'

Pierce's curiosity was further heightened but he said nothing, keeping his thoughts to himself as he watched her nervously shift her stance. He had no right to question her or ask more about her than she was willing to offer. He was a private person. His past was off limits so why should hers be any different?

His life had effectively started when he'd come to Uralla two years before. He had never spoken about his past or his family, except to say that his aunt had been given custody of him after his parents had passed away when he was a child. The circle of people his father and mother had once called friends had never tried to make contact after the tragedy so they hadn't factored into his thoughts as he'd grown older. When the parties on his parents' yacht had ceased, so had their friends' interest in Pierce.

However, their children had sought him out years later, when he'd been a young adult. At first he'd thought they'd actually cared about their friendship with him, but that belief had been short-lived when it had become clear these long-lost friends had only needed him to pay their tabs. It hadn't taken long for Pierce to realise that all they really valued was his family money—especially the women. All eager to snare a wealthy husband, they never tried to hide their love of the luxury lifestyle they assumed he would lavish on them if they were to become his wife.

Pierce wanted none of it. He wanted what his parents had never had. *Real* friends. The type that didn't care if your car was twenty years old and gave you a place to sleep if you needed it. Although he would never need to be given a helping hand with regard to money—he was indisputably one of the richest young men in Australia. His wealth, generated from his father's mining and real estate interests, was handled by his business manager in Sydney.

And so, one day, when he'd realised he wanted more from his life, Pierce had simply disappeared from high society and moved to a town he had heard about during medical school. A town that he hoped he would be happy to call home.

The townsfolk never asked more than he was willing to give, they never pried into his past, and he was happy with that arrangement. Everything he'd done after driving down the New England Highway and into Uralla was on the table. Anything before that was not discussed. The circus that had been his life had dissipated just as he had hoped. His new life was too quiet and uneventful to create any interest in the media—in fact, many thought that his inheritance was all gone, the proceeds lost to bad investments.

Out of the eyes of the press, Pierce quietly directed the accountant to make donations in the company name to deserving causes. A silent philanthropist, he never used any of the money in his personal life. And he wouldn't want it any other way. He knew who his friends were and without the family money there would be fewer enemies. Keeping his past to himself was working quite nicely.

Perhaps Laine had her reasons too. Clearly her accent was Australian, albeit with an international flavour, and he knew she was based in New York. He had just assumed she would have grown up in another big city like Sydney. But somehow she knew her way around Uralla.

'I know the town, I spent some time here eons ago,' Laine told him. She didn't want to get into it so kept the explanation brief. 'But it's immaterial. I just need you there at four-thirty and then in the late afternoon I thought we'd head over to Saumarez Homestead. They have a barn with a spectacular panoramic view. I would like to capture you in the doorway just as the sun sets.'

'Lighting, right?'

'Yes, lighting and amazing scenery. New England is a stunning part of Australia and I want to do it justice,' she said, then added, 'Besides, the early morning shoot will allow you to see patients during the day and then we can head out again around five in the afternoon. Minimal disruption to your day and daylight saving will add value to mine, giving me sufficient time to set up my equipment and still catch the sunset.'

'Yes, my patients,' Pierce remarked. He felt slightly guilty that being so close to this woman had made him almost forget the day ahead. No woman had ever made such an impression in such a short space of time. She was a conundrum. He wanted to know more about her but he didn't feel he had the right to ask too many questions. It was against his view of life, his belief in respecting privacy and boundaries. Suddenly those values began slipping as the desire to know everything he could about this woman began to grow. Her confidence was evident but it was not grandiose. She seemed so focused and serious. Almost a little too serious.

'You really do have a feel for this town. I'm assuming it wasn't a fleeting visit or, if it was, this sleepy enclave made an impression on you.' He wasn't able to mask his interest any longer—plus, there was also the chance she might open up just a little.

Laine took a deep breath. The town had left more than an impression. It had been the best and worst. The happiest and saddest. It had been her life and then it had ended. Laine knew she had to put the past behind her. She had an assignment to complete and a very different life waiting for her in New York and wherever in the world she was called to work next. Uralla had to remain business—sentiment didn't pay dividends for her any more.

'I will not intrude on any more of your time than I have to over the next couple of days, I promise,' she replied, ignoring his comment. 'But now I need to get these bags to my car and head back to my hotel. I have calls to make and emails to attend to this evening.'

'Sure. Let me take one of those.' Pierce accepted Laine's right to pass on answering him and reached for one of her bags, walking to the back door of the practice. It was an old red-brick house that had been converted into three consulting rooms, an office and a small surgery for minor medical procedures. The large backyard—complete with a clothesline on a slight Tower of Pisa lean and a wire chicken coop housing four large laying hens—had been retained, with patient parking relegated to the street. It was picture-perfect country rustic.

Looking at her surroundings, Laine realised she had almost forgotten the relaxed feel of the country. Her designer, sparsely decorated apartment on the fourth floor of a Manhattan apartment building had none of that ambience. And it was of her choosing. Nothing she didn't need and nothing she would miss when she was away. Streamlined and minimalist.

Focused on keeping childhood memories at bay, she followed Pierce through the yard and out of the back gate to where a large silver four-wheel-drive hire car was parked on the side of the road under the shade of a huge leafy tree. She opened the rear door and placed the equipment inside.

'I'm staying at the Bushranger Inn down the street. I can come past and collect you in the morning or meet you there,' she remarked casually as she closed the heavy door on her belongings. Trying to do the same to her thoughts, she made her way to the driver's side. It was the opposite side from the left-hand drive she was accustomed to but, as a New Yorker who mainly took cabs around the city, she found adjusting wasn't that difficult.

'What about I pick you up and I drive us there?' he returned.

'I'm perfectly capable of driving both of us,' she retorted, before she closed the door, turned on the engine and dropped the electric window. 'But since you don't want me to drive you, I'll meet you there.' Without another word, she put the car into gear and headed off in the direction of her hotel only half a mile down the road, leaving Pierce open-mouthed on the side of the road. Her exit was abrupt, to say the least.

Pierce had not meant to offend her. He had been trying to make up for his less-than-gracious attitude during the shoot with his offer. He quickly realised that what he had thought a gallant act had been something that she'd perceived as insulting, perhaps chauvinistic. He wasn't entirely sure. Clearly he couldn't win. She had driven off so hurriedly it had been as if she couldn't wait to get away from him.

'What the hell was that about?' he muttered as he walked inside. He was still shaking his head in frustration as he closed the back door and headed to the kitchen. Despite his best intentions to forget Laine, and her borderline rudeness, as he made his first coffee of the day the New York photographer had his full attention.

'Good morning, dearie. Who was that motoring off at lightning speed down the road?' came a voice behind him.

Pierce knew it was his receptionist Tracy, a retired nurse and wife of the former practice owner. Tracy worked three days a week, job-sharing with another local nurse.

'Morning Trace,' he replied, turning around with his coffee. 'The racing-car driver you just missed was the New York photographer in town to shoot the charity calendar.'

'Was she in a hurry or did you two have words? You seem a little stressed.'

'You might say that,' he said, then, noticing her face quickly develop a frown, he added, 'I thought I was being a gentleman, but somehow I still managed to offend her.'

'You know, if I'm to marry you off, young man you have to be nice to these young ladies. She was young, wasn't she?'

'Yes, young and very beautiful.'

Tracy watched his face curiously. She hadn't seen him look that way since she'd met him. The woman must be quite something for him to have this reaction.

'Then you need to find a way to see her again.' With that she put her lunch in the refrigerator and headed to the waiting room. Tracy knew that fewer words with Pierce always had a better response.

Pierce had already decided that was exactly what he would do after he finished the day. Thinking about how he could arrange it, he picked up his coffee, took a sip from the steaming cup and headed to his office to switch on his computer and check through the patient roster for the morning.

When Pierce had joined the practice two years previously, all the patient records had been hard-copy files with coloured coded spines. It had taken some convincing for the hesitant older partner, Dr Majors, to see the value in moving everything onto what Pierce had touted as a more efficient electronic system. It had meant hiring another administration person to transfer the patient records into the new format but after a sound argument from Pierce, Dr Majors had accepted a small trial. Once the older practitioner had seen the benefit of the system, he'd agreed that the new technology was needed across the entire practice and the surgery had made a much-needed move into the twenty-first century.

A few minutes later he stood in the doorway of the waiting room. 'Carla Hollis, can you please come in?' Stepping back, he let the young woman steer her pram into his consulting room, then closed the door and crossed back to his desk.

'So how is little James today?' he asked as Carla lifted

her baby from the pram. 'I see you've brought him in for his four-month immunisation.'

'I have, but I'm not sure, Dr Armstrong, he doesn't seem well today,' she replied, nursing the infant on her lap. His quickly wriggled his feet free of the blue cotton blanket.

Pierce wheeled his chair closer to the pair. 'In what way do you mean unwell? Can you be more specific?'

'He's had a slight runny nose for a few days now. It turned into a cough three days ago but last night I was up so often that I brought him into bed with us. He kept us awake for hours then finally stopped coughing about three in the morning,' she said, pulling her long blonde plait free of his chubby fingers. 'He still has an appetite and he's been breastfeeding so maybe there's nothing to worry about.'

Pierce took some disposable gloves from the dispenser on his desk. He slipped them on before he carefully unwrapped the little boy from his soft blue cocoon, lifted up his singlet and, in turn, placed the stethoscope on his chest then his back. Pierce pulled the clothing down again and placed a thermometer under his arm, holding it there for a few moments.

'Any persistent cough is a concern in an infant and James also has a slight fever,' he replied, after checking the reading. 'It's difficult to tell the difference between whooping cough and another respiratory infection, but I'd prefer to err on the side of caution. I'll take a swab of his nose to test for the Bordetella pertussis bacterium, which indicates whooping cough, but I won't wait for the results before we start antibiotics. The test can take time and it can quickly become serious in babies as young as James.'

'But didn't he have a shot for that when he was two months old?'

'Yes, he did,' Pierce responded as he stood, crossed to the consulting room trolley and collected what he needed to take a swab and returned to the mother and child. 'That was the first of the three immunisations he requires. One at two months, the next at four months and again at six months. Unfortunately, until he has completed all three he can still contract whooping cough.' Pierce gently held the infant's head steady, took a sample from his nose and placed it into a sterile lab container.

'But he will be all right, won't he?'

'I have no reason to think otherwise,' Pierce answered as he discarded his gloves, sat back down at his desk and began completing the online patient records. 'Has James been around anyone with a persistent cough?'

'We had family visit from Tamworth on the weekend and my nieces were coughing all night. I kept James away from them but my sister insisted on holding him,' Carla replied, as she lifted the child up and gently patted his back.

'If James does have whooping cough, it's very contagious. He may have contracted it from direct contact with someone infected with the bacterium—perhaps your sister—or by simply breathing the air within six feet of someone infected with the germs. The bacteria usually enter the nose or throat. We won't know for sure until the test result comes back but until then please keep his fluids up. We don't want to risk dehydration,' Pierce said, as he pulled the script request from the printer and handed it to Carla.

'If he becomes tired from coughing and can't take a full feed, you will need to give him small regular feeds.

Bring his bassinette into your room for the next few nights and keep an eye on him until the coughing has completely gone. Babies can develop apnoea as a complication of whooping cough, which means he may stop breathing for short periods.'

Suddenly the baby began a bout of coughing. It escalated quickly to a point where he was struggling for breath. Pierce immediately lifted him from his mother's arms and supported him in an upright position to make breathing easier. The cough was severe and Pierce immediately knew that James had been infected for longer than his mother suspected and was past home care with antibiotics.

'That's how he coughed all last night,' Carla gasped, and her eyes widened with concern at the infant's condition.

'It could be bronchiolitis or whooping cough but either way I want to transfer him to New England District hospital immediately. They are better equipped to help him through the illness. Antibiotics will need to be administered, as I first told you, but James needs to have oxygen delivered through a tiny mask during these coughing episodes.'

He stepped outside his consulting room and into the waiting area. 'Tracy, can you call for an ambulance, please? Relay that it is not an emergency but we need a monitored transfer to New England District. Carla can't drive and attend to James at the same time.'

Stepping back into the room where Carla sat, chewing her lip nervously, Pierce continued, 'James will need to spend a while in hospital, but I want you to have this in case you need me.' He handed her a card with his twenty-four-hour paging number. 'And don't hesitate to call if you have any concerns. One more thing, if it is confirmed that James has whooping cough, then the chances are high you will both will have contracted it, too. So if you get *any* sign of a cough, immediately begin antibiotics. If you don't, it may take six to ten weeks to subside and nothing will make the recovery quicker once you pass the initial two-week period. Please call your sister too and get her off to her family GP in Tamworth as soon as possible.'

'My husband was coughing last night too, so I'll get him onto the antibiotics tonight. Should I give him a cough suppressant so he can sleep?' Carla asked, as she gently placed the now quiet baby back into his pram to await the ambulance.

'I don't recommend it. I'd prefer to let him cough. It's what the body naturally does when it needs to clear the lungs of mucus and I prefer not to suppress that re-action.'

Carla stood up and took the new script that Pierce held out to her. 'I'll give the hospital a call later and speak to the paediatrician about the treatment plan for James.' With that he wheeled the pram through the waiting room and directed Carla into the spare consulting room. 'The ambulance should be here quite soon but until then you can wait here comfortably.'

Pierce explained to Tracy his reasoning for keeping Carla separate from the waiting patients. If he was correct with his diagnosis of James, he suspected that over the next few days there would be a few more of their family and friends appearing with whooping cough but at least keeping Carla isolated until the ambulance arrived might help those in the surgery that morning.

* * *

Laine turned into the narrow driveway of her motel, past Reception and continued driving down to her room. She pulled up at the front of the Ned Kelly room, her cosy home for the three-night stay. She had checked in a few hours earlier. She unpacked her equipment from the car and carefully stacked it up against the wall inside her room. It didn't take too long before the car was empty and her room looked like a photographic warehouse.

Tossing her sunglasses and keys on the bed, she crossed to the window and pulled it open to enjoy the fresh air. It felt so good to fill her lungs. It was a welcome change to the hotels where she routinely stayed. Her usual accommodation was elegant and never less than five star, but there was also never a window to be opened and always an abundance of pollution in most major cities when she stepped outside.

Laine stood motionless, looking out across the open paddock, and thought back to when she'd lived in the town. It had been over a decade ago but nothing much appeared to have changed.

Part of her wanted to take a walk around her old town. To feel like she belonged, the way it had been all those years ago. Now she was a stranger in her home town. But she didn't want to come face to face with the people who had been like her extended family when she'd been growing up—there was still the chance they might recognise her. It had been twelve long years and she certainly wasn't the Melanie they would remember.

Quite apart from her new name, she had grown out her trademark super-short pixie cut, the chubbiness of her baby face even as a teenager had been replaced by an elongated profile and her braces were long gone. The awkward teen with the tomboy dress sense, who would milk the cows, help to plant the crops, shoo away the crows and look forward to a twenty-minute car trip into Armidale as if there were no bigger treat possible, no longer existed. She had left that life far behind. She didn't belong in this town any more.

Laine walked away from the window with her heart suddenly, and unexpectedly, aching for her past. And even more for what had been taken from her. She kicked off her designer espadrilles and lay back on the bed, looking up at the ceiling. Her eyes closed and her mind slipped back to a happy time. A time when she'd felt loved and protected and wanted. Turning on her side, she felt a tear slip from her eye and roll down her cheek. It had been many years since she had stopped and yearned for that time in her life.

She wiped the tear away with the back of her hand, and silently berated herself for being swept up in emotions after only a few hours of being in the town. It was silly. Melancholy musings had no place in her life. She was an independent woman with no ties, just the way she liked it. *The way it needed to be*, she told herself, before she drifted off for a much-needed nap. The frantic six-week schedule she had given herself hadn't factored in any down time between shoots and flights and finally it had caught up with her.

Hours later she was woken from her slumber by a knock at the door.

Laine sat upright, staring at the wooden door, with no clue as to who would be on the other side. Waking with memories still so close to the surface, it quickly took

Laine back to a time when she would run from a knock
at the door. When she had felt sure someone was coming
to take her away from the loving home she had found.
Earlier in her childhood, the knock had signalled that
the authorities had been called and a decision made to
move her to the next placement. She became numb and
often didn't care as she'd been leaving a less-than-pleas-
ant situation, but all that had changed when she'd come
to live with the Phillips family and found a place she'd
truly wanted to call home. Then the knock would send
her scurrying to hide so that they couldn't find her and
rip her away from a place where she felt safe. Over time,
with help from her new parents, she'd learnt that a knock
did not signal something ominous. It merely meant visitors were arriving and she learnt to embrace the sound.

Then there was Manhattan, where no one knocked on
her door unexpectedly. They had to call from the lobby
and she or the concierge had to let them up. Laine liked
it that way.

She quickly looked around the clean motel room. The
housekeeping was done. There was no reason for anyone to be calling on her. No one knew she was in town.
The arrangement to use the McKenzie property had been
done by a third party so they had no knowledge she was
in town.

'Laine, it's Pierce,' came the deep voice from the other
side of the door. She could hear him clearly. There was
no other noise. No sounds of taxi horns or police sirens
or people partying in the room above. For a brief moment
Laine found comfort in the silence. It was so peaceful
until the knocking started again.

'I've finished up for the day and thought we might

grab a bite to eat,' he suggested tentatively through the still-closed door. 'If you're up to it.'

Laine was hungry but the thought of spending more time than absolutely necessary with Pierce was unsettling. He was an incredibly attractive man with charisma and home-grown charm and she was feeling slightly vulnerable, being back in this town. It was as if the warm memories of her past were trying to thaw her now cold outlook on life. She didn't like the feeling at all. She didn't like having her resolve questioned.

Pretending to be asleep wasn't as option as it was only seven o'clock. So, grudgingly, she climbed from the bed and made her way barefoot to the door.

'About dinner, I'm not sure,' she began as she opened the door. Pierce was leaning against the wall, dressed in jeans, one dusty boot having caught the lip of a red brick. His grey checked shirt was unbuttoned at the neck, hiding the perfectly toned chest she'd already been privy to. He was handsome in any light but it wasn't an arrogant or cocky assurance he had. It was the confidence a man had when he knew himself. One who wasn't searching for anything. One who had found what he was looking for. She wondered for a moment if Pierce had found himself in Uralla or had he arrived already content?

He dropped his booted foot to the ground and turned to face her. 'I'm heading to the top pub for a quick meal and I thought you might like to join me.'

His smile was perfect but more than that it was genuine. Laine was accustomed to the perfect smile that a model managed to show on cue but with no actual meaning behind it. Her stomach fluttered. Another feeling she was not expecting or enjoying. Her mind told her to feign a headache and slam the door but the clear country evening with a hint of his cologne convinced her heart to accept his invitation.

'I guess that would be okay.'

She was surprised by her own reaction. She was not spontaneous like this. She always weighed up all the options and then, after careful consideration through a jaded lens, she chose the one that would best fit her schedule. On the way to retrieve her purse from her backpack near the window, Laine heard alarm bells ringing in her head. They were as clear as every other sound she had heard since she had arrived in the quiet little town that morning, but they were in her own mind and her heart quickly shut them down as she slipped her espadrilles back on.

Something was driving her to spend time with the man at her door. And her cold New York reasoning was losing this battle. Her head was in a spin and she was going with it, even if it was against her usual calculated judgement.

'I think this will go well,' he remarked, as she closed the door to her room. 'Neither of us has to drive as it's walking distance so I can't offend you again.'

Laine allowed her mouth to curve into a smile as they made their way up the bitumen driveway to the main road.

'So they still call them the *top* pub and the *bottom* pub?'

'Yes, not sure why really but no one ever says meet you at the Coachwood and Cedar or the Thunderbolt, it's just the top or bottom pub.'

Laine smiled again at the way nothing had changed, but it was a bittersweet smile as they walked past the bottom pub and spied numerous patrons outside, enjoying a beer and a chat in the balmy evening breeze. She reminded herself she would only be in town for a few days and that after that her life would return to the one she knew. The life she had grown accustomed to. A life on her own on the other side of the world. And with any luck no one would recognise her tonight or any time over the next few days.

They meandered their way to their choice of venue for the evening, only a block away. It was a small town but the locals still managed to support two hotels and a number of cafés and restaurants.

Pierce held the door open and they stepped inside. It was hive of activity. It was mid-week and still busy. There was a drone of patrons' happy chatter and clinking of glasses as they walked through the front bar towards the dining section.

'G'day, Doc,' came a gruff voice just before they reached the dining area, followed by a hearty pat on Pierce's back. 'Who's the pretty lady? Even blind as a bat without my glasses I can see she's beautiful. And just to let you know, I'll be disappointed if you tell me she's your sister.'

Laine saw the older man smiling in her direction. She recognised him immediately but realised he didn't have the same recollection. Her stomach dropped. It was Jim Patterson, her father's best friend. He had more silver in his still thick wavy hair and his face was a little more lined but the twinkle in his blue eyes hadn't changed at all. For thirty years, the pair would relax over a cold beer on a Sunday afternoon on the back veranda. Jim was older than her father by quite a few years but they had struck up a friendship while working on the land as jackeroos when Arthur had just left school and Jim had been in his late twenties. Laine had gone to school with two of his four sons. She looked at Jim's face and for a moment she thought he might have remembered but she could see there was nothing. She was relieved that his vision was challenged without his glasses.

'Jim,' Pierce said, stepping back to let the old man closer to Laine. 'This is Laine. She's a photographer from New York.'

'New York, hey?' He laughed. 'Well, I'm pleased to meet you but old Uralla is a long way from your neck of the woods, young lady. What brings you from the Big Apple to our little town?'

'An assignment actually,' she replied, meeting the older man's handshake. 'I'm shooting a charity calendar to aid FCTP. Foster Children's Transition Programme. Pierce is my final subject.'

The old man nudged Pierce in the ribs and laughed again. 'So, you're a pin-up now? Uralla's own poster boy. Well, that's a hoot.' Then he turned his attention back to Laine. 'You're not shooting him in his boxers, though, are you, love? That wouldn't be something I'd want on the wall, but then again maybe the ladies would like it.'

Laine smiled at Jim and remembered he always had a great sense of humour. When he lost Claire he was beside himself with grief but the townsfolk lifted his spirits and made sure he was never alone. They cooked meals, helped him take care of his sons as the youngest was only eight, and they carried him through the sadness to a better place. And clearly he had stayed there and was back to his old self.

'Not his boxers. He's in jeans but that's about it.' Laine smirked as she watched Pierce's face fall.

'Enough of that,' he announced, changing the subject. 'I'll let you go, Jim, so we can get a table.' Turning his full attention to Laine, he added, 'Maybe we can talk about your history with Uralla? "Eons ago" was the term you used. I was hoping over a glass of wine you might elaborate on that just a little.' Pierce pulled out a chair for Laine.

Laine suddenly felt a cold shiver run over her before a large lump formed in her throat. Accepting the dinner invitation had been a huge mistake. She had been fooling herself to think she could enjoy dinner with Pierce and not have to talk about herself and her connection to the town. She didn't talk about herself. Not ever. Her private life was a closed book and she intended to keep it that way. She thought he had accepted that but apparently not. The night had to end. Now.

'I'm sorry, Pierce, I completely forgot there's a call I need to make to one of my editors in the US. I'll be crucified if I don't do it,' she lied, moving away from the chair and Pierce. 'You eat and if I finish quickly, I'll come back and join you,' she lied again, before she made her way back through the crowded front bar. Laine had no intention of returning for a dinner she anticipated would spiral into the Spanish Inquisition.

With that, she rushed out of the top pub, leaving Pierce alone, and made her way down the street. Anxiously she looked back over her shoulder once or twice and when she felt confident that Pierce was not following her, she ran into the bottom pub and sat down at the furthest table from the door. Her stomach was feeling empty from hunger and churning with nerves. She wasn't sure if the motel restaurant would be open, so she decided to grab a quick meal at the pub then head back to her room.

Dinner with Pierce would have been impossible. She had been naïve to accept the invitation and not expect that it would mean bringing up the past. Losing her family in Uralla gave her more heartache than she'd thought possible for one person to bear and she had no intention of discussing it.

Putting her life in Australia behind her had been easy in a big city with her high-profile career to keep her busy. And that's what she needed now. She didn't need dinner and question time with a country doctor.

'Here's the menu,' the young waitress said, as she placed the glossy card on the table for Laine. 'And we have some specials as well on the board over there. Can I get you a drink?'

Laine ordered a tonic and lime and glanced over the menu quickly, choosing grilled salmon. The waitress jotted down the order on her small pad, scooped up the menu and headed to the bar.

With a heartfelt sigh, Laine looked around the room. It was less noisy than the top pub but the locals were still engaged in friendly repartee and she could hear laughter and the clicking of billiard balls on the pool table in the next room. A dark purple-coloured outback mural decorated part of one wall. The old chairs she remembered had all been replaced with new light-coloured wooden ones but the atmosphere hadn't changed. Taking a sip of her drink, which had arrived quickly, she hoped the food would be served quickly too.

Laine wanted to finish the shoot, leave Uralla and head back to New York. This was her last stop of the calendar assignment. Editing would take another two weeks, followed by a few weeks off, and then in March she would be heading to Rome. After that who knew where she would be? It didn't matter as long as she was on the go and not putting down roots anywhere. There would be another shoot for the American arm of FCTP towards the middle of the year and then back to Sydney for a quick visit for the annual fundraiser around Christmas. Sydney, she told herself, *not* Uralla.

Laine would always donate her time and money to the cause and enlist celebrity associates to raise the charity's profile as needed, but coming to this country town would never happen again.

Looking back now, Laine realised that returning here had been a huge mistake. Little about the town or even where she was sitting had changed. But she had. The monthly Sunday dinners that she had enjoyed with her adoptive parents in this same room had been such a treat. They had not been a wealthy couple but they'd had an abundance of love and they'd given it unconditionally to the girl who had come into their lives and they had become a family. Over time, the townspeople had *all* unofficially adopted the twelve-year-old girl of no fixed address as their own and she had grown to love each and every one of them.

The sound of her plate of grilled salmon and cutlery being placed on the wooden table pulled Laine back to reality. She smiled politely at the young waitress then dropped her eyes down to the food in front of her. The generous serving reminded her of where she was again. In New York, an enormous plate would hold a tiny salad with a sliver of salmon, no oil, no dressing, but here the generous salad, French fries and grilled salmon with home-made dressing threatened to spill over the equally ample plate.

Their food was as generous as their love, she mused before she chided herself for being ridiculous. It had to stop. Large plates with birdlike servings enabled her to fit into her jeans, she abruptly reminded herself. This size serving was not for her.

She knew she needed to finish and leave. As she quickly ate, she replaced outdated memories with thoughts of the next day's shoot. The McKenzies' property would be the perfect backdrop and with any luck she would have the second shoot with Pierce done in an hour or so. The sunrise over the paddock with the single eucalyptus tree would be perfect.

She was almost finished with both her planning and dinner when a tall shadow standing over her made her raise her eyes from her plate to see Pierce standing before her.

'Why lie? If you didn't want to have dinner with me, just say so. I didn't see a gun or a club in my hand when I asked.'

Laine saw the disappointment in his deep blue eyes. It wasn't anger, it was confusion but it was a cold glare nonetheless. She hurriedly swallowed the salmon she was chewing, wanting to somehow disappear into the carpeted floor. She felt terrible, suddenly riddled with remorse that she had both been caught and that she had upset this man she barely knew. He seemed like a genuinely nice man. And she couldn't remember the last time she'd felt anything that resembled guilt. That was because she didn't have room for remorse and, she hastily admitted to herself, because she had no one in her life who would bring about those feelings.

She just as quickly realised that she didn't like the feelings that were at threat of being awoken. The sleeping giant, her heart, she wanted left alone. Untouched in the watertight vault she had built. Laine Phillips had no room for anyone but herself. There was no room in her life for more than the occasional fling.

One night now and then with a handsome, no-strings-attached man to remind her that she was a woman. To allow her to feel the warmth of another body but never the warmth of another heart. Her New York sensibilities kicked in. She didn't want this man to stir up feelings that made her question her choices.

'Why did you bother following me? I decided that I'd rather eat alone and was being polite. The whole idea of twenty questions over dinner isn't my style. I'm a private person, always have been, and I don't see it changing any time soon.'

'Fine, eat alone. I was just trying to be polite and show some country hospitality. And just for the record, I didn't follow you. My friends saw me walking back to my car after you ran out on me,' he said, not shifting his eyes from her but pointing to a group of men by the bar. 'I'd blown off our regular Friday night drinks with a lame excuse so I could have dinner with you. Guess it serves me right. Fastest karma ever.'

Without waiting for her response, Pierce left her sitting at her table and crossed to the bar to be greeted by the group. He kept his back to her. His broad shoulders seemed rigid and his stand was defensive, with his legs slightly apart and his arms folded. A couple of the men looked over at Laine and smiled. One raised his glass in her direction. She nodded back awkwardly.

Then suddenly she recognised one of them. It was Jim's eldest son, Mike. He hadn't changed much but, then, he'd already been a man in his twenties when Laine had left town. His resemblance to his father was strong, with thick brown wavy hair, deep blue eyes and an athletic build.

He did what Laine thought was a double take, and she watched him lean in and speak privately to Pierce. Her stomach dropped. Panic set in and her pulse began to race. Without hesitation she stood up, dropped her napkin on the plate and swiftly left the dining room, paying for dinner on her way out.

Her emotions were in turmoil.

Laine wasn't waiting around to find out if Mike had, in fact, realised she was an old family friend or if he was just talking about something unrelated with Pierce.

She was in a spin as she walked briskly down the street.

It was overwhelming. Being in this town and seeing old familiar faces was throwing her head first into a melting pot of comfort, joy and pain. Wounds she'd thought had healed, or perhaps buried, were suddenly feeling very raw. Laine had pushed any emotion away for so many years she had almost forgotten what it felt like. Being numb had become a way of life for her.

But coming back now, she could almost physically touch the kindness in the town. It was like an old blanket that could protect her if she allowed it to envelop her. Unfortunately for Laine, accepting their kindness would prise open her heart. And that could never happen. The way she lived her life now, there was no risk of ever feeling pain. There was also a lack of joy in the pure sense, but she found it to be a fair trade. No joy but no also heartache.

She definitely preferred it that way. Life was easier. And never suffering the incredible feeling of emptiness she'd endured at sixteen would be guaranteed if she never opened her heart.

Laine unlocked the door to her motel room, stepped inside and then slammed it shut on the world. The world she'd once lived in and the one to which she knew she could never return. She had to finish this assignment and get the hell out of town.

Pacing her room as the bath filled, she questioned her reasons for being there. *Was it a cruel act of the universe that brought her to this town?*

CHAPTER THREE

THE ALARM RANG on her phone, waking Laine from a deep sleep. It was a sleep that hadn't come easily so it felt disappointing to be woken up. She sighed, rubbed her eyes and rolled over in her tangled bedcovers to check the time. It was four in the morning.

Climbing from her warm bed, Laine made her way to the light switch and turned it on. She blinked as the stark light hit her still blurry eyes. She had bathed the night before so she just slipped into a pair of jeans, a T-shirt and grabbed a leather jacket. It was summer but the mornings still had bite. She chose some warm socks and knee-high boots instead of her espadrilles as she would be walking through the paddocks and that could be messy. She threw on a scarf for good measure.

Knowing the motel restaurant wouldn't be open this early, Laine had stopped at the supermarket on the way home from dinner the previous night. Quickly she finished a banana, half a protein bar and a glass of orange juice before she began the chore of loading the photographic equipment.

Pierce was fuming as he drove down the New England Highway, heading towards the McKenzies' property. He hadn't slept well at all. Livid described his mood. Getting out of bed at this godawful time for a woman as cold and dismissive as Laine Phillips brought his blood to the boil. But he knew that the shoot and in turn the fundraiser would be compromised if he didn't show up, so he had dragged himself out of bed, showered, shaved and dressed. Grudgingly, he also had to face the fact that it was Laine's face he'd pictured during his sleepless night.

Exactly who did she think she was? His jaw clenched as he remembered the feeling he'd had when he'd bumped into her into her having dinner alone. Walking out on him to eat dinner all by herself. It had been plain rude. He hadn't railroaded her into having dinner with him… or had he? He realised that arriving unannounced at her door hadn't given her much option other than to accept. But she seemed happy enough with the idea, he told himself, as he drove past her motel. He didn't want to look down the driveway but he did. And there she was. With the light spilling from her room and the glow from the full moon, he could make out all five feet four of her, alone and almost in the dark, lugging her equipment into the back of the rental car,.

He cursed as he swung the car back and drove towards her. *Little Miss Independence.* 'Here goes nothing,' he berated himself aloud. 'Prepare to be shot down again for trying to help!'

Suddenly the high beam of headlights heading down the driveway towards Laine's room blinded her. She put her hand up to block the glare.

'Need some help?'

Laine wasn't startled; she recognised the voice. She

had known it for only one day but it seemed very familiar. She hated that.

'I'm fine, really.'

Pierce jumped down from his four-wheel drive and reached for the heavy bag she was attempting to lift into the back of the car.

'I know you're perfectly fine on your own, you made that clear last night,' he retorted. 'But the sooner you're loaded and the shoot is over, the sooner I can get back to my patients. The first is at nine, so we need to get this circus on the road.'

Although, as his hand touched her soft skin, Pierce quickly realised he didn't want to get anything moving along. It felt warm against the cold of the morning. His mind wandered to how warm her entire body would be first thing in the morning lying next to him.

The thought of this irritating, argumentative, opinionated, gorgeous woman in bed with him was suddenly more appealing than any other thought he could muster. He had no idea what had come over him. His self-control was suddenly close to zero and he was always in control. There was something about Laine that puzzled and infuriated him. He didn't know what to make of her but she fascinated him like no other woman had ever before.

He gently tugged the bag free of her grip and placed it on the floor of the car beside the other equipment.

'Anything else?' he asked, looking around.

'No, that's it,' Laine replied, then matter-of-factly crossed the bitumen car park to close the door of her motel room. She was trying to ignore how good it had felt when his hand had touched hers momentarily. It had made her heart jump a little and her stomach turn in a curious, wonderful way. A way she had never felt before. She looked back in the moonlight at the man who was helping her and she suddenly wished her life was different.

He was so kind. Genuinely thoughtful and chivalrous. Not to mention more handsome than most models she had shot during her career. He was wearing black jeans, a white shirt untucked and a black leather jacket. Even without any effort on her behalf, she knew his shots would be stunning. The women would love him. He might not be the typical bad boy, but he had an edge.

The image was raw, the body was hot, but his eyes were warm and inviting. Summed up, the dream man. But the idea of accepting his kindness and giving it back was so at odds with how she lived her life. There was no room in her heart or her life for anyone. Besides, he wasn't her type. He was the staying kind. Nothing like the cold-hearted, indifferent bastards she dated. Those men made it easy to protect her heart. Leaving them before they left her was easy. She had done it enough times to know it was the best way for her.

Aware of other nearby guests still sleeping, Pierce closed the back of her car with a soft thud and headed back to his own.

'I'll follow you, then?' he asked, not wanting to have another argument. He was brutally aware that Laine was more independent than the fourth of July and needed, for some unknown reason, to call the shots, quite literally.

'Sounds like a plan,' she replied, before she climbed into her car, reversed into another parking space and turned the car round to face the street. Pierce followed suit and they were both on the New England Highway moments later.

Laine knew the area like the back of her hand. Although mindful of the interstate truck drivers who were hauling long loads through the night and into the early morning, she allowed her thoughts to return to the driver on her tail. She was confused as hell when it came to this man. With his looks, he could treat women badly and they would still flock to him, but he appeared to be gentleman.

She wished she could relax and enjoy his company but she couldn't risk it. She pushed the button to drop the electric window, needing air. Chewing nervously on her lips, she tried to return her focus to the road as she veered to the left and headed out to the property. In her rear-view mirror she saw the lights of Pierce's vehicle following her. Her focus waned as she pictured his strong, masculine hands firmly holding the steering-wheel and his hard, firm body pressed against the seat of his car. He was dangerously attractive. Thoughts of this country doctor that made her heart skip a beat had to end. He was off limits for so many reasons.

He'd surely had the perfect life, growing up, with two parents, a small dog, a white picket fence and siblings who were probably equally successful now they were grown up. A picture-perfect family photograph would have been sitting in a silver frame on the freshly dusted hallstand. Pierce would have arrived home from school to a mother in a floral apron, the smell of home-made raisin cookies baking in the oven.

Unlike her own childhood. More often than she cared to remember, Laine had arrived home from school to an empty house, a family she'd barely known, a tinned or frozen dinner she'd prepared herself and no time to do her homework because there had been so many chores with her name on them. And that had been her life in the better homes.

Then one wonderful day she'd found Maisey and Arthur Phillips. Two warm and uncomplicated people had opened their home and their hearts and had made her feel unconditional love for the first time in her life.

'Laine Phillips, you are so not his type,' she told herself. 'You don't bake apple pie and you don't do forever—or anything even close to that. You rarely go on a second date.' Laine reminded herself this was a job, and she was doing it for the charity and those who would benefit. She gave her time as often as she could to help a cause so close to her heart. That had to be her focus for the next two days. Nothing more.

Fifteen minutes later, and after travelling along a long dirt road, they were at the property. Laine checked her watch. It was just after five. This would give her time to set up the shot and have Pierce positioned for the sunrise. She was mindful of the family still sleeping inside, so she dropped her speed and cruised past the house as quietly as possible and pulled up near a wire fence.

'I will need your shirt off again,' she called across the paddock as Pierce climbed from his car.

'Let's just do the open shirt instead,' Pierce called back as he unzipped his leather jacket. 'It's damned cold out here this morning.'

'No, I don't want a shirt, open or not,' she responded as she opened the back of the car and began pulling out her equipment. She left her headlights on and faced them away from the house and onto the area she would be setting up. 'The moment *I'm* ready to go, you need to remove both your jacket and shirt.'

Pierce couldn't believe the words that had come from her mouth. His blood was boiling. 'If you think you can order me about in the name of charity you've got another think coming. Not sure what your problem is, but you need to sort it out and get back to me because I'm sure as hell not hanging around here, listening to you.'

Laine watched him take off across the paddock to his car, praying he would not start the engine and leave.

'I'm sorry,' she called to him. 'Hate me, but please don't go. We need this shot for the calendar.'

He paused, and looked back at Laine. She was standing alone in the paddock with everything set up. Damn her. Angrily he pulled the keys from the ignition. A scowl washed over his face as he slipped the keys in his pocket and made his way back to the fence to the fence.

'Let's just get this over with,' he said as he slipped off his jacket and shirt.

Laine didn't answer him. She was so grateful that he had not driven off and she knew she would have deserved it if he had left. Somehow she seemed bent on offending him, and she knew it was not always conscious on her part. It was just something she did to keep people, particularly men, at arm's length.

In silence, she set up the camera tripod and the large gold reflector. That would capture the light and give Pierce's sculpted body a golden hue, almost sun-kissed, as the sun rose. She pulled the camera body from her bag and attached the lens, then directed Pierce to the wooden fence post before she returned to switch off the car headlights.

She was very aware that the sun would soon be peeking over the hill soon and there was an urgency to capture that one special shot. She held a small meter up close to Pierce to check the amount of light available and then returned to her position behind the camera.

'Almost perfect,' she called, as she pulled a tan stockman's hat and an atomiser from her large backpack and rushed over to him.

Without warning, she placed the hat on his black hair and sprayed his already cold body with a fine mist of oil.

'Are you mad?' he yelled as he pulled the hat free. 'I'm already bloody freezing and now you cover me in oil—what the hell is up with you?'

He stopped his rant the moment her warm fingers began working the oil all over his cold, muscled chest. He looked down to see both of her hands moving slowly but purposefully across his bare skin. His raised his gaze to look at her beautiful face.

Suddenly his emotions took over and he took her wrists with his hands. He said nothing, searching her eyes for a reaction before he pulled her up against his body and kissed her. She froze as he first pressed his lips down on hers then unwillingly she melted into his kiss. A moment before he had been so angry but now his lips met hers there was no anger, his kiss tender and passionate. For a brief moment she relished being that close to him. The desire he was stirring within her was undeniable and it felt so good. She didn't want it to end.

But she had to pull away.

'No...we can't.' She struggled to speak as she could still taste his mouth on hers. Her heart was racing as she pulled her emotions into line and her body away from his.

He released her immediately. 'It was just a kiss. I wasn't about to throw you onto the ground and ravage you in the crops...not yet at least.'

Laine didn't respond but her heart was still racing. Her stomach still churning. Her mind still spinning.

'We have to keep this professional—'

'You're absolutely sure about that?' his husky voice questioned her. 'Because that kiss didn't feel at all like work.'

Her breathing was still unsteady, just like her voice. 'You took me by surprise, but it can't happen again.'

'Why not? Is there someone waiting back in the Big Apple with your name tattooed on his chest?'

'No, it's not that.' Her eyes rolled at the thought.

'So there's no one I have to duel for you?'

Hardly, she thought. No man she had ever been with would fight for her. She doubted if any of them had given her a second thought after she'd ended their brief liaisons.

Laine closed her eyes for a moment before she answered. 'No one is waiting but that's not the point. This is work. I don't mix pleasure and work. Ever. It's a rule. So let's forget what just happened.'

Laine knew she would never forget the kiss. It would be impossible to erase the tenderness and passion in his lips. But she had to try.

Pierce decided to play it her way—for the moment at least. He would acknowledge her rule. Then do his best later to break it.

'Okay, have it your way.'

She smiled nervously before racing back to the camera. 'Don't touch your body and please put the hat back on,' she managed to tell him after she drew a deep breath to steady herself. *What was happening to her?* Very self-consciously she added, 'The mist looks like sweat. Believe me, you look great. Just hold still…'

Pierce ran his fingers through his hair and pushed the hat back on, still smiling from the kiss and his intention for it not to be the last one they shared. At just that moment the sun rose and the most beautiful colours spilled over the hills and across the paddock and Pierce was lit by the gold and tangerine rays. Laine had positioned Pierce so that the glare of the sun did not make him just a silhouette. The sun was on her right side and it bathed him in warmth. Still reeling from the kiss, she felt strangely different, and a little light-headed.

Unsure what to make of it, she dragged her thoughts as best as she could back to the job. Capturing the beauty of the sunrise. Nothing could compete with the magnificence of what Mother Nature brought to the table. No photo-editing program could ever capture the jaw-dropping beauty that she was witnessing. Her camera shutter was clicking at lightning speed, just like her heart, as she directed Pierce to use the old fencepost as a prop. The single eucalypt was a black silhouette in the background.

Laine was struggling with her emotions and the almost overwhelming desire to rush back and finish what Pierce had started, but she couldn't. She had to focus on framing the shot. It was perfect. She quickly checked that she was happy with the colour rendition and saturation, and ensured the shadows were not too dark.

December would without doubt be her favourite month in the calendar. Uralla was truly beautiful. And Pierce was more handsome than almost any man she had ever seen. And his kiss was more tender than any kiss she had ever received. But it would be the only one they would share. She could never let it happen again.

Laine was painfully aware that if she wasn't very careful she might run the risk of getting a little too close to the man leaning on the fencepost. And logic reassured her that it would only lead to disaster.

Pierce was physically cold, and clenching his teeth

slightly to prevent them from chattering, but remembering the brief moment when his lips had met the warmth of Laine's made it bearable. Despite her pulling away, he had felt the way she'd instinctively responded. The way her body had pressed into his and the way she'd returned the kiss. Despite her icy demeanour, Laine had shown, albeit briefly, that she was all woman.

Pierce followed her directions. The focus and passion he witnessed as she released the camera from the tripod and moved freely on the ground near him, crouching and climbing as needed, kept the smile on his face. She was a complicated woman without doubt, but the love she had for her work was undeniable. It was as if she had opened a door and he was getting a view of the real Laine Phillips. And unfortunately for Pierce, he liked what he saw. And what he had felt in her kiss.

'That, as they say, is a wrap.' Laine tried to joke and remove the tension as she crossed to the car with her backpack. Once she put down the camera, she felt her shield had been removed. Hiding behind her professional demeanour was so easy with her camera in her hands.

She bit the inside of her cheek nervously as she stopped looking at Pierce through a lens and saw him standing so close to her. It was only a short time before that her body had been pressed against that nakedness. Pulling her desire into line, and her thoughts back to where they should be, she returned with a towel for Pierce. 'Here, take this and dry yourself off before you get dressed.'

Pierce had almost forgotten the cold. Watching Laine light up as she'd slipped into the role of professional photographer with ease, Pierce had felt an unexpected admiration. The way in which she had planned and executed the shoot had not only been skilled but also heartfelt in her desire to capture the beauty of the landscape.

And now he had felt her body against his, despite what she'd said about keeping things purely professional, she had definitely got under his skin. She was irritating, opinionated, abrupt and more defensive than any woman he had ever met, but it didn't deter him. In fact, he found that it spurred him on to know more about her. But time was limited. He was conscious that in just over twenty-four hours she would be gone. It gave him little time to be subtle.

He took the towel from her outstretched hand. 'Do you have any plans for dinner tonight?' he asked, then added for extra reassurance, 'No questions, just dinner.'

Laine stopped to consider the invitation. She wanted to say no, she knew in her head that she should say no, but something stronger, something she hadn't felt in years made her say yes. It was her heart talking again. This was the second time in as many days. What was it about Pierce that had her heart suddenly talking louder than her head? More than anything, she hated that she was listening.

She bit her lip and muttered, 'Okay. But on one condition…'

'Which is?'

'No repeat of what just happened. It can't happen again. This is just a calendar shoot, an assignment for me, that's all. There won't be another kiss.'

Pierce nodded. 'If that's the rule, I'll accept it.'

'Yes, it is.'

Pierce would accept it and then do whatever it took to *break* it. He wanted this beautiful, very talented conundrum more than he had ever wanted any woman.

'Okay.' He reiterated her low-key response as he slipped on his shirt and slowly buttoned it up, then put on his leather jacket. 'If we're finished up here, I'll head back to my surgery and see you out at the homestead around five.'

Laine was dismantling the reflector. 'Sounds good to me,' she said, alarm bells again ringing in her head. She was already questioning her sense in accepting the dinner invitation. 'Can you bring another pair of jeans? I'd like to shoot you in a faded old denim pair if you have one. Don't mind if they have rips in them—in fact, I'd prefer it if they did. The barn has a rustic feel and I'd like you to fit in with that.'

'Sure,' Pierce replied, and without thinking too much about it he began to help Laine put the equipment back in the car. They worked quickly and in moments both were ready to hit the road. It was still early and there were still no lights on in the house, which made Laine feel more relaxed. She would send an official thank-you note from New York and they would be none the wiser she had been there.

Pierce held back in his car so that Laine would exit the property first. There were still a few hours till he was needed at the surgery so he waved goodbye when they hit the New England Highway and headed home, planning on getting another hour's sleep.

Laine drove back to the Bushranger Inn, thinking about Pierce. The photos were great, she was sure. And he had been easy to shoot. She touched her mouth with her fingertips and thought back to the kiss and the way she had reacted. Her heart wished things could be different but they weren't. The idea of taking things further made her body sizzle with anticipation but her heart was now listening to reason. She couldn't afford to get involved. It wasn't in her plans. Not in Uralla, not anywhere.

She had another shoot that night and one she planned for early the next morning. Then she would be off. She'd be heading back to her real life in New York. The next day's shoot was for one of the major sponsors of the project and didn't involve Pierce. So after the session at the homestead and dinner there would be no further contact with him.

She drew in a deep breath and headed back down the highway. The sun was up now and there was a little traffic on the road but still not much. The driver of a small delivery truck waved at her as she passed him and she smiled and waved back. Her thoughts travelled back to her home and she smiled at the thought of the cab drivers leaning on their horns, a throng of people making their way down Wall Street, wrapped up against the freezing cold with a steaming coffee in one hand and their mobile phone in the other. Masses of people all heading to work, many in the same high-rise buildings with no time to stop and acknowledge each other. Their lives were frantic, stressful and for many, despite their social media updates, lonely.

Laine sighed as she remembered what she had left behind and what she had accepted in the trade. Manhattan was now home but Uralla was definitely tugging at her heartstrings. And a certain country doctor who certainly knew how to kiss was threatening to unravel her rules.

CHAPTER FOUR

'TREVOR JACOBS?' PIERCE called into the small waiting room. 'Please come in.'

The elderly man stood up slowly, folded his newspaper and slipped it under his arm before he crossed the room.

'G'day, Doc,' he said, as he entered the consulting room and took a seat.

'So, Trevor, what brings you to see me today?' Pierce enquired as he sat down and brought his patient's notes up on the computer screen on his desk.

Trevor drew a deep breath. 'It's the ticker, it's playin' up again. I was short of breath last night and again this mornin' and Betty reckoned I should get you to check it out.'

'Well, I'm glad you listened to your wife and came to see me,' Pierce remarked.

'As if I'd argue with Betty and live to see tomorrow.'

Pierce smiled. 'Okay, let's take your blood pressure and then I'll listen to your heart,' he said, reaching for the blood-pressure cuff. Wrapping it around the man's arm, he inflated it slowly and noted the result. 'And now if you could just unbutton your shirt?' Pierce began his examination. 'I need you to take a deep breath and hold it for a minute then slowly let it out. I just want to hear if there are any unusual sounds in your chest and also whether there's any build-up of fluid in your lungs.' After listening to his heart, he then lifted Trevor's shirt and placed the stethoscope on different places on his back, asking the older man to follow the same instructions. Then he checked the man's abdomen for swelling before he placed the stethoscope back on his desk and turned back to Trevor. 'One more thing then we'll be done. Can you just slip off your shoes and socks for a minute? I just want to check for any swelling.'

After completing the physical examination, Pierce washed his hands at the basin and returned to his desk.

'Is it bad?' Trevor asked, as he tucked himself in. 'Don't hold back, Doc, I can take it.'

Pierce considered the notes and turned his chair back to the man. 'It's nothing that we haven't discussed in the past, Trevor, but I want you to see a cardiologist in Armidale,' he began. 'Your heart appears to be struggling. It can't fill with enough blood or pump with enough force. The pumping action of your heart is getting weaker and that's why you are breathless and probably getting more tired.'

The old man nodded sheepishly. 'I'm exhausted by the day's end, sometimes exhausted by lunchtime. I've taken an afternoon nap a few times in the past couple of weeks.'

'I'm not surprised. Your heart is struggling to pump enough blood to the lungs, where it picks up oxygen, so that's why you're suffering from lethargy.'

'Lethargy? Isn't that some bug from air-conditioning units?'

Pierce looked at the man with a puzzled expression for a moment then realised what he meant. 'Not legionnaire's, Trevor, lethargy. It means tiredness.'

'Good.' He laughed. 'Bloody hate to add another problem to me ticker not workin'!'

Pierce smiled but continued, his tone stern, 'Because your heart is weakened, blood and fluid can back up into the lungs, and some fluid can build up in the feet, ankles, and legs. Yours are showing signs of swelling.'

'But I've done everything you told me, honestly. Betty is one tyrant and won't let me have my bacon and eggs any more, won't let me put bloody salt on anything. We walk every day for about thirty minutes and I haven't had a smoke for near on twelve months.'

'I know you're doing everything I have asked of you but unfortunately you still have some problems. Your blood pressure is very high and you need to see the specialist as soon as possible.'

Trevor shook his head. 'So that godawful oat bran that she makes me eat for breakfast hasn't made a scrap of difference, then?'

'No, Trevor, I wouldn't say that. It's all helped but I would like you to go to the Armidale in the next few days for some tests.' Pierce began inserting the different request forms into his printer. 'I'm ordering an ECG, which is a test to measure the rate and regularity of your heartbeat. The test can also show if the walls of your heart have thickened. I also want a chest X-ray to let me know whether your heart is enlarged or your lungs have fluid in them, both signs of heart disease, and I will ask for a blood test to measure the level of a hormone that increases in heart failure.'

'I'll feel like a lab rat at the end of that day, hey, Doc?'

Pierce signed each form as it was printed, knowing full well Trevor's humour was masking his concern.

'Trevor, they're routine tests and you've done every-

thing I asked of you so let's get this done and refer you to
a cardiologist at the New England District Hospital. Don't
worry and let Betty know if she has any questions to call
me.' With that he handed Trevor the printed forms and
gently patted his back. 'I'll ask Tracy to call and make a
time at the hospital for you as soon as possible and just
keep doing what you are doing.'

The old man nodded and tried to smile but it was half-
hearted and tainted by his anxiety as they made their way
back to Reception.

'Betty's okay, I hope? It's unusual for her not to be
here with you.'

'No, she's home with the grandkids today. To be honest, Doc, it was a relief to get out of there. I'm not sure
how from three married sons we got five granddaughters, not a grandson in sight. Each one has a squeal louder
than the other and they get vicious, really vicious over
a bunch of scrawny-lookin' dolls. I don't know what to
do with them. Trucks and cars, that's what I know, not
prissy dolls.'

Pierce smiled and watched the older man shake his
head as if he had spent the morning on a battlefield. He
hoped one day to have a family of his own. Apart from
his aunt, who kept in contact on the telephone, he had
no living relatives.

Although the last two years in this town had made him
almost forget that. He had made a great group of friends
and had been a part of their lives, their family events, the
odd Friday night watching televised sport, and Saturday
afternoon watching the local football matches, summer
barbeques, even birthday parties for their children. It was
a close-knit community and just what he had been searching for. Pierce was very happy to call it home.

It was also a far cry from the life he'd known as child. A life far removed from what he wanted for his own children in the future. An Australian citizen by birth, he had travelled extensively with his parents and lived abroad for part of his childhood; seeing Paris by the age of four, Tokyo's largest theme park for his sixth birthday, New York every year until he was ten, and finally an exclusive boarding school in Germany shortly after the accident when everything had changed. Although he'd never wanted for anything material, and his parents had always been there for him while he'd been young, he'd missed having roots and stability.

Pierce took a deep breath, pushing back those memories, and instead thought about Laine. She seemed to love travel, waking up in different cities, surrounded by strangers on her photo shoots all over the world, while he wouldn't mind if he never used his passport again. They were two very different people, with very different lifestyles.

Their personalities were also at odds, but still the woman was entrenched in his thoughts. She was nothing like anyone he had met, and neither was her kiss. He wondered if she might be like a chocolate éclair—sweet and mushy if any man ever had the chance to break through the hard exterior. Unfortunately there was little time for him to be the man to cut through that tough coating.

They had the final shoot at the homestead at five o'clock. Pierce planned on heading into Armidale for a nice meal. Laine had been unnerved enough by something to run away from him at the top pub and the bottom pub hadn't fared much better so he thought a fresh start in the nearby town would be great. He didn't want a repetition of the previous disastrous evening. Armidale was only fifteen minutes away and the short trip would give him a little more time with this gorgeous Aussie export, if she would let him drive.

He spied his well-worn denim jeans in a bag by the door ready for the final shoot and the final time he would see Laine. It was a strange and inexplicable emptiness that crept up on him as he thought that in a few short days she would be back on the other side of the world and there was little chance their paths would ever cross again. But the warmth in her kiss made him want more at least while she was in the same town.

Laine spent the day in her room, sitting on the bed poring over that morning's shots. She had grabbed a late breakfast at the motel restaurant after she'd returned from the McKenzies' property, then at about twelve she headed out for some lunch and returned to the quiet confines of her room again.

She lay back on the bed and closed her eyes and thought about Pierce. She had been scrutinising his shots for hours and in each one he was more handsome than in the one before. There would be little editing needed, just as she had suspected during the shoots. The difficult part would be selecting only one photograph. His striking face, complete with chiselled jaw, sculpted abs and powerful arms, would melt any woman's heart, and he was definitely the perfect Dr December. Although they would only be able to imagine the passion in his kiss. She had experienced it first hand but it would be her secret for ever. The tenderness and passion when he'd stolen that kiss would not be easily if ever forgotten.

He would indeed be a wonderful Christmas present for every woman who bought the calendar.

She wondered why there wasn't a Mrs Beaumont. Perhaps he was a confirmed bachelor, she mused, or just didn't want to settle down until he was older. She had seen the details on the registration form and had noted he was thirty-four. Still young enough to leave marriage for a few years, she thought.

'And why exactly that is your concern?' she muttered under her breath as she sat up, crossed her legs and twisted her hair into a high bun, securing it with a pencil. She hoped that changing her posture would bring the blood back to her brain, away from her heart, and stop her stupid train of thought. 'It was only a kiss and it will do no good thinking about a man like Pierce,' she berated herself. 'Love is for fools.'

'This is Dr Pierce Beaumont. I would like to speak with the paediatric resident regarding an infant admitted earlier today ago with suspected pertussis, James Hollis.' Pierce waited to be connected to the paediatric ward.

'This is Myles Oliver, the attending paediatrician looking after James.'

'Hi, Myles, Pierce Beaumont, the Hollis family GP in Uralla. Just wanted to see how James doing.'

'Thanks for getting James to us so quickly, Pierce. He's stable, we've him isolated from other patients and I've just broken the news to his mother that he may be with us for a few weeks. The coughing has become progressively worse over the last two hours so we have rostered nurses to watch him constantly for the next twenty-four hours. We're monitoring his heart and breathing.'

'So pertussis is the diagnosis?'

'Yes, there's a spate of whooping cough around at the moment. There's quite a few cases in the New England Tablelands region. It happens when some people in the community refuse vaccinations and, bingo, the society's immunity declines. Typically, it's the little ones like James who suffer.'

'What's your treatment plan?'

'Monitoring and antibiotics. He's still breastfeeding but if that slows he'll be given IV fluids. I'm keeping a close watch on the oxygen therapy.'

'Please keep me posted. I will try to get there tomorrow and see how his mother is dealing with it all. She'll need some support.'

'Great. See you then.'

Pierce hung up the phone and walked out to the waiting room.

'Tracy, can you block off a bit more time around lunch tomorrow? I want to check on James Hollis and his mother in Armidale.'

Tracy checked the diary for the following day. 'Not a problem, I can shift a couple of appointments around.'

CHAPTER FIVE

LAINE HEADED OUT past the Armidale airport to the homestead a little earlier than she needed to be. She loved the grounds and the ambience of Saumarez and she knew it would be months, if not years, before she was in a place so serene again.

As she drove along the narrow dirt road leading to the homestead gate, she gazed out at the wide-open paddocks dotted with small groups of cows taking shelter from the afternoon sun under the towering eucalypts. There were about fifteen other farm buildings on the ten-hectare grazing property and for obvious reasons it was a popular wedding venue. Laine could see why couples would choose the stunning backdrop.

However, she couldn't understand why they would want to get married. Signing up to depend on one person for the rest of your life was sheer madness, she had decided long ago. There was only one person in the world who would never let Laine Phillips down or make her feel secure then cut the rope, and that was herself. Laine Phillips was her own life partner and twelve years ago she made the only vow she'd told herself she would ever make, and that was to never depend on anyone else.

Still, it was a wonderful day and she wanted to enjoy

the serenity of the town while she could. She shook herself back into appreciating her wonderful surroundings. In no time at all she would be on another plane, beginning the long haul home to her high-rise apartment, so she decided to make the most of the open spaces.

It was very peaceful. She lowered the electric window and breathed in the warm, clean air. It took her back to a time when this had been all she'd known. No hustle and bustle, no traffic fumes, no rush to be anywhere and definitely no planes to catch.

Laine thought back to her very first plane trip at eighteen years of age. It had been an assignment she had secured for a small indie music magazine, photographing a grunge band in Melbourne. She hadn't wanted to admit to her boss that she had never flown before. Her nerves had mounted as she'd sat in the departure lounge, her boarding pass clutched in her shaking hand, but she'd known that if she wanted to forge a career overseas then she had to take the flight.

Her knuckles had been white and her stomach halfway up her throat when the plane had finally built up speed as it had thundered down the runway. When the huge and, in her opinion, much too heavy plane had finally become airborne, Laine's heart had pounded in her chest with such ferocity she'd thought it might possibly burst. She'd felt so light-headed that she'd doubted there had been any blood left in her brain. The fact that she hadn't passed out had been a miracle. But she hadn't, and it had been the first of literally hundreds of trips she was to make in the coming years. First they'd got longer and then they'd become a better class and over the years Laine had became accustomed to the business lounge in the international airports. But whenever the tyres of the plane lifted off the ground, she became Melanie Phillips for a few short minutes and wished there was another hand holding hers.

She came to a halt at the end of the gravel and dirt driveway as she found a place to park down near the closest of the large barns. It was Thursday and there were tourists, and probably some locals, she assumed, taking a guided a tour of the Edwardian mansion's thirty rooms and enjoying a leisurely stroll through the picturesque cottage garden, the picking garden and over the perfectly manicured lawns. But it was the outbuildings, complete with antique tools and equipment, that held more interest for Laine. They were a link to early pastoral life and would be a perfect backdrop for her final rustic shoot with Pierce.

She notified the caretaker of her arrival and then headed off to unpack her equipment and begin loading it inside the barn. The large door on the opposite side was open and the sweeping view was as breathtaking as Laine remembered. After stacking her equipment in one of the small rooms inside the barn and locking her car, she stood in the doorway and looked out across the paddocks. The other smaller outbuildings held farm equipment and the one closest was a chicken run filled with large Rhode Island reds.

Laine had been fourteen when she'd last stood in the very same place. It had been a wedding, a real barn wedding complete with white tables and chairs, home-made jam with checked gingham tops as wedding favours and a lot of dancing. She remembered her mother and father laughing as they'd danced all evening. With the back of her hand she wiped away a tiny tear that had formed at the corner of her eye. This was becoming a habit that she didn't much like.

'A penny for your thoughts?'

Laine knew the voice only too well. Dr December had also arrived early at Saumarez. She had no intention of letting him see her upset.

'I was at a wedding here many years ago. The bride was a local girl and the groom was a musician from Tamworth. It was one of the best times I had as a child,' she said honestly, and without turning around, before she dropped her voice to not much more than a whisper. 'Although, to be honest, it was so long ago I can only just remember the details.'

Pierce didn't hear the soft words she had muttered as he studied the silhouette in the doorway. She was still in her jeans and shirt but in the warm afternoon sun there was no sign of the morning's jacket or scarf. Her long wavy hair was hanging down over her shoulders and her feet were in flat brown sandals. Even without seeing her pretty face, Laine was still demanding his attention.

Her emotions back under control, she suddenly spun on her flat heels. 'So what brings you here so early?'

'I could ask you the very same question,' he returned, as he looked into the most stunning green eyes he had ever seen. Each time he looked at her face he found her more beautiful than before.

'Setting up for the shoot.'

Pierce looked around the empty, dusty barn complete with cobwebs strewn across the beams and smiled. 'Yep, this place is certainly filled with your equipment. Can't find a place to stand without tripping over a cord or light.'

Laine knew he had seen through her and decided to turn it into a factual conversation fuelled by her high-school studies as she turned around dismissively to the panoramic view again. 'Did you know that the property takes its name from the Dumaresq Estate in Jersey in the Channel Islands and it was the last stopping point for settlers moving north?'

'Yes, I did,' he replied in an equally controlled voice. 'And did you know that after Dumaresq's death the property was sold to a gentleman by the name of Thomas, whose family lived in the original slab homestead overlooking Saumarez Creek?'

'Fine,' she retorted, 'Mr Know-It-All, when was it built?' Laine didn't actually know the date or the last piece of information that Pierce had provided so this question was for her own interest and she couldn't verify his answer if her life depended on it.

'The date is somewhere around the early nineteen hundreds. There is nothing recorded to confirm the exact date.'

Intelligent and good looking, she thought to herself. A lethally tempting combination.

'I'm assuming we can't shoot with all of the visitors still around, so what if we have something to eat at the homestead café? They have the best scones, jam and cream.'

Laine was tempted. She knew the cream would be country rich, the jam would be home-made and the scones would be freshly baked. She had a mental picture of the steam escaping from the fluffy dough as she cut it open and covered it with fresh, fruit-laden jam and a huge dollop of freshly whipped cream. Her mouth was watering with the images in her head but she also knew that it went against everything her personal trainer would allow—no carbs, only low-fat dairy and no refined sugar. She bit her lip and knew there was only one choice to make.

'Do you think they'd have blackberry jam?'

Pierce nodded. 'Only one way to find out.'

The time passed quickly in the homestead café. Pierce didn't ask any questions relating to Laine's past and instead kept the conversation to her work and his role as one of the town's doctors.

'So what's the population here now?' she enquired, finishing the last bite of her delicious afternoon tea.

'Around twenty seven hundred, give or take.'

Laine was surprised. The town had had nowhere near that number when she'd left. It had grown but she knew it hadn't changed. Only she had and that was her issue.

'I think I'd better set up my equipment and you should put on something a little scruffy for this shoot.'

He playfully saluted her. 'The ripped jeans are in my car.'

In a different universe, she thought, this could end very differently. The handsome, eligible, intelligent, charismatic man sitting opposite her might ask her out, she would without hesitation say yes, and they would at the very least kiss goodnight in a few hours' time. But here and now they were two different people and it would end with a handshake after dinner tonight. No ifs, no buts. He was a charming man, with a good heart, and yet it would never work. It could never happen. They were so very different, although she noticed during their conversation he was as guarded about his past as she was about hers.

Not that she pried, but it was as if he hadn't had a life before he'd arrived in Uralla. Well, at least not one he cared to share with her. It seemed odd for a country doctor to be equally unwilling to talk about his past. There couldn't be anything too shocking or dark, she mused, or he wouldn't be able to practise medicine. He didn't appear overly scarred or bitter, unlike her, but she decided but there was definitely something Pierce Beaumont was hiding.

'Perfect,' she said as she took another shot. 'Now just lift your chin a little and lean back into the doorway.

Pierce followed Laine's instructions and she was able to capture the setting sun and the handsome subject, doing justice to both.

'Final shot now the sun's almost gone. Can you reach out and touch each side of the doorway,' she asked, as she lay on the ground, shooting up at his glistening torso. 'It looks amazing from here.'

Pierce couldn't help but agree as he looked at Laine lying on the ground in front of him. Her hair was cascading across the cobbled floor like a luxurious pillow and her long legs were poured into her tight blue jeans. Her white shirt was a little dusty and slightly open, revealing her lightly tanned cleavage in her white lacy bra. It took every ounce of self-control not to drop to the ground, pull her into his arms and kiss her again. And then more. The level of desire this woman was stirring in him was driving him crazy. But he had agreed to her rules. And he had to keep his word, even though it was killing him.

'Great job,' she announced, getting to her feet and dusting herself off. She ran her fingers through her hair and shook it gently. 'I may have picked up a little something from the floor but, what the heck, it will brush out and I have some amazing shots.'

Pierce was steeling himself against the doorframe. He took a deep and calculated breath and tried to keep his longing for the woman, so dangerously close to him, in check. 'I thought we might hit an authentic Italian restaurant in Armidale. Great pasta, the best wine and gelato better than you would find in Napoli.'

Laine stretched her back from side to side and then tucked in her dusty shirt. 'Sounds lovely but I think the way I look that we should go for drive-through hamburgers.'

'It's still early, we have time to change...' he began.

'Time maybe but I'm exhausted and lacking any energy to find fresh clothes in my suitcase and then head out again. It's been a long few weeks since I arrived in Australia and I could really do with a hot bath and an early night.'

Pierce wasn't about to accept her answer that quickly. 'Then what about the Chinese restaurant? It's a far cry from the Waldorf, so they won't mind how you're dressed. I'll stay in my ripped jeans if it would make you feel better.'

Laine smiled at his dining comparison. It was much better than the idea of heading out after her relaxing bath to find food. A quick meal on the way home would be the easier option.

'Sure. Why not?'

'Great. I'll help pack this all up and head to the club.'

Laine was already packing away her gear and feeling more tired by the minute. 'I'm sure I'll crash tonight and sleep for ten hours!'

They worked in unison, wrapping cords, packing up lights and putting everything away neatly in the allocated waterproof bags. Laine was grateful for the assistance and she couldn't help but notice how carefully Pierce handled everything. He was respectful of her belongings. That made her smile, just a little, as she zipped up the final bag.

'I'll follow you,' Laine said, as she closed the car door on the last of the gear and looked back at the tree-lined horizon one last time. Even in the dimming light it was stunning in its raw simplicity and she hoped with all her heart that she had captured the natural beauty of the land.

Pierce climbed into his dusty four-wheel drive, and headed out of the car park, along the windy dirt road and onto the New England Highway. He glanced back more than once, much more than once, at the car following him, wishing that the driver would stay a little longer in his town.

Fifteen minutes later the two cars pulled into the car park.

Laine jumped out of the car, hungry and tired in equal amounts. The evening was getting cool so she pulled her favourite designer sweater from her backpack and threw it over her shoulders. A quick Chinese meal, a goodbye, thank-you-very-much handshake with Pierce and then bed for a good night's sleep was Laine's plan. She pushed the image of their kiss from her mind. That would never happen again. Pierce had been professional during the shoot and she was relieved he hadn't tried a repetition of the early morning embrace when his lips had met hers so passionately. She wasn't sure she could pull away a second time.

'Let me get your backpack—you don't want to leave your laptop in the car.'

Laine looked at the man who was being so gallant. Most of the men she spent time with socially wouldn't give a damn about her possessions. Or even her for that matter, not truly.

With one hand in the small of her back and the other holding her backpack, he gently directed her to the door. It felt so good for him to feel the warmth of her body through her thin shirt. He knew he couldn't let his fingers rest there too long but he didn't want to pull away until the last possible moment.

Laine rested back a little into the softness of his warm hand. It felt good. His touch was strong but gentle. She didn't want him to move his hand away but she couldn't let him know that.

They entered the back way and climbed a flight of stairs into the bistro. It was busy for a Thursday night and they sat at the end of a long table. A number of patrons waved at Pierce and he acknowledged them in a similarly friendly manner. Laine was happy to be sitting away from the main crowd. She still felt a little uncomfortable in case anyone recognised her but with only Friday's shoot for one of the major sponsors in Armidale ahead of her, she was feeling a little more relaxed.

'White wine or something a little stronger after the day you've had?' Pierce asked with a teasing wink.

'My day was fine and quite easy,' she replied light-heartedly. 'To be honest, I'd rather stick to chilled sparkling water with a twist of lime.'

Pierce crossed to the bar and ordered the drinks while Laine looked over the menu.

Moments later he placed in front of her a tall glass with sparkling water, ice and a lime quarter sitting precariously on the rim. 'Spied anything you fancy?'

Laine thought better than to admit the truth. She fancied Pierce Beaumont. Laine Phillips, who travelled the world for a living, who refused to put down roots for more than a few weeks, the same woman who had a no-second-date rule, fancied the small-town doctor. It was ludicrous. And it wasn't going to happen. She had to finish dinner, shake hands and leave him at her motel-room door. It couldn't go any further, although the idea of spending the last night in town in Pierce's warm, strong arms was very appealing.

But Laine knew it couldn't happen. The night would no doubt be wonderful, he was such a caring man with a body that rivalled Adonis', and she suspected from the kiss that his skills as a lover would be perfectly honed, but then there was facing waking up in the morning. That awkward moment when she had to ask him to leave and say she would never see him again. She had done it more than once before and it had been easy, but this time she suspected it might actually hurt a little. It might be sad, it might even make her cry, and Laine Phillips didn't want any pain or sadness in her life.

She had to keep it friendly. But that was it.

'Special fried rice and lemon chicken sounds great to me.'

'I'm a black bean beef type of man so I guess that's our order done. Sit tight and I'll be back.'

Laine watched him walk away and this time she noticed the slight swagger in his long, purposeful steps. His broad shoulders, slim hips and perky rear could not be overlooked. He was the most handsome man in the bistro and from the way the women's eyes followed him she wasn't the only one who noticed.

The calendar would walk off shelves if he was the doctor for every month. Laine knew there would be no complaints if each of the twelve pages contained a different shot of her gorgeous dinner companion.

'So, no talk of the past,' he said as he sat down again.

'I learnt that early on, and I don't want you to walk out on me, so let's talk about the future. Where do you see yourself in five years' time?'

Laine sipped her icy cold drink and contemplated the question for a few minutes. 'I honestly don't know. I don't tend to think long term but I suspect doing much the same. Although I would like to increase my charity work. I believe in certain causes and in general they aren't high profile or on anyone's political radar and receiving oodles of money. So if I can help, I will.'

Pierce knew the woman sharing the table was a bundle of contradictions. She had an opinion about almost everything but she loved to listen; she tried to be cold and distant but she worked for charities that no one else cared about; she chose to be behind the camera when she was gorgeous enough to be on a magazine cover; and she had a deep appreciation of the Australian landscape and this little town in the middle of nowhere but chose to live in a high-rise apartment in one of the busiest cities in the world.

And he was confused, intrigued, curious but above all smitten. Laine Philips was fascinating for so many reasons and each minute he spent with her made him want her a little bit more.

But he couldn't let her know for fear of her bolting before her rice arrived.

CHAPTER SIX

LAINE RESTED HER head back and closed her eyes for a moment. She was in heaven.

'Was it as good for you as it was for me?' Pierce asked in a low, husky voice.

'Better, I suspect, much better.'

Pierce smiled. 'Maybe next time I'll have the chicken too, then. But mine was still great and the fried rice here is always good.'

She opened her eyes and looked at Pierce. 'Glad you talked me into coming here for dinner. With a belly this full I shall sleep like a little pig in mud now.'

Pierce chuckled. 'Bet you don't use that expression around your Manhattan friends, they'd have no idea what—'

His conversation was interrupted by a loud commotion by the doorway and then the sound of screeching tyres.

'Hell, no!' came a man's voice from the stairwell. 'I'll get the bastards who did this.'

Pierce stood up and, like most of the patrons in the bistro, made his way over to see what was happening.

'Sons of bitches. I'll rip their bloody arms off when I find them,' came another voice at top pitch.

'Any idea what's happening?' Laine called out in a concerned voice, hoping Pierce had seen something.

He shook his head in reply before he moved into the stairwell and out of her sight as he followed the men downstairs. As soon as he reached the ground he knew what had happened. It looked like a demolition yard. Almost every vehicle in the car park had been damaged. Windows were smashed, hoods and panels were dented and there were rubber burn marks on the bitumen leading away into the street. It appeared to have been more than one carload of perpetrators that had done the damage and sped away.

Pierce could see that the driver's door of his SUV had been scratched but it looked like they had been disturbed before they'd finished their handiwork on his. He looked over at Laine's hire car. The rear-view mirror was hanging down, with only wires keeping it attached, the front and back windscreen and the windows on the passenger side had been smashed. He raced over, fearing the worst. It was quickly confirmed.

All Laine's equipment was gone from the car. Everything had been taken, dragged out through the broken windows. He looked around on the ground and lying in the pile of shattered glass he saw two of her bags with the contents strewn across the bitumen. The lights had been trampled and the shards of broken glass were mixed with the glass from the windows. A tripod lay buckled and broken by the tyre and two camera lenses had been smashed against the building wall.

His head dropped into his hands. Laine would be devastated. He knew this equipment was very important to her. She had such pride and valued it all. To her, they were more than just work tools, she had an affinity and love of these objects.

The crowd outside was growing with all the bistro patrons pouring out to assess the damage. Something like this had never happened in the town, let alone this family-friendly restaurant car park.

'Did anyone see anything, anything at all?' an older woman, who Pierce recognised as one of the teachers at the local school, pleaded as she approached her car. It had been painted with a spray can of black paint. The roof had been smashed in, the tyres slashed and every window broken. It appeared to have taken the brunt of the attack. 'Who would do something so vicious? For no reason.'

'I saw them speed off, but they were too quick for me to get their number plates. I know they're not from around here, never seen them before,' one of the local lads told her.

'There were at least three carloads,' another older man added. 'That's why they were able to do so much damage so quickly. Rotten hooligans must have been driving through and decided to smash up some cars just because they could.'

Pierce quickly realised by the number of beer cans on the ground that it had been an alcohol-fuelled spree of destruction. 'Let's hope the driver wasn't drinking as much as it appears the rest were.'

'Oh, my God, what happened?' Laine gasped, as she reached the car park with the last of the bistro patrons. Then she spied her car. 'No, not my equipment, tell me it's not gone.' She looked at Pierce for reassurance he couldn't provide.

'I'm so sorry,' he said as he crossed to her. He wanted to almost barricade her from the desecration of her be-

longings. Pierce instinctively wrapped his arms around
her, pulling her close as she saw everything lying
smashed on the ground.

'Why? What sort of people do this?' She paused. It
suddenly felt so natural to be in the warmth of his embrace. For a fleeting moment she felt a level of comfort
that she had not experienced in over a decade. The softness of his chest, the strength of his arms wrapped around
her made her feel protected. She felt safe for the first time
since she'd left the town all those years ago. Her belongings were gone but somehow he made it almost okay. But
she had to snap out of it. Quickly she reminded herself
that she didn't want this feeling of dependence. She was
used to facing life's challenges alone. Pierce was not her
saviour. She could save herself.

Abruptly, she broke free of his hold and marched
around to inspect the damage. She grew angrier with
every step. 'The bastards have taken my cameras and
smashed everything else.'

Pierce was inspecting the damage when the screeching of tyres sounded not too far away and then the sound
of buckling metal. He rushed to the road to see the car
had spun and hit a metal power-line pole on the main
highway. The impact had been so great the rear of the
car was completely crushed. Three other men raced with
him to the scene.

'It's one of the hoodlum's cars. They must have turned
around and be heading back Tamworth way,' one of them
said loudly.

Pierce looked both ways on the highway before he
crossed with two of the men. Laine looked on anxiously
from across the road.

'Stop,' someone called to Pierce as he approached the

car. 'The fuel line must have been severed on impact, there's petrol leaking onto the road.'

Pierce saw the fuel slowing pouring from underneath the car. It was trickling towards the front of the car and the heat of the engine. He also saw the driver slumped over the steering-wheel. Quickly he prised open the driver's door, only to stop as flames could be seen emerging from the other side of the car.

'Step back,' the man called again. 'She's about to go up.'

Pierce could see the flames but he could also see the driver. He looked not more than sixteen and he was unconscious. There was no way that Pierce would walk away. If he didn't get him out, the boy would certainly die.

'He'll never make it,' another man called out. 'Get back away from the car.'

Pierce continued to struggle with the door until finally it opened. With only seconds to spare he pulled the young man from the car. As the boy's feet hit the bitumen the interior of the car was filled with the flames that had been lurking under the chassis. The other men rushed over and lifted the driver's legs and assisted Pierce to carry him across the road to safety.

'You're bloody crazy,' the older man said. 'He was one of the hooligans.'

In silence Pierce stared back at the car now engulfed in flames. His brow became clammy and his breathing laboured for a moment. Laine rushed over to see Pierce run his hands through his hair and watch in silence as the fire slowly took over the entire car, reducing it to a ball of fire and smoke. For a split second he was preoccupied, almost as if he was somewhere else completely. His far-away look didn't go unnoticed by Laine.

Abruptly Pierce turned his attention away from the burning vehicle and back to the young man. He knelt down and checked his vital signs. 'Can someone call for an ambulance and the firies, if you haven't already? Here's hoping there were no spinal injuries because I didn't have time to brace him.'

'Forget spinal injuries, he's bloody lucky to be alive, thanks to you,' the older man said, shaking his head in disbelief at what he had just witnessed.

Pierce checked the young man's airway before beginning CPR. The smell of alcohol was so strong on the boy that Pierce wasn't surprised he had lost control of the car. Laine watched on in awe at the way Pierce was handling the situation. He had risked his life for a young man who had been one of the group that had vandalised the cars. They had damaged everything in sight without remorse and yet he hadn't judged the boy's actions, he had saved his life. Completely selflessly he had stayed when he'd been told to run. The young man from the wrong side of the tracks owed his life to Pierce.

Pierce continued CPR until the ambulance arrived and the paramedics took over.

Laine doubted that she had ever seen such generosity of spirit in her life. Pierce was not just a handsome country doctor. He was a hero.

CHAPTER SEVEN

'YOUR TYRE IS slashed. Let me drive you back to the motel at least and we can get the hire company out to collect the car tomorrow.'

Laine looked down at the flat tyre. The shattered glass that had surrounded the car had been swept away, she assumed by the owners of the restaurant and no doubt the locals had chipped in to help out. Her torn bags and broken equipment had been placed neatly on the back seat. The car park mess had, for the most part, been cleaned up. She had forgotten how a small community rallied round and helped out. A mess like this would sit in a New York street until municipal services came and cleaned it up. She knew the foot traffic would turn up their noses and walk on by.

'Thank you, that would be great,' she said. 'I guess I can sort it out in the morning. It's not like there's anything worth taking now. It's all broken.'

All the commotion had finally subsided. The local fire truck and police had arrived on the scene at the same time. The fire had been quickly extinguished just as the rescue helicopter had airlifted the young man to hospital with head and suspected internal injuries. The police had taken statements and hoped, with the assistance of the injured young man in the days to come, all the culprits would be located and charged.

Not quite the evening Laine had imagined. Standing in the quiet of the car park with Pierce, she suddenly remembered she had a sponsor shoot the next morning at the local branch of a large national bank. 'Damn, my camera and my lights, I need them for tomorrow and they're gone. Thank God all of your shots are on the USB in my bag but everything I need for the sponsor shoot is gone and I have no way to get replacements here by tomorrow.'

'What if you purchase new gear at the camera shop in Armidale?'

'I can look into it but they may not stock everything I need. A lot of it comes from the overseas supplier directly. I can have it shipped but it will take a couple of days and the bank will be closed until Monday—'

'Tuesday, actually,' Pierce interjected.

'Tuesday?'

'It's a public holiday on Monday. Australia Day, so everything's shut.'

Laine just shook her head. 'But I need to be back in New York by then.'

'Then you'll have to miss the photo shoot in Armidale. No biggie. I guess it's just a country bank.'

'Don't say that,' she retorted. 'I promised the sponsor and I don't break promises. Whether the bank is in Wall Street or in Armidale, I said I would shoot it. And I will. I'll just have to make some changes to flights and get whatever equipment the Armidale camera shop doesn't have shipped to me from Sydney. Then let the bank know it won't be happening tomorrow. It can be done.' Laine was more than experienced at thinking on her feet.

'Great, then let's get you back to your motel so you can start making your calls and sending your emails.' He was still functioning a little on adrenalin and knew it would subside slowly, as would the vivid images that had come rushing back when he'd watched the fire envelop the car.

On the drive back to her motel Laine searched the net on her phone in silence but all the while was thinking about the way Pierce had looked back at the burning car. She wasn't sure she had a right to ask but something was making her want to know more about the man who had by his actions unwittingly proved himself to be so very different from the man she had imagined him to be.

'What happened back there?' Laine suddenly asked, as Pierce pulled the car to a halt in the car park at the front of her room.

'Running sheet, well, the vehicles in the car park were wrecked by some very troubled teens and then one wrapped himself around a pole, the car caught on fire and the young man was airlifted to hospital. But no one died so all in all a good outcome. Did I miss anything?'

'That's not what I meant,' she said. Undoing her seat-belt and turning towards Pierce, she brought her legs up onto the seat. 'I meant with you. I saw the look on your face as you watched the flames. It definitely wasn't fear, you'd just pulled the boy to safety, but there was something. I could see it in your eyes when you looked back at the burning car. I'm right, aren't I?'

Pierce turned his head to face his still slightly dusty driving companion. She was an amazingly beautiful woman but a woman with a question that begged for an answer. An answer he had never given before but one he now thought he might be ready to share. He hadn't struggled with the fire the way he'd imagined he might. The need to free the young man had been greater than the fear of the fire. Finally perhaps he had put that to rest.

He took a deep breath, put down the electric window and felt the evening breeze on his face. He said nothing as he gathered his thoughts.

'If you'd rather not talk about it, I understand. I really have no right to ask.'

'No, it's okay. I've never spoken about it and I guess I should and I suppose a car park is as good a place as any.' He lifted his gaze to the beauty of the now darkening sky. He didn't really notice the clouds that had formed streaks across the charcoal backdrop. His thoughts were travelling to a time in his past as he rubbed his neck.

'It goes way back. I was twelve, and I was with my parents in New York. It was November. My father liked to spend Thanksgiving there every year and watch the Macy's parade. We were staying in our condo, as we always did, and there was an explosion in the kitchen. They found out later it was a gas leak, my mother and father...' He paused for a moment. 'They were killed instantly. I had no idea at the time—'

'Oh, my God,' Laine gasped, and instinctively covered her mouth with both hands, her eyes wide in horror.

'The fire spread quickly,' Pierce continued matter-of-factly as his hands ran across the steering-wheel. 'I was forced out onto the balcony. We were fifteen stories up and the firies told me I had to jump. The ladders couldn't reach me and so I had no choice.'

'So you were alone on the balcony?'

'No, our neighbour's dog, Jackson, had been staying with us while they were away. He'd run through the smoke and found me, so I grabbed him as the fire took hold of the room behind us. When I saw the curtains finally go up in flames I climbed onto the railing and looked down at the fire trucks and the safety net below and I was petrified. I still remember fear running through me and the feeling of lead in my legs. They looked so small and so far away down on the pavement.

'I had no idea where my parents were and finally decided they must have left through the front door somehow. I'd been waiting for them to come and get me but the flames were too close and there was no sign of them. The idea that Jackson and I could die made me realise that I had to jump with him. No matter how frightened *I* was, I had no choice, I had to save him. So I stepped off the railing and just hoped to God they caught us both.'

Laine drew her legs closer to her chin and shook her head in disbelief. Pierce had been through so much and she had mistakenly thought his life had been easy. His words cut like a knife. How dared she have judged him on first sight? He hadn't judged the young man tonight. Instead, he had risked his life for a troubled young man he didn't even know. She had a lot to learn, she realised. And a lot she needed to forget.

Her illusions had been shattered and she was disappointed beyond belief with herself. The man she had imagined him to be had been one who had enjoyed a happy, secure family life, and it couldn't be further from the truth. She had envied him for something that he had never had. In fact, she had been more fortunate in having her parents until she'd turned sixteen, when they had been taken from her. She had been almost an adult and Pierce had only been a child when he'd lost his mother and father. And yet he never wore it on his sleeve. He didn't appear to be bitter with the world and yet he had every right to be an angry man.

'Hey, don't go quiet on me now,' he said, noticing her serious expression. 'It was a long time ago, over twenty years, in fact, and after tonight I guess I'm okay with fire, so I just need to work a bit on the height thing and I'll be as good as new.'

'And that's why you didn't want to go up the ladder. I'm so sorry,' she began, with concern etching her voice. 'If I'd known I would have found another way. I wish you'd told me. I thought you were just trying to be difficult. I must have come across as such an insensitive bitch.'

Laine wanted to reach out to him but not from pity—and neither was it the feeling that both owning the title of adult orphan made them in a way kindred spirits. It was more than that. It was his willingness to help another human being without hesitation. No preconceived ideas or prejudice despite what he had been though himself. And then to be willing to share something so personal with her. It took courage to be that vulnerable, that exposed, and she felt close to him for that reason alone. She had not witnessed that level of honesty in many years. Particularly not from herself. There was so much more to this country doctor than she had ever imagined.

'I didn't mean to go all serious on you.'

'Good. Now at least when you head back to the Big Apple you won't remember the Aussie doc as a pain in the arse without reason.'

'Far from it.' Laine's mouth curved into a smile and she leant over and did something she had never done. She tenderly kissed his cheek before she climbed from the car.

* * *

The idea came to Pierce in the early hours of the morning. As he tossed the light summer covers from his body and lay staring into the darkness he decided that he could not let Laine slip through his fingers. The kiss on the cheek had been a small step but a step at least. He knew he was right in thinking that underneath her chilly exterior lay a warm heart.

He rested his arms on the pillow above his head. There was no denying she had got under his skin. There was no point in trying to work out exactly when she had crept in. She just had. All he knew was that he had never felt this way before. And he suddenly realised he wasn't willing to let her walk away. Not without getting to know her a little better underneath that gorgeous armour.

It was just before three in the afternoon when he decided they could take a flight to Sydney to pick up what she needed for the shoot. The stores would be open on Saturday morning and they could call ahead and ensure everything was available. Then they could hire a car and drive to Toowoon Bay. His business manager could pull some strings and secure a villa for each of them at a beach hideaway for the weekend. It was a five-star resort, with stunning views over the South Pacific Ocean and the perfect getaway. They could stay Saturday and Sunday night. The practice was closed from Saturday until Tuesday morning so Uralla didn't need him and James was in excellent care in the New England District Hospital.

There would be uninterrupted time for Laine to relax with him. To get to know each other and see where it took them. Or at the very least he would have a fascinating and beautiful companion for the weekend.

They would have some time to unwind and maybe, just maybe she would let down those walls and he would get to know more about this stunning and aloof woman. For the woman who was consuming most of his waking moments was now disturbing his sleep. He pictured her beautiful face, her soft lips and her deep green eyes like emerald pools that seemed to harbour sadness but still drew him in. She knew a little about him—perhaps not everything but enough—and while he knew even less about her, Laine had captivated him in a way that he'd never thought possible. He didn't want to live with the regret of never knowing what might have been.

He had dated a number of women over the years. Some relationships had lasted longer than others but none had been overly intense. They had been pleasant but there had always been something missing. But now there was this woman, who had forced him up a ladder, stood him up for dinner, sprayed him with oil in a paddock before the sun had warmed the air, had returned his kiss with an unbridled passion that he couldn't forget—and he wanted to see what lay beneath her cool exterior.

'I'm not sure.' Laine stood in the doorway to her room dressed in denim shorts, a white halter-neck top and sand-shoes, with doubt evident on her freshly scrubbed face. She had listened sceptically to Pierce propose his plan for the two of them to fly to Sydney.

'Well, if you can think of a better way, be my guest,' he countered. 'But if you rely on a courier, then the equipment may not arrive here until late Tuesday. And that's still not a definite. You might be stuck waiting until Wednesday.'

Laine thought about what he was saying. She couldn't

afford to wait that long. 'I suppose it's the only way really for me to meet my deadlines and be back in New York next week,' she admitted.

Pierce hoped she would accept his invitation and they would spend time together. Despite the fact they'd only just met, he knew he was developing feelings for this complex, at times exasperating woman. He sensed inside her lay a heart of gold that had been broken more than once. He thought they weren't that different. Each had something in their past that they wanted to forget.

Whatever she was hiding or running from drove her to live in the fast lane.

His past had seen him abandon the fast lane and live in a quiet country town.

But he sensed they both wanted to leave something behind. Maybe they could do it together.

'We can fly up there, pick up the replacement equipment and stay a couple of days to unwind. I'm sure after the schedule you've had with this calendar shoot that wouldn't be a bad idea. Speaking from a purely medical standpoint, you need to rest and recharge sometimes. Now is as good a time as any. The bank won't be open until Tuesday, but you can shoot first thing and be on a plane back to the States by lunchtime,' he reassured her.

Laine eyed the man standing at her door. She was very confused. And it wasn't just his suggestion of the brief holiday by the sea that was confusing her. It was the feeling in the pit of her stomach whenever he was near her and now was one of those times. She didn't want to feel anything for this man. Knowing more about him now was making it harder to not feel anything.

He was so wrong for her, or, more truthfully, she thought, she was wrong for him. A wife and a family would more than likely be in this country hero's plans and Laine could never be that woman. Perhaps she was overreacting to his invitation. Maybe it was a purposeful trip to collect her gear and then have some harmless R and R, but what if it wasn't? She couldn't allow herself to feel something, anything, for this man. It wouldn't work and even if it did, it wouldn't last. Love didn't.

'Okay, I'm sensing you need time to think about it,' he said, breaking the silence between them. 'What about we head over to the car-hire company and report the damage and they can send someone to pick it up then we drive into Armidale, visit the camera shop and see if they will need to ship in anything and how long it could take. Then, armed with that knowledge, you can make your decision. And if we need to head to Sydney, I'll get my travel agent to do it this afternoon.'

Laine liked the new practical direction of his conversation. His almost businesslike suggestion made it easier to breathe. The thought of a weekend away with Pierce was making her feel uncomfortable. And that was her problem, not his, she knew. It would be so easy to enjoy a fling, she had done it before and no doubt so had he, but for some reason she doubted she would walk away as easily from Pierce as she had from the others. This man had the kind of heart and soul she had not witnessed in a very long time.

'How about you get your things and we head off?'

Laine nodded and took a deep breath, hoping they could keep it casual. Sort out the car, pick up some equipment and forget the idea of sharing any more time than necessary with a man who was making her feel more than a little special.

'Okay… I'll grab my purse.'

With just under two hours until the first afternoon patient arrived at the practice, they climbed into the four-wheel drive and Pierce steered away the topic from Sydney and gave Laine an update on the young man now in ICU in Tamworth.

'He survived the night and according to the resident his chances of a full recovery are around seventy per cent. But he was driving unlicensed, under the influence of alcohol and he's only fifteen. Children's services have been brought in. He's fostered and the family have asked for help.'

'So they're not abandoning him?' she asked incredulously.

Pierce shook his head. 'No, apparently they want to get him counselling so he'll get on the straight and narrow. He's only been with them for a few months. His last placement was in Sydney and that family let him run amok so his new family wants to pull him into line and help him. He's had a bad trot with quite a few placements, the resident told me. Must have been rough on the poor kid and he fell in with a bad crowd and acted up.'

Laine rested back into her seat with a smile. 'That's the best news. He's found someone who cares enough to ride out the bad stuff. He's fortunate, very fortunate,' she said. 'I just hope he appreciates what he has now. He's got to let go of the past and let them help.'

Pierce couldn't help but notice the emotion in her voice. Her work with the fostering charity was heartfelt. She was clearly a caring person with an obvious soft spot for children. There was little doubt in his mind that she was alone in the world by choice. But why she had made that choice confused him.

There was quite a lot about Jade that confused Pierce but even more that intrigued him.

'Do you want to have a family one day?' she suddenly asked. The discussion about the young man's new foster-family spurred her line of questioning. Family had meant nothing to Laine growing up and then it meant everything for a short while. Now she tried not to think about it.

'I suppose,' he replied, with his eyes on the road ahead. 'But I'm not in a hurry. What about you?'

'No,' she sighed as she looked out of the car window, her thoughts blurring the landscape. 'It's not for me but I'm sure you will.'

The tone of her response was not lost on Pierce. It was resolute with an underlying sadness.

Pierce didn't answer. He suspected she was right. He hadn't planned on it but deep down he knew he would love to come home to a family every night. His home had a yard big enough for a cubby house and a swing, even a dog. But he hadn't found a woman he had wanted to be with for ever. The woman he wanted to marry and be the mother of his children.

They headed to the car-hire company and explained the incident and arranged for a replacement vehicle to be delivered to her motel. Pierce planned on dropping Laine at the camera shop while he checked on James in the New England District Hospital only a few streets away.

'I know you have my phone number but I don't have yours,' he told her, handing her his mobile phone. 'If I'm going to leave you at the store, can you put your number in my phone so I can reach you if I'm delayed?'

'Sure,' she said, taking the phone and quickly entering her details before she slipped it back on the console between them.

Pierce pulled up not far from the camera store and said he would be back in an hour.

The store stocked most of Laine's needs and the staff were very helpful. They made some calls and informed her that if she chose not to travel to Sydney they could have the lenses she needed couriered in some time on Tuesday. Taking their business card, Laine headed down the main street, still unsure what to do. She really wanted to do the shoot first thing Tuesday morning and fly off by lunchtime but that would mean travelling with Pierce.

Confused about the decision she had to make, she walked around the shops. She had visited Armidale as a teenager a few times and her memories of it were with wide eyes like Christmas morning. Now, compared to New York, she realised it wasn't the big city she once imagined. It was a lovely town, clean and pretty, but when she'd been growing up it had seemed like a metropolis to her. The stores had seemed so large and the streets so busy, and it had been a treat to make a trip there. Nothing like the quiet town she called home. Now, all these years later, she appreciated the town for its relaxed ambience. No hustle and bustle, no tooting horns and mad foot traffic jostling each other for space on the kerb.

Finding an alfresco café, she sat down and closed her eyes for a moment and rested back in her chair. It surprised her how content she suddenly felt as she sat in the gentle warmth of the summer day, sipping her cool drink. The pace was so far removed from her usual life. She was eight thousand miles from her real home but suddenly she didn't miss it. She ordered an iced coffee and while she waited she reached into her purse for the business card and called the store.

'There's no need to bring in the lenses,' she told them. 'I'll pick them up in Sydney,'

She had done it. It was too late to turn back. The lenses could have arrived in time and she knew it.

She had made a decision to spend time with a man she liked. A man she admired.

The hospital visit was not as straightforward as Pierce had believed it would be.

Pierce arrived at the hospital to find that James had been transferred to Paediatric ICU.

'James unfortunately needed to be placed on a ventilator this morning. The oxygen therapy was failing him and his heart rate was falling. He also wasn't breastfeeding any more so he's on an IV to replace fluids,' Dr Myles Oliver, the paediatric consultant, told Pierce as they entered ICU together.

'How severe was the bradycardia?'

'Around fifty bpm while he sleeps,' Myles replied, as he checked the computer screen near the infant. 'But now we have the added issue of ventilation as little James's cough is compromising the pressure of the ventilator.'

'Is his mother aware of the complications?' Pierce asked, as he looked down at the infant unknowingly fighting the machine that was trying to keep him alive.

'She does know, and she's been great. Carla spent last night on a rollaway in the ward with James but now he's in ICU she'll be away from him when she sleeps.'

'If she sleeps,' Pierce replied.

'No, we will insist she leaves for a few hours' rest during the night. One of the nurses is walking with her to get a coffee now. She can't sit for hours without a break. It's not good for her or James if she's going without rest.'

Pierce watched as the ICU nurse gently stroked the child's arm as she checked the IV line.

'Honest prognosis?'

'James is an otherwise healthy baby. No issues with his health prior to this so we should be okay. We've had babies younger and less robust pull through, so without any further setbacks James will be fine. Although he'll be in hospital for a good month or so.'

'And you'll do a brain scan before discharging him.'

Myles walked with James to the door and out into the corridor. 'Yes, we'll be checking for any brain damage caused by the repeated low oxygen levels but I'm hopeful there won't be any problems if we can maintain ventilation. Great diagnosis, Pierce. The family knows that you got him here just in time.'

Pierce also checked if there had been any DUI admissions in A and E, but apparently not. The other youths had somehow passed through Armidale without incident. Their younger buddy had not been so lucky but hopefully he would leave that pack and turn his life around.

It was just over an hour before he called Laine, picked her up and they headed back down the highway to Uralla.

'I guess there's not a lot I can do in my room for three days, waiting for the equipment to arrive, and if it's not correct or gets mislaid then my next assignment in Rome will be compromised,' Laine said, looking straight ahead and trying not to make too much out of her announcement. It was logical and good business sense to fly away with Pierce. That was what she was telling herself, but inside she knew there was something more to it. Or rather someone who was making her want to take the trip.

'So you're accepting my invitation?'

'Sure, why not?' She knew she had all night to think it over and if she had a change of heart she would call and cancel and make do with the equipment she had purchased. It lessened the pressure. 'But I want to pay for my ticket. I'll write you a cheque or give you the cash. You're not paying for me.'

He could charter a plane to take her to Sydney without blinking an eye, but she wanted to pay her own fare. Pierce smiled at the gesture but he would not accept her money.

'How about you leave the air fares and accommodation to me, and you can buy lunch instead in Sydney? I like double ham on my sandwich so maybe I'll come out on top in this deal.'

After the serious but expected prognosis of his patient, this news lifted his spirits. He was still cautiously elated as he knew Laine had all night to think it over and perhaps get cold feet and change her mind. Although he hoped she just went with it and they had three days alone together. No cameras. No timelines. Just time by the sea with a beautiful and captivating woman.

'I'll pick you up around nine,' Pierce said as he dropped Laine at her motel door.

With her stomach starting to knot with apprehension, Laine took a deep breath and hesitated a little.

'Or perhaps ten's better?' he asked.

'No, no, nine's fine.' Laine was feeling so mixed up. She didn't know her own mind and she always knew and said what she wanted to. Now her emotions were suddenly in turmoil. A handsome man who she clearly found attractive wanted to spend time with her and she was feeling the same way and for some crazy reason she was as scared as hell. If this had been New York, she would run with it. Accept it for what it was. A few days of fun and nothing more. But Pierce was different. This town was different. And suddenly Laine felt different. And more than a little scared.

Pierce sensed she was feeling uncomfortable and he wanted to allay her fears. 'It's a great place. You'll enjoy yourself, just sun and beach and maybe a margarita or two.'

Laine swallowed the lump that had formed in her throat. It was hardly torture. Three days away with a handsome, kind and well-mannered bachelor. It seemed ludicrous to have doubts, but she did, serious doubts. Her barriers were unravelling a little more each minute she spent with Pierce. If she could just keep him at bay and keep herself in check it would be fine. There could be no fling. That was not negotiable. She spied him from the corner of her eye. Too damn good looking and she had the distinct feeling that it would take every ounce of her self-control not to be tempted.

'Okay, see you at nine,' she said, turning to go into her room. 'Unless something suddenly comes up.'

Pierce nodded. At least it wasn't a refusal but she had certainly kept the door open for a quick escape.

'See you at nine.'

Pierce arrived at eight-fifty the next morning and drove slowly down the motel driveway towards Laine's room. He felt apprehensive. The possibility that Laine might still cancel their trip away together weighed heavily on his mind. The fact that it did made him realise this woman meant more than any woman had ever done, particularly in such a short period of time. He knew it was crazy as she would never stay long term but he still wanted to

spend time with her. It had been only a few days and yet
he felt a connection that he wanted to explore on every
level. Toowoon Bay would provide the perfect setting.

He pulled the four-wheel drive up to her door. His
watch said five minutes to nine, so he decided to wait
in the car for a few moments. He didn't want to arrive
early or call to find Laine wasn't ready and give her a
reason to decline the trip. He had no intention of coerc-
ing her into going away but he sensed part of her wanted
to spend time with him too. Although, equally, there was
also something that was holding her back. Something
making her almost suspicious of him and not wanting
to acknowledge she might be interested in getting to
know him a little better too. Pierce wasn't sure what
had caused Laine to build these walls around herself,
but he wanted to try to break them down, just enough
to see the real Laine. Maybe the sun would melt them,
or the surf would wash them away. Or maybe he could
peel them away.

Laine saw Pierce's car drive up to her door. She had
spent the last hour sitting on the side of her unmade bed
in cargo pants, sneakers and a white T-shirt, with her
hair loosely tied in a low plait, wondering why she had
agreed to go away. Her overnight bag sat packed by the
door. A beachside resort in January meant a bathing suit,
sarong, shorts, two summer dresses and sandals. It easily fitted into a carry-on bag. She had packed the night
before, knowing if she didn't then she would more than
likely change her mind in the light of day. Pierce was a
lovely man but she didn't want a man like him in her life.
He would complicate it.

There was a knock at the door.

She dropped her head into her hands and drew in a

deep breath, stood up and in bare feet crossed to the door. This was without doubt a huge mistake. The third mistake. The first had been coming to Uralla and the second had been leaving her equipment in the car to be stolen. Could it be third time lucky or would this trip just be another disaster? she wondered.

'You're nothing if not punctual,' she remarked as she opened the door.

'So is the national train service,' he replied, a little deflated by her cold greeting. He had thought the day before that she had dropped her guard a little but now it was up like Fort Knox again. 'I was hoping for something a little more enthusiastic.'

'Nice shirt,' she said nervously, as she silently wondered what she had done. Going away with Pierce now seemed like a very bad idea. It wasn't him, it was most definitely herself she didn't trust.

Pierce could tell she was anxious. She hadn't greeted him by cancelling the trip but he suspected she was close to doing so.

'Thanks,' he said, glancing down at the navy cotton shirt he wore untucked over his beige shorts and leather loafers. 'A Christmas gift from Tracy, my receptionist, although I suspect her son Ben may have chosen it, he's the fashion compass of the town.'

Laine was trying to listen but her mind was spinning and she was barely concentrating. She wanted so badly to find an excuse, any excuse to cancel, but she couldn't verbalise a reason to say no to the man at her door. Try as hard as she could, it just wouldn't materialise. And a tiny part buried deep inside didn't want to cancel because that same tiny part wanted to spend time with this very handsome, very charismatic and, at times, witty doctor. He was growing on her and that was unnerving. She just wished she could block out that minority party in her head that was willing her to go away with him. She knew that no good would come of it. Now or later, if she even came close to falling for him, she would be hurt, that was certain.

'Well, I'm packed,' she said matter-of-factly, looking down at the overnight bag by the door.

Her tone and expression, similar to that of a woman heading to the gallows, did not go unnoticed by Pierce.

'If you don't want to go, just say the word. I can fly there, collect your gear and bring it back with me.' Pierce stepped back from the door and headed to his car. He wasn't about to force her to go. If she wanted to spend time with him, the invitation was there. If not then he would have a nice, albeit lonely weekend at the resort. At the very least he was sure he would enjoy a margarita by his private pool.

Laine realised that she had been less than gracious. Pierce was just being friendly and she was behaving poorly. Her problems should not be his. He wasn't asking for anything more than company for a few days. For her it would be a weekend with no deadlines, no clients, no temperamental models and apparently no strings attached. She realised she was making more of it than she should. Maybe it was all in her head. Or, more precisely, all in her heart.

'I'm sorry,' she called to him. 'I guess the equipment being stolen and the timeframe being thrown into disarray has played on my nerves. But that's no excuse. Who knows, a trip to the coast might be just what I need.'

Pierce paused in his tracks. 'No need to be sorry. You've had a rough couple of days and there's no hard feelings if you would rather stay in your room for three days of lonely editing, only stepping out for food and water.'

Laine smiled. She reasoned that few, if any, women would refuse a weekend away with such a charming man. 'No, you're not forcing me and I like the sound of margaritas after the last few days I've had.'

Pierce looked long and hard at Laine. She was the most complex woman he had ever met but he felt sure if she ever allowed him to truly know her, his effort would be rewarded tenfold.

'Then let's get out of here and get to the airport. Our flight is in about fifty minutes. Time for a temporary sea change.'

Pierce crossed back to her door and leaned in so close that she could smell the freshness of his still-damp hair from the shower and his woody cologne. Her pulse raced as her senses were filled with his masculinity, so near to her. He reached down for her bag and as he picked it up, his face swept dangerously close to hers. His soft lips were parted in a smile and she remembered vividly the tenderness that his kiss held.

She coughed nervously to pull her emotions into line. She felt overwhelmed but knew it was not his problem. There was so much tugging at her, so many feelings she'd left in this town and then there was Pierce, the last straw. She thought she might need that margarita sooner rather than later.

'So how long is this road trip after we finish our business in Sydney?'

'About an hour north,' he replied, as he opened the back door and placed her bag on the seat. 'Great scenery on the way, and the view the resort is spectacular.'

'Sounds good to me,' Laine said with a little sigh. Her feelings about the trip were not all that clear-cut but she intended on keeping it all to herself. Lifting the long strap of her handbag, she rested it on her shoulder and pulled the motel door closed. 'Let's go, then,' she said, as she climbed into his car and slipped on her oversized sunglasses. Pierce closed her door once she was safely inside, walked around to the driver's door and climbed in.

In no time they were at the airport, had checked in and were taking their seats on the forty-seater aircraft.

Laine buckled her seatbelt and made herself comfortable for the forty-five-minute flight. Briefly she looked out across the tarmac then turned to Pierce.

'So you can tell me to mind my own business, but what made you choose Uralla? I mean it's pretty much in the middle of nowhere and from what you said before, you lived in New York or at least spent some time there.'

Laine wasn't sure if Pierce would tell her the rest of his story or even part of it but she was hoping to hear just enough to remind her of their differences and throw any romantic overtones out the window before they took off. His desire to spend his life in a country town she hoped would send her heart back where it belonged. Tucked away from her lovely but all too perfect companion. She would for ever be a big-city dweller, at least that's what she told herself.

'I heard by word of mouth that there was the opportunity to be a partner in a country medical practice in a beautiful part of Australia and eventually buy out the retiring doctor so I thought, Why not? No traffic jams, no pollution and fresh eggs. Seemed like a great idea.'

He didn't want to spend more time discussing the family dynasty, money and scandal. He had left it behind and had never been happier. Now Pierce Beaumont was just a country practitioner with a real estate and investment portfolio that would anonymously support a great many causes indefinitely, and that was the only connection he had left to his family.

'I spent some time travelling as a child but I prefer this part of the world and I like to focus on the future. The analogy that the windscreen is so much bigger than the rear-view mirror is a valid one.'

Laine nodded in agreement. 'Isn't that the truth?'

For a moment they both looked out the small window in silence, each trying to forget something.

The plane had taken off on time and the landing was also on schedule. Pierce hired a car at the airport and headed to the camera store in the heart of the city. Laine had called ahead and said she would be collecting the lenses in person so they were ready when she arrived. Pierce watched as she walked around like a child in a candy store, looking at all the equipment. He could almost hear her squeal when she spotted a small sports camera she had been wanting and that too was packaged up with the lenses.

'You seem pretty chuffed,' he commented, as he took the heavy bag from the counter while she put her credit card back in her purse.

'Ecstatic, actually.'

Pierce was overjoyed to see Laine so happy. He wasn't sure why but seeing her smile made him just as happy. He didn't need another reason.

CHAPTER EIGHT

'MADAM'S MARGARITA, AS promised, and I took the liberty, considering the weather, of ordering the frozen variety.'

Laine smiled as she accepted the icy drink from Pierce. 'Perfect.' She sipped the salty, lime-flavoured cocktail and lay back on the sun lounge, looking through the palms to the holidaymakers on the beach, enjoying the perfect summer day.

They had pulled into the beachside resort an hour before and, just as Pierce had promised, they had separate accommodation. Laine felt guilty having asked for separate rooms when she found on check-in that he had booked her a spacious beach spa villa complete with private pool and sauna.

'I can't let you cover this, it's much too extravagant,' she told him.

'I insist. Besides, it was my idea, I needed a getaway weekend. Heading to Sydney to purchase your gear gave me the perfect excuse. It's nice to splurge now and then,' he said with a wink.

Laine graciously accepted but was relieved to discover his villa wasn't next to hers. No chance he would knock on her door in the middle of the night…and no chance she would impulsively knock on his either. She unpacked, changed into her red one-piece bathing suit and tied a sunset-coloured sarong around her hips before she made her way barefoot to the bar to meet Pierce.

'I agree, absolutely perfect,' he replied, but his remark was not in any way related to the drink. He was referring to the stunning brunette on the bar stool next to him. The open drape of the sarong exposed her long, honey-coloured legs, the scarlet swimsuit was cut low at the back and, at the front, shoestring straps held the plunging neckline in place.

Without doubt, Laine was the most gorgeous woman at the resort in Pierce's opinion and he didn't need to see another woman to know that was the truth. In his eyes she was by far the most gorgeous woman on the planet. Her body was lightly tanned, toned and healthy, her cleavage was small and appeared to be natural, which Pierce found even more appealing. Pierce found every inch of her body desirable. He could only imagine the parts not on display.

'I still can't believe I have my own pool, Pierce. Don't you think that's a little over the top?'

'Not at all. You need time out and you have it. Besides, you can always ask me to keep you company if you don't like swimming alone.'

Laine smiled. That was not the only pleasurable activity that they could share in her villa but she knew she wouldn't act on that thought.

'Do you surf?' she asked quickly, to change her thought pattern, as she looked out at the spectacular vista of beach stretched out before them.

'A little but I couldn't call myself a surfer.'

'So maybe we should stick to the shallows for a swim, then.' Laine looked across the crystal-clear water. It was enticing and the idea of swimming with Pierce in full view of the other guests made her feel safe. She didn't feel secure enough about her own feelings to swim in the villa pool alone with him.

'I don't claim to be a great surfer but we can venture into the ocean. I won't let you drown,' he replied, taking another sip of his drink. 'You can depend on me.'

Laine smiled in response. She had no doubt she could depend on Pierce but she never would.

The afternoon passed as they chatted about the resort over a light lunch, more talk about the stunning view of the beach and ocean, and even discovering that they had a mutual love of country music. Each claimed to have been a fan for longer, before they moved on to discussing Laine's return to the New York winter for two weeks and then her next shoot in Rome. Pierce suggested a swim. The water was perfect, initially a little cool against their warm skin as they plunged in but wonderfully refreshing.

Still lapping in the shallows at a leisurely pace, Laine watched as Pierce finally climbed from the water, his body glistening. His broad shoulders were tanned, his chest and torso were defined and muscular and, if possible, he looked even better soaking wet. He was drop-dead gorgeous. No debate about that. He ran his fingers through his thick black hair, walked over to the sun lounges they had claimed earlier on and, slipping on his sunglasses, lay down on the thick beach towel. There was no need to dry his body, the sun would do that quickly enough.

'I think you're blocking my sun,' Pierce remarked a few minutes later as Laine stood beside his lounge, slipping on her sarong.

'Pardon me,' she replied. '*Your sun?* How remiss of me not to watch where I was standing. I wouldn't want to cause you to have tan lines, now, would I?'

Looking up at the woman standing over him, Pierce wanted more than anything to pull her still-damp body onto his. To taste the sweetness of her mouth and then carry her to his villa and make love to her for the remainder of the afternoon and into the night. But that would never happen, she had made it clear enough. He had to get those images out of his mind. Still, he could enjoy the time he had with his stunning companion even if it was on her platonic terms.

'Well, if you agree to have dinner with me I'll forgive you.'

Laine laughed as she lay down on her sun lounge and slipped on her straw hat. 'I think I can manage that but not for a while yet. The sun is glorious and I have no intention of leaving here any time soon. I'll be knee deep in snow this time next week. Let me enjoy the sun while I can.'

'No argument from me. Let me know when you're hungry and until then I shall take an afternoon siesta.'

Laine worried that her sunscreen would have washed off in the water and reached into her bag, retrieved the lotion and, emptying some into her hand, began covering her exposed skin. Pierce watched from the corner of his eye as she stretched down and gently rubbed the sunscreen onto her legs and then her cleavage.

'Before I fall asleep, and you burn to a crisp, why don't you turn over and let me cover your shoulders and back,' he said, as he gently claimed the bottle from her hand.

Laine smiled nervously. The thought of his hands on her body was an incredibly unsettling thought. Her stomach fluttered a little and she felt her pulse race, although he hadn't done anything more than brush his hand against hers when he'd moved over to her lounge and sat down beside her.

'Thank you…' she began, then faltered as the dampness of his swimsuit felt cool against her bare skin and his hands moved slowly over her shoulders without warning. In unison, like two skilled dancers, his hands travelled lightly across her skin with the lotion then moved slowly down both her arms.

The warmth of his touch made her breathing a little staggered. The movements of his fingers on her skin made her feel light-headed as they traced their way up and down her arms and then travelled to her bare back. Suddenly the pleasure she was feeling abated as he reached for more sunscreen. She hated that she wanted to feel his touch again.

Closing her eyes, Laine was grateful she was facing away from him and didn't have to mask her smile as his hands returned to her body and he began covering her back with the now-warm lotion. Trickles ran down the curve of her spine and his fingertips caught them before they disappeared beneath the fabric of her swimsuit. His hands worked their magic all over her back and then without warning he slid her flimsy sarong to the side and began working his way down the backs of her legs.

Not flinching was almost impossible as he massaged her skin and slowly travelled down her thighs to the backs of her knees, where he paused for a moment, his lingering touch setting her skin on fire. Slowly he moved over the rise of her calves to her heels and then he gently worked the lotion into the soft, fleshy soles of her feet.

Laine kept her eyes closed and luxuriated in the feeling of his commanding hands on her bare skin. She couldn't remember ever feeling quite the way she felt at that moment. Her mind was floating, her body was more alive than it had ever been, and she was still partially dressed. His touch was intoxicating.

She was aware of every part of her body and could hear her own laboured breathing. She prayed he wouldn't stop.

'I think I've covered everything,' he announced, not wanting to stop or move away from her but realising he had no reason to stay. No reason that could justify keeping his hands on her body and feeling the softness of her skin or the warmth of her next to him for any longer.

Laine turned to face him. She looked up and softly thanked him before she turned away again. There was nothing else she could say. Although *Kiss me the way you did yesterday* was on the tip of her tongue, she knew she couldn't and she shouldn't. It wasn't right. Other than each having a past they would rather not discuss, they had little in common—in fact, they were miles apart, she told herself. And the following week they would be literally thousands of miles apart. It would never work. Despite their shared love of country music, they were two different people on very different paths in life.

Pierce closed the lid of the sunscreen, placing it down near her bag, and then without saying another word he returned to his own seat. Although he was still only a few inches away, it felt like a gaping chasm. He wanted so much more.

With their minds fighting an avalanche of emotions, they both lay in silence. There was nothing Pierce could say and nothing Laine wanted to say. And so the afternoon passed with sunbathing and the occasional casual remark. Pierce found it difficult to mask the desire he felt for her so he avoided being that close again.

Laine wanted to forget the breathlessness she experienced as his hands had slowly roamed her body so she also played her part in their newfound distance from each other. Hours passed with the arrival of two other couples, their laughter filling the air as they too enjoyed the brilliant sun-drenched day. But there was an awkward silence between Pierce and Laine.

'I think I might head in for a shower before dinner,' Pierce announced unexpectedly, as he stood up and gathered his belongings.

'It's much too nice to leave yet,' she replied in a sleepy voice. 'I might stay a while and meet you later. What time did you want to eat?'

Pierce studied her for a moment then drew a long and purposeful breath before he answered. He was frustrated beyond belief at the situation and his tone was abrupt. 'I don't mind. Perhaps I'll come back down here when I'm ready. You can always stay in your swimsuit for dinner.'

'Then if we don't need to change, why don't you stay a little longer, too?'

Because I can't, Pierce thought. *Because being near you is driving me crazy.* He needed to get away from Laine. She was more than just under his skin now. He knew if he had a cold shower and read a book it might help to snap him out of these ridiculous feelings. Something had to bring him to his senses and lying around with Laine in her barely-there bathing suit was not the solution. It was the problem.

'I think I've had enough sun for today.'

Laine watched Pierce walk away. It would have been so easy to reach out, take his hand and ask him to stay, but she knew better. He was a country doctor and she was not a fan of small towns any more, particularly the one he called home, so there was no point. In two days she would be leaving for her home in New York and Pierce would be the very kind and handsome man who graced the page of a calendar.

It was almost two hours before Pierce reappeared. He had showered and, in a still damp towel, lain on the freshly made bed, thinking about Laine. She was hauntingly beautiful but it was more than that. Pierce knew there was something in her past that was too painful to forget. She had obviously moved on, forged a life on her own, and a hugely successful life, but whatever had hurt her in the past was still there, driving her to be alone in the world. She was certainly an enigma and one he would not easily forget. But also not one he could solve.

He wondered if they were more alike than either of them imagined. Both wanted to move forward and never look back. But Laine seemed to take it one step further. Her journey forward seemed to be one she needed to do alone.

Later, dressed in white cotton shirt open at the neck and lightweight beige trousers with leather loafers, he took a stroll to the foyer bar to sit and enjoy a cool drink. The idea of sitting alone in his room was not appealing but sitting beside the object of his desire while she was sunbathing would be torturous.

The sun was almost ready to set and Laine had contemplated a few times making her way to her villa to change but had then decided, since she would be dressed in woollen leggings and a faux fur-lined parka in less than a week, she should make the most of the stunning summer weather. She also didn't want to be alone in the room with the object of her thoughts. Those thoughts had to be crushed. But finally, with no sign of Pierce and the sun showing signs of setting, Laine decided to head in to change for dinner after all.

She had a quick shower and slipped into an ankle-length white cotton sundress, flat gold sandals and pulled her hair into a high ponytail. Then she headed to the bar, suspecting that was where she might find Pierce. The fun-filled ambience had shifted gear. It was now more subdued, with almost romantic overtones.

Pierce was sitting astride a stool, waiting for her. His white shirt was unbuttoned slightly and contrasted starkly with his tanned skin. It would have been impossible for her not to admit to herself just how breathtakingly good looking he was at that moment. He was the stuff that sold magazines, that covered billboards and broke hearts, and yet she knew at least two of the three were not close to what he did. She had no idea if he broke hearts and she had no intention of finding out.

'So you changed after all,' he said, as he watched her walk towards him. Her dress was thin cotton and it flowed around her, allowing him to make out the curves of her body with each step she took. It was low cut and he could see the outline of her perfect breasts. He felt certain there was nothing between her skin and the soft fabric.

She became more desirable with every passing second.

'Well, it would look a little odd if you're dressed and I'm in bathers.'

Pierce just smiled, a knowing kind of smile. He knew there would be no complaints from him or any other man in the restaurant if she had glided in with just a flimsy sarong over her scarlet swimsuit. None at all.

'So, are we ready to eat dinner?'

'Well, I am. Are you?'

Pierce led the way to the restaurant with huge glass windows, allowing panoramic views over the beach. The sun had almost set as they were directed by the *maître d'* to one of the tables near the windows. Wild orchids and tealights dressed the intimate table that was to be theirs for the evening. They were so close to the beach that the crashing of the waves on the shore could be heard over the low chatter of the other patrons.

Pierce pulled out Laine's chair and once she was seated he made his way to the other side of the table and sat down.

Laine looked out across the expanse of white sand now lit by the moon. 'It's so beautiful here. Truly, it's the perfect getaway. There's no reason to leave, everything we could possibly want is right here in front of us and it's stunning.'

Again Pierce didn't disagree. He knew that everything he could possibly want was right in front of him. She was stunning and he was doing his best not to entertain thoughts that she would never reciprocate.

'Pre-dinner drink?' the waiter asked, as he handed them the menus. Flicking open the large white fabric napkins, he placed one on Laine's lap and another on Pierce's.

'I think I'll have my second margarita. You promised me three and I've only had one since we arrived almost seven hours ago.'

'Then two margaritas, please,' Pierce requested, handing the wine list back to the waiter.

Laine and Pierce both studied a menu. Each menu was filled with such an array of fresh seafood dishes that they both found it difficult to decide. Their drinks arrived as they were trying to make a final choice.

'The Moreton Bay bug tails sound delicious, what about you?'

Pierce looked over the menu a little longer. 'Think I'll go with the lobster.'

Laine smiled as she took a sip of her drink. 'Looks like we have a mutual love of seafood, then.'

Pierce signalled the waiter and placed the order, adding some mixed tapas for an appetizer.

'Not sure I be able to fit it all in but I'll try,' Laine remarked softly, then turned to look across the now silver ocean. The moon was hovering in a crescent shape and lighting the ripples in the water. 'It's so beautiful. Thank you for inviting me.'

'You are very welcome.'

The tapas and dinner were delicious, with the fresh citrus flavour in the salads being the perfect partner to both seafood choices.

'Shall we take a stroll on the beach? It's such a beautiful night and it's still early.'

Pierce was surprised by Laine's suggestion but happy to oblige as he wiped his mouth on the napkin and stood up to leave.

'But you'll have to roll up your trousers and lose the shoes,' she added.

The sand was still warm as they finally stepped onto the beach in front of the restaurant. Lanterns lit the area softly and made it easy for them to find their way to the water. Eager to feel the cool water on her feet, Laine tied up the hem of her dress in a knot so she could splash in the shallows.

'I should probably swim along the coastline for about five miles after all that I ate,' she said, as she felt the cool water wash over her feet.

'Great idea. I think that after about one mile cramps would set in and then shortly after that you could possibly drown.'

She looked up to see Pierce smiling back at her. 'You're a doctor, so you can save me.'

Pierce walked away from the water's edge and sat down on the soft sand, dropping his loafers beside him. 'Might not find you in the water. It's pretty dark.'

Laine walked back up to where he was sitting and lay down beside him. Untying the knot in the hem, her flowing dress spread out over the soft waves of the sand.

'I think you would find me.'

Pierce silently agreed. He would find her. He wouldn't let anything happen to Laine. She was the toughest porcelain doll he had ever met, but he knew underneath she still was a porcelain doll. Fragile and precious under a hardened exterior.

'Do you want another drink at the bar or do I risk inducing an alcohol problem?'

'No, I've polished off my two margaritas and that will be my limit for the entire weekend, I think,' she replied, looking up at the moon. It was a perfect night. The air was fresh but it was still warm enough to sit by the water and her companion suddenly became appealing on a level she'd never expected.

'Okay, no drink. What about a long walk or—?'

'How about we watch a movie?' She cut his line of questioning short. 'I'm sure they'd have cable or pay-per-view here, so why don't we watch an old movie?'

Watching old movies had been something she'd done

with her adoptive parents. To many it would seem normal, growing up watching television with the family, but in many of her foster-homes it had been rare or non-existent. She would be sent to her room as they wanted to watch their choice of programme and claimed it wasn't suitable for a child. She would be alone or sharing with a foster-sibling who was equally unhappy and they would hear the adults in another room, laughing and enjoying television, while they sat in the dark. She had always hoped one day to be a part of a family who included her, and when it had finally happened it had been as much fun as she had imagined. Sitting together, sharing a movie and pop-corn, was a joy. Now she wanted to share that with Pierce.

'Sounds great.' Pierce wasn't sure where this would lead but he also wouldn't refuse the opportunity to spend time with Laine. He had tried to stay away that afternoon but now, this close, he knew he would agree to pretty much anything she suggested.

'It's still early and if we stay out here eventually the mosquitoes will find us.'

Pierce stood and reached down for Laine's hand and pulled her up on her feet. 'A black and white movie it is, then.'

'Let's see if there's one that neither of us has seen,' she said, as her feet disappeared in to the soft sand and she again needed to lift up the hem of her dress as they walked back to the restaurant.

Laine made herself comfortable in a large armchair in the corner of the room and kicked off her sandals.

'That's not about to happen,' Pierce said, as he walked into the room with some iced water and found Laine huddled in the chair. 'Let me take the chair and you can make yourself comfy on the bed.'

'Are you sure?'

'I insist.'

'Always the gentleman.'

'Not always,' he muttered, as he reached for the remote control and found the movie channel on his way to the armchair. He, too, kicked off his shoes and made himself comfortable as Laine climbed onto the bed and fluffed up the pillows behind her back, before nestling into them. The ceiling fan above gently moved the warm evening air about the room.

As he scrolled through the selection Laine finally caught sight of the movie she wanted. '*Detour*, with Ann Savage.'

'Never heard of it,' he announced.

'Great, that means you will always remember me sitting in your room and watching this film noir thriller for the first time.'

Pierce knew it wouldn't be the movie he would remember. He would remember everything about Laine, more than she could possibly imagine.

'You seem to know all about it. If you've seen it then we should select something else. You said you wanted to see a movie that neither of us had seen.'

'I did and I meant it. I haven't seen this movie but I always wanted to. It was produced by a small studio in the mid-forties, it was low budget and they called the studio one of the poverty-row studios because they had so little money. But it's a classic.'

'If you say so,' he said, resting back into his chair as the movie started.

* * *

It was not only a long movie by most standards but Pierce noticed Laine fall asleep about thirty minutes into the film. He crossed the room and placed a lightweight blanket over her then went back to his chair. He worried that if the temperature dropped and there was an ocean breeze she might get cold during the night. With no conversation likely, Pierce watched the movie until the end while still keeping a watchful his eye on his sleeping guest. It felt good to have her near. The fact she was asleep didn't matter. She was close and he was happy.

He finally dimmed the lights and brought a chair from the desk alongside his armchair and stretched out. It wasn't the most comfortable of beds but it would do. He looked over at Laine. Her face looked so angelic as she slept, almost looked as if she were smiling. He drifted off to sleep wondering if she was dreaming and whether he featured within her thoughts.

Laine woke to see Pierce sleeping upright in the chair. 'You let me have the bed and you slept like that?' she said softly as she tapped his shoulder. 'You can't do that. I have a whole villa to myself and I'm taking your bed.'

Still drowsy, Pierce looked over at Laine. 'I'm fine, go back to sleep. Honestly, you need the rest.'

'That is taking chivalry to the extreme, actually the ridiculous,' she stated, sitting upright and trying to untangle her bed hair with her fingers. 'I'll leave, and you can get some sleep in your very expensive bed and I will go back to my equally expensive sleeping quarters.' She lifted her legs and swung around to find her shoes in the dim light.

'Your villa isn't next door,' he reminded her. 'You're across the other side of the resort. So stay here until morning. You're doing me a favour by staying. If you leave I will have to walk you all the way over there and then come back.'

'I'm a big girl. I'm pretty good at taking care of myself. Don't forget I live in New York so I think I can make a three-minute walk at...' She paused, looking unsuccessfully for a clock. 'Whatever time it is now.'

'Fine, be stubborn, but I'm walking you there.'

Laine reached inside her purse and discovered the swipe card for her room was missing, and quickly realised it was in her beach bag, not her purse.

'I can't believe it...'

'Can't believe what?' he cut in.

'My room card, it's in my other bag. The one I had with me when I was sunbathing. I'm guessing the front desk is closed at this ungodly hour.'

'Yes, I'm pretty sure you'd be right about that.'

'So now what am I going to do?'

'I think the universe has pretty much decided it for you.'

Laine knew he was right and she also knew that few women would be upset by the prospect of a night in the room of an eligible bachelor with the sex appeal of Pierce. But Laine was already struggling to keep their relationship platonic without staying the night with him. But now she had no choice.

'Fine, I'll stay. But you can't spend the rest of the night in that chair. We do have a king-size bed,' she said, swallowing her nerves. 'I think we can manage to share it for a few hours.'

'I'm okay here. When I asked you to stay the night, I wasn't asking to sleep with you.'

'Don't you think I know that? If you were expecting

me to *sleep* with you, I'd be leaving now even if I had to sleep in the foyer. But you have paid an exorbitant amount for two villas for us, and it's not your fault I forgot my room key, so I absolutely won't let you sleep on a chair.'

Pierce smiled. 'How can I refuse such a gracious invitation?' He made his way over to the other side of the bed in silence. He stripped off his trousers and unbuttoned his shirt, throwing it across to the desk and, wearing only his tight-fitting black boxers, he slipped into the bed beside Laine.

Not admitting she had watched him remove his clothing, and painfully aware that she had little under her dress, she softly said, 'I suppose I should do the same, otherwise my walk of shame in the morning will have the added embarrassment of having an incredibly creased dress.'

CHAPTER NINE

PIERCE WOKE IN the morning to a sight that made him smile. Laine was lying almost naked in his bed. His eyes appreciatively traced the curve of her spine as it disappeared under the covers. Her warm body was close to him but he knew he had no right to touch her. She had stayed because he asked her to do so, and he wasn't about to break the trust they were building by making a move in the light of morning. Although it took every ounce of self-control not to reach over and pull her into his arms and make love to her.

Moments later, Laine opened her eyes slowly, surveyed the room and immediately realised where she was. Sharing a bed with Pierce. Lying very still, she navigated the logistics of getting dressed without crossing the room naked to retrieve the dress that she had carefully draped over the armchair.

Unsure whether Pierce was still sleeping, she slowly turned in the bed, pulling the sheets with her to cover her breasts.

'Good morning, sleepyhead,' his husky voice breathed.

Laine was face to face with Pierce. Resting his head on bent arm, his dark, smouldering eyes were staring straight at her. His lips hovering very close to hers. Lips that only two days ago had kissed her so passionately. He was smiling and the dark stubble on his chiselled chin, now more pronounced, was shading his powerful jaw.

Laine gave a nervous cough. 'Good…morning.'

She drew the sheets more tightly around her. She wasn't scared of the man beside her, she was scared of her own desire. Inviting him to make love to her would be so easy but she knew it would put her at risk of being hurt. They would have to say goodbye in twenty-four hours and now, looking at him in the light of morning, she knew that would be painful. Now she actually cared. Life had dealt Pierce some hard blows and yet he had managed to stay afloat and not harden against the world. Just because he wasn't jaded, she had mistaken a genuinely grounded man for one who was privileged and spoilt by life.

'Would you like to take a swim to start the day?'

Laine could think of something she would prefer to do and was grateful that Pierce did not suggest it as she doubted she would be able to refuse. To stay wrapped in his strong arms, sharing his warm bed for the entire day would be heaven.

'Perfect,' she announced, pulling herself up in the bed, tugging the sheets with her as she moved away from his warm body. She struggled awkwardly to keep the sheet covering herself as she made her way to the edge.

A curious furrow deepened on his brow as Pierce re-alised her struggle. 'I'm going to hop in the shower while you manoeuvre yourself out of the oversized bandage you've made of our sheets.'

Our sheets. The words resonated with Laine. There had been no *our* anything for so many years. It had always just been hers. She hadn't shared anything since she'd left her family home. *Our* sounded wonderful but she knew even thinking like that was crazy. He was her travel companion, and she had to remind herself of that. There could never be *our* anything between them.

'Great,' she mumbled. 'I'll go to my room, do the same and meet you on the beach in fifteen.' Friendly plans. Perfect.

'Make it half an hour, it will take you fifteen minutes to find a way out of the strait-jacket you've created.' He laughed then climbed from the bed.

From the corner of her eye she spied his broad tanned shoulders in the early morning light. The muscles of his back were gently defined and the curve of his bottom was held firm in his tight-fitting black boxers. She pretended not to watch as he collected his belongings from his overnight bag and disappeared into the bathroom.

Laine waited to hear the water running before she undid the sheets and made her way to her dress and out of the door.

'Well, it didn't take you long to leave my room this morning,' Pierce began, as he stepped onto the sand. He was wearing the same navy swim trunks as the day before and carrying a towel and grinning as made his way to Laine, who was already lying in her red swimsuit on a beach towel. 'Not even a five-minute shower. I came out and there was no sign of you. You're quick.'

'I didn't want to waste a minute of the sun today,' she said, masking the real reason for her hasty exit. The idea of still lying in the warm bed when Pierce emerged from the bathroom with only a towel covering his wet body would have been too tempting for her.

But now, out in the sunlight, she was questioning if she should have given in to her desires after all. Her emotions were travelling like an out-of-control train and she had no idea where she was heading.

But it was a glorious day, and she intended to enjoy it.

Pierce dropped his towel beside her. 'Are you actually going to hit the water or just sit there all pretty on the beach?'

Laine glared at him. 'You're in so much trouble for that!'

Pierce hastily tucked his wallet, car keys and room card under the towel and raced to the water, with Laine in hot pursuit. His body disappeared beneath the waves before she reached the water's edge so she dived in after him. The water was crystal clear and Laine opened her eyes to see the stunning underwater world hidden to those on the sand. After a minute she rose to the surface, drew in a breath and submerged a little longer. On her second trip to the surface she found Pierce looking back at her.

'You constantly surprise me,' he confessed in a husky tone. 'I never thought of you like this. I thought New York may have taken the love of the great outdoors from you. But it hasn't so I guess I can't keep thinking of you as a prima donna now.'

'Me, a prima donna? First it's all *pretty on the beach* and now a *prima donna*! You're asking for trouble.' With her cupped palms full of salt water she playfully splashed his face before she swam off in the clear blue ocean.

Pierce wiped his face then swam in her direction. His powerful arms proved no match for her small strokes and he quickly caught up. 'Feisty in the mornings, aren't we?' he teased, as he swam alongside her.

Laine was so happy. The sun, the water, the man. The warmth and security she'd felt lying next to him in his bed. The trust she had found with a man she barely

knew yet suddenly found she understood. It was starting to wash away a lot of her resentment about life Down
Under. She didn't want to feel so carefree but she had
no choice. Suddenly the Laine of the last twelve years
was emerging from her lonely cocoon and spreading her
wings. And it was all because of the man swimming beside her. Pierce was changing her game plan and she was
helpless to stop him.

'I've booked a table for breakfast,' Pierce announced as
they walked dripping from the shallows onto the sand
and headed to their belongings. 'I thought we might be
hungry after lapping the coastline.'

'Absolutely starving,' she said softly, rubbing her hair
dry with her towel.

Pierce looked at the woman beside him and thought
she appeared different, a little less on edge. More playful
and relaxed than even the day before. Perhaps her walls
were crumbling a little.

'Great, let's head up there now. We can sit outside
under an umbrella in our swimsuits.'

Smiling they walked up to the alfresco section of the
restaurant, placed their towels on their chairs and sat
down in their still-damp swimsuits to order breakfast.
Pierce soon learned that 'absolutely starving' for Laine
did not extend to the bacon, eggs, grilled tomatoes on
toast with a cappuccino that he had chosen for himself.
Her order was Greek yogurt with a tropical summer fruit
selection, sparkling water and a long black coffee.

'In twenty years you'll have the better arteries but I
will have enjoyed my Sunday breakfasts far more, although you clearly have great genes and don't have to
worry anyway.'

Laine froze. Her look suddenly became serious and she didn't respond in any way to his compliment for a moment. No smile, no frown, nothing. Pierce was confused. He wasn't sure what he'd said that could suddenly dampen the otherwise great time they were having.

'Somehow I just did it again,' he said sombrely. 'Believe me, it was a compliment. Your mother was no doubt a beautiful woman.'

Laine looked into the warmth of his eyes. He had no idea what he had said that could have upset her. He deserved to know it wasn't him, it was the sadness of her past still darkening the present.

'I never met my mother,' she said with a sigh as she looked out across the blue horizon where the water met the azure sky.

Pierce looked deep into her eyes and reached for her hand. He didn't hesitate. It felt natural to comfort her. 'I'm so sorry. I didn't mean to upset you. It's the last thing I would want to do.'

Laine's lips curled but her smile was tinged with sadness. 'I know you didn't, Pierce.' She looked down and saw his hand covering hers and she didn't want to pull away. 'How were you to know your date for the weekend was abandoned at birth? Born to people who didn't want me or for some reason couldn't keep me, I'll never know.'

Laine was surprised it didn't hurt as much as she'd thought it would to say it. She'd never allowed the words to pass over her lips before and it wasn't as painful as she had imagined. Maybe she didn't care any more. Or perhaps it was the person listening who made it easier.

Pierce suddenly put the pieces together. 'So you became a foster-child. That's why you have an affinity with the charity?'

'Yes,' she said softly. 'I didn't have a particularly good time as a foster-child, way too many placements with families who didn't give a damn about me. Many foster-families are amazing, and many foster-children have wonderful lives, I know, but unfortunately I wasn't one of the lucky ones, well, not until the end. And by then, let's say the scars ran deep.'

Pierce looked at Laine with a newfound understanding. 'You're an amazing woman and you've achieved so much for having had such a sad childhood.' Pierce didn't pull his hand away. He wanted her to feel secure.

Laine continued, 'My final family, Maisey and Arthur, were the most loving people and they adopted me so they should take the credit for my success. I went to live with them in Uralla when I was twelve and they taught me what family really meant. I owe it to them to make the most of my life.'

He suddenly knew how she knew so much about the town. Everything fitted into place but he was aware there was still a lot of hurt and anguish she was carrying from her past. Although he wanted to know more about her upbringing, he did not want to cause her any further pain so instead he added, 'Well, they must be so proud of you...'

Laine hastily lifted her gaze to meet his and gently pulled her hand free. She didn't want him to know any more. To learn they had both died. She had already said too much. 'Enough about me. I wasn't twelve and left alone after being forced to jump from a burning building to save my life.'

'When you put it like that, it sounds dramatic. But we've both had quite rough trots in life and, hey, look at us now. We've done something right on our own, hey?'

'But surely you weren't on you own? You weren't even

a teenager.' Laine took another spoonful of her yogurt and wiped her mouth with the cotton napkin.

'In a manner I suppose I was,' he replied, pausing to take the last bite of his meal. 'My father's much older sister, Mabel, was given custody in the will and she'd never married, let alone had children. Growing up, I hadn't seen much of her so we weren't close and she wasn't in the best of health. Whatever the real reason, she said she wouldn't be very good as a surrogate parent. She worried that a boy raised by his maiden aunt might miss out on a balanced upbringing so she sent me to boarding school overseas. In hindsight maybe it was a sensible decision but at twelve it was hard, suddenly being thrown on a plane to the other side of the world after losing my family.'

Laine shook her head in disbelief. 'That would have been terrible. You would have still been grieving.' She drew a breath and continued shaking her head. 'Now I'm not sure who had the worst childhood. Close contest really between you and me.'

'Mabel did what she thought was right. I guess we can safely say we've survived the worst, so we will get through anything life can throw at us.'

'Maybe,' Laine said sombrely. 'Or perhaps we're so battle worn we won't survive the next heartbreak.'

Pierce looked at Laine for a moment and knew that her grave outlook on life was colouring everything else in it. 'You're an amazingly resilient woman and, who knows, perhaps the universe is done testing both of us and it'll be smooth sailing for the next sixty years.'

'Who knows…?'

Laine finished her sparkling water and looked out over the beach in silence.

Pierce noticed the distance in her eyes. Her pain was

almost palpable and he didn't want her to start rebuilding the walls around her heart. He now understood her need to protect herself but he wanted her to feel safe with him. To be able to lose the need to be on the defensive and just enjoy their time together. He needed to turn the day around. Quickly.

'How about you and I head off for a nice drive to a place the concierge told me about this morning? It's a native animal and bird reserve and rainforest about thirty minutes from here called the Forest of Tranquillity. We can stay cool amongst all the greenery,' he said, standing and extending his hand to her.

Laine looked at his hand and then her gaze lifted to linger on the curves of his handsome smiling face for a moment. Then, surprising even herself, she reached up and rested her hand in his and her lips curved to a smile as she nodded.

Pierce was pleasantly surprised at her reaction. Perhaps there still was a chance for them. He wasn't sure what the chance would be but he wanted to explore whatever direction it took.

'Should I change?' she questioned him.

'Not a thing,' he told her, insisting that a sarong over her swimsuit was perfect attire for wherever they went, and pointed out that he was in swimming trunks too. He didn't bother with a T-shirt as the day was perfect and if the weather forecast was correct, in just a matter of hours it would be a scorching hot summer's day.

'It's a rainforest on the Australia Day long-weekend. It's not Park Avenue,' he said, opening the car door for her. 'Dress code around here on a one-hundred-degree day is "remain decent but no need to overdo it"!'

Laine laughed as he closed the car door. She could

learn a lot from Pierce. He was good for her and she knew it. He put the past where it belonged. She hoped one day to be able to do the same. She just didn't know how long it would take.

The day passed quickly as they made their way around the rainforest sanctuary in the slowing rising temperature. They enjoyed an Australia Day celebration barbeque lunch before they headed off again on the forest walk.

'Let's do a spot of bird-watching,' Pierce said light-heartedly.

'Definitely haven't done that before,' she said, 'unless you count avoiding pigeons in Time Square.'

Pierce rolled his eyes. 'Then you are in for a treat, because you will witness over one hundred and twenty birds here.'

'Really, one hundred and twenty here today?'

'Well, you may have to spend a few weeks or maybe months for them to all to return home but it says here,' he told her, pointing to the coloured brochure in his hand, 'that one hundred and twenty-six species of native birds have been recorded in the sanctuary.'

Laine playfully hit his shoulder. 'You're crazy…like one of those over-enthusiastic biology teachers.'

'Maybe I missed my calling,' he replied, as they sat down on a wooden bench under the shade of a tree. 'I could become a professional bird-watcher. I'd just need some binoculars and a safari suit. Now, that's a fashion statement that needs to be brought back. What do you think? With your fashion contacts, can you make it happen?'

Laine listened to his silly ramblings as she stretched her legs out in front of her and looked up at the perfect blue sky peeking through the dense greenery. Their surroundings were stunning.

'Unfortunately, not even my favourite fashion bible could resurrect that disaster. Besides, I'm not sure you have the patience required to wait for one hundred and twenty-six birds to return home.'

Pierce smiled. Perhaps not. But he did have the patience to wait for Laine to fall for him, he thought as he watched her suddenly jump to her feet with the arrival of a small yellow and grey plumed bird. She began to take photos with the new camera she had purchased in Sydney. The day was relaxing just as Pierce had hoped and he noticed Laine's mood lift, just as he had planned. Pierce smiled as he watched her face light up, waltzing around happily taking snaps of the birds in their natural habitat. He thought back over the last few days and how only week ago he hadn't even known the woman who had his complete attention now.

Laine turned around to see Pierce leaning against a low wall of uneven rocks. His suntanned chest was bare, his bathers hung low over his taut stomach and his gorgeous face was radiant with the most perfect smile. *Perhaps returning to Uralla and meeting Dr Pierce Beaumont wasn't a mistake, after all*, she thought to herself as she snapped his photo. Perhaps, for some reason, it was meant to be.

The day turned into evening and they chatted happily as they drove back to the resort with plans for a refreshing swim in the private pool in Pierce's villa before dinner.

They were alone in the secluded villa garden as the sun set.

'Thank you for a lovely day—in fact, two lovely days,'

Laine said, as she sat on the pool's edge, dangling her feet in the water as she dried off in the warm evening breeze.

Pierce swam over to her and looked up into her beautiful smiling face. 'You are more than welcome but I should be the one thanking you for agreeing to join me.'

Laine looked down at his handsome warm face and realised the last two days she had spent with Pierce had melted the last of her reserves. Suddenly she didn't want to hold back any more. She slipped her still-wet body back into the water and into his arms. Without thinking, she kissed him. Then, feeling scared at what she had done, she pulled away.

Pierce pulled her back towards his hard body and kissed her with the passion of a man possessed. His lips kissed hers with desire that he had never felt before. His hands caressed her body, sliding over her shoulders, teasing the straps of her swimsuit as he threatened to slip them off. Slowly she opened her mouth and kissed him with abandon. She wanted him too and she was not going to hold back. He pressed her against the pool edge as his hands slipped down the small of her back and rested on her bottom.

'I think we should take ourselves inside,' he breathed softly into her ear, and he kissed her neck.

Laine nodded and, holding her tiny waist, he lifted her from the water and placed her on the pool edge before he hauled himself up beside her. His tender kissed trailed across her shoulders and up her neck until he reached her eager mouth.

He had a look in his eyes that she felt in her heart.

Standing up, he reached down for her hand. Only this time he knew he wasn't offering a drive into town to distract her. They were about to become lovers. Laine willingly allowed him to pull her into his arms again. Strong, warm arms that she knew would hold her all night. Neither said anything as he scooped her up in his arms and carried her to the bed, their kisses becoming more intense with each step.

He wasn't waiting a second longer to have her. The room was lit only by the moonlight but it was enough for Pierce. He could see her beautiful sparkling eyes looking up at him as he slowly slipped her bathing suit from her body, kissing every part of her body as he inched the suit down. Finally he threw the swimsuit across the room, his own swimming trunks joining hers a moment later on the floor. Then his mouth slowly, purposefully began kissing his way up back her body again.

'Are you sure?' he asked huskily, as he slipped on the protection he had taken from his wallet.

Laine moaned her answer and pulled him to her. She was more than sure.

CHAPTER TEN

THEY LAY IN each other's arms for the longest time. Laine had floated to a place she never knew existed. She named it bliss in her head and hoped to visit again very soon. Pierce silently declared himself the luckiest man in the world. Both realised they were falling in love.

Pierce was not yet ready to tell Laine.

Laine was not yet ready to tell herself.

'Can I say, you're an amazing woman,' Pierce said, cupping her face in his hands and kissing her softly.

Laine kissed him back and pressed her body into the warmth of his embrace. His naked body felt so good next to her. Without doubt he had been the best lover— kind, considerate and passionate. Smiling to herself as she looked over his shoulder at the desk where, after throwing the contents of the desktop on the floor, he had made love to her, she added *surprisingly innovative* to the mental list.

'I definitely can't take all the credit for the last...how many hours?'

'Don't know, don't care,' he said, as his hands gently roamed her body and he listened for signs of her pleasure, lingering when he heard a response.

'I would love to continue this all night,' she murmured

as his kisses moved slowly down her neck, 'but we might need to eat or they'll find two bodies in the morning, wearing big smiles but bodies none the less.'

Pierce smiled and lay back down on the pillow. 'Point taken.'

Laine rolled over to face him. 'I'm thinking that I rather like our state of dress, so what if we order room service then only one of us has to leave bed?'

Pierce replied as he looked at the woman who was closer than any woman had ever been to claiming his heart. Her long brown hair was trailing across the pillow, framing her smiling face, and the sheets were barely covering her body. There was none of her earlier modest sheet wrapping. 'And that *one* would be me?'

'Do you mind?'

Pierce climbed from the bed. 'Not at all, but I'll need some swim trunks and a menu.'

'I think they're both on the floor,' Laine told him with a grin. 'The menu was on the desk a few hours ago but it's definitely not there any more.'

'And the swim trunks were on me a few hours ago and they're definitely not any more either.' A wicked glint appeared in eye and he leant back down on the crumpled sheets and began kissing her again.

'I'm thinking grilled chicken salad,' she told him, as she gently pushed him away.

The order arrived a short time later. Pierce carried it to the bed as Laine emerged from the shower and sat down beside him in a towel with her hair up in a clasp.

'I'm so ridiculously hungry,' she began as she picked up a fork and began selecting pieces of grilled chicken from the salad plate, ignoring the leafy mix and tomatoes.

'I think I know why,' he replied with a smirk as he cut into his steak.

Laine ignored his remark and continued eating. There was nothing left on her plate when she had finished. Not even a basil leaf. 'Do they have strawberries and cream on the menu?'

Pierce removed the tray from the bed and carefully placed it on the floor near the door. He slid over to Laine, pulled the clasp from her hair and slowly opened her towel, revealing her naked body to his appreciative eyes. 'Let's forget the strawberries, keep it simple and just order whipped cream.'

It was after midnight when they fell into a deep, satisfied sleep. Laine was secure in the strong arms that encircled her. Pierce held everything he knew he could possibly want in the world. The empty dessert bowls lay on the floor with the other dishes.

Pierce awoke in the morning as the sunlight crept through the blinds and spread across the bed. Laine was still in a deep sleep. The trip, he decided, had definitely been the best idea he had ever entertained. With careers on different continents, Pierce had no idea how their relationship would work but he decided then and there that he would make it happen somehow. Staring at the patterns the sunlight and blinds were making on the ceiling, he decided he would not give up easily.

Laine opened her eyes, in more ways than one.

She woke to realise the enormity of what she had done. She had broken two rules in one night. She had slept with one of her *models* and she had slept with someone she cared about. Even worse, someone who cared about her.

It had the makings of a disaster…yet she had never been so happy in all her life.

Pierce noticed her stirring and, lifting the mass of messy brown locks away from her neck, gently began kissing her bare skin. The stubble on his chin was tickling her but the desire he stirred again overrode everything else. Gently he rolled her on her back and looked into her eyes. His gaze was intense, as if he was looking into her soul.

'You must know how I feel… I…'

Laine put her finger to his lips and then followed it with a kiss. She was scared he might say he was falling in love with her. She didn't want him to spoil it. Her own heart was saying it too and now she realised she wasn't ready to hear the words. She might *never* be ready to hear them. They lived on different continents, lived different lives. It was overwhelming to think that she could be falling in love. It could never happen.

As the sun hit his chiselled jaw, once again darkened by a fine covering of stubble, she told herself she had no choice but to accept they were like two ships who had collided for one amazing night.

Pierce pulled away. 'We can make this work. If you want to see where we can take it.'

Laine closed her eyes. 'Let's not—'

Suddenly the ringing of Pierce's mobile phone interrupted her answer.

'Now, that's got to be worst timing,' he muttered in an irritated tone as he reached down to find it on the floor. Immediately he knew the caller from the screen. 'Hello, Tracy, what's happened?' Pierce knew that she would never call him on his time off for anything short of an emergency.

'I'm sorry to interrupt your time away, Pierce, but Trevor Jacobs had a heart attack last night. The hospital called. Betty drove him there yesterday for the tests you requested and he suffered the episode in the waiting room. His children and grandchildren have arrived at the hospital and the attending doctor wondered if you might be able to head there later today. The whole family is worried the shock might be too much for his wife. I've taken the liberty of changing your flights to the earlier one. You'll need to be at Sydney airport in an hour and a half. I knew you'd want to be here.'

'Thanks, Tracy,' he said, swinging around to put his feet on the floor. 'Betty will be beside herself so we'll need to keep an eye on her. Tell the attending doctor I'll be there by lunchtime.' With that he ended the call.

'Is everything okay? Laine asked, sitting up in the bed and twisting her hair away from her face and into an untidy plait. 'Is it a patient?'

'Yes, and it's serious so I'm sorry but we'll have to cut our stay short by a few hours and take an earlier flight. I need to be back there as soon as possible.'

They drove back to Sydney and caught the next flight to Uralla. Pierce was preoccupied with Trevor and decided to leave their talk until that night. He invited her to dinner at his place, where he planned on telling her how he felt over a candlelit meal.

Their time away had been wonderful beyond belief and Laine thought he was the most amazing man but he was a country doctor who loved his life in Australia and she was a photographer with a life wherever she was booked. She had already broken two rules she had never broken before, and having dinner tonight would be breaking her no-second-date rule. And she already had doubts. She couldn't keep breaking her rules or she would have nothing to hold onto. Her rules protected her. They were her constant. If she broke the final rule and allowed this fling to turn into a relationship she risked everything. She risked her heart. That was something she couldn't do.

'I'll call and pick you up as soon as I've checked on my patient,' he said, kissing her cheek before she alighted from the car.

She was still happy inside that she had got to know the real Pierce and that he too knew more about her, but it was a bittersweet happiness. 'You should get going,' she finally muttered, and leant in to give him the last kiss she knew they would ever share. It was warm and tender and it made her want to cry. Pierce was a good man and he would make someone happy one day. He would have a family and a wonderful life but it wouldn't be with her. She already felt as if she needed him in her own life, and it had to stop—immediately.

'I'll see you tonight,' he said huskily as his lips left the softness of hers.

She didn't answer him.

Her walls were slowly being built up again and it was a quite conscious move on her part. She needed to block him out. She needed to protect herself. She had been stupid and reckless in letting Pierce in and thinking that she would be all right. Being in Toowoon Bay had not been the real world. It had been a beautiful dream and she had just woken up.

Standing outside her door, watching the man who had stolen her heart drive away, she knew she would leave today before he returned. She wasn't strong enough to love another person and let the universe play Russian roulette with her heart. But she doubted if she found herself in his bed again that night that she would be strong enough to leave. It was only lunchtime. She would head to Armidale, finish the shoot at the bank and catch the plane that afternoon. It might hurt him that she was gone without saying goodbye but it was what she needed to do.

Pierce arrived at the hospital fifteen minutes later to find Trevor's family gathered outside ICU where he had been transferred.

'Tell us what's happening,' Trevor's eldest son pleaded. 'I don't understand the medical mumbo-jumbo. We didn't know Dad even had a heart condition. He kept it from all of us. Is he going to make it?'

'Let me speak with the cardiologist and I'll let you know.' He paused and not able to see Betty, he asked the young man, 'How's your mother handling this?'

'Her granddaughters are distracting her but we're worried about them both. They're inseparable. Forty years of marriage and even though Dad's a grumpy old man at times, they've never had a cross word. She won't be able to go on without him.'

'Let's hope that's not something she has to contemplate. Keep a watch on your mother and I'll let you know in a few minutes how your father is getting on,' Pierce said, patting the man's back before hastily entering ICU after washing his hands. There he met the attending physician, Eric Milburn, who Pierce knew socially.

'Hi, Pierce, the family are all extremely anxious, as you've probably seen.'

'Yes, they're wanting me to update them. What's the prognosis?'

'Late last night I would have said grim and that's why we called the family here as we didn't think he would make it through the night. Somehow he's managed to turn a corner. We're all baffled, to be honest, but very pleased.'

Eric discussed at depth with Pierce the surgical intervention required as they worked though the case notes. It was nothing that Pierce had not seen before and he was elated at the news. He had arrived prepared to hear a dire prognosis. 'I'll let the family know.'

'Cautious optimism,' Eric told Pierce, as he removed his gloves and left ICU. 'And he will still be hospitalised for quite a few weeks with the surgery he has ahead.'

Pierce thanked Eric and left to speak to the family. Betty was now standing with her sons, awaiting the news of her husband.

'The doctors need to monitor your husband closely after his heart attack, and it's hospital procedure if there's the slightest indication of any injury to the heart to keep a patient in ICU.'

'How long will he stay here?' she asked, her face dressed with worry.

'It depends on how his coronary arteries are functioning. They're the arteries supplying blood to your husband's heart. If they're not working properly then his heart can't work either. They are also assessing the damage to the heart that may have occurred during the heart attack.'

'And how bad do they think it is?' the eldest son asked.

'Luckily, because he was already at the hospital and seen immediately, his chances of recovery are quite good, but he will need a stent to keep the walls of the coronary artery open and allow the blood to pass through.'

'When will that happen?' asked the taller of Betty's sons.

'They will ensure he is stable then schedule the surgery. Once your father has recovered completely from the operation and the cardiologist is satisfied, he will go home. He will need lots of rest. I will insist on that, but you all need to take the next few days slowly. It's been a shock to you all. I'll speak to you as soon as I know anything more. I'll update you and go over everything, including the recovery plan for home.'

The family had a lot to take in and there was still a long road ahead for their father but they thanked Pierce for his part in sending Trevor to hospital for testing.

'Thank you from the bottom of my heart,' Betty said, with tears running down her softly wrinkled cheeks. 'If you hadn't insisted on him having the tests, we might have lost him.'

'Trevor did the right thing and followed my instructions, so you can also give credit to him and the hospital for Trevor's prognosis. Of course, there's still a way to go. You may have a few more hurdles in store, but his spirit and the love he has out here will give him the best chance of making a great recovery.'

After leaving Trevor, Pierce checked in on James and found that he was stable. Myles was hoping to wean him off the ventilator within a few days. Now satisfied with the progress of both of his hospitalised patients, Pierce turned his attention to Laine. She was a wonderful woman and he intended to tell her that and more when he held her in his bed that night.

* * *

Laine's plane was due to touch down in Sydney at around
the time she knew that Pierce would be arriving to collect her. The bank had agreed to the shoot being brought
forward and she was able to wrap it up in just over an
hour. Then with another hour to spare she headed to the
airport, stopping to mail a letter before she dropped off
her hire car and boarded the plane. Her heart was heavy
as she sat on the small runway in the plane that would
take her away from Pierce for ever.

It was for the best, she kept reminding herself. She
had been single for a very long time and for good reason.
The thought of caring for another person scared her to the
core. Her hands were shaking and she hid her tears behind her sunglasses. Only the night before she had shared
this man's bed but in the light of day she had panicked.
The reality had been too much for her. She admitted to
herself she was a coward when it came to love. Although
she wished it to be different, she wasn't brave enough to
risk heartbreak. She buckled her seatbelt, knowing there
was no other way. As the plane picked up speed down the
runway, Laine closed her eyes and prayed she would not
live to regret leaving this town, and this man.

After leaving the hospital, Pierce headed to the jewellery store, where he looked for something special. Immediately he spied the stunning platinum chain with a
solitaire diamond drop. It was perfect. The shop assistant gift-wrapped the piece and Pierce was on his way
to the woman he knew had won his heart. The feelings
he had for Laine were real and he intended on letting her
know. A puzzled frown crossed his brow when he saw her
rental car was missing from the motel car park. Pulling

up outside her room, he dialled her number but her phone was switched off so he made his way to the motel office.

'Miss Phillips checked out this afternoon. It must have been just after lunch.'

Pierce headed to Armidale, thinking perhaps she had changed the time of the shoot and she was planning on staying the night with him. No point in keeping her motel room when she clearly wouldn't need it. He smiled to himself. Ever the consummate professional, her phone was probably turned off while she was working. The drive took fifteen minutes, and after parking behind the bank he walked along the side street with a smile a mile wide.

He had to admit he was in love. It had happened faster than he'd thought possible. But it had happened. This crazy, independent woman from the other side of the world had stolen his heart as quick as lightning. She was self-sufficient, opinionated, feisty, mysterious and challenging in so many ways. But she was also the one for him.

Entering the bank, his face fell when he saw there was no sign of her. No lighting, no equipment, no Laine.

'She left about an hour ago,' the bank manager told him. 'She brought the shoot forward, said she had an afternoon flight to catch.'

Laine didn't switch on her phone when she entered the Sydney terminal. She knew that Pierce would try to call. Most likely demand an explanation and attempt to talk her out of her decision to end it before it had really begun. It was easier if he just got the letter. No man before Pierce had ever made her question being alone and she didn't know if she could give him a good enough

reason. The letter would put everything in perspective
and he couldn't make her doubt her decision if she never
heard the warmth in his voice again.

Pierce raced to the airport, desperate to see her. To find
out what had happened. Her phone was still switched off
so he knew there must be an emergency, a reason for her
sudden departure. He couldn't fathom that she wouldn't
just leave without an explanation.

Numb best described his mood as he left the airport
twenty minutes later, knowing that Laine really had
caught the afternoon flight. The kiosk attendant told him
that she'd sold the stunning brunette a coffee before her
one-thirty flight. She confirmed it was the same stunning
woman who had flown in five days before with a trolley load of equipment. The airline staff weren't allowed
to confirm it was her but it didn't take much to work it
out. Laine had left town without so much as a goodbye.

As he lay in bed alone that night he knew that a farewell
call would never come. Sydney was less than an hour's
flight. They had shared that flight together that morning. There could be no emergency that wouldn't allow
her to call and let him know. He realised she had breezed
in and out of his life and there was nothing he could do.
Nothing he would do.

He had fallen in love with a beautiful woman with a
life and successful career overseas and for some insane
reason he'd thought they would have a future together.
That was not going to happen. He was suited to living
in Uralla whereas Laine, he knew in his heart, was not.
She was a woman with no ties and the world at her feet.
She had a way of life and an attitude that was more in

line with a big city. He could call but he wouldn't. Laine had switched off her phone for a reason. And he would accept it. He had to face the cold, hard fact that a country doctor would have no long-term appeal to a woman like Laine. And he didn't want his old life back. He liked his life just the way it was. New York was no place for him and apparently Laine felt the same about Uralla.

She had made her decision and looking at the diamond pendant on the dresser he knew he had to let her go.

CHAPTER ELEVEN

THE INVITATION FOR the gala ball and launch of the 'General Practitioners of Australia' calendar in Sydney arrived in the mail early one September morning and tugged at Pierce's heart just a little. It had been almost eight months since Laine had left and not a day went by when Pierce did not think about her.

He knew in time he would stop and some days he came close but then something would remind him of the stunning brunette who had crept under his skin and into his heart. Casual talk of Toowoon Bay by a friend, the mention of New York in passing, the sight of the ladder he'd climbed the day they'd first met...anyone holding a camera.

He'd had no choice but to let her go. She wasn't interested in a relationship with a country GP. And Pierce did not want to step back into the limelight that he had left behind. They had different priorities.

'Not interested,' Pierce muttered, as he threw the gilt-edged invitation in the bin and returned to the computer screen and his emails.

He had been expecting the invitation. His business manager, on Pierce's instructions, had contacted the charity and offered the use of Sydney's newest hotel at no

cost to host the event. It was a hotel that Pierce owned.
An investment that the business manager had convinced
Pierce to make six months before when the original inves-
tors had needed to sell. It had been nearing completion
when they'd run short on finance and there had been a
concern it would sit as an eyesore on the Sydney skyline
if it wasn't completed.

Pierce had agreed to take it on but wanted nothing to
do with the running of it. He doubted he would even visit.
It would give a good return and help fund his charities
so that was all the level of his involvement until it came
time to name it.

Pierce had thought long and hard about it. He had seen
the photos. The hotel had an elegant yet strong façade. It
was nothing like any other hotel on the harbour. Luxurious, yet almost minimal. Understated and timeless. The
only hotel with a helipad for a discreet escape. He knew
there was only one name it could carry, the one person
he knew who personified the hotel. And so it became
The Lainesway Hotel.

'Not interested in what?' Tracy asked as she entered the
room to put a new disposable covering over the examination bed.

'Nothing. Nothing at all.'

'Fine, don't tell me,' she replied. 'But I think you need
to get out. Come to our place for dinner on the weekend.
Sitting here talking to yourself is not a good sign.'

'Then perhaps you could send the next patient in and
I will have someone to speak to.'

'Trevor cancelled.'

'Why?' Pierce asked firmly. 'It's important I still

monitor him. I don't want him getting cocky on me and letting his appointments slip.'

'I told him that and he'll be in to see you tomorrow first thing. Apparently the *New England Focus* magazine is over there now, doing a photo shoot of the giant dolls' house he built for his granddaughters and also one to auction for the cardiac unit annual fundraiser. They are doing a feature story. It's taken him the best part of six months but the houses are magnificent.

'Fine, but if he cancels again, I will personally drive over and bring him here.'

'Don't worry, I told him that he's on your radar and he won't get away with anything.' Tracy laughed. 'But back to you talking to yourself—what was the topic of conversation? You didn't seem very happy.'

'Just the invitation to attend the calendar launch in Sydney. No way in hell am I going.'

'Why not? It sounds like fun. There might be some eligible women for the eligible doctors.'

No doubt, he thought, but more to the point there would be a certain photographer. He had no interest in seeing the woman whose name was emblazoned on the invitation: *World-famous photographer Laine Phillips*.

'I think you should go,' Tracy told him, as she bent down and collected the invitation from the recycle bin and began reading in earnest. 'Ooh, and it's at the The Lainesway Hotel. That's the lovely new hotel overlooking the Sydney Harbour. I read about it in the paper. It would be a lovely evening, you can get all gussied up and have an amazing time.'

'Is anything private any more?' he asked, taking the invitation back from her and tearing it into uneven strips before throwing it back in the bin.

'Come on, you might meet a nice lady. You need to be thinking about getting married and having children, and you clearly haven't tried to meet anyone around here.'

'I'm too busy.' Pierce continued typing and tried to ignore the direction of the conversation.

'You shouldn't be too busy for love,' Tracy said with a huge smile.

Pierce turned from the computer screen and stopped what he was doing. 'I don't think travelling to Sydney to be humiliated in a topless photograph will secure me a lifelong partner.'

'But it's for charity.'

'And?'

'Charity events bring out very nice people, it's a well-known fact, and one of them might be lovely enough to catch your eye.'

Pierce loved Tracy, always the optimist and now she was running around with a cupid's bow, trying to find him a wife. But try as he may, he couldn't imagine falling in love again. He'd thought he would be over Laine by now but he wasn't. He thought he was going mad some nights as he lay in his bed, thinking over in his head about their time together.

The anger had passed, and so too had the denial. He'd quickly realised Laine wasn't coming back. It had all been said so eloquently but so coldly in her letter that had arrived the day after she'd left town. In it she'd explained that although she'd had a wonderful few days it had been nothing more than that. A wonderful few days. She hoped he hadn't read any more into it and she apologised if she had led him on in any way. The letter had finished by telling him that she would always think fondly of him.

The letter had hit the wall in a crumpled ball. It had

been seven months and twenty five days before the glossy invitation had arrived in the mail. Not that Pierce had been counting the days since she'd left.

'What was the charity again?' Tracy enquired, as she took the seat where the patients would normally sit during a consultation.

'Foster Children's Transition Programme.' Pierce eyed her becoming comfortable in the chair and wasn't sure if he liked that idea. It suggested a motherly advice session he didn't want or need.

'That's a wonderful cause, you should consider supporting it.

'I did,' Pierce retorted. 'I posed for the ridiculous calendar, remember?'

'I knew you were posing but I never met the photographer. She'd left before I arrived that day and you did the other shoots away from here and you never seemed to want to talk about it,' she announced, her voice not hiding her disappointment in not being included. 'But it's a very worthwhile cause. Our close friends fostered a child many years ago. The Phillips family, they lived in our street.'

Pierce stopped what he was doing at the mention of the name.

'Yes, Maisey and Arthur Phillips. They fostered a little girl for a short time and then finally adopted her. She was a real sweetie and the apple of her father's eye. They couldn't have children of their own but anyone would have thought she was their own flesh and blood, the way Arthur treated her. He taught her all about photography when she was growing up. It was his hobby and he had the biggest collection of cameras of anyone I knew. She'd run around town taking pictures of anything she could.'

'Yes, well, it's a small world. The photographer for my shoot, Laine Phillips, was their daughter,' he said, drawing a deep breath and speaking matter-of-factly so his voice did not betray his emotion.

'What was her name?' she asked.

'Laine. She shortened it from Melanie when she left town.'

Tracy paused as she pictured her angelic face as a child. 'Melanie Phillips was here?'

'Yes, in the flesh, but she didn't want anyone to know. She liked to keep to herself. Too many memories, or so she said.'

Tracy sighed. 'That's sad. I know everyone would love to see her. I'm surprised that she wasn't recognised.'

'I don't know what she looked like then but now she's…' He paused, thinking about her beautiful face, her smile, the way her long brown hair had spread across his pillow that morning. 'She's a stunning woman. She might not be the girl you all remember.'

'Why do you say that?'

'Quite the big city attitude. Think she's outgrown Uralla. But I gather she was looking for bigger and better when she left town as a teenager. Outgrew it then so it definitely wouldn't hold any appeal now.'

'She didn't *outgrow* it, Pierce. She left after her parents died. Maisey and Arthur were killed in a car accident about twelve years ago, when Melanie was only sixteen. We were all worried sick about her and we tried to rally round and help her out but she wouldn't have a bar of it.

'Almost overnight she changed personality from happy and outgoing to fiercely independent. She shut us all out. It was like the shutters came down on her heart and there was no way in. That was one of the saddest times for the town and then even sadder is the fact that Melanie just took off a few weeks later and no one's ever heard from her since. Nothing. It's like she fell off the planet.'

The words hit him in the chest. So she had run away from loss in Uralla just as he had done from his loss in New York. They were more alike than he'd realised. It was her way of dealing with sadness. To run away and pretend she'd never cared. It all fitted into place like a jigsaw but it didn't solve anything if he didn't do something about it.

'Tracy, can you book two seats on a plane to Sydney for the first Friday in October?' he said, after confirming the date on the almost unreadable invitation. 'I think I might just head over for the calendar launch after all. Will you be my date?'

'That sounds wonderful. So you want me to RSVP for you?'

'No, I think I'll decline as a calendar model, but I'd like you to buy two guest tickets. I don't want the fuss. I'd prefer to just melt into the background and watch the proceedings.'

Tracy wheeled her carry-on luggage off the plane and down the air bridge into the bustle of the terminal. It was just one night so her evening dress, shoes and accessories were all inside the one bag.

'I'm so excited!' she exclaimed as they hurriedly made their way to the cab rank. Pierce loaded her bag in the trunk of the cab, along with his suit bag containing his black tuxedo and a small leather carry-on.

'The Lainesway Hotel, please.'

'But the dinner isn't for hours. Aren't we going to our hotel first?' Tracy asked.

'About that,' Pierce replied. 'I saw you booked a very nice hotel but I changed the booking. We're staying at The Lainesway. And I have booked us each a suite. No arguments, you deserve to be spoilt.'

'But I was trying to be economical.'

'And I love you for it…but economical is not the way I want to tonight to play out.'

Tracy had settled into her suite when there was a knock at the door.

'Who is it?'

'Pierce. May I speak with you for a minute? I need you to do something for me.'

Tracy opened the door and invited him in. 'Do you need something pressed?'

Pierce smiled as he crossed the carpeted floor to a modern-style chaise longue by the huge floor-to-ceiling window. Gold silk drapes framed the view of the Sydney Opera House jutting out into the blue harbour waters. 'Ever the mother, aren't you? But the answer is, no, I don't need you to do anything before the gala. I need you to do something at the gala.'

'What would that be?' she asked, sitting on the edge of her bed where her long black beaded evening dress was draped.

'I'm not sure if you know that there will be an auction of the twelve framed calendar shots this evening, with the proceeds going to the charity.'

'No, I didn't, but that's a good way to generate more funds. It does sound like such a worthy cause. When I think of Melanie and all she went though as a child before she moved to Uralla, it breaks my heart.'

Pierce suddenly wondered if Laine was in her suite

yet and if she was looking at the same view. And was she thinking about their time together? She was incredibly independent and distant at times, but underneath her armour she was loving and caring and scared. He just needed to make her understand that a life and love like they could share was worth the risk.

'I said that's a good idea.' Tracy had raised her voice a little to bring Pierce back from his reverie. She was puzzled by his behaviour but decided not to ask too many questions and accepted that he obviously had a lot on his mind.

'Yes, yes, it's a great marketing idea,' he said, standing up and moving away from the window. 'Anyway, I would like you to buy them for me.'

'All of them?'

'Yes, all twelve.'

'And exactly how much is that going to set me back? You pay me well but I don't think well enough for that.'

Pierce laughed. 'No, what I should have said was *on my behalf*. I will be giving you a cheque for the amount I wish to pay at auction and it's well above what they would be expecting. There shouldn't be any competition from other bidders.'

Tracy suddenly wore a puzzled expression. 'Any reason why you would want to hang pictures of yourself and eleven other doctors you don't know in our office?'

Pierce shook his head and grinned. 'I don't want to keep any of them. I'm happy to give them away. Perhaps the nurses at the hospital can take one each, except mine. That can be boxed up somewhere, never to be seen again.'

'Then why exactly do you want to buy them if you don't want them?'

'It's for a good cause.'

Tracy knew better than to delve further. Pierce was a lovely man but there were some parts of his life he guarded and clearly this was one of them. She checked her watch and then went to the luxurious marble bathroom to run a bath. 'I think I'll soak for a while. I don't often have the time to take a bubble bath but it's quite a special night tonight so I'm going to spoil myself. There's still over an hour until cocktails,' she called out over the sound of the running water. 'You can just leave the cheque on the desk and I'll bring it down with me.'

Pierce pulled the bank cheque from his inside jacket pocket. 'It's here by your purse.'

Tracy returned to the bedroom to collect her make-up and while she was there she picked up the cheque. 'I'll do it now so I don't forget…' She paused to read the details and her voice became a shrill scream. 'Are you mad? One point two million dollars for some photographs?'

'I know it seems a lot…'

'It doesn't *seem* a lot,' she replied. 'It *is* a lot and it's mad. Photographs of people you don't even know for that much money. I wouldn't pay that much for photos signed by the entire Royal family…and I adore the monarchy!'

'Look, I don't have time to go into everything now, you need to get ready for tonight and I don't want to rush you so I'm going to leave. You have the cheque so I will meet you downstairs in an hour and a quarter, and can you please bid for the photographs?'

'A million dollars?' she declared, still in shock as she walked in to turn off her bath.

'Yes, a million dollars for a worthy cause, and don't worry, I can afford it. I have money put away for a rainy day,' he called to her.

Tracy walked back into the room with her arms folded

across her chest. 'I'm not worried about the money, I know you can well afford it. I'm worried about the reason behind it.'

Pierce was taken aback by her comment. 'What do you mean by "I know you can well afford it"?'

Tracy sat on the edge of the bed and clasped her hands in her lap. 'Pierce, do you honestly think that my husband would have sold his practice to you and let you take over the care of his patients without knowing everything there was to know about you? He loves the people of this town and he wanted to hand them over to someone who would do the right thing by them. He had to be sure.'

'But neither of you ever asked me about my past or my money.'

'There was nothing we needed to ask you. Gregory made enquiries before you arrived. We might be country folk but we're not silly. You were the son of a very wealthy parents who died when you were a child, you attended a private boarding school in Germany from the age of ten until seventeen, when you returned to Sydney and to study medicine. You were well respected by your peers and your grades were exemplary. When you arrived in Uralla two years ago you didn't bring up your family or any of what we knew so we didn't either.

'My husband believes you judge the man on his own merits, not his family money. You were a great young doctor and just what the people of the town needed. There was nothing shady in your past, just a lot of money. To be honest, we weren't sure if you had given it away or something had happened because you hardly live an extravagant life here in town, although we did notice a lot of anonymous donations to the local schools after you arrived. Perhaps a coincidence,' she said, looking directly at him, 'but we think not. You're a good doctor, who always buys a lot of raffle tickets and fundraising lamingtons, that's all that matters here.'

Pierce was flabbergasted. 'I can't believe you never said a thing in all this time. No one in the town knows? Or is everyone aware and not saying anything?'

'No one knows and it's not their business. You're just the nice young doctor who everyone respects and trusts, and that's all they need to know. You don't flash your money around, well, not until tonight anyway. So how would anyone know? It won't come from me or Gregory, so unless you suddenly turn up with a flashy imported sports car, the town will never know.'

Pierce was still in shock. His secret had been kept by them for the last two years and he'd had no idea. The day was certainly not as he had expected but nothing about his life had been since Laine Phillips had come to Uralla. She had turned his life upside down and now he wanted to turn hers around and make her understand that real love was worth the risk.

'Okay, we can talk later. But now I'll leave you to soak and I'll meet you downstairs in an hour.

Pierce stood in the doorway of the ballroom dressed in a black tuxedo with satin lapels, a crisp white shirt and black bow-tie. His black hair was slicked back and his skin freshly shaven. The grand ballroom of The Lainesway Hotel was at capacity with over five hundred guests. The event organisers had done their work in publicising the night.

His gaze slowly, purposefully roamed his surroundings. Twelve stunning crystal chandeliers hung in the grandeur of the softly lit room. The walls were appointed with Tasmanian pine and sophisticated fabric panels. Huge white and black floral centrepieces with steps of tealights decorated each table. Then he saw her. Like a Grecian goddess she moved through the crowd. Her floor-length one-shouldered white dress was trimmed with gold stones and it caught the light. Her long dark hair had been twisted into a chignon at the nape of her neck. She was breathtaking.

Although he wanted to approach, he decided to leave their meeting until the auction so he took his allocated seat at a table with Tracy.

The fundraising auction for the twelve calendar framed prints began shortly after main course. All were signed by the photographer and being put up for auction individually. They were on easels across the stage but each was hidden from view with a black covering.

'I thought we might have some fun—mix it up and start with December then work our way backwards,' the auctioneer announced, with Laine standing by his side. 'Each of the doctors is here tonight and has kindly agreed to step up to the stage during the auction and also to sign their print. That is, except our first lot tonight. Lot Twelve, Dr December. Dr Pierce Beaumont sent his apologies, so I'm sorry, ladies, he won't be here to sign this one, but we have the eleven other doctors.'

'I have been able to make it. I'm here,' Pierce called in a husky voice.

'So much for melting into the background,' Tracey muttered, as she sipped her champagne.

'Did I just hear something?' the auctioneer enquired, looking out to the audience.

Pierce stood and made his way through the tables to the stage.

Looking directly at Laine, he answered, 'There's no-where else I'd rather be than here tonight.'

Laine froze. Her heart began to race. She'd had no idea Pierce would be attending. Her acceptance to attend had been given on the assurance that he had declined.

Pierce made his way to the stairs and then took his place beside Laine and his photograph.

'I thought you weren't coming,' she managed to mutter, without meeting his gaze, her heart racing so fast she thought she would pass out.

'I wasn't but then curiosity got the better of me. I thought I'd like to see which photo you chose. Was it at the McKenzies' property or perhaps me perched atop the ladder?'

Pierce watched Laine's eyes narrow as the auctioneer crossed to the easel. She wouldn't look in the direction of her work, and she seemed very nervous. Pierce had no idea why until the auctioneer slowly lifted the dust cover and the photograph was revealed. Laine hadn't chosen any of the staged photographs. Instead, she had enlarged and framed one from their day in the rainfor-est, taken only hours before they'd made love. It wasn't a planned shot, there was no posing or design. It was as spontaneous as the moment she'd slipped into the pool and into his arms.

Their time away had meant something to her. This was the proof he needed.

'Well, it seems that all the framed photographs will in-deed be signed tonight,' the auctioneer said with a cough to clear his throat. 'So I'll start the bidding for Dr Pierce Beaumont at five hundred dollars.

A very elegant, manicured hand went up to the right of the room. 'Five hundred.'

'Five it is,' the auctioneer announced.

Another French-manicured hand was raised. 'Six hundred dollars.'

'Six hundred I'm bid.'

A third female hand was raised. 'One thousand.'

'I'll take one thousand from the lady with the lovely voice at the back.'

'One hundred thousand dollars.'

The room fell silent for a moment then burst into noise. Those closest, who had heard Tracy's bid, gasped. Those who hadn't been listening started chatting wildly amongst themselves, trying to understand what was causing such a reaction. Trying to catch up with what had just happened.

Laine's eyes widened in shock.

'Did I hear correctly? Did someone just bid one hundred thousand dollars?' the auctioneer asked loudly, the wooden gravel in his hand.

'Yes,' Tracy replied. 'One hundred thousand dollars per photograph, and I want all twelve. I can give you a cheque for one point two million now.'

Tracy had never done anything that exciting in her life and she blushed a little when she realised the entire room was looking at her. She nodded and acknowledged the attention.

Pierce stood smiling on the stage next to the unveiled photo. He hoped his generous donation would kick-start the rest of Sydney society into opening their cheque books. He knew that many there were spurred on by the need to outdo each other so he hoped he had set the bar high enough that all of the foster transition centres would be funded by the evening's donations from the well-heeled guests. If not, he would cover them himself anyway.

He posed for the media after signing the photograph then turned to speak to Laine. But she was gone. As quickly as she had appeared on the stage, she had disappeared. Pierce looked everywhere but she had left the ballroom.

Immediately he called for the event co-ordinator and questioned her about Laine's whereabouts.

'She wanted to be alone. She's on the rooftop.'

'The rooftop?'

'Yes, it's a secure area. There's a door that leads to the rooftop from the eighteenth floor stairwell but unfortunately I gave her my only pass, but I can give hotel security a call and get another one. I'll be right back.'

Pierce watched as she walked away but then as an afterthought added, 'Miss Laine has booked a helicopter to collect her from the rooftop and take her to a large private yacht in fifteen minutes. She has a photographic assignment on board for the next two weeks. It's anchored just out of the harbour and due to sail at midnight.'

CHAPTER TWELVE

PIERCE DIDN'T WAIT for the co-ordinator to contact Security. He made the call himself. They sent one of the guards, and on learning that Pierce was the owner of the hotel, the guard accompanied him to the stairwell and to the rooftop door, but as they tried to open it they found it was jammed.

'It's as if there's something leaning against it,' the guard said with a puzzled look on his face. 'Definitely won't be anyone going out this way tonight.'

'Is there another way?' Pierce asked, not bothering to hide his desperation to get to Laine in time.

Rubbing his chin, the guard looked at Pierce. 'It's that important?'

'Nothing more important in the world right now.'

'Then come with me.'

The guard took Pierce in the opposite direction and they climbed down two flights of stairs until they came to another secure doorway. The guard again used his pass to open the door that led onto a balcony.

'And now exactly where are we and why are we here?' Pierce asked, as he stood in the cool breeze on a balcony sixteen floors above the street. He didn't care to look down, preferring to look across the lights of the city skyline and then lifting his gaze upwards to the darkened sky now strung with stars.

'Well, just around here is a fire escape,' the guard began, as he walked with Pierce slightly to their left. 'It leads to the rooftop and the helipad.'

Pierce followed the young man and quickly came across a black metal ladder attached to the rendered wall. Pierce studied it carefully and noticed it had bolts every six inches holding the framework in place. It was his only way to Laine. Looking at his watch, he knew that there was less than ten minutes until the helicopter arrived. He tilted his head to see the end of the fire escape. He assumed that was the rooftop and where Laine was waiting for her lift to the yacht.

'Are you okay, climbing the fire escape?' the security guard asked.

'I guess I've run out of other options,' Pierce answered, without looking away from the framework he was about to ascend.

'She must be very special. Not sure I'd be doing it.'

Pierce turned his gaze to the uniformed man. 'Very special.' And with that Pierce removed his tuxedo jacket, undid his bow-tie and the top button of his shirt and put his foot on the first rung of the ladder. His stomach churned and his heart raced as he lifted his weight to the next rung. His hands held tightly to the sides of the framework, turning his knuckles white as pulled himself up yet another step. Pausing for a moment, he took a deep breath and kept her beautiful face in his mind as he continued the climb. Rung by rung he thought about Laine, of her laughing as they'd raced to the water's edge, the kiss he'd stolen just before the sun had risen on the farm, her lying naked in his bed.

He was going to reach her, come hell or high water.

Finally he reached the top and as he stepped onto the rooftop caught sight of her silhouette. She was standing alone, looking up into the sky.

Pierce cleared his throat. 'A penny for your thoughts.'

She spun on her heel to see Pierce standing on the rooftop.

She couldn't believe he was there. She had blocked the doorway to make sure he couldn't reach her. She didn't want to be that close to him again. Ever.

'What the hell are you doing up here?'

'Trying to convince you to give us a shot,' he replied, stepping carefully towards her. Looking across at the doorway, he noticed it was blocked by a planter. 'I wanted to tell you that eight months ago but you didn't give me a chance. You ran away, and tonight you blocked my way to reach you.'

Laine followed his eye line to the barred doorway. 'I didn't run away. I finished what I came to do and I left. But why are you here, and...*how*?' She stumbled over her words, aware that Pierce had found the only other way to reach her. He had climbed an outside fire escape on top of a multi-storey building. She wasn't sure how he'd done it. His fear of heights should have prevented him but somehow he'd managed. Somehow he hadn't let that fear cripple him. Somehow he had come to her despite his fear.

He walked across the rooftop to her and reach for her hands. 'Because I want you. And I wasn't about to let anything stop me.'

Laine tried to control her emotions but she was struggling. Each moment it became harder not to fall into his arms. But she couldn't. The helicopter would arrive any minute and she could leave him. And never look back.

'I told you how I felt in my letter. It was just a few days we shared, nothing more.'

'And the calendar photograph of me, how do you explain that?'

Laine pulled away but he caught her wrist, pulling her back to him.

'It was good lighting.' It was so much more and they both knew it. It had been her favourite. It had reminded her of an incredibly special time and she'd wanted the world to see it.

'That's the worst excuse ever. The lighting on any other photo would have been better and we both know it,' he said, looking intensely into her eyes. 'It was what happened a few hours later, wasn't it?'

'I liked the photo, let's leave it at that,' she replied in not more than a whisper, not daring to look at him.

'I'm not buying that. And I'll stay right here until I hear something that convinces me to go.'

'You're a wonderful man, but I don't want or need a relationship. I don't want to depend on someone.'

'Not someone, *me*. I want you to depend on me.'

She shook her head. Her walls were crumbling. She felt the months apart vanishing in the warmth of his touch and it frightened her. 'I can't, I'm not brave enough. Pierce, I'm not worth it, just let me go.'

'That's where you are wrong,' he told her, his hands holding hers even more tightly. 'You are worth it, and so much more, too.'

Laine felt tears welling in her eyes and spilling down her face. No man had ever wanted to risk everything to love her. She was finding it more difficult by the second not to accept his words. He had overcome a huge obstacle to be standing there with her. Maybe he had enough belief for both of them but even if she could take her fear out of the equation there were practical barriers too. 'I have no idea how *we* could work, it's not even close to feasible. Are you forgetting that I live in another country? In a city you hate. A city that brings back memories you can't live with.'

'I can put memories where they belong but I can't live knowing you're somewhere without me. Memories we both need to put to rest are keeping us apart. We can build new happy memories together. We can both let go of the past safe in the knowledge we have each other. Eight months have passed and I don't love you any less than the day you woke in my arms. In fact, I think I love you more.'

'That's ridiculous,' she said, pulling her hands from his and walking away. Looking out across the water, she could see the lights of the harbour and the yacht moored waiting for her. 'We barely knew each other then.'

'Then tell me, if you didn't feel anything, why did you run away from me? Why couldn't you say goodbye to my face?'

Laine knew what Pierce said was true. She had been falling for him then and not a day had gone by that she hadn't thought back to the time, however brief, that they had shared together. Maybe he was right, maybe it *was* love, but she was scared. So scared that it would end and she would be left alone, her heart broken all over again. She had nothing to lose in telling him the truth so she turned to face him. Her expression told the story.

'I was scared, Pierce. There, I said it. I was scared then, and I'm scared now. I'm frightened to my core that you will leave one day, that something might take you away from me. I couldn't bear to be without you, to be alone again.'

'And what are you now?' he demanded. 'You're *alone*, Laine. You had me, you still have my heart, but you're alone. We wake up without each other and you go to sleep without each other. How could it be worse than that?'

'But I never really had you, it was only a weekend.'

'A wonderful weekend that we could turn into a lifetime if you'll let it happen. I'm admitting that I love you and I think you might just love me,' he said, reaching for her hands again and holding them tightly in the strength of his own. 'If you didn't love me just a little then you wouldn't have chosen that photograph and you wouldn't have run away and you wouldn't be shaking right now.'

Laine looked away in silence. All of it was true.

'And you wouldn't be crying…'

Pierce smiled and using the softness of his hand he wiped away another tear as it trickled across her cheek then gently cupped her face as he looked into her eyes.

'I don't want to live without you. I can't. The last eight months have been empty. My life has been empty but I didn't know it until I met you. You challenge me, you make me feel alive, and I want you more than any woman I've ever met. I can practise anywhere in the world and you can take photographs anywhere. The possibilities are endless—we just have to decide what suits us. And our children.'

'Children? How do you know I even want children?'

'Because you have devoted your life to helping them. We can foster, we can adopt and even throw in a few of our own. But that's much later. What do you say? Maybe we can pass on the wedding for the time being if it's too much too soon, just live with me. Wake up in my arms and make me the happiest man alive.'

Laine's head was spinning. Suddenly, looking at the man standing before her, she realised she was about to be just as crazy as Pierce had been moments ago when he'd climbed the fire escape. Maybe he was right, maybe she *was* ready to be loved. And to love him back.

She closed her eyes and suddenly knew that what she was about to do was the right thing. She had no choice, her heart was overruling her past and his heart was putting it where it belonged, drowning out her doubt and convincing her to take the leap of faith and give in to love. He had shown her how to be brave.

She stood on tiptoe and kissed him. 'I'm not exactly sure how we'll sort out the practicalities but we will if you love me.'

Pierce pulled her into his arms and kissed her and then kissed her some more.

'My love for you is greater than you will ever know. I didn't come here with an empty promise. I want you to know you can trust me, lean on me and know I'm never leaving your side for the rest of my life.'

He swept her into his arms, pulling her body even closer to him. Brushing away the tendrils of her hair that had fallen across her face, he kissed her the way he intended to do for the rest of their lives.

And for the first time in her life, and over the sound of the helicopter approaching, Laine said the words *I love you*.

EPILOGUE

'THE HOME IS AMAZING,' Laine said, her eyes bright with excitement. Slowly, taking in every detail, she surveyed the ground floor of the accommodation for foster-children transitioning from home care when they turned eighteen. 'Thank you, Pierce. It's more than I had ever dreamed possible.'

'You, my darling wife, are more than welcome. Your dreams are my dreams and I have the means to make them all come true.'

'I know that now, but there are many men in the world who wouldn't share their wealth the way you so willingly do with others in need.'

Laine walked over to one of the huge murals that decorated the inside walls. Pierce had commissioned a group of street artists to paint inside the three-storey building with colourful and uplifting work that would make the new residents feel at home.

'I absolutely love this,' she said, before she rushed off to look at the other rooms. Pierce had designed the interior layout and she had done the decorating, except for the mural, which was a surprise.

There were study rooms filled with desks and computers, a games area, a laundry, a commercial-size kitchen where the residents could hone their cooking skills, a home theatre and a huge dining room where everyone could eat their evening meal together like a big extended family. Each young person had their own room and was responsible for their own laundry and there were kitchen rosters. It had not been designed as a holiday home but a real home with rules and responsibilities. Trained house mothers and fathers would provide guidance and counselling to these young adults to help them on their pathway in life.

'This is one of the happiest days of my life,' she announced, as she walked back to her husband filled with pride at what they had accomplished together.

'This is just the beginning,' he told her, and pulled her into his arms. 'This is the pilot transition home, and once we gauge its success and make improvements where required, then we will begin the process of building one in each capital city. Australia can lead the way and this programme can be a model for others.'

Laine knew the excitement she heard in his voice was real. The project meant as much to Pierce as it did to her.

'You are the most generous, wonderful man in the world. I'm so proud of you,' Laine said, as she leant her head on her husband's shoulder and looked again at the community home they had built for at-risk teenagers.

'Not nearly as proud as I am of you, Mrs Beaumont,' he said, before he kissed her tenderly. 'I don't know how you do it. A working photographer, an interior decorator for this project, a mother of two foster-children and now one on the way!' His hand rested protectively on Laine's tiny bump, which was only just showing through her thin summer dress. 'And not to forget, the most loving wife. I am the luckiest man in the world.'

Looking in to the warmth of his smiling eyes, Laine felt her heart flutter as it always did when he held her. 'I think I'm the fortunate one, Pierce. You convinced me to break all my silly rules and now you have my heart for ever.'

* * * * *

SNOWBOUND
WITH THE SURGEON

BY
ANNIE CLAYDON

MILLS &
BOON

Published in Great Britain 2014
by Mills & Boon, an imprint of Harlequin (UK) Limited,
Eton House, 18-24 Paradise Road, Richmond, Surrey, TW9 1SR

© 2014 Annie Claydon

ISBN: 978-0-263-90809-1

Harlequin (UK) Limited's policy is to use papers that are natural,
renewable and recyclable products and made from wood grown in
sustainable forests. The logging and manufacturing processes conform
to the legal environmental regulations of the country of origin.

Printed and bound in Spain
by Blackprint CPI, Barcelona

Dear Reader

When I was writing my first book, one of the (many) details I worried about was the fact that I'd described a very sharp frost and frozen pipes before Christmas. Would this be entirely believable? In the previous few years we'd had mild winters, without any really cold weather before Christmas. But the unpredictable British climate came to my rescue, and December 2010—the winter before that first book was published—was one of the coldest we'd experienced for a hundred years, with enough snow to make my December cold snap seem a little bit understated!

So this time around I've no qualms about giving my characters something a bit more extreme to deal with. Dr Neve Harrison doesn't have the luxury of being able to give in to adverse weather conditions. She's struggling to get to all her patients, despite heavy snow and blocked roads. So when Joe Lamont turns up on her doorstep, ready and able to help, it seems that her luck has changed.

Together, they're more than a match for those adverse weather conditions—but Joe himself is a more daunting proposition. His secrets threaten to break Neve's heart, and deprive her of the thing she wants most in the world.

I hope you enjoy Joe and Neve's story. I'm always thrilled to hear from readers, and you can contact me via my website at www.annieclaydon.com

Annie x

Dedication

To Noreen, who taught me how to end well.

Recent titles by Annie Claydon:

A DOCTOR TO HEAL HER HEART
200 HARLEY STREET: THE ENIGMATIC SURGEON
ONCE UPON A CHRISTMAS NIGHT…
RE-AWAKENING HIS SHY NURSE
THE REBEL AND MISS JONES
THE DOCTOR MEETS HER MATCH
DOCTOR ON HER DOORSTEP
ALL SHE WANTS FOR CHRISTMAS

**These books are also available in eBook format
from www.millsandboon.co.uk**

**Praise for
Annie Claydon:**

'A compelling, emotional and highly poignant read that
I couldn't bear to put down. Rich in pathos, humour and
dramatic intensity, it's a spellbinding tale about healing old
wounds, having the courage to listen to your heart and the
power of love that kept me enthralled from beginning to end.'
—*GoodReads* on
ONCE UPON A CHRISTMAS NIGHT

'Well-written, brilliant characters—I have never been
disappointed by a book written by Annie Claydon.'
—*GoodReads* on
THE REBEL AND MISS JONES

CHAPTER ONE

THIRTY PACES TO her gate. Neve counted them all. After that, ten paces would be enough to take her up the front path. It turned out to be eleven because she slipped on the ice, grabbing at the porch rails to steady herself and wrenching her shoulder as her heavy medical bag fell to the ground.

She waved her hand in front of the sensor for the porch light, and nothing happened. The electricity was still off, then. All the same, the cast-iron stove in the kitchen would be throwing out heat, and she couldn't wait to get inside. Just as she was about to savour the moment of sliding the key into the lock of her own front door, her phone rang. Dammit. If she had to go out in the snow again tonight…

If she had to go out again tonight, then so be it. She'd turn around, slide back down the front path and hope that it wouldn't take twenty minutes to start her car this time. The vision of sipping a hot drink and letting her toes thaw in front of the stove, which had carried her through the last hours of a very long day, began to recede.

'Yeah, Maisie. What have you got for me?'

'Good news…'

'Really?' Neve took the risk of further disappointment

and opened the front door, stepping inside and dumping her bag in the hallway. It wasn't much warmer in here, but the kitchen door was closed against the chill in the rest of the old farmhouse. 'Is it safe to take my coat off?'

'Aren't you home yet?'

'Just. It took me over an hour to get back from my last appointment. The road through Cryersbridge was blocked by a car that slid out of control, and we had to wait until it was towed.'

'You must be frozen. Are you in the warm now, pet?' Maisie Johnstone was the wife of the senior partner of the Yorkshire practice that Neve had joined eighteen months ago, and sometimes took it upon herself to mother Neve. That was okay. Neve could do with a bit of that at the moment.

'Hold on…' Neve tramped through to the kitchen, her boots shedding shards of ice onto the carpet. Opened the door, and the heat hit her like a soft, welcoming pillow. Light flared as she struck a match and lit the candles on the kitchen table, and she shed her coat and sat down. Pulling her boots off with one hand, she pressed her phone to her ear with the other.

'Fire away, Maisie, I need some good news…'

She heard Maisie's chuckle at the other end of the line. 'Some of the local practices have got together with the healthcare trust to organise a group of volunteers with four-wheel-drive vehicles. The idea is that they'll help doctors and district nurses who are having difficulty getting through to patients. You've got your very own escort for tomorrow.'

Neve swallowed hard. This sounded too good to be true, and if the general trend for today was anything to go by, that meant it was. 'Who? Is he local?'

'Lives in Leminster. He's from Canada, so I suppose he must know a bit about snow.'

'Sounds promising.'

'It is. Joe's a nice guy. Outdoorsy type. Moved here just before Christmas last year. He was on crutches then, but that was only for a couple of months. He built a front porch for Edie Wilcox last summer and put in grab rails so she could get in and out of the house…'

'Wait… Who's Edie Wilcox?' Maisie had lived in this area all her life and seemed to know the life histories of everyone within a thirty-mile radius.

'She lives in Leminster. Married old Stan Wilcox and they argued for thirty-seven years non-stop until he dropped down dead from a heart attack. She was devastated and didn't go out of the house for a couple of years…'

'She doesn't go out?'

'Oh, that was twenty years ago. She goes out all the time now. Likes to terrorise the tourists in the summer. Edie's a tough old bird and proud with it. She won't let the social services past the front door, but she must have taken a liking to Joe because she let him do a few alterations to her cottage to make it a bit easier for her to get around.'

Neve's head was beginning to swim. Maisie had been invaluable in helping her to settle in and be accepted by the community, but there was always the danger of going into information overload.

'So his name's Joe? The guy with the four-by-four?'

'That's right. Joe Lamont. He was going to call round to see you this evening, just to make contact, but I expect he's missed you if you've only just got home. Did he leave a note?'

'I don't think so. Hold on, I'll go and see.' Neve scooted down the hall to the front door, treading on a piece of ice and feeling it melt through her thick woollen socks. 'No, nothing here.' Shivering, she hurried back to the warmth of the kitchen.

'I'll call him, then, and let him know you'll be in contact.'

'That's okay, I'll call him now…' Neve found a pen and scribbled the number that Maisie recited onto the back of her hand.

'You're all right out there, are you? You know you can always stay with us.'

'I'm fine. Thanks, Maisie, but I've got all I need.' She had food, heat and plenty of candles. The farmhouse kitchen extended the full width of the back of the house, and was big enough to easily accommodate a table and chairs next to the cooking area, and a sofa bed at the far end by the old stone hearth. Right now, the sofa bed was the only thing she needed.

'Okay. I'll give you a call in the morning. Stay warm.'

A cup of tea, and then she'd call this guy and get some sleep. Neve filled the kettle and set it to boil on the stove.

The front door rattled, as if something heavy had struck it. Neve wondered if she should go and see what it was and decided against it. If that was the porch collapsing under the weight of snow on the roof, then tomorrow morning would be soon enough to find out.

Two more thumps and the muffled sound of a voice. Someone was outside. Neve picked up a candle and ventured into the hall.

Movement, and a flare of light ahead of her made her jump. Stupid, it was just the candle, reflected in the hall mirror. Perhaps it was the flickering light that made her look like something out of a horror movie, a chalk-white face with dark circles under the eyes. Neve grimaced at herself in the glass, swiping her free hand through her unruly blonde curls in an effort to make herself look vaguely presentable.

'Who's there?'

'Joe Lamont. I'm looking for Dr Harrison.'

'What…?' Neve bit her tongue. There wasn't much point in asking what he was doing out on a night like this if she was going to leave him standing on the door-step. She pulled the door open, and a gust of freezing air blew the candle out, leaving her staring at a large, black shadow.

'Come in. I was about to phone you.'

'Thanks…' The figure kicked his heavy boots against the doorstep, and stepped inside, pushing the door closed behind him. 'Your doorbell isn't working.'

'No, the power's off. Wait there a moment. I'll just open the kitchen door to give us some light…' Suddenly, a torch beam almost blinded her, and a gloved hand found hers.

'Here. Take this.'

For a moment all Neve could register was his smell. Warm and clean, the kind of scent produced by the chem-istry of soap and skin, rather than anything you got from a bottle. Then he put the torch into her hand, stepping back almost immediately, as if to give her some space.

'Thanks.' She had a strong temptation to shine the light in the direction of Joe's outline, but Neve resisted it and turned, leading the way through the hallway. 'Come through.'

She shut the kitchen door behind them, watching while Joe pulled his gloves off and unzipped his heavy jacket.

He was tall, with what looked like broad shoulders, but that might just be the bulk of his clothing. In the torch-light, his cheekbones looked as sharp as knives.

'Are you okay out here on your own?'

His voice was deep, with the trace of a Canadian accent along with a little of the cadence of the Yorkshire village he'd made his home. The kind of voice you'd want to hear if you were in trouble. Neve almost began to wish she was.

'I'm fine, thanks. I have heat and light.' She switched off the torch, and in the candlelight his features seemed to soften.

He looked around. 'And food?'

'Yes.' Enough to keep her going for another day. 'I'm making tea—would you like a cup?'

His gaze flicked quickly around the room, as if he was still unconvinced about something, then he nodded. 'Thanks. That would be nice.'

'Sit down.' She waved him towards the table. 'And why don't you take your coat off? You'll melt in here.'

He slung his coat over the back of a chair and sat, running one hand absently across the scarred oak tabletop, his fingers seeming to explore the grain. 'You get hot water from the stove?'

'Yes. The power goes out from time to time here, so I had an oil-fired stove put in.' It appeared the questioning wasn't over quite yet. That was okay, he could ask. Neve had made sure that she could deal with pretty much anything the world chose to throw at her, and she had the answers.

The touch of humour that twitched at the sides of his mouth suited him. 'I guess I'll just stop with the neighbourly concern, shall I?'

'It's appreciated. But not needed at the moment.' She hid her smile behind the open door of the larder, reaching for the biscuit barrel and laying it on the table next to the teapot. 'Help yourself.'

He took the mug of tea that she slid across the table towards him with a nod of acknowledgement. He seemed… tense wasn't the word. He seemed watchful, taking in everything around him, as if he needed to keep an eye on the world to keep it spinning. Neve began to wish that she'd found the time to fold the sofa bed back up this morning. Hopefully, any stray underwear would go unnoticed in the candlelight.

'You're not from around here?' His attention was fixed on Neve now and, before she could stop it, her hand flew to her hair to smooth it back. 'The South somewhere?'

'London.'

He nodded. 'I must be improving. When I first came here, all I could hear was that everyone had British accents.'

'And you're from Canada…?'

His smile had the same sense of discipline about it as all his other movements did. Graceful, economical, and with a sense of purpose about it. And gorgeous.

'Right in one. Most people reckon I'm from America.'

'Actually, Maisie told me. I imagine you've got a lot more experience of driving in these conditions than me.' Best get back to business. That smile, the relaxed, watchful curve of his body was distracting her.

'A bit. It's a little different at home…'

'Snow's snow, isn't it?'

'My Inupiak granny wouldn't agree with you there. She lived on the ice when she was a child, and could write a book about different kinds of snow.'

That explained his striking looks. Raven-dark hair that grazed the collar of his thick sweater. Dark eyes and proud cheekbones. 'So how did you end up in Yorkshire?'

'My other grandmother came from around here. Her family went to Canada when she was a child, but she used to tell me stories about England. I decided to pay a visit and ended up staying.' He looked at his tea, as if taking a second sip was yet another thing that required a thought-through decision. 'It's a good base to travel to Europe from.'

Neve would have thought that London would be better. But Joe didn't seem the type to spend much time worrying about what other people thought. 'You travel a lot?'

He shrugged. 'A bit. I've seen most of Europe. Africa, Asia.' He made a small, dismissive movement of his hand, as if this all meant nothing. 'How long have you been here?'

'Eighteen months.'

'Love at first sight?'

'Eh?' Suddenly she was falling into the depths of his dark eyes. Not quite love at first sight, but there was definitely something about him...

'You fell in love with this place. Like me.'

Nothing like that. Yorkshire had been somewhere to run to, and the most lovely thing about this particular location was that it was remote. 'I'm growing to love it. Maisie's been very good to me.'

He nodded. 'She's a force to be reckoned with, isn't she? When she called me, asking for help, there was no saying no...'

'But I thought... Aren't you a volunteer?'

'Seems I am now.'

Neve's heart sank. 'So Maisie talked you into this. Listen, if you don't want—'

'It's okay. I was getting a little cabin crazy doing nothing at home, and I was looking for a way to help. Maisie just saved me some trouble.' His dark gaze sought hers. 'I have winter tyres fitted on my four-by-four, and they'll cope with just about anything. And snow chains, in case we run into any trouble. You'll be quite safe.'

'I don't doubt it.' He didn't need to reassure her. Maisie had vouched for him, and in any case there was something about Joe. If you were in the habit of trusting people on the basis of ten minutes' conversation then he'd be the one to pick.

'Maisie said you were covering the north side of the practice's catchment area.' He reached over and slid a map out of his jacket pocket, spreading it on the table. 'Here...' His finger described a loop.

'Yes, that's right. We've split the practice up into three, and each one of us is covering one section. We're holding temporary surgeries in church halls and so on for people who find it difficult to get to the main surgery, and taking on all the visits for our own area. Cuts down on the travelling.'

'I imagine you're still pretty busy, though.'

'Yeah. With only two weeks to go before Christmas...' She shrugged. 'Everyone seems to rush for the shops and the doctor's surgery around now.'

He nodded, surveying the map thoughtfully. 'You've drawn the short straw, this is some of the most difficult terrain in the area. Couldn't you have asked to swap with a doctor with more local experience?'

Neve felt her spine stiffen. One of the reasons she'd

come here was to escape being told what she could, and couldn't, do.

'We each took the area closest to where we live. I can handle it.'

'I dare say you can.' He flashed her a disarming smile. 'What time do you want me tomorrow?'

Six o'clock, with a cup of fresh brewed coffee and a gently warmed croissant. The fantasy was inappropriate on almost every level she could think of, and Neve let it slide.

'If nothing else urgent comes up, I'll be starting in Leminster at nine tomorrow. I can drive over and meet you there…'

He shook his head. 'I'll pick you up at eight-thirty.' He re-folded the map and stood up. 'I'd better get going now. I'm on my way to the supermarket in town…'

'At this time of night?'

'I promised to pick some things up for someone. Can I get you anything?' He gestured towards the large, well-scraped jar sitting on the kitchen worktop. 'Some more peanut butter?'

He didn't give up, did he? But she *was* going to have to stop off at the shops tomorrow if she didn't ask for more supplies now. 'Um…perhaps one or two things. If it's no trouble.'

'No trouble. Give me a list…'

CHAPTER TWO

A BOWL OF steaming porridge, a banana that had seen better days, coffee, toast and the last of the peanut butter would be enough to keep her going for the morning. By twenty past eight, Neve had tidied up and folded the sofa bed, and her deliberations about whether it was entirely wise to tidy her duvet away upstairs in the freezing bedroom were interrupted by the sound of a car outside in the lane. She dumped the duvet back onto the sofa and ventured into the hall, peering outside.

The trees were laden with snow after a fresh fall during the night. Clear blue skies, and sparkling white fields. The landscape had a kind of rugged beauty about it, an implicit challenge to either respect its rules or fall foul of them.

And talking about rugged beauty…

Joe had just got out of the driver's seat of a black SUV. The high chassis and large wheels looked more than capable of tackling the rough terrain they were going to face today. He looked pretty capable, too. Tall and broad, standing for a moment to assess the sky and the road that twisted away into the distance, then shouldering a large canvas bag and turning towards her house. The gate was packed round with ice and snow and refused to budge, and he swung effortlessly over the low front wall.

It looked a bit eager, but she opened the front door anyway, not waiting for him to knock. 'Hi. You made it…'

He shrugged, as if making it here hadn't been in question. Kicked off his boots and strode into the kitchen, dumping the bag at her feet.

'Hope this is what you wanted…'

Neve bent to look inside the bag. Everything on her list and more. A hand of bananas, a bag of apples and a punnet of strawberries. She looked up at him silently.

'I saw that your bowl was nearly empty.' He gestured towards the one wizened apple in the fruit bowl.

The idea that Joe had been silently noting and assessing everything wasn't particularly comfortable. 'Thanks. That was thoughtful of you.'

'You're welcome.' He fished in his pocket and brought out a note and some change, putting it down on the table.

'Is that right? Surely you spent more than that?'

He shrugged. 'I shopped around. And someone gave me the strawberries yesterday.'

Neve gave him a long, questioning look and then gave up. If Joe wanted to operate on a need-to-know basis, then so be it. She hurried to stow the non-perishables in the larder and then opened the back door, pulling a heavy-duty plastic box inside and putting it on the table.

He was quietly watching her every move, and Neve felt her brow crease with anxiety. That old feeling of having something to prove to someone. She thought she'd left that behind her when she'd turned onto the M1 motorway from London, and headed north.

'Let me…' She was struggling with the clips on the box, and before she could protest he'd spun the box towards him and knocked a lump of ice out from under the lid, wresting it open.

Inside, there was half a pint of milk and a carton of juice, both frozen into solid lumps. One of his eyebrows arched, and Neve felt her hackles rise in response to the unspoken question.

'What…?' She should probably just leave it. Neve tipped the remainder of the shopping into the box and clapped the lid back on, fastening it securely.

'Nothing… If I'd realised you were so short of supplies, I could have brought a few more things in for you.'

'I'm fine. I told you that last night.' She heard herself snap at him and reminded herself that Joe was a volunteer, doing this out of the goodness of his heart, and that she ought to make an effort to get along with him. 'Are we going to get going, then?'

'As soon as you tell me where.' A hint of emotion tugged at the corner of his perfect mouth.

Neve sat down at the kitchen table. Maybe she was overreacting. It wasn't Joe's fault that the quiver in the pit of her stomach whenever she saw him reminded her of all the promises she'd made to herself about never letting a man walk all over her again.

'This is my list. We're due in Leminster first and then whichever order is easiest in terms of the driving.'

'Right.' He pulled the map from his pocket, spreading it on the table, one finger tracing the pattern of the other addresses on the list. 'So if we drive north from Leminster…' He swept his finger across the map in a rough circle, indicating forty miles of driving through blocked roads and over sheets of ice.

'That would be ideal. Can we make it?'

'Let me worry about that.' He picked up his gloves from the kitchen table and folded the map, his frame suddenly taut and eager. A glimmer in his eyes seemed to flash out a warning to the world that obstacles weren't a problem, and only existed to be overcome.

She'd find out soon enough if Joe was as good as his word. Neve picked up one of the bags of medical supplies, which lay ready by the door, and Joe got to the second before she could. 'Let's go, then.'

She was silent as Joe drove along the winding, treacherous road into Leminster village. Wary of him maybe?

Joe dismissed the thought. Neve struck him as the kind of woman who wasn't afraid of anything. When her blue eyes had flashed with stubborn resolve, all his senses had tingled painfully back to life, reminding him that once he'd lived for the kind of challenges she faced now. Her scent and the way she moved only added to the temptation. He dismissed those thoughts as well.

Joe had put himself on trial here. When he'd first come to the village he'd deliberately avoided anything that was even remotely connected with his former life, but now there was a need he could fulfil. If he could do this, without getting involved with the medical side of things, that would be a final step towards putting his old life behind him.

He drew up outside the church hall in Leminster. A surgery had been arranged for those who could make it here, and outside the new fallen snow was already churned and flattened by the passing of feet. Inside, the occasion appeared to have turned into an impromptu coffee morning.

From the relaxed smile on her face when Neve walked

into the hall, one would never have guessed that she was probably counting faces, wondering whether she was going to be here all day. She walked briskly into the middle of the noisy throng and clapped her hands.

Silence. Joe allowed himself a smile. That was an achievement in itself.

'Who's here for me?' She made it sound like a party, and that she was excited to see that so many people had turned up. Three-quarters of the hands in the room shot up, and she tried again.

'One hand for each patient, please.'

Most of the hands went back down again, leaving six. She gave a dazzling smile in response and received a low rumble of approbation from the assembled company.

She had a nice way about her. In Joe's experience, if you wanted to know about a doctor, you looked first at their patients. And if the faces here were anything to go by, Neve was one of the best. Her style might be a little different from his, a little more long-lost-relative and a little less here-comes-the-cavalry, but that was no bad thing. Joe reminded himself that he was here to drive, nothing more.

'Who's first?' Someone pointed to Fred Hawkins, sitting in the corner of the room, and he reached for his walking stick.

'That's okay, Fred. Finish your tea, it'll be a couple of minutes before I get settled.' She flashed Joe a smile then turned to the church warden, who guided her away into one of the small rooms at the back of the hall.

Although the intention behind holding a surgery here had not been primarily to carry out a fact-finding mission regarding Joe Lamont, it did turn up a lot of information. Fred Hawkins confided that he was a 'useful enough carpenter' while Neve was trying to listen to his chest. Lisa Graham chattered about him incessantly as Neve examined a lump on her young son's leg, and Ann Hawkins, headmistress of the local primary school and the wife of Fred's second cousin, proffered the information that Joe had built an adventure playground for the school a few months back.

'He was quite a talking point for a while...' Ann winced as Neve removed the dressing from her swollen finger to reveal a cut.

'Do you have any loss of sensation? Here?' Neve worked gently along the main nerves.

'No. It's a real addition for us. The kids love it.'

'Right. I'm going to put some adhesive stitches onto the cut and I'll prescribe antibiotics, just to be on the safe side.'

Ann nodded. 'Thanks. He doesn't seem to have anyone. Not that some of the younger women haven't tried. I had to have a word with one of our teaching assistants about staring out of the window all moony-eyed at him when she was supposed to be doing her job.'

Neve hid a grin. It appeared that Joe-itis wasn't just confined to the teaching assistants. The school's head teacher had been infected with the epidemic as well, along with what sounded like half the village.

'So what exactly does he do?' Neve's curiosity about Joe had been growing, and she gave in to the inevitable. 'His job, I mean.'

'I heard he was ex-army.' Ann pursed her lips thoughtfully. 'I don't know if that's true. He doesn't seem to have a job now. Unless of course he's doing something on the internet in the evenings.'

Professional gambler? She imagined that Joe would

have the perfect poker face if he put his mind to it. Writer? Internet entrepreneur? Combination of all three?

'There were a few rumours going round, but they were just idle talk.' Ann dismissed any further speculation with a disapproving twitch of her mouth. 'But, then, people will wonder.'

True enough. The secret to keeping a secret was never to let a soul know that you had one. Neve had never told anyone about her marriage, and so the awkward questions about why it had been such a disaster never occurred to anyone.

'Hold still, Ann. This will sting a little bit.'

Ann winced as Neve cleaned and disinfected the wound. 'He wasn't well, of course, when he first came here. You know his grandmother was born in Leminster? Fred remembers her from way back, when he was just a boy. Says she was a pretty little thing.'

Perhaps that was why the village had taken Joe to their hearts. The prodigal son returned. But in Neve's experience, any respect you got from the close-knit communities around here was generally earned and not just doled out on account of who your grandmother was.

'Right, then, Ann.' She handed her the prescription. 'I want you to take these for a week. Can you get to the chemist today?'

'Yes, no problem.' Ann got to her feet. 'I suppose you're back on the road again now. You must be busy.'

'Yes. It's a lot easier with Joe doing the driving, though.'

'Mmm. With the weather like this, you need someone to help you.'

By the time Neve had finished, Joe had been persuaded up a ladder to fix Christmas decorations to the high ceil-

ing beams and had helped move the piano to make room
for the Christmas tree. It was something of a relief to
retrieve his coat and follow her back outside to the car.

'What's that you've got?' She nodded at the plastic
food container in his hand.

'Chocolate cake. I said it was a bit early for me, so
there are two large pieces here for later.' He wondered
whether she'd greet this latest offer of food with the same
prickly indignation she'd shown that morning.

'Oh, nice. I like chocolate cake.' She had a particular
flair for confounding his expectations, and Joe found
himself smiling.

The first real obstacle of the day presented itself a mile
down the road, in the shape of a white minibus. It was
blocking the road ahead, almost invisible against the
drifting snow, only the bright flash of a logo on its side
clearly distinguishable.

Joe slowed and stopped. 'Television crew.'

'How do you know that?'

'I heard they've been filming around Leminster. Community in crisis, that kind of thing.'

Neve was frowning at the vehicle. 'Looks as if the
community's dealing with the crisis a bit better than they
are.'

'Yeah. Perhaps they can film themselves.'

The sound of a racing engine drifted towards them
and the wheels of the minibus spun uselessly. Joe swung
out of the car. 'Hey. Hold up. That's not going to get you
anywhere…' he called over to the driver and the engine
stopped abruptly. One of the doors opened and a woman
got out.

Joe knew what was needed, and it didn't take much to

persuade the woman to leave things to him. He trudged back to his own vehicle, nodding grimly at Neve and opening the tailgate.

'What are we going to do?' She scrambled out of her seat, almost losing her balance on a patch of ice and grabbing at him to steady herself.

'Maybe you should stay in the car.' Much as he liked her weight on his arm, it wasn't going to get the van on its way.

'What, and comb my hair? Check my make-up?'

Joe straightened up. However much he got snagged on her protective spikes, he still couldn't help but smile at her. Maybe it was the vulnerability behind that tough exterior. Or the bravery that met everything head on. 'If you use the rear-view mirror, don't forget to adjust it back the way you found it.'

A moment of fleeting outrage and then she relaxed. 'Sorry. It's just that I've been managing on my own for a while now...'

'I know.'

She leaned back against the car. 'So what are you going to do?'

'I should be able to dig them out. Might need to give them a tow but I hope not. It'll take time to get the snow chains on the wheels to give me the extra traction.'

'What's that for?' She pointed to the large bag of cat litter that he'd dumped in the snow beside them.

'It'll soak up the water around the wheels and give something for them to grip onto.' Joe reached for the fold-up shovel that he'd stowed in the boot, snapping it open.

'You have a cat?' No detail was too small to escape her interest and Joe couldn't help grinning.

'Why would I have cat litter if I don't have a cat?' He

picked up the bag and started to trudge back towards the stricken minibus.

'Let me know if you need a hand,' she called after him.

'Sure. Let me know if you can't find your comb.'

Neve remained where she was, leaning against the side of the SUV. Two men had got out of the minibus and Joe had set one of them to work with the shovel while he spread the cat litter around the wheels. The woman Joe had been talking to had left them to it and was headed in Neve's direction.

'I'm glad you guys turned up.' She was grinning brightly. 'Your friend seems to know what to do. What are you doing out today?'

'I'm a doctor. I have house calls to make.'

'Ah.' The woman nodded enthusiastically. 'And your partner?' She gestured over towards Joe. 'He's a doctor too?'

'He's a volunteer. He's helping with the driving.'

'Nice one. As we're stranded here, perhaps you could give me an interview.' The woman didn't wait for Neve's answer and gestured over to the second man, who was standing by the stricken vehicle, watching Joe. 'Camera, Nick…'

'I don't think we have time. We have to get on…'

'Just for a minute. We won't keep you.'

Neve bit back the temptation to say that the news crew was already keeping them, by dint of their minibus blocking the road. 'I have patients…'

'I promise we'll be finished before you know it. Or you could go over there and pretend to help, if you prefer.'

No, she didn't prefer. The last thing Neve wanted to

do was to embarrass herself with Joe by pretending to help him for the cameras.

'Joe…' She marched over to the minibus, where he was now shovelling ice and snow from under the chassis. 'We'll be going soon, won't we?'

He straightened, taking in the hastily assembled tripod and camera. 'She's asked you for an interview, hasn't she?'

Neve shifted uncomfortably. 'Yes. But I've told them there's no time. We have to be on our way…'

He grinned. Joe was enjoying her discomfiture a little too much. 'I'm afraid it'll be a short while yet. And I don't dig well with an audience. Perhaps you can keep them amused for a few minutes.'

'Thanks a lot.'

He shrugged. 'Thought you wanted to help.'

Not what she'd had in mind. Neve turned on her heel and walked back to the camera.

'Ready?' The woman smiled brightly at her. 'Perhaps if you could take your hat off so we can see your face.'

She was going to have to do this. Neve stood on the spot the reporter indicated and removed her hat, smiling uneasily. The camera swept across the snow-covered hills and then homed in on her.

'How are you coping in these difficult conditions? Are your patients going without the medical help they need?'

An image of Maisie on the phone, reassuring worried callers that the doctor would be able to see them, flashed through Neve's mind. 'No, we're seeing everyone. We're coping very well.'

'But your resources must be strained to breaking point. How long can you go on like this?'

'As long as we need to. We expect snow during the

winter here, and we plan for it. It's business as usual, and that's not going to change.' Neve tried to put all the gravitas of her profession behind the statement. Difficult when a blast of icy wind had just slapped the side of her face, almost taking her breath away and making her nose drip.

The sound of the minibus's engine choking into life saved her. Joe was in the driver's seat, gently rolling the vehicle forward and out of the patch of slush that its spinning wheels had produced.

'Sorry. Got to go.' Neve almost skipped over to where the empty cat-litter bag and the shovel lay, picked them up and carried them back to Joe's car. Then she got in, shutting the door firmly. The news crew took one last shot of Joe walking back to the SUV, then there was a scramble to get the camera packed up and they were on their way, Joe following the minibus as it nosed its way along the narrow, snow-filled lane.

As soon as the road widened, he flashed his headlights and a brief, assertive blast of the horn signalled the driver of the minibus to pull over. Joe overtook it, and in a sudden show of bravado he put his foot down, a shower of powdery snow flying up from the wheels as they accelerated away.

'Show-off.'

He chuckled. 'You looked a bit put out by some of those questions.'

He'd noticed. No surprise there, Joe seemed to notice everything. 'Well, really. What did they expect me to do? Go on TV saying that my patients will be lucky to get a visit this side of next week?'

'I imagine that's what they wanted to hear.'

'Well, tough. I'll make it through to everyone...' It

occurred to Neve that Joe had a part in that now. 'I meant *we*.'

He gave her a melting grin. 'Yeah. We'll make it.'

After eleven hours, half of it spent huddled in the passenger seat of his car and the other half seeing her patients, Neve still shone. In Joe's experience, that took some doing. When they drew up outside her house that evening, she heaved a deep sigh of contentment.

'Look…'

He looked. Welcoming light glowed from the porch. 'Your power's back on?'

'Yes.' Her smile made it seem like the end of a perfect day, rather than the first piece of good luck that she hadn't had to work hard for. 'Will you come in for tea?'

The warmth of her rambling farmhouse kitchen. The warmth of her smile. In a past life, which seemed so distant now it was if it had all happened to someone else, Joe wouldn't have hesitated to say yes.

'No. Thanks, but I should get going. I'll see you in the morning. Same time?'

'Tomorrow's Saturday. Aren't you taking the weekend off?'

'Are you?'

She shrugged. 'Not this weekend. I'll be off next weekend.'

'Then I'll see you in the morning. Eight-thirty.'

Her smile made the whole day worthwhile. 'Shall we say nine? I think we both deserve a lie-in.'

'Nine it is.'

'Thanks for all you've done today, Joe. I really appreciate it.'

It had been his pleasure. Having her rely on him,

bringing her safely home again had made Joe feel strong again. As if he'd flexed muscles that had been long under-used and had found, almost to his disbelief, that they had taken the strain. But he shouldn't go too far.

He carried her bags up the path for her, setting them down on the doorstep and turning back, before the lure of refreshments got too great. Got into his SUV and waited until she was safely inside the house before he started the engine and drove away. Neve was just the kind of woman who could tempt a man into believing that he could be whatever he wanted to be. And in Joe's experi-ence, the one good thing about having found your break-ing point was that you knew for sure that some things were out of reach.

CHAPTER THREE

'How are we going with the list?'

The list had been the overarching purpose of their lives for the last three days. How many people were on it and where they lived. It was a challenge and a reason for Neve to spend her days with him. Joe was getting to love the list.

However much he loved it, he didn't get to spend a lot of quality time with it. While she let him get on with his side of things, assessing their route, driving and the odd spell of snow clearing, the list was Neve's responsibility, and she seemed to function best when it was under her control.

'Not bad. Just four more. We need to go up to Holcombe Crag, and there are three more between there and Leminster.'

'Where first?' Joe had no inclination to involve himself in the decisions about who needed her most urgently, and was always careful to let Neve set their priorities.

'What do you think? I guess it would be better to go up to Holcombe Crag while it's still light.' She reached for the bag of toffees on the dashboard, offering him one, and when he shook his head she unwrapped one for herself.

'Probably, but don't worry about that. If the others need to be seen first…'

'No, they're all routine visits. They could wait until tomorrow morning if we don't get time today, but Nancy Olsen's got a young baby so I'd like to see her this afternoon.'

Joe nodded, and started the car. 'Holcombe Crag it is, then.'

Neve had been watching the clouds draw across the sky as they approached the crag. 'Are we going to make this? It looks as if the weather's closing in.'

'We'll make it. There's plenty of time to get up there and back before it gets dark— Is that your phone, or mine?'

'Mine, I think.' Neve unzipped her jacket and pulled her phone from the inside pocket, studying the small screen. 'It's a text from Maisie.'

'Another house call?'

Neve shook her head and read from the screen. '"*Local radio news. Car carrying father and young son found abandoned in your area this morning. Search under way. Keep your eyes open.*"'

Neve texted a short acknowledgement back to Maisie and put her phone back into her pocket. 'Anyone walking in this weather is going to be freezing.'

Joe nodded, his brow creased. 'Hopefully they've been able to find some shelter. Shame they didn't stay with the car.'

'I hope they find them soon.'

'Yeah. When we get to Holcombe Crag I'll take a look around. Might get lucky.'

* * *

He turned off and took the track that climbed towards Holcombe Crag. At the best of times it was a steep hill to climb, but now the ice and snow seemed an impossible barrier. But Joe took it calmly and steadily, confident of what the vehicle could do and not asking the impossible from it. He drew up outside the single-storey, stone-built house, which clung to the slope three-quarters of the way up the crag.

'If I walk up to the top, I'll get a much better view.' He'd extracted a pair of field glasses from the boot of his car, which seemed increasingly to Neve like an Aladdin's cave of useful items. 'How long will you be?'

'I think Nancy would appreciate some a little extra time.' Neve looked at her watch. 'Shall we meet back here in half an hour?'

He nodded, dropping his car keys into her hand. Joe always carried her bags from the car, and this sudden break with what had become a small, comfortable ritual between them unsettled her. He must be worried.

She watched as he strode away from her. Strong, steadfast. However much she tried not to depend on him, however misguided it felt to allow any man to shape her fate, he was still becoming an indispensable support to her in this hostile landscape. She dismissed the thought and turned towards the house.

When Nancy opened the door, beckoning her inside, the smell of baking bread assailed her, and Neve's mouth began to water. 'Thanks for coming, Doctor. I'm so sorry to bring you all this way, but I'm worried about Daniel…'

Neve laid a reassuring hand on her arm. 'I'd rather you called if you have any concerns at all. Let's take a look at him.'

Neve was taking her time with each patient, aware that asking someone to pop back to the surgery if things got any worse wasn't a viable option for most people at the moment. But after a careful examination, she found baby Daniel was suffering from no more than a slight cold. Neve reassured Nancy and allowed herself to be tempted into the kitchen for fresh-baked bread and strawberry jam.

'Will you hold him while I put the kettle on?' Nancy smiled down at her son, and he stretched his arms up towards her face, mimicking her expression.

'I'll make the tea.' The bond between them was so precious, too beautiful to break, even for a moment. Neve couldn't help feeling a little stab of envy.

'That's okay.' Daniel gurgled with joy as Nancy planted a kiss on his forehead, before delivering him into Neve's arms. 'See you later, my sunshine...'

Daniel's tiny fingers curled around hers when she tickled his palm and he looked up at her solemnly. Neve no longer had to steel herself to be around babies. The pain of her own loss had slowly given way to gnawing regret for what might have been, and when she smiled at Daniel and he rewarded her with one of his own, everything was suddenly right with the world.

'Can you see Joe?'

Nancy leaned across the sink to get a better view out of the window. 'No. He was at the top a few minutes ago, but he must be on his way back here now.' Nancy turned, seeming to need the reassurance of checking once again that her own child was safe. 'I can't stop thinking about them out there. I hope someone finds them soon.'

'Have you heard any search helicopters?'

'Yes, I heard one go over about half an hour before you got here. I called Daryl when I heard about it on the radio and asked him to keep his eyes open.'

Word of mouth. Passed from wife to husband, friend to friend. Everyone in the area would be on the alert. 'They'll find them.'

Nancy grimaced. 'I hope so. It's snowing again and it'll be dark soon.'

Neve's phone rang, and she fished it out of her pocket one handed. 'Yes?'

'I see them. The man's on his feet, and walking. I'm on my way to them now.' Joe was breathing heavily, as if he was running.

'Where are you? I'll come out and meet you…'

'No… Neve, listen. I need you to stay there…'

It wasn't a matter of what Joe needed. 'I'm a doctor. I can help these people…'

'Which is why you need to organise things there. You can't get to them before I do, and our first priority is to get them into the warmth. I'll bring them to you…'

He was right. Neve didn't like it very much, but this wasn't the time to be squabbling over who did what. 'Okay. We'll get things ready to receive them here. Call me when you reach them and let me know what condition they're in.'

A grunt of assent came down the line and then it cut off. Joe must be putting all his energy into getting to the man and his son.

'What can I do?' Nancy took little Daniel from Neve's arms and put him into his baby bouncer.

'We need somewhere warm to bring them.'

'Okay, the sitting room's best. I've got a fire going in there.'

'That's great. Have you got some spare blankets or a duvet we can use?'

'Yes, of course. What about a hot bath?'

'No, not until we see what condition they're in.' If the man and his son had been out for any length of time in these conditions, the boy could well be hypothermic, his smaller body less able to resist the freezing conditions than an adult's. Warming him too quickly could cause shock or heart problems.

The smile on Nancy's face told Neve that she knew nothing about that, just that the man and his son had been found. Neve hoped that her bright optimism turned out to be justified, and set about helping to warm blankets and fill hot-water bottles.

Just as the wait for Joe's call was becoming intolerable, her phone rang again.

'Joe…'

'I'm with them. The boy's shivering and drowsy but conscious. The man's able to walk.'

Joe wasn't wasting any words, but that was all she needed to know. If the boy was still shivering, then his small body hadn't given up its fight to stay warm yet. 'Okay, that's good. Can you get back here with them?'

'That's the plan…'

'Right. I want you to carry the boy. Be sure to do it carefully, Joe. You must avoid bumping him around any more than absolutely necessary. That's important.' Hopefully the boy wasn't cold enough yet to make him susceptible to internal injuries, but without seeing him Neve couldn't be sure.

'Gotcha. I understand that precaution. I want you to do something for me.'

'Yes…' Anything.

'We're about a mile from you, in a westerly direction. I want you to turn my car and put the headlights on, full beam. Stay on the line, I can hear you through the earpiece. Do it now.'

'Okay, on my way.' Why did he want her to do that? It didn't matter. Neve slung on her coat, grabbed the car keys and signalled to Nancy that she'd be five minutes.

She heaved a sigh of relief when the car started first time. Carefully she manoeuvred it until it was at right angles to the house, hoping that this was in approximately the right direction.

'Joe… Joe…?'

'I see you. Move about ten degrees to your right…'

She rolled the car forward and then back again, turning in the direction he'd told her, frantic tears forming in her eyes. She could see the reasoning behind this now. The storm that had been threatening was now right overhead, the light was beginning to fail and it was snowing heavily. Neve couldn't see Joe, and it followed that he probably couldn't see the house. The lights were a beacon for him.

'How's that?'

'Good…' His breath was coming fast now, and he must already be walking. Every step brought him nearer. 'One more thing…'

'Yes, Joe. I hear you.' Neve wanted to stretch out and pull him back to her. If willpower alone could have done it, then he was already home and dry.

'If we don't make it back, I want you to stay where you are. You can't find us in these conditions. All that will happen is you'll get lost as well. Have you called the emergency services?'

'Yes, I got on to Maisie. She's liaising with them.'

'Great. Sit tight and wait for them… We're on our way, a mile out in the direction of the beam of the headlights. Have you got all that?'

She couldn't answer. Couldn't tell him that she'd just leave him out there if he didn't return.

'Have you got that, Neve? Say it…'

'Got it, Joe.' It wasn't going to happen. It was only a mile. He could walk that, even in these conditions.

'Good.' Another pause, as Joe caught his breath. 'See you soon.'

She wanted to tell him to come back to her, but she couldn't find a way to say it. 'Yeah. Very soon.' She almost choked on the words. And then determination took over. 'Stay on the line, Joe. I'm going to keep talking…'

'Yeah… Good girl…'

'Girl?' She grinned desperately at her phone. 'I'll give you *girl*, Joe Lamont. You get back here now, and I'll show you…' Just how much of a woman she was.

'Yes, ma'am…'

'Shut up and walk…'

Nancy's husband Daryl had been summoned from his workshop, which lay thirty feet to the rear of the house, but there was nothing that he could do, other than wait. Neve sent him inside with Nancy, asking them to stay by the phone and keep Maisie updated. She stayed in the car, talking to Joe, straining her eyes into the increasing gloom for any sign of him.

He was beginning to weaken. She could hear it in the few words that he managed to spare for her. His voice was shaking from the cold, and from the effort of walking through the snow. Neve looked at her watch. He must be close by now. Maybe if she went to the edge of the beam of the car headlamps, she'd see him.

Joe had told her to stay here. Ordered her to stay here, actually. And she'd obeyed him. When had that started to happen? The inevitable consequences of that particular slippery slope were suddenly forgotten. She caught her breath, staring into the swirling snow, and slowly the shapes of two men became visible. Joe's jacket was wrapped around the bundle in his arms, which must be the child. A man stumbled alongside him, relying on him for both support and direction.

'I see you, Joe...'

He didn't reply. Just kept walking. Neve wrenched the car door open, stumbling towards Joe, vaguely aware that Daryl had appeared from the house and was running towards the small group. They both reached them at the same time and Daryl took the man's arm, winding it around his shoulders and supporting him towards the house.

She took Joe's arm, and he seemed to straighten, relieved of the burden of the man he'd been supporting. Something stopped Neve from taking the bundle from his arms. He'd carried the boy for a long, painful mile, and he deserved to be the one to bring him inside.

When Nancy ushered them into the hallway, Joe gave up his precious cargo, delivering the boy into Neve's arms. 'The boy...Charlie. Four years old... F-father... Michael.'

Neve felt Charlie moving fitfully against her. Quickly she looked around, assessing the situation as best she could. Joe's waterproof trousers and heavy boots had kept his legs dry, but his sweater was wringing wet and he was shivering, from cold and exhaustion. Michael had a heavy coat on and seemed dry, but looked near to collapse.

'Daryl, take Michael through to the sitting room. Nancy, will you help Joe, please? Get those wet clothes off him.' Neve followed Daryl through, laying Charlie down on the blankets that were warming by the fire.

Carefully she stripped the boy of his coat and wellingtons. By some miracle, Charlie was dry. It was a hard-won miracle, though. His father must have carried him for miles to keep his legs dry in the snow, and Joe had wrapped his own coat around him to protect him from the snowstorm.

Daryl was helping Michael off with his coat and into a chair by the fireside. 'Daryl, will you check that none of Michael's clothes are wet, please? I'll come and look at him in a minute.'

'No... See to Charlie. Please...' Michael's agonised voice.

'That's what I'm doing, Michael. Stay where you are and rest now.'

Neve had already taken the things she'd need from her medical bag and they lay ready for her. Quickly she checked Charlie's pulse and reactions. Good. Better than she'd hoped. The low-temperature thermometer read 32 degrees. Much better than she'd dared hope.

All the same, she followed the guidelines for a more severe case. Wrapping the baby hot-water bottles that Nancy had prepared, she placed them under his arms and at his groin. Then she wrapped Charlie's body in the duvet, leaving his arms and legs free.

A tear squeezed from beneath Charlie's closed eyelids, and Neve bent over him to hold him still and give him some comfort. 'Okay, Charlie. You're all right. Lie still for me, sweetheart.'

'Dad...' The little boy let out a whimper, which stretched into a moan.

'Charlie...' Michael's voice came from behind her.

'Your dad's here, you can see him in a minute.' Charlie's eyes opened. Took their time focussing on her, but surely and steadily found her smile. 'Hello, there, sweetie.'

'Charlie...do what the doctor tells you, darling. Daddy's here...' Michael's voice broke, as if he was crying.

'He's doing well, Michael. You did a good job, keeping him dry. He has mild hypothermia, but I'm warming him now and he should be fine.' Neve allowed herself to hope that the worst was over.

CHAPTER FOUR

SHE HAD EXAMINED Charlie thoroughly. No sign of frost-bite and his core temperature was beginning to rise a little. Michael had allowed her to check his pulse and reactions quickly, before sending her back to Charlie's side.

Nancy appeared in the doorway, alone.

'Is Joe all right?' Neve had suppressed the urge to go to him, knowing that Charlie and Michael were her first priorities.

'Yes. I sorted out a sweater of Daryl's and he shooed me out of the bedroom.' Nancy grinned at Neve. 'Guess he's shy.'

Neve suppressed a smile, trying hard not to think about what Joe had to be shy about. 'Go and knock on the door. Make sure he's all right and tell him to come in here, by the fire.'

'Right. Daryl, will you go and check on the soup I've got on the stove?' Nancy disappeared, and Daryl got up from his perch on the arm of the sofa, leaving Neve alone with Michael and Charlie.

'Michael, I'm going to take your boots off and have a look at your toes.' She bent down at his feet.

'Please…' Michael shifted his feet away from her. 'You should be with Charlie.'

'Charlie's right here, Michael. I've already examined him very carefully.'

'No.' Michael's jaw set stubbornly. 'You don't have my permission. Now, go to Charlie.'

Legally speaking, there wasn't much Neve could do. Michael might be under stress, but he was certainly competent to make this decision. In his place, she would have done the same herself.

'Michael, I assure you that I've done everything I can for Charlie—'

'I know the law. I can and will prosecute you for assault if you lay one finger on me.' Michael's eyes were blazing. And Neve knew that all the medical knowledge in the world wasn't going to help him if he wouldn't allow her to touch him.

Joe towelled himself dry and pulled on the T-shirt and sweater that Nancy had left out for him on the bed. He wasn't shivering so badly now, but he knew that the cold ache in his bones would take a while to subside.

He sat down on the bed, resisting the temptation to wrap himself in as many blankets as he could find, curl up and sleep. Maybe there was something he could do to help Neve.

She'd given him no quarter when he had been out in the snow, straining to see the lights from the car. She hadn't cajoled him on or spoken soft words of encouragement, she'd bullied him forward, her voice stronger and more compelling than the storm. He couldn't help smiling to himself when he wondered whether she'd consider carrying out some of those threats she'd made.

There was a knock on the door and Nancy's voice

sounded. 'Neve wants to know whether you're okay in there. I'm making a hot drink.'

The rejuvenating feeling that Neve hadn't forgotten about him drove Joe to his feet. 'Thanks, Nancy. Just coming.'

As he approached the sitting room he heard Michael's voice, raised in panicky desperation, and Neve's quieter tones.

'I know the law. I can and will prosecute you for assault if you lay one finger on me.' Michael was pointing to Charlie, insisting that Neve return to his son. Joe's respect for the man grew.

'Neve, why don't you go to Charlie and I'll help Michael with his boots?'

She turned at the sound of Joe's voice, her gaze searching his face. He knew what she was looking for. Some sign that he was up to the job he'd just appropriated for himself. Beckoning him over, she spoke quietly to him.

'You must be very careful. If he has frostbite you can damage his toes very easily. Don't rub his feet to warm them…'

Joe nodded. 'I've been trained in dealing with cold-weather injuries. I've seen frostbite before.' And somehow he just couldn't let go, even though he knew he should. The exhilaration when he knew he'd found Michael and Charlie, the rush of achievement when he'd carried Charlie into the house were still too recent to let him back away now.

She thought for a moment then made her decision. 'Okay. But talk to me, Joe. Tell me everything you see, and let me make the decisions on treatment.'

'Understood. You're the boss.'

He summoned up a relaxed smile and moved over

towards Michael. 'Guess you drew the short straw, mate. Let *me* help you.'

Michael nodded, leaning towards him. 'I'm sorry…'

'You don't need to apologise.' Joe almost envied Michael. The kind of love that had driven him on through miles of freezing terrain, and then to reject Neve's offer of help so she could tend to Charlie, was something special. Something that Joe had once wanted for himself, but had given up on.

Michael nodded. 'Dr Harrison…'

'Neve.' She turned to face Michael. 'My name's Neve.'

Michael nodded. 'Neve…I'm sorry, I shouldn't have shouted at you…'

'Don't be. Charlie's a lucky kid to have a father who cares so much about him.'

The tenderness in her eyes would have made a stone weep. Suddenly there didn't seem as if there was enough air in the room for the four of them, and Joe instinctively held his breath.

'We're both lucky that you and Joe were there when we needed you.' Michael spoke quietly.

She gave Michael a smile.

Joe thought the responsibilities that she shouldered for her patients, the ones that Michael shouldered as a parent, were the kind of privilege that *he* had shown himself to be unworthy of. But maybe, just for this afternoon, he could help them both.

'Let's get your boots off now, eh?' Michael didn't argue and Joe reached for the laces, untying them and easing his boots open as far as they would go before he slipped them off. Then his socks. Neve nodded in approval when he asked her to double-check Michael's toes, and Joe tucked a warm blanket around his feet, turning his attention to Michael's hands.

'The last two fingers on his left hand are swollen and red. They feel cold and hard to the touch. No blisters.' He knew this was frostbite, but still he kept his word, relaying everything he saw to Neve without any diagnosis.

'Okay.' Neve turned to look, giving him a quick nod. 'I don't want to attempt rewarming unless we know that we can complete it. I'll give Maisie a call, see what's happening with Search and Rescue.'

'I should have stayed with the car.' Michael was shaking his head, his eyes still fixed on Charlie, as Neve pulled her phone out of her pocket.

'Hindsight's always twenty-twenty.' Joe didn't have the heart to tell Michael that he was right.

'This is all my fault...'

'Hey. Enough of that. You carried Charlie for miles to keep him dry. Never underestimate how important that was.'

'If it wasn't for me, he wouldn't have been in that situation in the first place.'

'I heard that your car ran off the road.' Neve had finished her call and put her phone down on the floor beside Charlie's makeshift bed.

'Yes, we skidded on a patch of ice and ended up in the ditch.' Michael shook his head. 'The battery on my mobile was flat, we've got no power at home, and we stayed in the car for a while. No one came by and I thought that I could walk to the next village, but I got lost. So stupid...'

'You were pretty shaken up by the accident?' Her question seemed casual, but Joe was beginning to divine where she was headed with this.

'Yeah. I couldn't think straight...' Michael began to realise where this was going too. 'It's no excuse.'

'You probably couldn't think straight because you were in mild shock. A car accident will do that.' Joe added his own voice to reinforce Neve's point. 'You acted on instinct, and that instinct was all about getting Charlie to safety.'

Michael fell silent. If he couldn't bring himself to agree, at least he was thinking about it. Joe caught Neve's eye and she shot him a smile.

'What did Maisie say?'

'Search and Rescue are sending a couple of vehicles. One's fitted out as an ambulance and they'll be able to take Michael and Charlie straight to the hospital.' She shrugged. 'Apparently the helicopter's a no-go.'

'Yeah, they can't land in this visibility.'

She gave him a long look. Joe's mask had slipped again, this time unintentionally.

'That's good to know.' Her tone left him in no doubt that there would be questions later. 'So we'll commence rewarming Michael's fingers. We'll need a bowl of warm water...'

'Thirty-seven to thirty-nine degrees centigrade. For thirty minutes.' He was teasing her now, showing off. Or maybe just trying to reassure her that he knew what he was doing and that she'd been right to trust him. 'Aspirin?'

'Yes, there's a packet in my bag.' She looked up at him, her wry grin taunting Joe. 'I'm sure you haven't forgotten the list of contra-indications...'

By the time the rescue team arrived, Charlie was awake and alert, seemingly none the worse for his experience.

Michael had seemed to gain in strength as soon as he'd seen that his son was doing well, and under Neve's watchful eye both of them had managed to drink some soup.

'They'll be all right?' Nancy blinked back the tears when she planted a kiss on Charlie's forehead, before the little boy was bundled up in blankets, ready for his trip to the hospital.

'I'll call in the morning and make sure. They're safe now.' Neve took her hand and squeezed it. So much had happened this afternoon. Everyone had played their part in keeping little Charlie safe.

'I guess we should be on our way too...' Joe was reaching for his coat. 'We can't thank you enough, Nancy.'

Nancy shrugged. 'The word "privilege" springs to mind.'

She'd summed it up completely. Neve had seen her share of people fight for life in a hospital setting, but somehow this was so much more raw, so immediate. Now that it was over, Neve wanted to retreat into a corner and weep at the thought of the sum of human endeavour that had wrought today's miracle.

Strike that. She wanted to cling to Joe and weep. Then she had a couple of questions for him.

She gave Nancy a brief hug, pulling away before the lump in her throat strangled her. 'Thanks for everything. I'll call you in the morning.'

The front door opened and Daryl burst in, bringing a blast of cold air with him. 'I don't think you two are going anywhere tonight.' He dropped Joe's car keys into his hand. 'I got the worst of the snow off the car and went to start the engine to clear the windows. The battery's flat.'

Neve's hand flew to her mouth. That was her fault. In the joy of seeing Joe and Michael emerge from the storm and her haste to get them inside, she had forgotten to switch the car headlights off.

'Joe…I'm so sorry…' He was sure to be angry with her. Who wouldn't be?

He dismissed her crime with a shrug. 'No problem. I've got a set of jump-leads.' He turned to Daryl. 'If you can give me a start, I'll take the car for a run to charge the battery up and come back for Neve.'

'You will not!' Nancy glared at him as if he'd just suggested burning the house down. 'I'll get some dinner and you'll both stay here tonight. Daryl can plug the battery in to charge in the garage.'

'That's too much trouble…' Neve was caught agonisingly between two sets of inconvenience that her mistake was going to cause. She didn't want Joe out there on his own in this weather, but Nancy and Daryl had already done enough.

'Nah.' Daryl grinned at her. 'If you want trouble, try telling Nance that you're not staying.'

Nancy nodded. 'And while I'm making dinner you can go over to Daryl's workshop. He's got a few new designs that he's dying to show off…'

The no-nonsense, make-yourself-at-home hospitality hadn't once suggested that Neve was at fault for the dead battery. It had just been one of those things. Daryl had spent a while in his workshop with Joe, and when Neve had been sent over to fetch them for dinner, they had been deep in conversation over the custom-made furniture that was the product of Daryl's growing small business.

Neve was shown to the spare room, and a bed was made up for Joe in the sitting room. Nancy and Daryl bade them an early goodnight, leaving them sitting together by the fire.

'I suppose I should turn in as well.' Neve wasn't tired, and the events of the day were still jostling for attention in her head, but now that she was alone with Joe she didn't know how to ask the questions that had been bugging her all afternoon.

'Yeah? Not on my account. I'll be staying up a while longer.' He was sunk deep into an armchair, his legs stretched out in front of him.

'Are you okay?'

'Why wouldn't I be?' A question to deflect a question.

'I noticed you were…limping a little.'

'When did you notice that?' The soft words were a challenge. Only go here if you dare.

'When I was walking behind you, on the way back from Daryl's workshop. You were favouring your right leg.' She met his gaze and remembered warmth tingled through her senses. That same intimate connection that had seemed to reach out and pull Joe from the cold embrace of the storm. 'I'm a doctor. I notice these things.'

He nodded. 'It's an old injury. I still limp a little when I'm tired. It's nothing.'

'Are you sure? I can take a look…' Here, at the warm fireside, taking a look was unlikely to remain strictly professional. It might not be a good idea. But, then, Neve's reasons for asking weren't strictly professional either, however much she wanted to pretend they were.

'I'm fine. Truly.' The silence in the room enveloped them. Warm, melting, as if they were curled up together beneath a thick blanket.

'Comminuted fracture of the left femur.' He smiled lazily. 'You were looking at my legs.'

'Was I?' More like staring. Neve felt herself redden.

'I have a titanium intramedullary nail.' He laid his hand on his left leg, splaying his fingers as if to shield it. 'Eighteen months ago. Pretty much a complete recovery.'

She was trying not to think about the force that it took to break the long, sturdy bone that ran from his hip to his knee. 'That…must have hurt.'

'Yeah. At the time. They did a good job of patching me back up, though.'

There was something more. Something floating in the air between them that Neve couldn't quite catch hold of. Maybe she was just tired.

'I should go to bed.' She got unsteadily to her feet. 'I'll see you in the morning.'

'Yeah. I'm going to sit up for a while.'

Was that an invitation? Or just a statement of fact? It was difficult to tell what Joe was thinking at the best of times, and it would be good to go now, before she said something that she was going to regret in the morning.

'Goodnight, then.'

'Neve…'

'Yes…?'

'Thanks for…' He broke off for a moment, staring thoughtfully into the fire. 'I heard every word you said. On the phone.'

Her cheeks were burning now. Exactly what *had* she said? She could hardly remember. 'I'm…I'm sorry, I…'

'Don't be.' He cut her off abruptly. 'At one point I was practically carrying both Michael and Charlie and I didn't think I could go much further. Then you told me to move my sorry arse.'

Neve winced. 'I said that?'

'Yes.' He looked up at her, his gaze threading its way

into the pleasure centres of her brain. 'I think your exact words were…'

He broke off as her cheeks burned redder. 'I forget your exact words.'

She remembered them now. And it was definitely time to leave. 'Right. Good. Sleep well.'

He flashed her a grin. 'Goodnight.'

Joe walked into the kitchen, ran water into a glass and took long swallows from it. Perhaps he'd been living the quiet life for too long here. Today had been a taste of his old life—the challenges, the keen exhilaration of overcoming them. Only there had been a difference. Before he'd been fighting for a principle, an abstract notion of saving the world. Today it was Neve that he'd come back to, her face that he'd imagined in front of him in the snow.

He needed to take it down a notch. Things had worked out today, but he couldn't rely on that. Couldn't rely on himself to come through on a regular basis, and in Neve's world that was what you needed to do. That was what he had needed to do, and he'd been found wanting.

Joe returned to the sitting room, laying the quilt from his bed for the night on the floor in front of the fire. Slipped off his jeans and sweater and sat down on the quilt. He'd done this practically every night for a year now, and it calmed him and helped him to sleep.

Closing his eyes, he worked his fingers along his leg, massaging the knotted muscles. Stretching his legs, and then his arms and shoulders. Letting his mind and body relax into the familiar routine. Almost…almost banishing her face from his thoughts.

CHAPTER FIVE

NEVE SAT ON the bed in the spare room, staring at the nightdress that Nancy had left out for her. She could hear Joe moving around quietly in the kitchen. Then silence.

She padded to the door and looked out into the hallway, unable to shake the feeling that there was still unfinished business between her and Joe. The sitting-room door was ajar, a line of light filtering round it. Unthinkingly, with the mistaken instinct of a moth attracted to a naked flame, she was drawn towards it.

She'd meant to knock on the door, but instead she stopped short. Joe was sitting cross-legged in front of the fire, dressed in just a pair of boxer shorts and a T-shirt. A slow, thoughtful set of movements set the muscles of his back and shoulders rippling beneath the thin fabric, like the movement of a stream running over smooth, water-worn boulders.

Despite his bulk, he was supple. Neve doubted whether her own spine could take that degree of rotation. She swallowed hard, trying not to think about how it might feel to be tangled in the strong, demanding, grace of his body.

Then she saw the scars. She'd expected the ones on his leg, a long surgical scar, together with a deep jagged gash where the break must have occurred. His left arm came as a shock, though. A wide, dark mark running up from his elbow and disappearing beneath the sleeve of his T-shirt. Another, thinner this time and bearing the faint marks of stitches, on his forearm. She caught her breath, stuffing her hand into her mouth to stop herself from crying out.

She should go. Keep her tears for him for somewhere else. Neve was pretty sure that Joe would have no time for them.

'Why don't you come in?' His voice was low, and he didn't turn to meet her gaze.

'I…I'm sorry.' She hissed the words in a whisper. 'I didn't mean to…interrupt you.'

He twisted round to face her. 'You didn't. I was just stretching, and I'm finished now.'

There was no way she could turn her back on him and walk away. No way in the world. Neve padded into the room, closing the door behind her. It seemed somehow wrong to sit on the higher level of the sofa and look down at him, and there was plenty of room to sit down on the quilt, where she could face him.

'This helps? Your leg…'

'Yeah.'

'It's…a nasty injury. Once you leave the hospital, the after-care is…' She ground to a halt. She was babbling anyway. Searching desperately for something to say.

He ran his fingers along his arm, pressing hard, as if the scars might rub off in his hand. They didn't. They were there, and Neve couldn't unsee what she'd seen. Wouldn't have done so for the world.

'You can ask.' He shrugged slightly. 'Or maybe you already know some of it.'

She was about to protest that she knew nothing, that she hadn't been thinking and drawing conclusions. But that would insult his intelligence. 'You're a doctor, aren't you? You were in the army and…' She waved a finger at his arm. 'I guess that you were injured.'

The flash of surprise in his eyes told her that Joe hadn't reckoned that she'd seen quite so much. Then he nodded. 'Royal Canadian Medical Service. How did you work it out?'

'I heard…from someone…that you'd been in the army.'

'Village gossip?'

'Yes. And you said you had medical training and…' She shrugged. 'I can't explain it, I just recognised the way you acted around Michael and Charlie.'

He shook his head, as if that was something he'd feared hearing. 'I guess you can't leave these things behind.'

'Why would you?' Neve couldn't imagine leaving being a doctor behind. It was her reason to get up in the morning. The one piece of her identity that her ex-husband hadn't managed to strip from her.

'It's not what I do any more.'

'Why not?'

A flash of defiance in his eyes. He seemed about to tell her to go away and mind her own business, and then his expression softened. 'My contract of service with the army expired a couple of weeks after I was injured and I didn't re-enlist. It took a while to recover, and I'd done some thinking in the meantime.'

Which didn't go anywhere close to answering the question. Neve tried another. 'How were you hurt?'

'An ambush. I don't remember all the details.'

Most people started off with what they did remember,

not what they didn't. It was as if not remembering was Joe's primary purpose.

'You had other injuries? Apart from your leg?'

He nodded. 'Ruptured spleen, partial kidney failure. Abrasions, lacerations…' He reeled off the list with a kind of detachment that Neve recognised. Designed to insulate you from the pain. 'Broke three fingers.'

He was holding up his right hand, flexing the fingers, and Neve noticed that one bent at a slightly different angle from the others. Somehow the crooked finger brought the horror of the rest of his injuries into sharp focus. Neve began to feel slightly sick.

'I guess it's not unusual. Not being able remember something like that.' She was struggling to keep the tears away. Wanting to convince herself that he'd been spared the trauma of those memories, even though she didn't believe it for a moment.

'No, it's not unusual.' He reached forward, and before she could flinch back he'd brushed a tear from her cheek. 'You don't want to do that. I'll be thinking that it's okay to feel sorry for myself any moment now.'

'And that would never do?'

'No, it wouldn't.' He shot her a look of rebuke. 'It's amazing what modern medicine and a good health package can do. It may not be very pretty, but everything works now.'

'It's…' Neve was suddenly lost for words. She'd talked to people about scars a hundred times before. This was different, she wasn't at work now. 'The scars aren't what I notice about you, Joe.'

He raised one eyebrow in an expression of disbelief, which melted into a wry smile. 'Thanks.'

If she could only tell him what she saw. The proud

tilt of his head, a body that had survived so much and yet remained graceful and strong. Any woman would want him…

Don't go there. Just don't.

'You were really good with Michael today.'

He shrugged. 'I was just helping out. You were the one in control.'

'I feel a bit of an idiot now, telling you what to do.'

'You shouldn't. Michael and Charlie were your patients and it was absolutely right that you should have the final say in their treatment. And, as I said, I don't practise as a doctor any more.'

There was no physical reason for that. Maybe an emotional one? PTSD? Neve couldn't believe that Joe no longer wanted to be a doctor. This afternoon he'd seemed to come alive. She shook her head slowly, not sure what to say.

He puffed out a breath. 'It's my decision, Neve.'

'I respect that.'

He nodded. 'I'd appreciate it if you didn't mention it to anyone else.'

'No, of course not. It's not up to me to tell anyone.' Without meaning to, she'd found Joe's weak spot. The fault line that, if tested, might spread into a network of cracks, ready to shatter.

'I should go to bed. Let you get some sleep. I'm glad you're okay. I was worried about your leg.' She wanted to reach out and touch him. But Joe was too proud for anything that seemed like sympathy, and right now he seemed too fragile as well.

'Wait.' It was Joe who reached for her.

There was no thought in his mind about trying to make Neve understand his decisions, or chasing away the feelings that had precipitated them. All he knew was that she was a woman, and he was a man. That she was beautiful in the firelight and that he wanted her. Did it need to be any more complicated than that?

Her eyes widened in surprise, but when he pulled her hand up to his lips she didn't resist him. This was the vision he'd held in his head, the one that had made Michael's weight seem like nothing.

'I really should go.' She didn't move.

'Yeah. You should.' Joe reached for her, pulling her close between his outstretched legs. She smelled so nice. Her hair brushed his cheek. Silk against his stubble.

She turned her mouth up towards his. Waiting. He let her do just that for a moment and then *he* couldn't wait any longer. Joe kissed her.

Her weight in his arms. Her softness. They were just right. Her lips were just right, too. Curving against his into a smile, which lit her beautiful blue eyes. Teasing him just a little and then giving him what he wanted. Another kiss.

'This isn't the place…' She ran her fingers lightly along the line of his jaw.

'No. You're quite right.' Joe kissed her again.

'Or the time…' She kissed him back.

'No, it's not the time either.'

'And there are about a hundred other reasons why I ought to go to my room.' Her little sigh of regret sent a thrill through Joe's already inflamed senses.

'Probably two.'

She turned her gaze onto him. Pensive, gorgeous, and enough to break him into a thousand pieces if she took it into her head to do so. 'Goodnight.'

Every bone in his body ached for her. Neve was the

kind of woman who could get a reaction out of a stone, and Joe let her go.

She left him with the taste of one last kiss on his lips and a hunger that no amount of work on his taut muscles was going to calm. One last flash of emotion from her lovely eyes and then she closed the door quietly behind her. Joe flopped onto his back in front of the fire, his hands covering his face. What in the world was he going to do now?

Neve heard the sounds of voices outside the house and rolled over in bed, covering her head with the thick, warm duvet. Just a few moments more. A couple of minutes to persuade herself that she could still taste Joe's kisses on her lips.

Last night her wakefulness had been punctuated by dreams of him. Holding her, kissing her. Dreams that had turned into nightmares, stark images of Joe broken and bleeding. When she slid out of bed and walked to the window it was almost a surprise to see him in one piece, clearing the snow from his car with the usual powerful grace that characterised all his movements.

By the time she got to the kitchen, the newly charged battery had been secured in the car and had jolted the engine into life. Breakfast was made, and Neve noted with satisfaction that little Daniel's cough was much better today. Then they thanked Daryl and Nancy, and took their leave of them.

Alone in the car, it was as if nothing had changed. Joe was the kind of old-fashioned gentleman who opened doors, carried bags, and it seemed that extended to not mentioning the indiscretions of the night before to anyone, not even the willing co-conspirator in those indiscretions. The kisses, which had made the world a different place this morning, were hidden behind his relaxed, watchful reserve. Along with the scars. Along with all the other things that Neve dared not ask about.

'If we stop by at yours, then I can take you on to Lemister for your surgery. I'll go home, and you can pop in when you've finished.'

'Yes, thanks. I could do with a change of clothes before I take on the morning. And some more coffee.'

Joe chuckled. 'I'll make the coffee.'

Joe closed the front door of his cottage, took off his coat and slung it onto the sofa, ignoring it when it slid off the cushions and onto the floor. He hadn't slept much last night and had watched the feeble rays of the morning sun creep into the room, shedding light on a situation that was already clear to him.

He'd thought that he could remain detached from the medical side of things. With any other doctor he might have stood a chance, but Neve... She was beautiful, committed and she reminded him of all the reasons he'd become a doctor in the first place. He wanted to be back in that world. And he wanted her.

Joe shook his head. If a broken leg and a few scars were all there was to it, it would have been easy. Not easy perhaps, but he could have beaten the emotional and physical trauma. But the terrible guilt, after a woman had died needlessly on his operating table, was a different matter. The family's grief, which had turned to anger, and the beating that had followed that had seemed like a kind of justice.

No one who made those kinds of mistakes deserved the title of doctor. It was as simple as that. And Joe could wish as hard as he liked that he could turn back time. He couldn't, and that was all there was to it. Taking the stairs two at a time, he made for his bedroom.

'You're not allowed in here.' Joe frowned at the little black cat curled up on the bed, and Almond took no notice. She knew she wasn't allowed in the bedroom, and chose to ignore that fact whenever the door could be pushed open by applying her weight to the bottom corner of it.

'All right, then.' He tickled Almond's neck and she rolled over for more. 'Guess you want some breakfast.'

When he'd started working with Neve, Joe had made an arrangement with his cleaning lady to leave food out for Almond every afternoon, in case he was late home. It had turned out to be a wise piece of forward planning. There was still some food and water left in Almond's bowls, and Joe washed and refilled them, setting them back down on the kitchen floor. Then went upstairs again, to pull off his clothes and scowl at himself in the bathroom mirror.

'Stupid…' The hissed word provoked a yowl from behind him. Almond had a habit of following him wherever he went, and Joe had got used to watching his feet for her. 'Not you, Almond. I'm the one that's the idiot.'

An idiot who was feeling rough around the edges from lack of sleep, and whose head hurt from thinking about all the things he knew he couldn't have. He turned on the shower, and Almond retreated behind a towel that drooped from the rail.

What had made him think that Neve would want him anyway? When he turned, the mirror reminded him of the dark welt that curved across his shoulder and down his back, the scars on his side and arm. The short, jag-

ged scar across his temple, usually hidden by his hair
unless he slicked it back or decided on a buzz cut. The
list went on. He was damaged goods. And although he
seldom stopped to consider it these days, he looked like
damaged goods as well.

Joe decided to leave the shower until later. Neve would
be a couple of hours, and that was time enough to work
some of this nonsense out of his system. A strenuous
workout was what he needed. That, and not dwelling
on the way that Neve wrinkled her nose slightly when
she smiled.

CHAPTER SIX

JOE'S COTTAGE WAS at the other end of the high street from the church hall, one of a row of three. When the front door opened, a small black cat appeared from behind his legs, dabbing one paw delicately on the ice and then retreating back to claw at the leg of his jeans. He bent to pick the animal up, and it dug its claws into his dark, hooded sweatshirt and started to purr.

He was clean-shaven, his hair slicked back and still a little wet from the shower. Somehow the tiny animal, tucked against his chest accentuated the breadth of his shoulders.

'Come in.' The front door opened straight into a small, comfortable sitting room, and he ushered her inside.

It was a nice room. Old beams across the ceiling contrasted with pale paintwork. There was a little brick fireplace, and a TV was tucked in the corner, dwarfed by piles of books. A brightly coloured armchair and an old leather sofa.

'What's its name?' She wanted to touch Joe, but she wasn't sure how he'd react to that. Instead, Neve crooked her finger and held it out to the cat, who sniffed at it and then allowed her to fondle her neck.

'*Her* name is Almond.' He grinned. 'When I first got

her, someone said that she was as sweet as a nut. She's a Yorkshire cat, so I guess that a Yorkshire expression will do for her.'

'Actually, I think you'll find that expression is used all over England.'

He shrugged. 'Well, she's an English cat, then.'

'So she had to be Almond, or Hazel or... Pea...?'

He chuckled. There was something about the flex of his body, his wet hair and the scent of soap on his skin that spoke of exercise and then a shower.

'Have we got time for some lunch?' His voice cut through Neve's sudden vision of taut muscles, sheened with sweat. 'I'm starving...'

'Yeah. I called Maisie and there are no visits for this afternoon. Apparently the off-roading club has got involved with the driving and the other doctors can easily cover the rest of today so we've got the afternoon off.'

He nodded, seemingly in no hurry to take her home. 'Lunch it is, then.'

He'd led the way through to the kitchen extension at the back of the house and was staring at the contents of the refrigerator when the phone rang. Joe frowned at the instrument then clearly decided that answering it wasn't going to be too much of an interruption.

'At least it's not yours. I don't get those *drop everything and come quick* calls any more.' He picked up the receiver and barked his name down the line, in an unmistakeable invitation to keep it short.

'Edie...?' His gaze left Neve, and he suddenly began to concentrate on the call. 'What's up?'

'Cough mixture...? Yes, of course I'll fetch some, but don't you think you'd better see the doctor?'

He stiffened, holding the phone away from his ear, as

an incomprehensible stream of invective sounded from the other end of the line.

'That's as may be, Edie. I'm bringing the doctor round to see you.' He listened again. 'No, actually you don't have much choice. Just grin and bear it.'

He chuckled, and then put the phone down, turning to Neve.

'Who was that? Did I hear mention of the word "doctor"?'

'Yeah. I'm really sorry about this, but it's Edie Wilcox. She says she's got a terrible cough, and she doesn't sound too good. She doesn't want to see the doctor.'

'So we're going round there?'

He nodded, grinning. 'Yeah. Thanks.'

He picked up a couple of energy bars from the top of the refrigerator, handing her one and tearing into his own while he put his coat on. Picking up her bag, he held the front door open for her.

'After you, Dr Harrison.'

'I hear you did a few jobs for Edie.' She had to walk fast to keep up with Joe.

'Yeah. She can be a bit ferocious, but the trick is to show no fear…' He turned into a tiny front garden, the steps and front path edged with a secure, workmanlike handrail.

'Right. Gotcha.'

Edie took a long time to answer the doorbell, and when she did she was wearing a heavy coat over a nightdress and slippers. She was a tiny, birdlike woman, with bright, sunken eyes and flushed cheeks. Joe stepped forward, holding out his hand.

'I…don't need…'

'I know.' Joe's arm extended protectively around her back, not touching her but there in case she faltered. He guided her into the small, neat sitting room, and she sat down heavily in an easy chair.

'All I need is some cough mixture. And a dash of brandy.' Edie's words were full of bravado, but her eyes told a different story. They were fixed on Joe, almost pleading that he stay.

'Sure you do. But will you do me a favour and let the doctor have a look at you first?'

Edie nodded. 'You're fussing, Joe.'

'That's right. You know Dr Harrison?'

'No.' Edie shot Neve a hostile look and Neve remembered Joe's words. Show no fear.

'Mrs Wilcox.' Neve stepped forward confidently, holding out her hand. 'I'm Neve.'

'Nice to meet you, Dr Harrison.' Edie tightened her lips. Obviously a lady who needed to know you for at least ten years before she'd deign to call you by your first name. Unless, of course, you happened to be Joe.

That was fine. Pulling herself up to her full height, Neve shot Edie a firm look. 'I'd like to take a look at your chest, if that's all right with you.'

Edie folded her arms across her, pulling the coat closed. 'If you say so, Doctor.'

'I'll go and make a cup of tea.' Joe began to retreat.

'Don't you make a mess in my kitchen.' Edie rapped out the words like a command, but her face had softened when she'd looked at him.

'I'll put everything back where it was…' Joe's voice came from the hallway, and Neve closed the door behind him.

'You're the doctor that Joe's been driving.' Edie wasn't

going to submit herself to an examination before Neve had given a full account of herself.

'Yes, that's right. I couldn't have managed without his help this past week.'

'He didn't bring my shopping until half past eight the day before yesterday.' Edie tightened her lips, as if shopping in the evenings was another thing she didn't particularly approve of.

Neve suppressed a smile. 'We didn't finish until seven that day.' Joe had made no mention that he would be doing Edie's shopping, and Neve had supposed he would go straight home. But, then, the more she found out about Joe, the more she realised just how much she didn't know.

Edie gave a little nod. 'He's a good man.'

'Yes, he is.'

That settled, Edie relaxed her grip on her coat enough to allow Neve to examine her. 'I hope you're going to warm that up.' Edie was looking at her stethoscope as if it were an instrument of torture. 'Dr Johnstone never does.'

Neve knew for a fact that the avuncular, friendly senior partner of the practice *always* warmed the diaphragm of his stethoscope before placing it on a patient's skin. She let that go and handed the instrument to Edie.

'Here. Hold the end in your hand for a moment to warm it, while I take your temperature.'

Joe took his time making the tea. Edie's stubbornness could be immoveable at times but, then, Neve's smile was irresistible. Somehow he didn't give much for Edie's chances.

He didn't give a great deal for his own either. He'd thought about coming up with an excuse that would make him temporarily unavailable to accompany Neve, ending their relationship there, but he'd made a promise and he wouldn't go back on that. In any case, the idea of another volunteer encroaching on what he now saw as his territory was unthinkable.

Like it or not, Joe knew he would see it through to the end. He heaved a sigh, placing cups and saucers precisely onto a tray. He waited before pouring the hot water from the kettle into the pot, knowing that Edie would complain if the tea was stewed. Joe found some biscuits in the scullery and tried to divert himself by arranging them in different patterns on a plate.

When he heard Neve's footsteps in the hall, he set the kettle to boil again. She was smiling. His brain—or maybe his heart—took special note every time she smiled.

'Edie wants to know what you're doing. She says that your grandmother would be horrified at the way you make tea.'

Slowly, irrevocably, Neve was beginning to turn his world upside down and make him doubt every part of his carefully constructed life here. When she was around he had to remember to stop grinning like a fool, staring like a moonstruck child. 'She must be feeling all right, then.'

'She's got a nasty cold, but she'll be all right in a few days.'

'Her chest's clear?' Joe wondered whether that might be misconstrued as fussing. Or a comment on how thorough Neve had been in her examination.

'Yes. But it would be good to keep an eye on her.'

'She has a daughter in the village. I'll give her a call.'

'Good.' She turned her attention to the tea things. 'Edie told me to remind you to warm the pot.'

He rolled his eyes. 'Edie's mission in life is to teach me how to make a decent cup of tea.'

'And has she?'

He shrugged, laughing. 'I'm a work in progress. She did mention once that my tea wasn't too bad. I think she wasn't feeling up to much that day.'

'Well, I'll leave you to concentrate, then. I'm just going to wash my hands.'

Neve had obviously made the mistake of leaving her stethoscope lying around, because when Joe walked into the sitting room Edie had the instrument plugged into her ears and was listening to the chest of her old ginger cat. Clearly she was feeling better and her irrepressible interest in life was resurfacing. He put the tray down and tapped her on the shoulder.

'If you put it there, all you'll hear is Errol digesting his breakfast.'

Edie didn't reply but moved the diaphragm of the stethoscope. She listened intently and then nodded. 'Well, he's alive. Not that you'd know it. He hasn't moved recently.'

Joe grinned. 'And what did the doctor say? Are *you* alive?'

Edie gave him one of her looks. Most people seemed to think that Edie's glare could fry you on the spot, but Joe was somehow immune to it. Perhaps because he got her sense of humour.

'She says that you've been fussing. Sit down, you're making the place look untidy.'

Joe sat. Edie asked for no quarter, and gave none. She'd never referred to his injuries, other than to nod approvingly when he'd thrown the walking stick away and expect him to carry her shopping. She was pure gold.

'Nice girl. Pretty, too.' Edie lost interest in the stethoscope, having learned everything she could from it, and turned her attention to Joe.

'Yes. Only she's not really a girl…'

'None of them are these days.' Edie seemed to have regained the rest of her usual feistiness. She might talk tough, but underneath it all she'd been feeling ill and worried and Neve had obviously seen that and put her mind at rest. 'And I may be old, but I'm not blind.'

'I can see that.' Joe grinned at her.

'Don't try getting around me, Joseph Lamont. Try that smile with her instead.'

'I don't know what you mean.'

'Yes, you do.' Edie waved an imperious finger at the tray. 'Did you warm the pot?'

'I did.'

'Then perhaps it'll be drinkable.' Humour sliced the faded blue of Edie's eyes. 'I won't have a biscuit just yet. Don't want to spoil that pretty pattern you've made until she's seen it.'

Edie's daughter had arrived and ordered her upstairs to bed in no-nonsense tones that bore a remarkable resemblance to those of her mother. Neve packed up her things, flashing a querying look in Joe's direction when she found a ginger cat hair on her stethoscope, but he just shrugged with a look of mock innocence. Then they were ready to go.

'Lunch?'

'Sounds good.' Neve had rather hoped that Joe hadn't forgotten he'd promised her lunch.

'How about the pub? It's nothing fancy...'

Nothing fancy was just what Neve wanted at the moment. 'Sounds perfect.'

They tramped towards the painted sign, which showed a white deer, its breast pierced by an arrow. 'I'm told this is the oldest building in the village.' He grinned at her.

'You've heard the story too?'

'Oh, yes.' He grinned. 'King Henry VIII took time off from a royal progress to do some hunting in the area, and *The Bleeding Hart* was named to celebrate that. In the summer it's crammed with tourists.'

'But you're a local now?'

'I've moved around so much that it only takes a couple of weeks before I reckon I'm local...' Joe shrugged. 'As far as everyone else is concerned, I'm working on it.'

He ducked through the low doorway, and led the way to the bar. Beamed ceilings, slightly sloping walls and an eclectic furnishing style gave the impression that the place had been here since the year dot, and the soot-scarred fireplace attested to a succession of roaring fires, just like the one that blazed there now.

'A pint, thanks, Mark.' Joe indicated the tap that bore the insignia of the local bitter and turned to Neve. 'What'll you have?'

She leaned across the bar, squinting at the chalked board above Mark's head. 'Hot punch sounds good.'

Mark nodded and Joe handed her a menu. 'What are you having?'

'Shepherd's pie. Runner beans, carrots and...' She turned to him, unable to make a decision. 'I suppose chips on the side is a bit much.'

'They do very good chips here.' Joe grinned.

Neve's ex-husband had always ordered for her when

they'd gone out to eat, taking it on himself to watch her waistline when he did so. It appeared that Joe had no such concerns, and if she wanted to resist temptation, she was going to have to do it all by herself.

'No…I won't have chips. I'll have apple pie to follow. With cream.' She was reaching inside her coat, but Joe had the better start. He signalled to Mark to make it two of everything and handed him the money, waving away the note she proffered from her purse.

'Thanks. My treat next time.'

'I'll look forward to it.' Joe grinned and picked up the drinks, navigating past the clusters of chairs and tables to a seat by the fire.

'So how did you get to know Edie Wilcox?' Neve took a sip of her punch and nodded in approval.

'She gave me the evil eye a couple of times when I first got here. Looked as if she might kick the crutches out from under me. The first time she spoke to me was in the village shop. She took one look at me, pointed to the chair by the counter and told me to sit down because I was making the place look untidy.'

Neve snorted with laughter. 'And did you?'

'Yeah. I was fed up with everyone back home wrapping me up in cotton wool, and I'd had about as much sympathy as I could take. Edie never gave me a shred of it.' He took a draught of his beer.

'But she looked out for you?'

'Oh, yes. She goes to the village shop every morning, and before I knew it she was expecting me to walk her down there and back, nice and slowly because of her bad leg. Funnily enough, as soon as I started to be able to walk a bit faster, her bad leg got miraculously better.'

'She had your measure, then.' Neve chuckled.

'Is it that hard?'

'Don't know. Is it?' A now-familiar tingle registered at the back of her neck. Danger? Pleasure? A bit of both?

'There isn't that much to know.' Joe took another draught of his beer. 'You've heard it already.'

'Really?' She raised one eyebrow, just to show that she didn't quite believe him. He nodded, as if he was perfectly aware of that but there was nothing he could do about it.

'Yeah. Really.'

There was no shortage of things to talk about over lunch, or afterwards when he took her home. Village gossip, the weather. The price of apples. All the things that didn't really matter all that much. Neve reflected that Joe must want it that way.

They were caught in a no man's land somewhere between friends and lovers. Not wanting to go back, not daring to go forward.

'I'll see you tomorrow, then.' Neve made no move to get out of the car, but sat staring at her front door.

'Yeah. Same time?'

'That would be great, thanks.'

For a moment she thought that he might reach for her. Maybe she ought to give him some sign. He couldn't know that the constant craving for his scent, his skin had given him the right to hold her. It had given him the right to break her front door down, carry her upstairs and do pretty much anything he pleased.

'Right.' Suddenly he swung out of the car, fetching her bags from the back seat and carrying them up the front path. Neve followed, her steps slowed by indecision, waiting for him to make the first move. Wondering whether she should.

He dumped her bags on the front doorstep and turned, striding back to the car. The grin that he shot her from the driving seat ought to have lost some of its potency at this distance but somehow didn't. Then the car began to recede slowly away, down the snow-filled lane.

CHAPTER SEVEN

THE RING OF the doorbell synchronised perfectly with the time pips for eight o'clock on the radio. Almost as if he'd been waiting, at the other end of the lane, to time his arrival. Neve decided to enquire no further. Enquiring no further seemed to be exactly what Joe wanted.

He seemed more relaxed this morning, less restless. He wished her a cheery good morning and they took the road that wound its way to Cryersbridge, through the village, and to the nursing home on the other side, drawing up in the wide, snow-filled drive.

'You should come inside.' He hadn't moved to get out of the car when they came to a halt. 'I'll be a while, I've a few people to see here and there are some things I've promised to do for the district nurse. You'll freeze out here.'

He nodded, getting out of the car without a word. The manager of the nursing home waved to them from the window, and a wall of heat hit Neve when she opened the door and ushered them inside.

'Dr Harrison, thanks for coming. The surgery said you'd be here this morning, but I wasn't expecting you until later.'

'I had some help. This is Joe Lamont, he's been driving me for the last week. Joe, this is Jane Matthews.'

Joe's smile turned the warmth of Jane's up a notch. 'They're still serving breakfast in the dining room. Go and get yourself a cup of tea and sit in the lounge if you'd like.'

The invitation wasn't all just good hospitality. Neve imagined that the residents hadn't received too many visitors in the last few days, and a new face was always welcome.

He turned a look of untrammelled pleasure onto Jane, as if she'd just invited him to the Queen's garden party. 'Thanks, I'd like that.'

'Good.' Jane looked around quickly and, finding no one available to show him the way, pointed to her left. 'The dining room is through there, you can't miss it. Just introduce yourself…'

'Sure.' Joe turned quickly, and strode away in the direction of Jane's pointing finger.

'Is that it, then?' Neve had seen six of the residents, redressed a leg ulcer, and made sure that the various bumps, wheezes and an unexplained watery eye were nothing serious and could be managed here.

'There's Stuart. Dr Johnstone usually sees him…'

'Ah, yes. Fairly new resident, became very distressed when he moved here. Dr Johnstone has him on a mild anti-depressant. How's he been?'

'Much better. He's joining in with some of the activities now. Still keeps himself to himself, but some people prefer that.' Jane grinned. 'He has good days and bad, but on balance the good ones are getting more frequent.'

'Okay. I'll find a quiet corner and have a chat with him.'

'Great. Thanks.' Jane led the way back to the main sitting room, scanning the circle of faces from the doorway.

'Hallie, have you seen Stuart, love?' Jane's teenaged daughter had obviously been pressed into service while the home was short-staffed, and was dispensing tea and biscuits from a trolley.

'In the small sitting room, I think.' Hallie leaned towards her mother. 'With the new guy. Who is he?' One look at the grin on Hallie's face told Neve that she was referring to Joe.

'Don't get your hopes up, he'll be gone soon. He's driving Dr Harrison today.'

Hallie wrinkled her nose, and shot Neve a look of undisguised envy. Suddenly, seventeen seemed a very long time and a whole world of complications away.

The small sitting room was bathed in light. The high windows caught the best of the morning sun, reflecting off the snow outside, and the room was bright and warm. Joe was sitting in an armchair, next to a wiry, neatly dressed elderly man, whose lined, weather-beaten face attested to a lifetime spent outdoors.

'What did you do, then?' Joe's face was alive with interest, and Neve hung back in the doorway, waiting to see how Stuart would respond to him.

'Pulled 'er out wi' a tractor. But that road through the fells is always like that in winter. Summat to do with the way the wind blows. The snow just piles up through there.' Stuart leaned forward, tracing his finger across the map in front of them.

'And what about here?' Joe indicated another spot on the map, about a mile south.

Stuart's face became suddenly confused. 'Depends.' Uncertain anger sounded in his voice. The notes had stated that Stuart had mild dementia, and his reaction was typical. He was lashing out at Joe before he'd admit that he couldn't remember.

Joe didn't miss a beat. No surprise, no trying to get Stuart to explain. Just what Neve would have expected from a doctor who was sensitive to his patients' feelings as well as their medical needs. 'Yeah, I guess so. Probably best not to risk it. I'm thinking that going this way is the thing to do. It's further but more sheltered.'

Stuart looked carefully at the map. It was difficult to say whether he was really following Joe's line of thought, but that didn't matter. Joe had neatly skirted the lapse in memory, and Stuart's self-respect remained intact.

'Yes. That way's sheltered. That way's best.'

Joe nodded. 'Yeah. Thanks, Stuart, that's good to know.'

'Seventy years on the land, in all sorts of weather. You pick up a few things.' Stuart was no longer a frail old man who wasn't of much use to anyone. 'I'd take you myself, but…'

'You've done your share, mate.' There was respect in Joe's voice but no pity.

'That I have.' Stuart nodded sagely. 'That thing over there's crooked.' A sudden change of subject, as different thoughts jostled for supremacy in Stuart's mind.

'The tree?' Joe followed Stuart's gaze towards the brightly decorated Christmas tree in the corner of the room.

'No, the star on the top. The girls can't reach it…'

Joe took the hint. Striding over to the tree, he reached up and adjusted the star. 'Better…?'

'That'll do.' Stuart suddenly seemed to realise that Neve was in the room. 'Who's this?'

Joe looked round and caught Neve staring at him. 'It's the doctor. Looks like I've got to go now.' He collected his map from the coffee table and held out his hand to shake Stuart's. 'Thanks for all the advice.'

'No trouble. I seem to be always here now, if there's anything else you want to know.'

'Thanks, Stuart. I'll know where to find you.'

Joe had already done what Neve was here to do. Get Stuart talking, without making it too obvious that she was here to assess his mood and how much he could re-member. She sat down next to the elderly man.

'I'm just here to have a chat. Why don't you stay a moment, Joe?'

She thought that the look she shot him implied that the invitation to stay was anything but casual. If Joe could talk some more to Stuart, and she could just listen, that would probably answer all the questions she had. But Joe, it appeared, had other ideas.

'I've got to go and clear the snow from the car.' He grinned at Stuart. 'Kick the tyres…'

Stuart nodded. 'What have you got fitted?'

'High silica snow tyres. I don't know what everyone around here has against snow tyres, no one seems to fit them. They're standard practice in Canada.'

Stuart chuckled. 'You need a tractor, boy. Get over anything.'

'I dare say. Bit chilly for my passengers, though.' He gave Stuart a parting smile, and then he was gone.

She was obviously angry. Neve was having difficulty marching in two feet of snow, but her face was a picture as she toiled across to the car. Pink with exertion, her lips pressed together in a sure sign of emotion, she was intoxicating. He twisted the ignition key, trying to keep his mind away from those thoughts. The engine almost choked into life and then died.

'Thanks for that.' Joe expressed his wry gratitude to the treacherous gods of fate. If he tried again too soon he'd flood the engine so he was going to have to leave it now and sit with her for a few awkward minutes in the car.

He got out of his seat and opened the tailgate so she could put her bag inside.

'Car won't start?' She turned her lovely blue eyes up towards him, trying to catch his gaze. There was more than a hint of fire in them, which made him want to kiss her.

'Give it a minute. It'll start.'

She nodded and walked to the passenger door, getting in before Joe could close the tailgate and get around there to open the door for her. As she wished. He trudged back to the driver's door, kicked a minuscule shard of ice from one of the tyres in an attempt to put the awkward moment off, and then got into the car.

Her hands were clasped in her lap and she was staring straight ahead, as if assessing the road in front of her. Joe wondered if he should get out and clear the windscreen again.

'You might have stayed.'

Yes, he might have. But that wasn't what he did any more.

'I had to come out here and get the car started.'

'Right.' She turned her gaze onto him, bright and

angry, and it rocked him to the very core of his being. 'Go on, then.'

'Give it a minute. I don't want to flood the engine.'

She frowned at him. It seemed that he wasn't going to get off the hook that easily. A part of him embraced that, aching for more, and Joe wondered again if he hadn't been living the quiet life a little too long.

'You're Stuart's doctor. It wasn't appropriate for me to hang around.'

'Why don't you let me be the judge of that? I wasn't asking you to do a full-blown assessment of him, just to keep him talking a little while longer.'

'And you're not capable to talking to someone?' Joe was in no doubt that Neve had handled Stuart with compassion and sensitivity. What he couldn't fathom was why she had seemed so set on dragging him in to help.

'Of course I'm capable of talking to him. I could ask him the questions if you think that's going to do any good.'

The standard set of questions, things that everyone was supposed to know, which were designed to assess dementia patents. It was likely that Stuart had come across them before, and he might recall their purpose. If he knew why Neve was asking the questions but couldn't remember the answers, it was just setting him up for failure and humiliation.

'You didn't, did you?' Concern for Stuart snagged at him, and then he remembered that this was Neve he was talking to. Of course she hadn't. 'I'm not sure *I* know who the prime minister is over here…'

The temperature in the car shot up. 'Stop being a smart-arse, of course I didn't. But the map and his local knowledge were a great way to get him talking and assess what he remembers.'

That hadn't been Joe's intention, he'd just fallen into conversation with Stuart and had recognised the frustration of a man who felt that he was no longer of any use to anyone. It had been the act of a human being, not a doctor. But the knowledge that Neve was right cut him to the bone.

'Look, we both have a job to do. We don't have to be overjoyed about it, but we need each other right now. So let's just get on with it, shall we?'

She flushed red. 'Okay, so I need you. Is that what you want me to say? I'm not quite sure how you need me…'

Joe wasn't sure quite why he needed her either. Other than that the air seemed thin, almost unbreathable when she wasn't there. There was an insistent rapping on the misted car window beside him and Neve jumped.

The window slid down, and he saw Hallie outside, shivering in just a blouse and cardigan. 'Stuart says to pump the accelerator. You'll need to start in second gear.' She turned, without waiting for an answer, and skittered back to the warmth of the house.

He already knew that, but he wasn't going to deprive Stuart of his moment of glory. He gave a wave to the figure at the window, twisted the ignition key and the engine growled into life. A quick thumbs-up in Stan's direction and they were ready to go.

'Where next?'

'Straight through the village then take the first left. There's a house about two hundred yards down.' She seemed to have made the same decision as him.

Arguments about who did what, and why, were sheer self-indulgence. They needed to save their energy for the road ahead.

CHAPTER EIGHT

SILENCE HAD GIVEN way to frosty formality and then to studied good manners. By the time they drew up outside Neve's house the day had worn them both down, and a couple of smiles that weren't strictly necessary had passed between them.

'I've been thinking…' Neve took a breath. Letting Joe drive away without clearing the air between them had become impossible.

'Yeah?' He leaned back in his seat, stretching his legs as much as the footwell would allow. Cautious. Watchful as ever.

She'd better make the admission now, before she lost her nerve. 'I was angry.'

Joe grinned. 'Now tell me something I don't know.'

All right. This was a different way of handling it. Not quite the way her ex-husband had approached anything that even approximated disagreement on Neve's part but, then, the one thing that didn't seem to register with Joe was her mistakes.

'I'm sorry.' It was easier to apologise when an apology wasn't demanded.

'No, you were right. I might not practise, but that doesn't absolve me from being a human being. Staying

around and chatting to Stuart was what anyone would
have done.'

Joe had clearly been thinking too. Coming around
to her way of seeing things. It was a novel experience.

'Come in and have some tea.'

'You're tired.' The look that ignited in his eyes told her
that Joe was wondering the same as she was. Whether tea
was the only thing he was supposed to be coming in for.
The thought of Joe's embrace, testing her to the brink of
exhaustion, flooded through her senses.

'I'd like some company.'

He reached forward and found her hand. When he
pulled her glove off, it felt as if he was undressing her.
He laid his gentle fingers around hers, and it was as if
they were naked already. Neve leaned forward, brushing her lips against his.

The suddenness of his next move activated his seat
belt, and for a moment he was pinned against the seat.
Cursing, he punched the release, twisting round and pulling her into his arms. Sudden heat jolted through her
when he kissed her.

'Come inside.' The gear shift was in the way, and
the steering-wheel wouldn't allow him to get as close
as she'd like. Their clothes wouldn't allow him to get as
close as she'd like.

'If I let you go…?'

'You're going to have to. One step back and two steps
forward.'

His lips curved against hers. 'I like the way you
think…'

She liked the way he thought as well. There was no
rushing up the front path, struggling with her keys. He
opened the front gate for her, his hand on her back while

she opened the front door. Treating her as if she was something precious. He would ask, but he didn't just go ahead and take.

As soon as they were inside, she wound her arms around his neck, pulling him down for another kiss. She felt his hands around her hips, lifting her upwards and against his body, and she wound her legs around his waist, just making it clear, if either of them was in any doubt, what was coming next.

Separated by layers of high-performance down and waterproofing, she couldn't feel the lines of his body. All she could feel was his strength, supporting her weight, crushing her close until she couldn't breathe.

'Upstairs…' She took just enough time out from kissing him for that one word.

'I *really* like the way you think.' The curve of his body was urgent against hers, but he seemed intent on taking his time. 'I want to undress you. Piece by piece.'

Just the thought made her head swim. 'Go on…'

'And then I want to touch your skin.' He nuzzled against her neck, his breath caressing her ear. 'Fingers… Then lips…'

This was too much. If he didn't stop asking and start doing, she was going to faint. 'Upstairs. Now, Joe.'

She unwound herself from him, difficult though it was, then led him up the stairs and into her freezing-cold bedroom. Went to flip on the light and Joe caught her wrist before she could do so, pressing her fingers against his lips. In the darkness she felt him pull off her coat and then the padded liner, then he walked her backwards until she fell onto the bed. Bending, he pulled her boots off, then her thick woollen socks. She shivered a little in the cold air.

The hall light, filtering in through the half-open doorway, was enough to see his shape. The delicious shadow of his bulk loomed over her, as he hurriedly shed his coat and boots, pulling off his sweater. Then his warmth enfolded her again, and he unbuttoned her thick cardigan. Slid his hands inside, and then pulled it off, along with the sweater she was wearing underneath.

'Joe…' She pulled at his shirt and he dragged it over his head. Her fingers slid to the button on his jeans and he slipped out of them. It was the fastest she'd seen a guy undress in her life.

'Thermal vest…' His lips were close to her ear again. 'Very practical.'

The way he was taking his time, easing her out of it, exploring every new inch of skin with his fingers, wasn't at all practical. It was a simmering, languid testament to his intentions of taking his time with her.

'Condoms. In the drawer…'

'Later. This is all for you, honey.' Joe was gently slipping her slacks down, kissing the skin on the inside of her leg as he went. His words echoed through her consciousness, like a golden, erotic promise of what was to come.

'What about you…' He silenced her by cupping her breast with his hand, brushing gently against the nipple. All hell broke loose, fire shooting through her body as if it had just been injected straight into a vein.

'You first.' His hand slid around her back, unhooking her bra with an uncommon dexterity. She felt the soft cotton of his T-shirt, brush against her stomach…

'Joe, wait.' It took all her strength to push him away, even though he drew back at the slightest touch of her fingers. Every ounce of her self-control.

'What is it, honey?' She could see the outline of his

face in the darkness. Feel his hand, resting lightly on her stomach.

'Not like this, Joe.' He probably hadn't even thought about this. It was just instinct, born of the feeling that his body was broken and disfigured. But he was about to squander their precious first time, rob her of the chance to share it with him.

Neve rolled away from him, leaving him stretched out on the bed. Stumbling over to the window, she drew the curtains, although there was no one outside. Then she picked the matches up from the mantelpiece, half closing her eyes against the sharp flare of light as she struck one of them.

There were four large candles, standing on the mantelpiece, in front of a huge, heavy framed mirror. As she lit them, light slid across the contours of her body, caressing her curves.

What had he been thinking? Neve felt good, she smelled good and she tasted wonderful. But she looked stunning. Long, slim limbs, beautiful breasts... She was enough to bring a man to his knees.

'That's better, isn't it?'

'You're beautiful.' His voice came out hoarse with emotion. Not like him at all.

'And you...' She sashayed back over to the bed, and climbed onto it. He could see the high brass bedstead now, and the thought of her gripping hard onto the rails nearly destroyed him. 'You are not going to get away with this.'

She rolled him onto his back, sitting astride his stomach. Joe had a horrible feeling he knew what was coming next. She bent over him, running her tongue around the edge of his ear. 'What did you think? That I don't want to see you?'

That had crossed his mind. But largely it had been un-thought, an instinctive need to give her pleasure, feel her break in his arms.

'Or did you reckon on making me scream first, before you got rid of this.' She pulled at his T-shirt. 'Maybe I wouldn't notice quite so much then.'

He hugged her close. She seemed to know his inten-tions better than he did, right now. 'It's a thought. I par-ticularly like the screaming part…'

She giggled against his chest. Clearly she did too. 'Yeah, well there wasn't going to be any screaming be-cause I don't scream in the dark. It's a lonely place, the darkness.'

Suddenly it was. Suddenly the one thing that Joe wanted was for her to see him, all of him, just as he was. Maybe accept him a little.

'So we've got some light. What now?' She might have the courage that he didn't.

She reached over to the bedside table, opening the drawer with one hand, and drawing out a pair of scissors. The blades gleamed in the flickering light.

'Take it off, Joe.'

'Or what?' He tucked his hands behind his head. He'd never had a woman cut his clothes off before. Not when he was fully conscious, anyway. Even that thought didn't break through the depth of his longing.

'This better not be your best T-shirt.' She tugged the hem out from under her, and snipped at it. The sound seemed like the tearing of all his inhibitions. Then the first long cut. He could feel the touch of cold steel against his stomach.

'Careful….' Joe swallowed the words. He knew she wouldn't cut him, and he didn't much care if she did. It was the newly born hope that he so wanted to preserve. And she could destroy it now, with one look.

'You trust me?' She slid her hand under his T-shirt, and he felt her fingers against his skin. Her mouth curved into the most beautiful smile he'd ever seen.

'Yeah. I trust you, honey.'

Carefully, slowly, she cut the T-shirt off him. Stopping to kiss his chest. Making sure that he knew she liked what she saw. More than that. Her body couldn't lie, and she was turned on by what she saw. Joe reached for her with trembling fingers, caressing her, and she cried out.

The scissors clattered onto the floor beside the bed. Her hands tugged at his boxer shorts, and Joe lifted his hips, so she could pull them off.

'Nice.' She kissed him on the lips. 'Very nice. Very big…'

He held her still on top of him, his hands clasped around her waist. 'That's all because of you…'

'Look…' She forced his head to one side, so he could not longer look straight at her. Then Joe realised that there was another mirror in the room, on top of the dressing table. She must have turned it slightly when she'd got up to light the candles, because instead of sitting straight it was trained right onto the bed. 'What do you see, Joe?'

'You and me…'

'Just that?' She smiled at him in the glass.

'Just that.' Nothing else. Two bodies, both taut and trembling, ready for each other. The scars were still there, but right now they didn't seem to matter.

He pulled her down so he could kiss her breasts. Heard her sigh, so he kept her right there, using his mouth to make her cry out. Once wasn't going to be enough, it never could be, and he kept going until every breath was a moan.

Her whole body was aching for his. She told him that. Neve was unused to telling anyone anything very much in bed, but he'd needed to hear it at first. And then it was like a glorious affirmation, building the heat between them until she felt drops of sweat prickling on her spine.

'What was I thinking?' He whispered the words against her ear. 'I love the feel of your skin against mine and I nearly...'

That didn't matter. Nothing mattered other than one thing. 'Now, Joe. Please...now.'

He flipped her over, with as much effort as it took to turn a page, his body taut and strong against hers. The sound of tearing fabric as he pulled her knickers off only added a delicious twist of urgency. When she felt his fingers, trailing down her belly, parting her legs, she almost blacked out from sheer sexual need. Her body responded almost immediately to his light, deft touch.

He kept the orgasm rolling. Didn't stop, just changed the rhythm. Kissed her, caressing her through the aftershocks and into a deeper need, one that could wait until they'd wrung the last drops of sensation out of each and every moment.

She flung one arm out, reaching for the condoms, and missed the box completely. His longer reach got them, and he tipped the box upside down on the bedside table, catching one of the foil packets up in his fingers.

Neve didn't even notice the break when he put the condom on because he was whispering in her ear. Words of one syllable that made it more than plain what he was about to do. Warm caresses that told her he was going to do it with feeling.

Slowly, he slid inside her. She moved convulsively and he shook his head, letting a little of his weight pin her immobile beneath him. 'Hold up there, sweetheart. I'm not going to manage long and slow if you keep this up.'

His olive skin against her pallor. The muscles of his shoulders and arms flexing as he moved. That conscious hesitation before each caress, which let her feel everything before he even touched her, and then again when he did.

He guided her legs a little higher, settling them around his waist and choking out her name as he did so. He slid his hand around her to the base of her spine and lifted a few inches, thrusting inside her again.

'Oh!' Suddenly the soft, warm pleasure spun into something more urgent. Joe's gaze was on her, watching every reaction, as he changed the angle slightly and thrust again. This time he got things more blissfully, agonisingly right than she had even realised was possible.

When she came for the second time it was like electricity running down his spine. As if somehow he could feel what she felt by some process of osmosis, or mind-melding, or whatever the hell else it was that seemed to bind their souls together. And then his whole world seemed to disappear into a vortex of wanting her, turning him into a mess of sheer feeling.

It took a conscious effort not to collapse on top of her in the almost overwhelming aftermath. Carefully, shakily he rolled them both over onto their sides, covering her with the duvet, and she snuggled in tight against him.

He let out a sigh of pure contentment. Somehow the

most beautiful woman in the world found him attractive. He couldn't account for it, but he wasn't going to argue with it. Maybe, just maybe this could work. He could try to settle, piece together his life. He had made a plan out of having no plan, so far. Maybe that could change.

He was clutching at straws, but straws were all he had right now. He watched her sleep for a while, and when she stirred he watched her wake.

'Hey, you…' She curled her arm around his neck, pulling him in for a kiss. 'How long…?'

'Half an hour. You okay?'

'Better than okay.' She grinned up at him. 'Are you hungry?'

'Yeah I'm hungry. For you…'

She bumped her cheek against his shoulder. Didn't care that it was resting against puckered, scarred flesh. She didn't seem to even notice it. 'What are you, superman?'

'I said I was still hungry. Didn't say I was in any state to do anything about it.'

Neve smiled lazily up at him. He liked the way she could hardly keep her eyes open. She was soft, and warm, and it made him feel good to think that their lovemaking had unravelled her as much as it had him.

'Be sure to let me know when you are.'

He chuckled, smoothing her shining curls back from her brow, and she shifted a little against him until she found a position she liked, her limbs tangled with his. He held her while she drifted off to sleep again.

Later, much later Joe carefully moved her head from his chest and got out of bed. The air was icy cold. He slipped into his jeans and sweater, and made his way downstairs to the kitchen. A quick reconnoitre of the refrigerator, and he decided that bacon sandwiches were just the thing.

When he returned to the bedroom, wafting the scent of the food in her direction, she reacted by wrinkling her nose slightly. Joe smiled to himself, murmuring quietly into her ear.

Her eyes snapped open. 'You, Joe Lamont, are an angel.'

He grinned, putting the plate down on the bedside table and handing her a napkin.

'Take your clothes off...'

'Before or after I pass you a sandwich?' He raised an eyebrow in query.

'Ow...I love bacon sandwiches and I'm so hungry...' She teased him for a moment, then her earnest blue gaze found his. 'Before. I like to see you naked. Unless you have a problem with that?'

Not one. In fact, this was the first time he'd felt anything apart from hesitancy about undressing in the last eighteen months. He took off his sweater and jeans, and she smiled, that beautiful smile that made him feel like a million dollars.

'Better?'

'Much. Bring the sandwiches with you when you come back to bed....'

CHAPTER NINE

THEY ATE AND TALKED. Drank coffee and talked. Embraced, in the comfort of her bed, which was so much warmer with him in it, and talked.

'I got it at auction. It's old...' He'd asked her about the brass bedstead.

'It's great. Really solid.' He tested his strength against one of the bars.

'Yeah. Took me days to clean up, but I was really pleased with it. You know the auction house just outside Cryersbridge?' He nodded. 'I got nearly all my furniture there.'

She'd furnished her home with good-quality, second-hand furniture, all restored and polished up to look better than new. It wasn't a low-budget option, it would have been cheaper to buy from a furniture warehouse, but she'd chosen well and the pieces matched the style of the old farmhouse, solid and attractive.

'So...what? You threw away all your old furniture?' She never seemed to talk about what she'd done before she'd come here. She talked about London, her family, her childhood. She talked about medical school, but the years in between then and now hardly seemed to exist for her.

'I was staying with my parents for six months before

I moved up here.' She drew the bedcovers around her as if she was suddenly cold.

'And before that?'

Neve obviously had an issue with whatever had come before that. She was almost like a cornered animal, suddenly motionless with terror. But he'd asked now, and dropping the subject wasn't going to make her feel any better. The only thing he could do was make the answer a bit easier. Joe took a wild guess. 'I imagine you probably lived with someone…?'

She nodded, watching his face. 'I was married… There hasn't been anyone for two years…'

A jealous guy, then. In Joe's experience, women didn't get that defensive without some reason.

'I have an admission to make to you, too.' He looked at her with mock solemnity.

'Yes?'

'You're not my first either…'

She was laughing now, and that was just the way he wanted her. Not worrying about what he'd think of her past. History was history, and he was the one holding her tonight.

'You mean you haven't been saving yourself for me?' She nudged at his shoulder playfully. 'I'm disappointed.'

The thought occurred to him that he just might have done, if he'd known. 'No. I've had a girlfriend before… two, maybe.'

'I bet you've had hundreds.' She ran her hand across his chest in a gesture of possessiveness, and he was surprised at how much it pleased him.

He pretended to count on his fingers. 'Not quite that many.'

'Never…married, though?' She almost managed to make the question sound casual.

'No. I moved around a lot.' Joe had never been short of female company, but he'd always put his career first. When that had come crashing down he'd been left with nothing. He reached for her, pulling her against him, the touch of her skin somehow reassuring.

'Are you hungry?' She picked up his arm, looking at his watch. 'It's getting late.'

'Starving. I'll cook for you, if you like.'

She considered the idea. 'You cook?'

'Of course I do. I eat don't I? Trust me, once you've tasted my crème brûlée, you'll be putty in my hands.'

'I wouldn't bank on it.'

'You don't like crème brûlée?'

She tapped one finger on his chest, as if to catch his attention. 'I'm not putty in anyone's hands.'

It had just been a throwaway comment, but she seemed to have taken it seriously. Joe caught her hand, pressing her fingers to his lips in a gesture of goodwill. 'I'll remember that. Although I can't promise that I won't find I'm putty in *your* hands from time to time.'

She ignored the observation. 'And talking about ground rules...'

'Were we?'

'I just...' She sat up in the bed, wrapping one end of the duvet around her body. 'I'm not the clingy type. I really like being with you Joe, but I'm not going to ask you to spend every waking moment with me. You don't have to take responsibility for me.'

Somehow he felt deflated. Joe told himself that this was what he wanted. He was in no position to make any promises to anyone about where he'd be or what he'd be doing in six months' time. But on another level he was upset. He cared for her. He wanted to take care of her, and that entailed a bit more than just meeting up a couple of nights a week for sex. He adjusted the thought slightly. Amazing sex.

'Does that mean I can't cook for you?'

'No, of course not.'

'Or that you can't cook for me?'

'No. I just don't want you to feel that I'm dependent on you...' She shrugged. 'You know.'

No, not really. It had never occurred to Joe that Neve was dependent on him. She was fiercely, gloriously independent, and that was one of the things he respected about her.

'You're worrying about nothing, honey. Aren't things just fine the way they are?'

She leaned in for a kiss, and the baffling question of what on earth they'd been talking about for the last few minutes seemed suddenly unimportant. 'We'll eat, then?'

'Yeah. Is it okay for me to put my clothes on?'

She pursed her lips, as if thinking about the proposition. 'Just for a little while. I wouldn't want you to catch a chill.'

Waking up with Joe was lovely. This wasn't the first time she'd woken curled in his arms, but this time they couldn't love each other back to sleep again. She had to go to work.

Even so, the dash for the shower and a rushed breakfast was far more fun when Joe was around. And when Maisie phoned through the list of calls for the day, Neve didn't care how long it was, just that it meant that Joe would stay with her.

He wasn't like her ex-husband. Joe wasn't jealous or controlling and he didn't seem to feel the need to micromanage every part of her life. But, then, Matthew hadn't been like that when she'd first met him. Neve had often wondered how much of a part she'd played in the catastrophic change, which had turned the man she'd married into the man she'd divorced.

This time she had to do better. She'd married Matthew and then allowed him to walk all over her, submissive to his wants and needs. This time she'd be different. She'd make the ground rules clear from the very start and stick to them. She mustn't give Joe any reason to change.

But nothing could take the bright sheen off today. The feeling of being fully awake, having been half-asleep for such a long time. She and Joe worked doggedly together through her list of patients, and Neve left the tough questions until later.

'So we're done? Would you like to go and get something to eat?' They'd driven to all corners of Neve's allotted area so far today, and they were now on the south side, closest to the surgery and the town.

'I got a text from Maisie just now. Just one more to go.'

He nodded, keeping to himself whatever disappointment he felt at the thought of dinner being once more postponed. Another way that he wasn't like Matthew. Matthew would have phoned ahead, booked a table at the restaurant of his choice, and if anyone had upset his plans there would have been hell to pay.

Today was turning into a game of spot the difference. Neve hadn't given Matthew so much thought in months. She followed Joe to the car and consulted her phone, reading through the details of her next patient. 'Infected tattoo.'

'Where?'

'I don't know, Maisie didn't say. But apparently it's very swollen and beginning to suppurate.'

Joe rolled his eyes. 'I meant where's the house, not the tattoo. I'm the driver, remember?'

'Ah. Silly me.' She grinned up at him. It seemed that the separation of their roles was a joking matter now, instead of something to argue about. 'Only about two miles up the road. Here's the address.'

The snow had been melting all day, and driving conditions were getting easier. The two miles were accomplished with no delay and they drew up outside a large house, screened by trees and settled into the side of a hillside. Obviously newly built, it was a clever mix of local materials with modern design, the soaring glass windows framed with stone and the unusually angled roof clad with slate.

They stood for a while in the huge, glass-sided porch before the door was opened by a young man dressed only in pyjama bottoms, who looked as if he had just woken up.

'Dr Neve Harrison. I've come to see Andrew Martin.' Neve smiled at the youth, who seemed almost puzzled to find that someone was standing on the doorstep.

'Yeah. I'm Andrew.'

'Can we come in?' Joe stepped forward, and Andrew shrugged and nodded.

Andrew turned, and Neve caught her breath. On his shoulder blade was a large, swollen lump. At one time there might have been a design there, but that was now obscured by scabs and oozing sores. She flipped a glance at Joe, who took Andrew's arm, supporting him into the lounge.

It seemed a bit of a pity to sit him down on the plush leather sofa, but Joe didn't hesitate. Andrew slumped forward, his head resting on his knees, while Neve snapped on a pair of surgical gloves, handing another pair to Joe, who took them as automatically as they were offered but didn't put them on.

'What do you think?' As usual, he was standing back, not expressing any opinion of his own.

'Could be a reaction to the ink. It looks as if there's red and blue in there and they're the most likely colours to cause an allergic reaction. Or, more likely, it's infected.' She tapped the side of Andrew's face gently. 'Andrew... Andrew.'

'Yeah...'

'How long ago did you have this tattoo done?'

'Last week. Me and my mates went into town, and we all had one.'

'Is there anyone else here, Andrew?'

'Nah. My folks are away on holiday.'

Neve could smell stale alcohol on his breath. She mouthed to Joe to go and look in the kitchen and he nodded.

'Ow!' Andrew flinched when Neve gently touched the edge of the lump, to feel its consistency.

'Looks pretty painful.'

'Well, yeah.' Andrew's voice was heavily laced with sleepy sarcasm.

'Okay. Who called the surgery?' She couldn't imagine that Andrew had. He could hardly string a sentence together.

'My girlfriend. She's got a job in a bar. Had to go to work.'

Joe appeared in the doorway, and she met him there. 'The kitchen's full of beer bottles, pizza boxes and ashtrays. Smells like marijuana.'

'Right. Well, either he's got the mother of all hang-overs, he's doped up to the eyeballs or he's got an infection.' Neve sighed. 'Probably all three. His skin feels warm to the touch.'

'Hospital?'

'Yes, we can't leave him here.' Neve pulled out her phone.

'We'll take him.'

'Is that okay? It'll probably be faster.' Neve had heard that the emergency services were still very stretched, and it was likely to be a long wait.

'Yeah. If he throws up on my back seat, I'll send his parents the cleaning bill.' Joe quirked his mouth downwards and strode towards Andrew. 'Come on, mate, wake up. We're going for a ride.'

Neve called Maisie and sent Joe to find some clothes for Andrew. The lad protested mightily when Neve tried to position a temporary dressing over the sore on his back, and Joe was suddenly there, grabbing his flailing arm and gently holding him still. Then Joe got him into his clothes, and together they supported Andrew into the car, Neve making him as comfortable as she could on the back seat, while Joe wound the seat belt around him.

'Okay?'

'Yeah. Let's go.' Neve settled into the seat next to Andrew, and Joe slid the car out of its parking spot and back onto the road.

Andrew had been seen almost immediately after Neve had briefed the triage nurse at the hospital. She found Joe in the A and E waiting room, reading a magazine about agricultural machinery, which someone had obviously left behind.

'What's the story?' He hadn't betrayed any clinical interest in the sore on Andrew's back when it had been right there in front of him, but it appeared that now was a good time to catch up on the details.

'They agree with me that it's an infection. They're keeping him in tonight because he's so out of it, and it looks as if he's developed a mild case of sepsis.'

Joe nodded. 'Good. Any news from Maisie?'

'Yeah, she's managed to contact Andrew's mother on a mobile number in the family's medical records. They'll drive back from London first thing in the morning.'

He put the magazine down on the chair next to him, stretching his arms. 'So are we done now?'

'Yes. Although would you mind if we popped in to the surgery? I could do with restocking my medical bag with a few things, and as we're so close…'

'No problem.' His mouth twitched into the smile that he'd given her last night. 'I can have a cup of tea with Maisie. Thank her for asking me to drive the most beautiful doctor in town.'

'You will not!'

She saw hurt in his eyes, but he covered it quickly with a grin. 'Ashamed of me?'

In her desperate attempts not to make any of the mistakes she'd made in the past she'd forgotten that Joe was vulnerable too. Neve stepped forward, between his outstretched legs, planting a kiss on his cheek. No one in the crowded waiting room looked round, they all had their own problems to think about. But the public acknowledgement was still thrilling.

'No. I just want you to be my little secret for a while…'

'*Little* secret?'

She leaned a little further forward, feeling his hands

around her waist, supporting her weight. 'Great big beautiful secret,' she whispered in his ear, and he chuckled.

'Yeah. That's more like it.' He dropped a businesslike kiss on her cheek, and stood up. 'As we're in town, we could get something to eat and pick up some shopping if you like. The big stores are all open late this week.'

'Christmas shopping…?' Neve had hardly thought about when she was going to do the rest of her Christmas shopping. There was still another week to go, and she'd been so busy for the last couple of weeks.

'Most of my presents are already on their way to Canada, but I still need to pick up a few bits and pieces. How about you?'

Neve shrugged. 'I want to get a drill for my dad. Mum says his old one is making a funny noise.'

Joe grinned. 'Great. There's a DIY place not far from here. We could go there, if you want.'

'Just to have a look maybe. Not to buy.' It must have been apparent that many of the Christmas presents her family had received over the last few years had been chosen by Matthew, but her mum and dad had pretended not to notice. Neve had promised herself that this year she would choose her dad's present on her own, even if she knew nothing about power tools and was worried that she'd get the wrong thing.

'Sure. I'm always up for browsing around the DIY store.' He grinned at her. 'Particularly with you.'

Neve might as well have stayed in the car for all the notice that Matthew had ever taken of her when they'd been out shopping. But Joe seemed so different.

She should stop the comparisons, even if Joe did come off better every time. Joe was his own man, just as she wanted so badly to be her own woman. She'd fought so hard not to let Matthew define her, and she shouldn't let him define Joe either.

'The DIY store it is, then. I'll look at the drills, and you can look at everything else.'

CHAPTER TEN

FIRST THEY CALLED in at the surgery, and then went to the little Italian restaurant just around the corner for a hurried meal. Then they got down to the serious business of shopping, making for the glittering windows of one of the larger department stores.

'Right.' He stopped short inside the swing doors, apologising as someone elbowed him out of the way and rubbing his hands together as if this was a foray into the unknown. 'I know what I want to get.'

'That's a start...' Neve took the scrap of paper that he'd extracted from his wallet and focussed on the writing. A round, woman's hand. And this perfume was a classic.

'It's for Edie. I asked her daughter what I should get.'

'This is pretty expensive...'

He grinned. 'Yeah, that's what her daughter said. But I want to get Edie something nice, she's been very good to me. And she can't really afford this on her pension.'

Neve smiled up at him. 'You know what, you're a really nice guy.'

He gave her a look of mock horror. 'Be quiet! If Edie gets that idea into her head, I'll be done for. Do you know where the perfume is?'

Neve swept her gaze over the sea of heads, located the

perfume counter and beckoned for him to follow her. 'It should be somewhere here…'

While she methodically inspected each of the displays, Joe was picking up random tester bottles, sniffing tentatively at the tops.

'You have to spray it if you want to know what it's like.' She leaned towards him. Even with the heavy scent of cosmetics and perfume hanging in the air around them, she could discern his warm, clean smell. Like a creature sniffing out its mate.

'Think I'll pass on that.' He put the bottle down quickly.

'Not on yourself…' She sprayed a tester strip, waving it under his nose.

'Ugh! That's horrible!' He grabbed another bottle at random, spraying it onto a second strip.

The scent's strong statement hit her like a punch in the face. She'd never liked it, but it was Matthew's favourite. And the most shaming part of it all was that Neve had let him dictate that she wear it all the time.

'Hmm…' He shrugged, discarding the bottle, and a sudden calculating glint showed in his eyes. 'So which one do *you* like? What do you wear when you're off duty?'

'The same as when I'm on duty. Nothing.' Neve was done with having anyone else buy personal things for her. Clothes, shoes, perfume. That was her territory now.

'Ah.' He bent towards her, and she felt the scrape of his stubble against her neck. 'That's why you always smell so gorgeous.'

'Stop it.' She loved it, but Christmas shopping was serious business. 'Focus, will you?'

'Right.' He scanned the length of the display in front of them. 'Is that it?'

An assistant appeared out of nowhere, flashing Joe a glittering smile. 'These, sir?' She spread manicured fingers over the range, from relatively inexpensive to don't-even-think-about-it.

'How about that one?' Joe pointed to a generously sized bottle, somewhere in the middle, and turned to Neve. 'I don't want to embarrass her...'

'I think it's a lovely present. Although I imagine that Edie will tell you that you've got the wrong thing.'

''Course she will. That's half the fun.' He turned to the assistant, pulling his wallet out of his pocket.

'Gift-wrapped, sir?'

'No, thanks. I want to wrap it myself.'

The assistant threw him a more spontaneous smile. 'Would you like one of these?' She reached under the counter and drew out a small tester pack, prettily packaged and containing tiny amounts of six different perfumes.

'Oh. Thanks very much.' Joe took the pack, stared at it, and handed it awkwardly over to Neve. 'That's probably more your department.'

She took the pack and stowed it in her handbag. 'Thanks.'

He nodded, and turned his attention back to the assistant, handing her his bank card. Neve curled her fingers around the packet in her bag. The scents looked nice, and she might just try one of them. But it would be *her* choice when she did.

Joe brightened considerably once paper and ribbon had been chosen and they were heading for the DIY store. He seemed to have the geography of the large tin shed well fixed in his mind, and Neve followed him past seemingly endless shelves of paint and tools until they got to a small enclosure, where an assistant guarded the power tools.

'You're looking for something, sir?' The assistant approached Joe.

'Not me. The lady's looking for a drill.'

'Ah.' The assistant glanced at her and walked over to the smallest drill in the display. 'Something like this, perhaps?'

Joe didn't look very impressed. 'What about this one?' He ran his finger along a large, complicated-looking model.

'Very heavy for a woman.' The assistant was still speaking to Joe, as if Neve didn't exist.

Joe seemed to have already dismissed the man's advice and didn't bother to explain. 'Well, perhaps we'll try a couple out and get back to you.'

With that Joe turned to Neve, beckoning her over to where he was standing. 'What do you think?'

'I don't know, really. Which one do you think's best?' She could hear his opinion at least.

Joe puffed out a breath, as if the question was a hard one. 'It depends on what kind of work your dad wants to do.'

'Nothing in particular. Drilling holes in the wall to hang pictures. He built a garden shed once.'

'Well, these are two good general-purpose ones. Do you want to pick them up, see how they feel?'

The question threw Neve completely for a moment. *She* should see how they felt?

'Yes… Yeah, I do.'

Joe grinned, signalling to the assistant to unlock the

demonstration models. Then he dismissed the man again, and put one of the drills into Neve's hands.

'How am I meant to hold it?'

'Put your finger on the trigger... No, you'll need to be able to reach the trigger lock as well. Like this...'

Suddenly he was at her back, his arms stretching around her, his hands over hers, holding the drill. Instinctively she moved in closer.

'That's it. How does that feel?'

It felt great. His arms around her. His taut, unyielding body at her back.

'Lovely.'

'The drill.' She could feel his breath on the back of her neck. 'Focus...'

'Oh. Yes. I don't really have anything to compare it with.'

'All right, try the other one.' Joe reached for the second drill, putting it into her hands.

'Oh, this is better. More balanced.'

Joe nodded. 'Right, well, there are a few other considerations.'

Corded or cordless, what kinds of bits to buy, power rating, speeds, gears, torque. There was much more to it all than Neve had suspected, and Joe seemed to have a handle on it all.

'So, which one do you think?'

He couldn't have said a nicer thing if he'd tried. But even though Joe had given her all the information, she was still undecided. 'Do you mind if I just look at them all again quickly?'

'Take your time. I'll be over there.' He pointed to a display of unlikely-looking tools, which Neve couldn't fathom the use of.

She made her choice, sorted through the boxes to find one that wasn't crushed or dented, and found Joe immersed in conversation with another man who was browsing the shelves.

'Decided?'

'Yes. What do you think of this one?'

Joe gave the box she was carrying a glance. 'I think he'll really like it.'

It was late when Neve carried her precious parcel out of the DIY store. Joe had automatically reached for it, the way he always did when there was anything to carry, and had grinned when she'd snatched it from him. This she was carrying herself.

They didn't discuss where they were going, just drove. Out of the lights of the city, plunging into the darkness of the country lanes, where only the car's headlights illuminated their path. When Neve had first come here, the darkness on roads without streetlights had been intimidating. Now it was the bright lights of the city that seemed wrong, polluting the atmosphere and blocking the soft glow of the stars on a clear night.

The car began to shudder, and Joe cursed under his breath, easing his foot off on the accelerator and bringing the vehicle to a gentle halt.

'What's the matter?'

'It feels like a puncture. Stay there, I'll go and see.'

'Okay.'

The rosy glow retreated a little and Neve got out of the car. 'Do you have—?'

She slipped forward and suddenly she was falling into the darkness. Cushioned by her bulky clothes and the deep snow, she rolled down the bank beside the road.

She was vaguely aware of Joe's shout, and then she hit the bottom.

She lifted her head, and there was Joe, at the top of the bank, a dark shadow behind a torch beam, which urgently swept the bank, before coming to rest on her.

'You okay?'

'Yes, I'm all right. The snow broke my fall.' She struggled to her feet and then slipped over again and decided to stay put until Joe had found something else to do other than stare at her.

'I said to stay there.' His voice was edged with frustration.

'I heard you. I'm not in the habit of obeying instructions without question.' She folded her arms across her chest defiantly.

'So I've noticed. Are you going to get up?' He had the demeanour of someone who could wait.

'Not just yet.'

'You'll get soaked.'

'That's why I'm wearing waterproofs. So I don't get wet.'

Suddenly he moved, sliding sideways down the bank, the arc of powdered snow that flew from his boots glistening in the waving torchlight and spraying her jacket. He was still on his feet when he reached the bottom.

'Stop showing off.'

'Then get up.' He grinned, holding up a handful of snow and training the torch onto it, just in case she'd missed his intention. 'Or else…'

There was only one possible answer to that. 'Or else what?' Neve flopped back into the snow. 'I thought you had a tyre to change.'

'I thought you were going to stay in the car.' He

planted his feet on either side of her hips then dropped to his knees, brandishing the snowball.

'Don't you dare, Joe.'

Too late. His eyes, the curve of his lips dared everything. And she dared him right back, her body melting, ready to be moulded into whatever shape he wanted.

He ditched the snowball, pinning her arms down over her head. 'You think I don't dare?'

'I think you *do* dare.'

So did she.

He bent, kissing her. She'd been missing that kiss all day. Not the brief brush of his lips against hers but a searching, demanding onslaught that melted the last remains of her resistance. His gloved hand slid across the outside of her waterproofs, finding the exact place where her breast was under layers of clothing.

The torch had gone out and they were in complete darkness. She felt his hand pulling her knees apart, and then his body settling onto hers.

'You can't. Not in this temperature.'

His chuckle sounded in her ear and his stubble scraped her cheek. 'I like a woman who knows the limits of human physiology.' His body began to move against hers, a delicious friction that could only arouse, not satisfy. 'What about the limits of human imagination…?'

She was there already, her body trembling for his touch. Neve groaned with frustration.

'So you'll help me change the tyre, then? Hold the torch steady and hand me the lug wrench when I ask for it?'

'Yeah.' Anything…

'And you'll come back to my place tonight?'

She hadn't intended to. He seemed to sense her hesitation and his hand slid to the back of her leg, pulling it up and around his hips. 'I'll make it worth your while.'

'I know.' She felt a tiny, cold trickle at the back of her shoulder and shuddered. 'By the way, I think the high-performance waterproofing's just stopped performing.'

He was standing over her almost before she could even register that he was gone, pulling her to her feet and brushing the snow off her back. 'Are you okay?'

Stupid question. 'Fine. Hurry up with that tyre.'

CHAPTER ELEVEN

THE THAW WAS well under way now. When Neve woke the following morning the snow in Leminster High Street, outside Joe's window, was almost gone. And even when they drove out into the countryside the roads were clear, the snowploughs and the warmer weather having done their job.

They were finished by five in the evening, and this time Neve was less of a walkover. Tomorrow was Saturday and she had the weekend off. She told Joe that she needed some sleep and he made no comment, other than quirking his lips down in an expression of disappointment.

'You fancy the movies tomorrow afternoon, then? Is there anything you want to see?' He seemed unwilling to leave until he had a firm date fixed for when he'd see her again.

'Yes, a couple of films. Why don't you come round for lunch?'

The familiar ritual of getting out of the car and letting Joe carry her bags to the door followed, then a kiss, light on her lips, as if anything more would be too much of a temptation.

'Goodnight, honey.'

They'd been together now, non-stop, for more than sixty hours. Almost enough time to work a virus out of your system, but Joe was more tenacious than that and she wasn't even beginning to work up a resistance to him. Leaving him was more difficult than she'd thought.

'Goodnight, Joe.' She'd see him tomorrow. And tonight she would get some sleep.

The house was clean, a bunch of flowers stood on the kitchen table, and the potatoes were peeled and ready in a pan on the stove. Neve had woken at her usual time that morning, had got out of bed and been unable to linger over breakfast. At some point she'd probably sleep for twelve hours straight, but right now she felt more awake than she'd been for months. Years.

At twelve sharp she heard the doorbell. Dropped the knife that she had just used to skin two large onions and ran to the door.

'Hey, there.' He grinned.

She'd missed that smile. Missed his warm body next to her in the bed, which was far too cold to sleep in without him. The sofa bed in the kitchen, which had seemed so cosy before, now felt deeply unsatisfactory.

'Hi.' She stood back from the door and he bent to pick up the post from the mat, handing it to her before he tramped through to the kitchen. No kiss.

He remedied that as soon as she'd put the bundle of letters down on the table, catching her in his arms and moulding her against him. 'I missed you last night.'

'Yeah? I would have thought you'd be sleeping like a baby...'

'Nope. I was thinking of you.' He was clean-shaven

this morning, his cheek smooth against hers, still cold from the air outside.

'What were you thinking?'

He kissed her. Yeah, she'd been thinking that too…

'I was wondering what you were going to make me for lunch today.'

'Oh, really?'

'It's important.'

She unclasped his hands from behind her, walking to the stove and picking up the frying pan. 'Bangers and mash.'

'Nice. Local sausages?'

'Of course. From the farmers' market.'

Joe grinned. 'You really are my kind of woman.'

Neve laughed. 'And you really are easy, aren't you.'

'Me?' He put his hand on his chest with an expression of disbelief. 'I'll have you know that I'm not even slightly easy. Are you making onion gravy?'

'I thought you might take charge of that.' Neve walked to the table, sorting through her letters. A couple of bills, which she put to one side for later, and a bunch of coloured envelopes.

'Why don't you open them?' He nodded towards the mantelpiece, which was already two deep in Christmas cards. 'I think you've got about a square inch of spare space up there.'

She grinned and started tearing the envelopes open. 'Ah. That's nice.' A shower of glitter fell from the front of the card and she brushed it off the table. 'Auntie Maureen.' She showed him the inside of the card.

He nodded in approval, taking the card and looking at the snow scene on the front. 'Have you got a tree?'

'Not yet. I've been too busy.'

'You want me to pick one up for you? I could go on Monday, if you're not going to need me to drive you.'

'I don't think I will. We're planning to resume the normal rota on Monday so I'll be over at the surgery. And I thought I might give a tree a miss this year as I'm going back to London for Christmas.'

'That's only for a couple of days, though. Christmas lasts longer than that.'

Christmas seemed to have already started, and would probably last right through till March at this rate. 'Okay, then. If it's no trouble, thanks.'

Neve tore open the last of the envelopes. A thick, heavy card, which looked like something that a company would send, well designed, tasteful and completely lacking in any sparkle. When she flipped it open she felt the smile slide from her face and crash to the floor.

Happy Christmas.
    I saw you on TV the other day, and realised that
I love you more than ever.
    Let's talk in the New Year.
Matthew

Matthew's precise, rather too artful script, with a flourish at the end of his name and two kisses. Neve closed the card and then decided she didn't want it anywhere near her. Or Joe. As casually as she could she tore it into two, walking over to the kitchen waste bin and dropping it inside. Then, for good measure, she threw the onion skins from the chopping board on top of it.

'I'd better start on lunch if we're going to get to the pictures in time.'

He didn't reply, and when Neve turned to look at Joe

his eyes were thoughtful. She almost wanted him to ask, but perhaps he didn't want to know. She turned back to the onions, slicing them into halves.

He was quiet on his feet when he wanted to be. She didn't hear him cross the room and Neve started when he wound his arms around her waist from behind. 'Anything you want to talk about?' He brushed a kiss against the back of her head.

'Not really.'

He took the knife out of her hand and put it down on the chopping board, turning her round to face him. 'And I suppose that's just the onions...' His finger brushed at her cheek.

'Actually, it is.' The card from Matthew had surprised and unsettled her. Nothing more. She had no tears for him, and no love left either. If he got in touch with her again, she'd tell him so.

'Then you won't mind telling me who the card was from.'

That was different. How Joe might feel about the card *was* important. But Neve couldn't lie to him.

'It was from my ex-husband. I didn't even know he had my address.'

'You didn't tell him where you are?'

'When I left London I wanted to leave my marriage behind. It wasn't as if I was talking to him about anything else.' Neve heaved a sigh. 'He saw me on TV doing that stupid interview, and I suppose it's not too difficult to find someone once you know their general whereabouts.'

He nodded, his face grave. 'He hurt you that much?'

'It's history, Joe.'

'Yeah. But sometimes the past leaves scars...'

'Yes.' Her fingers found his lips, trying to brush the words away. 'I'm sorry, Joe.'

'Don't be. It was just something that happened.' His face softened again. 'Sometimes I wake in the night and it's as if I'm right back there.'

Neve caught her breath. 'You said you didn't remember...'

He shook his head, as if that was a minor detail. 'What I'm saying is that when you're hurt, physically or emotionally, the shock of it stays with you. You think you've healed, you may look as if you've healed, but it takes a while before your emotions catch up with that fact.'

She hugged him tight. There weren't any words. None that made much sense anyway. She felt his chest heave as he took a breath.

'Don't you think it's time to talk about it?'

Joe had watched Neve tentatively taking hold of this new relationship, acting sometimes as if it might burn her. He knew that she'd been hurt and that at some point it was all going to come to a head. It seemed that now was that point.

'What do you say I make a cup of tea?' There was something to be said for Edie's obsession with the perfect cup of tea—it served to lessen the tension a little. And while he was busying himself, it seemed to give Neve some time to think. As soon as he sat down she started to talk.

'I married Matthew when I was twenty-three, not even out of medical school. He was intelligent and charming. He'd made a lot of money in property when he was very young, and he wanted to give me everything.'

'Sounds like a good start.' Joe reached for the teapot and began to pour the tea.

'Yeah, I thought so too. Then the moods started. This little thing wasn't right or I hadn't looked smart enough for his friends. He was working pretty hard and I thought that he was just under stress.'

Alarm bells started to ring at the back of Joe's head. He ignored them and nodded her on.

'Before long he was dictating practically everything. Where we lived, who we saw, what kinds of things I wore. My perfume…' The words seemed to stick in her throat.

'And so you left him.' Joe reckoned that was a pretty safe assumption.

'No. I should have done, I know, but I wanted my marriage to work. I thought it was my fault. Can you understand that?'

'No.'

She flushed suddenly, bright red, tears forming in her eyes. Then came the anger. Anger seemed to be Neve's answer to everything that touched her personally, and Joe imagined it was what had got her through. It drove her to her feet, her face distorted. 'Then you should go.'

'Wait. Hold up there…' Joe was on his feet too. 'Will you just sit down? Please.'

'You either get it or you don't, Joe. I can't explain…' Neve sat back down with a bump, glaring at him.

'What I don't understand is why a guy would want to change anything about you.'

'Stop being nice.'

'And stop being so damn angry, Neve. You're an intelligent, capable woman and you push me away because of what another guy's done.'

'I know. I'm sorry.' She stared at him, one lonely tear tricking down the side of her face.

'What? What is it, Neve?' The suspicion of something dark throbbed insistently in his head, making him feel sick to his stomach. 'Did he ever hurt you?'

'He…' The dark red flush of her cheeks was like his own scars, a badge of shame at having been hurt.

'Okay.' He reached across the table, his hands trembling as he took hers. 'You took me as I am. We can do this together.'

He steadied his gaze on hers. Somewhere, deep in her eyes, he found the strength to stay calm and just listen to what she had to say.

She took a deep breath. 'I was pregnant. We didn't plan it, but I was so happy. I thought Matt would be too, but he said it wasn't the right time. He reckoned it was best for me to leave it a few years, get more established with my career, and then…then *he'd* think about it. I didn't see it at the time but he was just terrified that someone else might take his place. That he wouldn't be my top priority any more.'

Joe's felt his lip curl. 'His loss. His weakness…'

'My weakness, too. I knew in my heart that our home wasn't the place to bring up a child but I tried to persuade Matt. We argued about it for weeks, and it was the one thing I never backed down on. Then one night I told him I was leaving. He punched me in the face.'

Rage. All Joe could think about was finding this guy and… But punching the walls because he couldn't get his hands on the brute who had hurt her was the last thing that Neve needed from him right now. Slowly he reached out, brushing the side of her face. 'What happened then?'

'I ran. He was very angry and he grabbed hold of me

but I managed to get away from him. I got into my car and drove away... I shouldn't have been driving, one of my eyes was beginning to swell, but...'

'You were protecting your child.'

'It seemed like that at the time. I was turning into my parents' road when a kid on a motorcycle shot out in front of me out of nowhere. I swerved to avoid him and went into someone's front wall.'

'You were hurt?'

'I wasn't going very fast and the airbag saved me from anything but a jolt. But my face was bleeding and someone called an ambulance and they took me to hospital. My mum told them I was pregnant and they checked me out and said everything was fine...but two days later I lost my baby.'

Joe had already guessed that she must have lost the baby. But still there were no words.

'I'm so sorry.'

'Thank you.' She gave a trembling smile and Joe almost choked with emotion. 'When Matthew came to see me and said it was all for the best, that we could put everything behind us and start again, I threw him out. After that, my dad wouldn't let him into the house.'

'I'm glad your parents were there to support you.'

She pressed her lips together. 'I should take my share of the blame, too.'

How did she work that one out? 'You know, don't you, that it's unlikely the car accident caused your miscarriage. In the first trimester the baby's very well protected...'

'That's not the point, Joe. If I'd left when I first knew I was pregnant, there's a chance...' She shook her head.

'You can go around in circles like that for ever, Neve.'

In his moment of greatest need Joe found himself cling-ing to the training he'd been given, the profession that he had promised he would never again practise. 'As a doc-tor, I could tell you all the statistics, all the probabilities. You know them as well as I do.'

She looked at him steadily. 'I thought you didn't admit to being a doctor any more.'

'Some things are more important than the rules you make for yourself. I won't let you believe that this was your fault.'

'How can you really know?'

'Because I know you, Neve. I know that you were thinking always of your child and that you did every-thing you could.'

'I can't forget, though…'

'Nor should you, ever. But grieving is a process. It's a way of making peace with the past so that you can move forward.'

Her gaze searched his face, as if looking for clues. Joe didn't have any. All he could do was be there for her.

'You know the two things I've always wanted were to be, a doctor and to be a mother…' She gave him a teary smile.

'Not a wife?' Joe wouldn't much blame her, after what she'd been through.

'Yeah, a wife too, one day. I didn't want to mention that in case I frightened you off.' She gave a little laugh-ing shrug, and suddenly the tension in the room broke.

'You don't frighten me…' The thought of hurting her suddenly terrified Joe.

She chuckled. 'I know. That's one of the things I like about you.'

'Well, I think you'd be a great mother. I already know

you're a great doctor.' Joe's heart began to thump in his chest. If the lesson from Neve's past told her that she'd married the wrong man, that she should move on and find someone who could be a good father to her children, the lesson from his told him that he wasn't that guy. He wasn't someone who could be trusted with the welfare of others.

But the hope on her face was so precious to him. He should concentrate on that and not his own doubts.

'Thank you. I really appreciate what you've said.'

'I just told you what I see.'

She rose from her chair and perched on his lap. Joe pulled her in close, allowing the happiness of having her in his arms block out everything else.

'You want to risk some lunch, then? Since I don't frighten you…' She smiled up at him.

'Yeah. Let's take a chance on it.'

CHAPTER TWELVE

THE HOURS HAD slid by, like honey on his tongue. Lunch, and then the drive into town for the cinema. But in the darkness of the auditorium it was impossible to keep himself from his thoughts any more. By the time the lights came back up he'd lost the plot of the movie but the scenario that had projected itself in his head was entirely clear to him.

'You're very quiet.' She nudged him gently in the ribs as they walked along the lane to her front gate. 'Didn't you like the film?'

'No, it was fine...' Joe had no feelings one way or the other about it.

'I thought the part about waiting for the information to download from the laptop was a bit much. If the guy had just tucked it under his arm and run off with it, he'd have been free and clear before the guards arrived.'

Joe felt himself smile, almost against his will. Neve obviously hadn't liked the film any more than the other movie-goers he'd heard talking about it on the way out. But she didn't let the little things in life get her down, she just smiled about them. He felt an overwhelming urge—no, a duty—not to quash that irrepressible optimism.

'I guess they had to get the chase over the rooftops

in somehow.' That was about the only part of the movie he remembered.

'No, you must have nodded off, that was later.' She took out her keys, letting them both into the house, and Joe followed her into the kitchen. 'Mind you, that chase over the roof was another thing. He'd have broken a leg, landing on the pavement after that fall, not just got up and run away...'

She stopped talking and looked up at him. He saw the concern grow in her face, the unmistakeable flash in her eyes that signalled she knew that something was wrong. 'Why don't you take your coat off, Joe?'

'I'm...not staying.' He had to be careful what he said. Neve was vulnerable, and he shouldn't make this all about her. It wasn't, it was all about him.

'That's okay.' Her mouth twitched downwards. 'You can have a cup of tea, though, can't you?'

The urge to say yes, to allow the evening to drift gently to a point where he would take her to bed and hold her for the last time, was almost irresistible. But Joe knew how to resist the irresistible. And however many other faults he might have, he'd never acted dishonestly just to slake his own libido.

'No. Neve, I think that we should take a break.'

Her hands clenched tightly together, making a small wringing motion. He could almost see the cogs whirring in her head. Dammit, she was doing just what he didn't want her to do and blaming herself.

'That's...that's okay. Whatever you want, Joe.'

'It's not what I want. But I haven't been quite honest with you.'

She sat down at the kitchen table with a bump. 'There's nothing that you can say that I won't listen to...'

He knew that. But it was complicated, and now wasn't the time to burden her with it. 'I'm going back to Canada. In a couple of weeks' time.' The move came as news to him, as well as being an obvious shock to her. But the lease on his cottage was up in the new year, and he could pack up and move in a couple of days.

'I don't believe you.' She jutted her chin at him determinedly.

'I know I should have told you…'

'I don't believe you, Joe. I just don't believe that you'd sleep with me without telling me that.'

It was almost a compliment. It would have been unthinkable to Joe as well, and the fact that she knew that warmed him, when he shouldn't really have been taking any comfort from any of this.

'Neve, I—'

'Take your coat off.' A tear rolled down her cheek.

He couldn't deny her that one thing. He threw his jacket across the back of a chair and sat down opposite her. 'Neve, I am going to go back home. I've been thinking about things and…' Only the truth was going to do. A watered-down version, at least.

'When you told me about your marriage I was furious with the guy who hurt you. And then, when I thought about it, I realised that I'm no better than he is. I don't want to see you hurt again, you don't deserve that.'

'Then don't do it.'

'That's exactly why I'm doing this.' She'd played right into his hands but it gave Joe no pleasure. 'I can't give you the things you want and it would be dishonest of me to string you along.'

'Is that a way of telling me that you changed your mind?'

'No. It's a way of telling you that I can't give you what

you want. A lot happened to me when I was in the army, and I'm still struggling with that. I don't want to…I *can't* take responsibility for other lives any more.'

'You don't have to take responsibility for me.' She seemed to stiffen, starting to withdraw from him. It was the beginning of the end, and now Joe just wanted to get things over quickly.

'Look, I know that this is something that's way in the future. But one day, if things work out between us, it's natural to want to settle down and have children. I can't do that and I don't think I'll ever be able to. It just isn't in me any more.'

'I haven't asked you for that, Joe. We've known each other…what…two weeks. Less than that…' He could see in her eyes that she'd thought about it. He'd thought about it too. The connection between them was too strong not to have wondered if it might last a lifetime.

'I know. But if two weeks turned into two years, then my answer would still be the same. Then I'd be the guy who strung you along, who never told you. So I'm telling you now.'

She looked at him blankly. She knew as well as he did now that this wasn't going to work.

'You deserve—you need—someone who wants the same things as you, Neve.'

Anger flared in her eyes. The final denial of how much this hurt. 'Don't be so bloody arrogant. Who are you to tell me what I need?'

The man who loves you. The man who's going to leave you. Joe reached for his coat.

'If you go now, you don't come back.' She flung the words at him. That was okay. Joe knew that this was his fault already. He stood, hurrying for the front door before his courage failed him, half expecting, half wanting her to follow. She didn't. He closed the door behind him, got into his car, and drove away.

Thinking about it was useless. Something had happened to Joe, something he wouldn't talk about, and Neve couldn't work out what it was. She'd looked up PTSD in her medical books and on the internet, dwelling on the parts that mentioned feelings of guilt and inability to commit. But that wasn't the whole story. And he had it right in one respect. If their relationship had survived, if they'd got married, then Neve would have wanted children. If Joe hadn't, it might well have been a breaking point.

She'd feel better about this once she got it into perspective. She'd known Joe for a total of two weeks, then he'd made it clear that he didn't want to take things any further. It really didn't qualify as the romance of the century, and mooning around as if it was was plain stupid. Three days at home with her family, over Christmas, would stop her from thinking about him for every waking moment and dreaming about him when she finally succumbed to sleep.

The week dragged by in a numb succession of coughs, colds and sprains, and finally it was Friday morning, Christmas Eve. Neve was up early to finish her packing, ready to catch the train down to London at midday. The bedroom was cold, and when Neve opened the curtains to peer outside, she realised why. From the look of the lane outside, it had been snowing all night.

'Damn!' Possibly not the most festive of reactions, but she had to travel today. Grabbing her laptop, she got back under the bedclothes and searched for updates on whether the trains were running.

It was the first thing in days that made her feel even remotely like smiling. Trains to London were on time and, despite adverse weather conditions, no delays were expected for intercity services. She might have to walk to the station but she'd get there. Neve snapped her laptop shut with a grin, put a thick cardigan on over her pyjamas, and hurried down to the kitchen to brew some coffee.

Two hours later she was ready to go, with an hour and a half before her train left. Before she put three hundred miles between her and Joe.

Her phone rang. Despite herself, Neve's first thought was that he'd called to wish her a happy Christmas.

Clearly not. Neve shook her head and swiped her thumb across the screen.

'Hi, Maisie. How's the mulled wine going?' Neve had shared her recipe with Maisie the previous day.

'Neve. I'm sorry to do this to you…'

Neve resisted the temptation to throw the phone out of the window. 'What is it?'

'Emma called. She's on her way back here for Christmas, and the train she's on has broken down in the tunnel, just before you get to Leminster.'

'Yes, I know where you mean…' Neve wasn't quite sure what she could do about Maisie's daughter being stuck on a train.

'Apparently they waited an hour and a maintenance crew arrived. The driver got off the train with them and started shovelling snow or something, and then he collapsed. They got him back onto the train and Em's doing her best—there's no phone reception in the tunnel but she's passing messages back to one of the crew, who talked to Ted. He says it sounds like a mild heart attack.'

'All right. I'm on my way, Maisie. Let Emma know if you can. Have you called the emergency services?'

'Yes. Ted's on his way too, but he just phoned and said that the snow's pretty deep and it's slow going.'

'Yeah, I reckon I'll have to walk it but it's not far. I can get there much quicker than either Ted or the ambulance. Tell him to come back home and I'll call and let you both know what's going on.'

'Thanks, Neve. Would it help if I called Joe?'

She didn't want to see Joe. She didn't need him, she could handle this on her own. 'It's okay. There's no way he can get through any quicker than I can.'

'Okay. Well, let me know if there's anything you need.'

'Will do. Thanks for calling, Maisie.'

A short, strained laugh. 'You don't mean that.'

'Yes and no. I wouldn't have forgiven you if you hadn't.'

Neve ended the call, and sat motionless, looking at her phone for a moment. She had no idea of the situation on that train. And yet she'd just made a judgement call.

It was a bit rich, calling it a judgement call. There wasn't much professional judgement involved, more personal hubris. She sighed, running her finger down her contacts list. Joe answered on the second ring.

'Neve... Hi.'

His voice sounded relaxed, pleased she'd called. How could he have forgotten so soon that they were supposed to have just broken each other's hearts?

'Joe, there's a train stranded in the tunnel just out of Leminster. There may be a casualty...'

'You need me to drive you?'

'No. The quickest way from here is to walk across

the fields. I may need some medical assistance, though, and you're the only other doctor in the immediate area.'

There was a pause. 'Neve, I don't think that's appropriate.'

Anger flared. She'd just put her pride aside and called him, and he'd turned her down flat. Fine. She could manage without him. In fact, she could probably manage a great deal better without him. 'Okay. Whatever you say.'

She ended the call, without waiting for his reply. If Joe said he wasn't coming, she had no time to mess around talking to him. She had to hurry.

Quickly she packed the things she might need into one bag and pulled her coat and boots on. Her luggage, one small case with her clothes in it and a larger one full of presents stood ready behind the front door, and she pushed them ruefully to one side. Christmas was going to have to wait.

It was still snowing, and it was hard going down to the end of the lane. But the road beyond was relatively clear. Neve took a moment to look to her left, in the direction of the station, and then turned right. Two hundred yards further on there was a footpath, which skirted the fields and then ran parallel to the railway line.

It took ten minutes on a good day to get from here to the tunnel. But today, with a heavy bag to carry, and in the deep snow, she'd be lucky to make it in twenty. She put her head down and started to walk.

She would have seen the figure walking towards her across the fields sooner if she'd not been concentrating on each step she took. Trying not to slip on the uneven ground. Trying to walk as fast as she could. When she did look up, it was within shouting distance.

Joe. His hood almost covered his face, but his bulk, the grace with which he strode through the deep snow were unmistakeable. Neve cursed herself roundly for the moment of sheer happiness that forced itself on her before she had time to think.

'I thought you weren't coming,' she shouted to him—*at* him—as the gap closed between them.

'I changed my mind.'

He must have changed it pretty quickly. Even at the punishing pace he was keeping up, it would have taken him at least as long as it had her to get to this point. 'Right…' Neve was too out of breath for argument.

'Let me take that.' He fell into step beside her.

'I can manage.'

'Give me the bag.' There was a glint of no-nonsense steel about him. The same set determination that she'd seen on Holcombe Crag where practicality, not etiquette, was the order of the day. Neve pulled the strap of her bag over her head and gave it to him.

'Thank you.' He hooked the strap over his shoulder.

What for? She was just getting the job done, in the best way she knew how. They'd make better time this way, and that was all that mattered.

'Why are you here, Joe?' She didn't stop walking.

'You asked me to come.'

'Yeah, and you said that it was inappropriate. You've decided to come and watch?'

'No, I decided it was inappropriate of me to not to offer help in this situation.' He seemed as intent as she was in keeping this on a purely professional basis. He wasn't there for her. He was there for the people on that train.

'Your experience?' Irrational disappointment lend harshness to her words.

'Military general surgeon. I also have experience of combat casualty care.'

Neve nodded. Joe had better experience of dealing with the kind of situation that might be waiting for them than she did. Whether he had the heart to use that experience remained to be seen.

CHAPTER THIRTEEN

She needed to start working with him, not against him. If Neve wanted Joe to come through for her, she needed to give him a bit of support and stop treating him like the guy who'd broken her heart six days ago. Even if he was.

'The situation is that there's a man on the train who may have had a mild heart attack. There may be other injuries that I'm not aware of.'

'We'll find out soon enough.' Up ahead the line disappeared into a tunnel, banked with snow. 'I think I see the back of the train.'

It was snowing heavily now, and visibility was limited, but there was a bright flash of colour at the mouth of the tunnel. As Neve watched, a figure in high-visibility gear detached itself from the opening, waving at them.

The ground sloped down towards the railway line and there was a line of bushes curtaining a chain-link fence and barring their way. Joe began to slide carefully down the slope, and Neve followed him.

'Careful…these have thorns…' The bushes were designed to keep people out, forming a deep, prickly, hedge. Joe started to break a path through them, holding the spiny branches to one side so she could get through.

'We're going to need to climb— Ow!' Neve caught her sleeve on a thorn, and Joe turned to unhook her.

'One thing at a time.' He broke his way through to the fence, just as the man in the high-vis suit reached the other side. 'Dr Neve Harrison and Dr Joe Lamont.'

It was the first time she'd heard him say it, and there was no time to even think about what it meant. Joe pulled a small pack from his back and unzipped it.

'We didn't know which way you'd be coming. I'll have to go back down and get some wire cutters.' The man turned and started to pick his way back down the embankment.

'Yeah, right. We'll wait.' Joe's tone was heavy with sarcasm as he drew a pair of wire cutters from his pack.

'Does this count as vandalism of railway property?' Neve murmured the words to him.

'Guess I'll find that out later. If anyone asks, I forced you into it.' The ghost of a smile tugged at his mouth and then he turned, snipping at the links of the fence.

'I should be doing that.' The man toiled back up towards them again.

'Sorry.' Joe slipped the cutters into the pack and held the gap in the fence open for Neve to step through. 'It's already done.'

Neve suppressed a smile. When she was through to the other side, Joe handed her the bags and followed her.

'You'll have to follow my instructions. Health and safety rules…' The man seemed intent on emphasising that he was in charge here.

'Fine.' Joe started to stride on ahead. 'And you'll have to keep up.'

Neve slithered down the steep incline of the embankment behind Joe, almost losing her footing. But Joe was there, one arm held out towards her to steady her.

'Keep away from the rails. Don't touch anything.' Joe's advice seemed the most reliable and Neve nodded. 'Here. Just slide down this last bit and I'll catch you.'

Neve tried to keep her balance so that Joe wouldn't have to grab hold of her, but she couldn't. She skated down the last couple of feet of the embankment, right into his arms.

No eye contact. Joe seemed suddenly to be looking one way and Neve the other. He set her unceremoniously back onto her feet, turning towards the mouth of the tunnel.

'I've got to stay here with the phone.' The railway guy was breathing heavily from the effort of keeping up with them. 'Adam Grimshaw's my boss, he's the one you need to speak to.'

'Okay, thanks. Up here?' Joe pointed to a steep gangway that had been lashed together to give access to the last door of the back carriage.

'Yep. Want a hand?'

'No, thanks, we're good.' Joe climbed up to the open door, depositing the bags inside, and reached down towards Neve, wrapping his hand around her arm. Her boots slid on the gangway, but he steadied her and pulled her up into the train.

It was dark inside the carriage. Joe bent to open his pack and withdrew a couple of torches, handing one to her. When he switched his on, playing it around the carriage, Neve could see another railway employee hurrying towards them, one hand raised to shade his eyes from the torchlight.

'You're the doctor?'

'Drs Harrison and Lamont. We've been told to ask for Adam Grimshaw.' Neve stepped forward.

'That's me. I'm co-ordinating things here until we can get everyone off the train. Thanks for getting here so quickly. The driver's ill and there's a woman been injured as well.'

Two casualties. Neve turned to Joe. 'I'll take the heart attack, you have a look at the other injury.'

He nodded, his face tightening into a mask. 'Right you are.'

Whatever his reservations, it seemed that Joe was going to do it. That was all she needed to know.

The man led them through the connecting doors to the next carriage. Groups of people sat in the darkness, and every face turned towards them, pale in the torchlight, as they hurried down the centre aisle.

'All right, folks. Stay in your seats, please. Doctor coming through.' Adam's voice rose above the hubbub of murmured questions.

The next carriage was full of people. The same pale faces, the same questions, only this time the sound of a young child crying sliced through the air. Neve made a mental note that as soon as the emergency cases had been seen, she'd find the mother and make sure that both were all right.

'We got everyone together in the middle carriages to keep warm.' Adam was talking as he hurried along the aisle. 'The driver's pretty poorly, and your girl Emma's with him in the front carriage. There's also a woman passenger who was hurt when the train stopped suddenly.'

Adam seemed capable and to have everything under control. Not easy on a train full of cold, frightened people and in virtual darkness, apart from the flickering emergency lights. 'I've been through and asked everyone if they're okay. There are a few cuts and bruises, but I let them stay in their seats. One of them's a child and her mother wanted to keep her away from the more serious injuries.'

Joe's voice sounded from behind Neve, calm and confident. 'That's good. Can you go round again? If anyone seems asleep and you can't wake them, or they seem disoriented, let us know. Sometimes adrenaline can mask shock or other injuries for a while.'

'Will do.' Adam held the connecting doors open for Neve, and she stepped through into the front carriage.

She could see Emma's face at the far end and walked towards her. A hand reached out from the darkness and grabbed her arm.

'You're the doctor. My wife's hurt...' A man had tight hold of her arm.

Joe was there. 'All right, mate.' His fingers curled around the man's wrist, applying brief pressure below the thumb, and the grip on her arm relaxed suddenly. 'I'll see your wife.'

She nodded at Joe, and made for the end of the carriage, not looking back. There was no choice now. Joe was going to have to come through for her.

The young woman was weeping softly, and a brief glance was enough to tell Joe what was wrong. Another woman, sitting next to her, was supporting her arm, stretched out awkwardly, to accommodate the metal spike that disappeared through a hole in her sleeve just below the elbow and seemed to be running straight through her arm.

'What's her name?' He turned to the woman's husband.

'Her name is Jan... You're a doctor?'

'Yes, Dr Joe Lamont. If I can just get a bit closer…'
Joe craned over, training the light from his torch onto
the spike, which he could now see was a knitting needle.

'Jan, my name's Joe. I'm a doctor.'

Her face was pale and her eyes red from crying, but
she seemed alert enough. 'They said you were coming…'

The look in a person's eyes when they knew that they
were hurt and that someone was there to help never failed
to move Joe. 'I'm going to get a few things but I'll only
be a moment. Then I'll take a proper look at your arm.
Okay?'

'Yes. Thanks.'

At the other end of the carriage Neve was kneeling on
the floor, bent over a middle-aged man, who was lying
on a makeshift bed made out of passengers' coats. She
was talking quietly to him.

Joe puffed out a relieved breath. The man was obviously conscious, and it seemed that Neve had everything
well under control. He quickly selected what he needed
from her bag and, turning, nearly crashed into Jan's husband, who was hovering in the darkness behind him.

'Is there anything I can do?'

'Yeah. I want you to sit down opposite your wife.
It'll hurt when I cut her sleeve, and she's going to need
you there.'

He shepherded the man back up the carriage and
slipped past him, carefully supporting Jan's arm while
the woman who had been holding it ducked out of the
way. Then he sat down next to Jan, training the light of
his torch onto the knitting needle. It was bent from the
impact that must have driven it through her arm, and
Joe's initial plan was to leave it in situ.

'Okay, Jan, let's see if I can't make you a bit more comfortable before the ambulance gets here.' Joe smiled at her. 'First of all I want to check that you're not hurt anywhere else. Did you bump your head at all?'

'No.'

'Good. I'm going to open your coat and feel your tummy and legs. Just to make sure.' Joe was confident enough that Jan was able to tell him if she had any other injuries, but he wasn't going to leave it to chance.

Joe handed the torch over to the woman who had been supporting Jan's arm, and indicated where he wanted her to shine its beam. Putting on a pair of gloves, he opened Jan's coat, feeling her stomach, back and legs carefully, watching for any signs of pain and alert for the sticky feel of blood. 'Does this hurt?'

'No.'

He finished his careful probing and tucked Jan's coat back around her. 'Good. You're doing fine. I'm afraid I'm going to have to cut your sleeve so I can get a look at the wound now.'

'That's okay. I never much liked this coat.' Jan seemed calm enough, but Joe was watching her carefully. The emotional effect of seeing something passing through your own body wasn't something that it would be wise to ignore.

'I'm not going to touch the knitting needle yet. It's best to leave it where it is and let them remove it at the hospital.'

'Okay. It looks so weird, though…'

'I know. I want you to take your husband's hand and look at him. Can you do that?'

Jan summoned a smile. 'Yes, I can do that. The look of love, eh?'

Joe chuckled. 'That's right. Straight into his eyes.' Joe

wondered what it would have been like if someone—who was he trying to kid?—if Neve had been there to hold his hand when he'd been hurt. Whether it would have made any difference at all.

'You think this is the time to mention our anniversary…?'

'I think it's an excellent time.' Joe's heart thumped in his chest. Jan knew beyond doubt that her husband was there for her, without having to ask or even think about it. It seemed to make all the difference to her.

'Anything you want, babe.' Jan's husband rallied, sliding forward in his seat and taking hold of her hand, and Jan turned her head towards him.

'Just you.' Jan silently mouthed the words and her husband gripped tight onto her hand.

Joe began to cut the thick woollen material of Jan's coat, carefully freeing it on both sides from the metal spike. Then the material underneath. The wound was oozing blood, but that was already beginning to congeal around the shaft of the knitting needle.

'We're good, Jan. It's not bleeding too much. I'm going to put padding around it to protect it a bit and stop it from moving.'

Jan shot him a teary smile. 'Thanks… It hurts pretty bad.'

'Yes, I know, and we're going to do something about that. I want you to sit tight, and I'll go and get some pain relief for you.' He slid out from his seat, indicating to Jan's husband exactly how he wanted him to support her arm while he was gone.

'Joe. Cardiac arrest…'

Neve's voice rose above the quiet voices in the carriage, and for a moment Joe froze. He'd been here before.

Left one patient to tend to another, and that time he'd made the wrong choice. Suddenly the quiet, focussed confidence that had grown as he'd carefully tended to Jan shattered into smithereens.

'Joe…' Her voice again. Joe made his decision.

'Stay there. Just as you are.' Jan's husband gave him a quick nod. 'I'll be back as soon as I can.'

Neve was still kneeling on the floor next to her patient. Another young woman, who must be Emma, was shrinking back from them, her hand over her mouth in an expression of helpless horror. Joe ignored her for the moment, bending down next to Neve.

Suddenly everything came together. Like two parts of a machine, snapping into place and humming smoothly into life. Without a word, Joe lifted the man, supporting him while Neve snatched the cushions out from under him.

'How long…?'

'Twenty seconds. Start CPR.'

Joe was already there. 'Tell me you've got a defibrillator in your bag.'

'Yep. Emma, we need some light, please. Over here.'

There was no time to thank Joe for coming through for her. Gerry had been awake and talking when Neve had arrived, and suddenly this. His heart, already weakened by the heart attack, had stopped pumping blood, and he had begun to die before her eyes. Neve opened her medical bag and pulled out the defibrillator, taking the pads from their protective wrapper.

'Got a razor?' Joe had already got the coats covering Gerry out of the way, and bared his chest.

'Yep.' One glance told her that she was going to need

it. Neve pulled the disposable razor from the side pocket of her bag, and while Joe continued CPR a few quick strokes of the razor made two patches in the dense mat of springy chest hair, large enough for the pads to stick properly.

'Ready for defibrillation.' The shorter the interruption in CPR, the better, and Joe needed to know exactly when to stop.

'Okay. On your call.' His voice was calm and steady.

'Checking... Stand clear.'

Joe moved back. 'Safe.'

Neve pushed the button and Gerry seemed to stiffen slightly. 'No response. Resume CPR.'

Joe clasped his hands again, pushing rhythmically on Gerry's chest, replicating the beat of a heart that currently wasn't capable of doing its job. The CPR would keep blood circulating around his body until the defibrillator could recharge and another shock be delivered.

'Ready.'

'Okay.'

'Checking... Stand clear.'

'Safe.'

The same smooth procedure. It was as if they'd planned it all in advance, choreographed each move. Somehow their training, undertaken on different sides of an ocean, and their experience, also different, dovetailed together in a smooth, unbroken pattern.

'I've got a normal sinus rhythm.'

A little choking sob came from behind her, and the beam of the torch quivered. Emma had done well but this was a lot for a twenty-year-old law student, whose only medical experience came second-hand from her father.

'It's okay, Emma.' Joe's voice, quiet and reassuring.

'You've done really well. Just give us another few minutes and then I promise you can fall apart. What's his name?'

'Gerry.' The light steadied as Emma took a deep breath and gulped back her tears.

'Thanks.' Joe bent over the man, whose eyelids were beginning to flutter. 'Gerry. Can you hear me, Gerry?'

There was no reply, but Gerry's eyes were open now and struggling to focus. 'Gerry. Just lie still now.'

Gerry's heart was beating now, the rhythm regular. Neve kept watch on the small monitor of the defibrillator while Joe put a cushion under Gerry's head, talking to him all the time, reassuring him.

'Give me the torch, Em.' Neve shot a smile towards Emma. 'And would you slide my medical bag over here, please?'

Emma did as she was asked. 'There you go.'

'Thanks.' Neve found the pulse oximeter, clipping it on to Gerry's finger to check the oxygenation level of his blood. She nodded with satisfaction. Not bad, considering what he'd just gone through. Minutes ticked by.

'Are you satisfied that he's stable?' Joe murmured the question for only Neve to hear.

'Cautiously.' No one was in a position for anything more than that at the moment. 'Why?'

'I've got a woman back there with a knitting needle stuck through her arm.'

'A what?'

'Yeah. I want to get her some pain relief.'

'Okay. Look in my bag. I have paracetamol, or morphine if that's not enough…' She was keeping her eyes on Gerry, not looking at Joe. If Joe had a case that

needed morphine then he was going to have to handle
that himself.

'Thanks. I think the paracetamol should be enough
for now. Won't be long.'

'Right. And can you see if you can find out about the
ambulance?' Gerry was back with them again, but he
was very weak. Even if he maintained this improvement,
they had a ninety-minute window to get him to hospital before he started to suffer irreversible complications.

'Will do.' She heard Joe get to his feet. Almost felt
him walk away. It was a cold feeling, almost annihilating
the calm confidence she'd felt when he'd been there by
her side. Neve took a breath and concentrated on Gerry.

'How is the ambulance going to get to us?' Emma's face
was pale in the torchlight. Joe had been gone for ten,
precious minutes.

'They'll find a way, Em. We'll just keep things going
here until they do. Right?'

Emma nodded. 'Yes. Should I hold his hand or something?'

'That would be good.' Emma needed something to do
almost as much as Gerry needed the comfort. 'We need
to keep him calm and quiet. Reassure him.'

Emma took Gerry's hand between hers. 'Gerry, it's
Emma. Just lie still and rest. The doctor's here and you're
going to be all right.'

It was a rash promise, and one that Neve didn't know
whether she was going to be able to keep. She saw
Gerry's fingers curl around Emma's and prayed that she
could.

She heard footsteps behind her and Joe knelt down

next to her. 'The first ambulance is about five minutes away and there's another behind it.'

'How are they going to get to us?' Neve didn't much want to see Gerry being carried over the fields to the ambulance.

'They're coming via the road that runs along the other side of the tracks.'

'Isn't it blocked?'

'Yeah. But apparently they've got a snowplough with them.'

She felt the light touch of his hand on her back. Didn't he know that he'd lost the right to do that? All the same, she was glad of that small reassurance.

'How did they manage that?'

Something that looked like a smile tugged at his lips. 'Who knows? Just be thankful they did.'

In less than five minutes a commotion at the entrance to the carriage heralded the arrival of the ambulance crew. Neve got to her feet and quickly briefed the young, sandy-haired man who accompanied them and who had introduced himself as a doctor.

The EMTs were gently transferring Gerry to a carry-cot, wrapping him in blankets and clipping an oxygen mask in place.

'How's your route back out of here?' Neve asked the doctor.

'We managed to get pretty close. Your colleague's helping the railway guys to clear a path up the embankment for us.' He grinned at her.

Neve had wondered where Joe had disappeared to, supposing that he was keeping out of the way now that the ambulance had arrived. She should have known better.

'Ready to go?' One of the ambulancemen caught the young doctor's eye.

'Yes.' He consulted Neve's written notes, which detailed exactly which drugs she'd given Gerry, along with the readings she'd taken from the portable defibrillator. 'We're good.'

'Safe journey.' Neve slipped her hand into Emma's as they watched the ambulance crew carry the portable cot down the narrow aisle.

'Thanks. We'll be fine. We've got a clear route back again. Are you coming with us? There'll be a spare seat up front.'

'No, we've got people I need to stay with here.' She squeezed Emma's hand. 'Do you want to go, Em?'

'I'm staying too.' The look on her face was remarkably like Maisie's when she had something that she was determined to see through until the end. The young doctor's mouth curled into an easy smile, which was all for Emma.

Neve squeezed Emma's hand. 'Perhaps my colleague... Tell him that I said I can manage here now.' The intimacy of working with Joe to save a man's life had been fragile and transitory, over before Gerry had been strapped into the carry-cot. All the same, the thought that he would probably jump at the chance to be out of here made her feel suddenly cold.

'Okay, will do.' The doctor shot one last grin in Emma's direction and she returned the compliment. Then he hurried along the aisle to catch up with the ambulance crew. Neve swallowed the tears that sprang inexplicably to her eyes and focussed on the woman that Joe had seen halfway down the carriage. She still had a job to do.

CHAPTER FOURTEEN

NEVE TOOK A deep breath and approached the small group. 'Hi. My name's Neve. How are you doing?'

'Not so bad. How's that man?'

'Stable. The really good news is that he's on his way to hospital now. And the other piece of good news is that another ambulance should be here for you very soon.'

'Thanks.' The woman was obviously in pain but Joe had done a good job of making her comfortable, her arm supported on a couple of bags, cushioned with a soft jacket. She had a fire blanket over her, and when Neve touched her other hand, it was warm.

'Do you have any discomfort anywhere else, or is it just your arm?' She should check that nothing had been missed.

The woman's lips twitched into a smile. 'No, nothing else. Joe, the other doctor, asked me that, too, and checked me over.' She gave a shrug, wincing as the muscles of her shoulder pulled at her injured arm. She seemed bright enough. And the grin she'd given when she'd talked about Joe checking her over seemed a perfectly understandable reaction from a patient who was alert enough to appreciate it. Joe could be as professional as he liked, you still couldn't change human nature.

'How did you do it?' Neve carefully inspected the dressing for any signs of new bleeding.

'Jan was holding her knitting up, counting the rows, when the train stopped and she fell right onto the needle,' the man sitting next to her chipped in.

'Good thing it was just my arm.' Jan rolled her eyes. 'It was one hell of a jolt.'

Neve had noticed that the floor of the carriage was at a slight angle, and as soon as she got the chance she should ask exactly what had happened here. 'Joe's given you something for the pain?'

Jan smiled, reaching under the fire blanket and taking out a piece of thick card, trimmed to make a label and secured around her neck with strips of gauze and surgical tape. Clearly marked on the card were the time, date and the dose of paracetamol that Joe had given.

'Right. Looks as if all we need to do is wait for the ambulance, then.'

The second ambulance crew appeared in the doorway of the carriage a few minutes later. Jan was helped to her feet and secured in a carry-cot, and her husband shook Neve's hand before he left.

'Tell Joe thank you as well.'

'Yes, I will.' She probably wouldn't get the chance. Joe was gone now, and he wasn't coming back. Soon he'd be on his way back to Canada. Perhaps it was better this way. While Neve still had the other passengers on the train to think about, she couldn't curl up in a ball and cry. She took a deep breath and opened the connecting door into the second carriage, looking for Adam Grimshaw.

Expectant faces turned towards her. Then there was a murmur of conversation.

Someone started to clap. Then someone else. By the time she got to the centre of the carriage everyone was applauding. She wasn't as alone as she'd thought, but still the one person that she wanted wasn't here. Neve held up her hands for silence.

'Thanks, everyone. The two people who were hurt are on their way to hospital now…' She was interrupted by the murmur of approval which went around the carriage.

'When can we get out?' A man's voice from the corner.

'I don't know any more than you. I'll try to find out.'

'Can't we walk along the tracks? Go the same way that you came in?' Another voice.

'No.' Neve remembered what she'd heard from the TV about the dangers of passengers getting out of a stranded train. 'It's not safe. And, anyway, there's no transport. We'd be stuck miles from anywhere. If you think it's cold in here…'

A murmur ran around the carriage and then another voice rose above the rest. 'Best to stay here.'

One voice of sanity at least. A few others joined in, and the mood swung back in favour of staying put. Neve caught sight of Adam, entering the carriage from the other end, and hurried towards him.

'Did you get to check on everyone, as my colleague asked?'

'Yes. There are two more minor injuries for you to see. A woman with a swollen hand and the child. Do you want me to get them brought down to you?'

'Yes, as long as the front carriage is stable. It seems to be listing to one side…'

Adam nodded. 'The wheels of that carriage hit a lump of ice and slid off the rails. They're stuck fast now.'

'You're sure?' It all sounded a bit precarious to Neve. 'Is there any danger of the carriage tipping any further?'

'No, I've been down there and taken a look. The front wheels are wedged between two rails. That carriage, and the rest of the train for that matter, isn't going anywhere. We're working on evacuating into a rescue train.'

'Some of the passengers are talking about walking along the tracks. I said it was a really bad idea and that we should wait.'

Adam nodded. 'Yeah, thanks. If anyone else asks, stick to that message. It's much too dangerous to have a whole train full of people walking along live tracks. I've had some flasks of coffee sent along the line and hopefully that'll give everyone something else to think about.'

'Coffee?' Neve could really do with a cup of coffee right now, and she expected that Emma could too.

Adam grinned. 'I'll have a flask sent along to you straight away. It's the least I can do.' His face reddened slightly and he held out his hand to Neve. 'I've known Gerry for thirty years and he's a good mate. Thank you.'

Neve took his hand and he gripped hers tightly. 'I'm glad I was here to help.'

'I want to thank Emma too. There was no one on the train who had any medical knowledge, and she stepped forward like a good 'un, even though she was shaking like a leaf.'

Tears brimmed in Neve's eyes at the thought of Emma, afraid and alone. At least she had her training and experience to guide her. 'I'm just going to talk to her now. She's a bit shaken up, and if you have a minute I'd be really glad if you could say a few words to her.'

'It'll be my privilege to shake that girl's hand.' Adam seemed to realise that he still had hold of Neve's, and let it go suddenly. 'I'll go and get the coffee and I'll be right there.'

When Neve re-entered the front carriage, Emma was sitting on her own at the far end of the carriage, hugging her coat around her tightly, her face streaked with tears. Neve made a beeline for her.

'Hey, Em.' She sat down next to her, putting her arm around her shoulders.

Emma nodded an acknowledgement. 'Where's Joe?'

'He's gone with the ambulance.' Neve heard her voice break slightly.

'Do you think Gerry's going to be all right?'

'He's on his way to hospital.'

Emma quirked her mouth downwards. 'I didn't know what to do, Neve.'

'That's okay. You kept your head, and you called for help. Then you did what your dad told you until Joe and I got there. That was more than enough.'

'But if I'd been able to see the signs perhaps I could have done something earlier so he didn't go into cardiac arrest...'

'Em, listen.' Neve took Emma firmly by the shoulders. The girl knew just enough to realise what was happening and to blame herself for it. 'Gerry's heart was weakened by the heart attack and that's what precipitated the arrest. There was nothing you could have done. The only reason that Joe and I got here in time was because of you.'

'I'm going to learn how to do CPR.' Emma's voice was small, but a note of determination had crept into it.

'That's a good idea. Everyone should.'

Emma nodded, wiping her face with her hand. 'Perhaps Joe will teach me.'

'Perhaps he will.' Unlikely. Unless he and Emma could

fit the lessons in some time in the next few days before he left.

'Perhaps I will what?'

A deep voice sounded behind them. Neve didn't dare look up.

'Joe! You came back!' Emma didn't have any of Neve's hesitation in expressing her joy.

'Of course.'

'I thought you'd gone with the ambulance.' Neve heard her voice shake. Her heart had wanted him there so badly, even though her head had patiently explained that it wouldn't be for long and that there would only be more tears when he did leave.

'I was on the embankment, helping the crews up with the carry-cots.' He smiled at Neve, and then turned the voltage up to full when he grinned at Emma. 'How's it going, Em?'

'We're glad to see you.' Emma sprang to her feet and delivered the hug that Neve hadn't offered. Joe held her tight, his hands spread across her back. Neve knew how reassuring that felt. It would be downright mean-spirited to begrudge Emma that comfort.

She saw Adam at the entrance to the carriage, carrying a flask and some polystyrene cups. 'Why don't you go and get some coffee, Em? I think that Adam wants a word with you.'

'Oh. Coffee.' Fortified by the hug, and the thought of a hot drink, Emma started to pick her way down the aisle to the other end of the carriage, leaving Joe and Neve alone.

Neve reckoned he would probably find something else pressing to do now, something that would discreetly avoid the need for any conversation between them. But instead he sat down opposite her.

'What's that all about?' He nodded towards Emma's receding back.

'Adam wanted to thank her personally for coming forward to help.' She twisted round in her seat, watching as Adam took Emma's hand and shook it, receiving a brilliant smile in return.

When she turned back towards Joe he was nodding in approval. 'She deserves a bit of recognition. This must have been very difficult for her.'

'Yes, it was. And for you, too. Thanks for being here, Joe.'

He leaned forward, propping his elbows on his knees. Joe had a knack of conjuring up their own little world, making it seem as if they were alone in a crowd. Shielded by the high backs of the seats, it was as if there wasn't another person for miles.

'I don't deserve any thanks. I almost didn't come.'

'I know. But you did come, and you made all the difference. That's what matters, not what you almost did.'

For a moment that precious connection flashed between them, as if it had never been broken. Then he shook his head. 'You know there's more to it than that, Neve.'

'I know that I didn't give you much encouragement.' Neve didn't want to think about what the consequences of her own angry pride might have been.

'You called me.'

'I hung up on you.'

'You had every right to be angry. Anyone who thinks that saving a life isn't appropriate isn't worth much.'

'Anyone who gets over their own personal feelings and does the right thing is worth something. Worth a great deal, actually.' Joe had hurt her badly but lashing out like a wounded animal wasn't going to help either of them.

He deserved better than that, and the thought occurred to Neve that maybe she did too.

'I'll remember that. Next time I manage to get myself into this kind of situation…'

She twisted her mouth. 'Which I imagine is going to be a very long time in the future, if you've got any say in the matter.'

A short burst of wry laughter. 'Yeah. Probably.'

'In the meantime, remember this. Gerry. He's the guy you helped save. Remember his name.'

He swept his hand across his eyes, as if he suddenly felt weary. 'Will you do me a favour?'

'Depends what it is.' Making up your mind to act like an adult only extended so far. The fragile, uneasy truce between them could only stand so much pressure.

His gaze focussed on hers, and heat seared through her senses. 'You're a great doctor and… Next time anyone tells you that you need to change, could you just laugh in their face, please?'

'I'll think about it.'

He nodded. 'Okay. That's good enough.'

There weren't going to be any next times for her and Joe. He wasn't going to say that he'd suddenly seen the light, that his confidence had been restored and he was taking up medicine again. He wasn't going to believe that they could try again. Miracles like that didn't happen. Not in a matter of days at least, and in a few days' time he'd be on a plane on his way back to Canada.

'Emma…thanks.' He stood suddenly, and Neve turned round to see Emma, balancing three polystyrene cups of coffee, each perched on the lid of the other. He lifted one out and handed it to Neve.

'Ah. Thanks. I could do with that.' The chill in the

carriage was beginning to work its way back into her bones. 'Have they brought our next patients through yet?'

'They're on their way. In fact, the first one's here now.' Emma grinned at her.

'I'll go.' Joe signalled towards the other end of the carriage that he'd be right there. 'Sit for a minute and drink your coffee. I'll call you if I need you.'

Neve sipped her drink, smiling as Emma proudly told her what Adam had said to her. She was unable to sit still for very long, though. And when she stood up she was drawn to Joe, as if by some irresistible magnetic force.

He was sitting at the other end of the carriage next to a young woman, a little girl of about three on his lap. He was persuading his young patient that having the small cut on her arm cleaned wasn't so bad after all.

'First I'm going to clean your arm with this, Daisy.' Joe had an antiseptic wipe from Neve's medical bag in his hand, and Daisy took it from him, rubbing it onto the sleeve of his jumper.

'No, honey, on the skin.' Joe pulled up his sleeve, his arms still around Daisy. She responded to his prompt and scrubbed mercilessly at his forearm.

'Ow…' He gave a little grimace of mock pain. 'It stings a bit, but that's because it's working properly.'

He pulled another wipe from the packet and Daisy smiled up at him. 'Snap…'

'Of course. I forgot that.' He snapped the edge of one of the surgical gloves he was wearing against his wrist. 'Ready now?'

Daisy nodded. Joe started to clean the wound gently, holding her tight when she squirmed and whimpered a little. 'I'm sorry, honey. Nearly finished.'

It was almost too much to bear. The tenderness. The

softness of a child against the war-torn ruggedness of the man. The final straw was that Daisy looked a little like Joe, dark hair and big brown eyes. He'd make a great father...

You're out of order... She had no right to even think that. Absolutely no right to pretend that Joe wanted the same as her. He had his own life, his own aspirations, and they had nothing in common with her own.

'You're a very brave girl, Daisy. Now I'm going to put a little sticky plaster on the cut, which you mustn't take off...' He showed her the stitch. 'It doesn't hurt.'

'Snap!'

'That's right. Thanks for reminding me.' Joe snapped the surgical gloves again, and Daisy laughed up at him. This was torture.

He decided on two stitches, clearly veering towards the safe side. He applied them so swiftly, so expertly that Daisy hardly blinked. 'Now I'm going to put a bandage over the top, just to keep everything in place...'

That was it. Neve couldn't watch any more. Adam was guiding a middle-aged woman through into the carriage, holding her bags for her, and Neve turned and plastered a bright smile on her face to greet them.

CHAPTER FIFTEEN

Now that there was nothing to do but wait, time seemed to slow to an interminable crawl. Joe had responded to Daisy's demands for a story and then delivered her back into her mother's arms. Neve was busy with a woman who looked as if she had a sprained wrist, and Emma was sitting at the far end of the carriage with her nose in a book.

Seized with restless energy born of dissatisfaction with the world rather than enthusiasm for the job in hand, he walked to the other end of the train to liaise with Adam and see whether he could get any reception on his phone. Two bars was a hollow victory, because there was no one he wanted to call. It seemed that everything he'd ever wanted was right here. Close enough to touch, but not his to take.

'What's the story, then?' It was Emma who caught Joe's attention when he walked back into the front carriage, his heart grumbling with discontent.

'It'll be a while.' He threw himself down in the seat opposite Emma and Neve. 'Hello, there, sweetheart…'

Emma was struggling to hold Daisy on her lap as the child reached for him, and Joe felt a sharp, instinctive tug of warmth.

'Here, you take her. She doesn't want me any more.' Emma grinned, lifting Daisy across the small table between them, and the little girl reached for him with an eagerness that almost shattered his heart.

Her hands were a little cold, and Joe unzipped his jacket, letting Daisy snuggle into his body heat. Maybe she needed her mother...

'I want a story.' Daisy's mother was deep in conversation at the other end of the carriage, and her gaze flicked up automatically at the sound of her child's voice. Then she smiled at Joe and turned back to the woman with the injured wrist, obviously reckoning that he was the man for that particular job.

'Okay, Daisy. What about the one about the penguin and the polar bear?'

Emma giggled. 'Aren't penguins at the North Pole? And polar bears at the South?'

'Other way round. That's the whole point of the story.' Joe hadn't dared look at Neve, but now he chanced a quick glance. She was staring fixedly out of the window at the dark walls of the tunnel.

'Hmm. Talking about impossible treks, is there any news about when we'll get out of here? Or are they going to send turkey sandwiches and candles down the line for tomorrow?' Emma grinned at him. 'Or perhaps *we* could walk home.'

Joe rolled his eyes. 'We can't walk along the line, Em.'

'How dangerous can it be? You and Neve did it.'

Neve seemed to wake from her reverie at the sound of her name. 'We walked a few yards in order to get here in an emergency. It's miles to the station behind us, and to get to Leminster we'd have to walk through the tunnel ahead, in the dark.'

'All right, so we can't move, and we can't walk. What *can* we do?' Emma stirred restlessly, and Daisy turned her big brown eyes onto Joe.

'They're backing a rescue train down the track towards us. It'll get as close as possible to the front of the train, and we'll all walk through into it. Then it's just a few minutes to Leminster station.'

'So it won't be long, then?' Neve was looking at him now, her eyes suddenly filled with tears.

'No. Not long.' It was Joe's turn to avert his gaze. He got to his feet, taking Daisy with him, and started to walk along the carriage. 'This story's about a penguin and a polar bear, and a very, very long walk.'

It was almost an hour before Joe heard the sound of activity coming from the front of the train, which signalled that the rescue train had arrived. It took another half an hour to manoeuver it into position and rig up a walkway between the trains. When the time came to evacuate the carriages, everyone queued quietly, waiting their turn for the railway staff to help them across the gap. Joe carried Daisy across and, with a trace of reluctance transferred her into the arms of her mother on the other side.

There was another wait while the walkway was dismantled, but at least this train was warm and there were hot drinks, sandwiches and unblocked toilets. Finally the train started to move slowly up the track to Leminster station.

When they arrived everyone made a beeline for the warmth of the waiting room, where a surprising number of people were gathered, waiting for the train to arrive. Joe hung back, watching while Neve made sure that the woman with the sprained wrist and Daisy's mother both had someone to take them home.

Emma had someone too. A greying, middle-aged man broke his way through the crowd, and Emma fell into her father's arms, talking volubly. The man listened, pride and relief shining from his face when he looked at his daughter, and Joe looked away, suddenly feeling as if he was being intrusive. This was their world, not his.

For a moment Neve was alone at the station. No one had come for her. He watched as she shouldered her bag and began to walk slowly towards the exit.

Neve's face hurt from smiling, and her heart hurt from pretending to everyone who wished her a happy Christmas that she too was looking forward to tomorrow. It was time for her to get going. It was already dark and she had a long walk ahead of her.

'Neve! Wait!' Ted's voice rang out, and Neve turned to see him hurrying towards her, his arm wrapped protectively around Emma.

'Thank you for everything, Neve. Maisie sends her love, too.' Ted's look said it all. It wasn't just Gerry who had needed saving. Emma had been spared the agony of having to watch a man die and being able to do nothing about it.

'I'm glad I was there.' Ted raised his eyebrows in disbelief and Neve grinned at him. 'Well, you know...'

'I know.' Suddenly she was no longer the most junior doctor in the practice, in need of support and guidance. She was an equal, who had done her job well and gained his respect. 'We'll give you a lift home.'

'That's okay. It'll take you out of your way and it's going to take ages. Probably quicker if I walk.'

'Not in the dark and with that heavy bag.' Ted's decision on this was obviously final.

'Perhaps you can just put my bag in the boot of your car. I'll drop by and collect it after Christmas.'

'I'm taking you.' Joe's voice boomed out from behind her and Neve jumped. If only he'd stop creeping up behind her...

She should be careful what she wished for. Joe almost certainly wasn't going to be doing it again. It was tough to creep up behind someone from a different continent.

'Joe Lamont?' Ted stretched his free hand out towards Joe and the men shook hands. 'Ted Johnstone...I'm Emma's father. Pleased to meet you. My wife's been singing your praises.'

'My car's five minutes down the road. I've just checked with the station staff, and the trains down to London are still running.' Joe was looking at Neve.

Ted brightened. 'In that case, we won't keep you. Travel safely, eh?'

'Er...yes, I will.' Neve was about to protest that she wasn't going anywhere with Joe, but that would mean that Ted would insist on taking her home. Get one good Samaritan out of the way at a time.

Happy Christmases were wished all around, and Ted turned, hurrying Emma to his car, his arm still firmly around her. Joe picked up Neve's medical bag and started to walk, realising after a few steps that she wasn't with him.

'What?' He turned and faced her.

'I don't need a lift, Joe. I'm going home.'

'Yeah, we'll pop in at your place, collect your bags...' He stopped suddenly. 'You've no intention of going down to London tonight, have you?'

'It's too late. The local train services are probably disrupted and it'll take me for ever.'

'I'll take you over to Leeds and you can get the intercity train from there.'

He still hadn't given up on the hope that Neve had successfully managed to put aside hours ago. 'I appreciate it, Joe. But I'd have to go back home and get my things, and then goodness only knows how long it'd take to get to Newcastle. It's too late. I'd rather stay here.'

'I'm happy to try. If there's a chance…'

'There's no chance.' Joe was just clutching at straws, and even if there had been some chance of her getting down to London, Neve wouldn't have gone with him. The grim perversity of wishing he was there when he wasn't and then, when he appeared, wishing he'd go away had to stop. She had to say goodbye to him and mean it.

He thought for a moment. 'All right, then. I'll take you home.' Neve opened her mouth to protest and he held one hand up to silence her.

'Don't make a liar out of me, Neve. Ted only left you behind here because he thought that I was driving you. I know you think you can manage everything by yourself, and if anyone can then it's you. But, just this once, you're coming with me, if I have to sling you over my shoulder and carry you.'

He wouldn't. Neve looked at his face, set with determination, and decided that he probably would. He certainly could, she knew just how strong Joe was. And he didn't seem to appreciate the irony of his insisting that she get home safely and then breaking her heart all over again by leaving her there.

'Okay. But you take me home and then you go.' Somehow it didn't seem so bad when she was in control of things.

'All right.' He turned and started to walk again, and this time Neve followed him.

Joe hadn't wanted any of this. He would have driven her all the way to London, rather than take her back to her dark, silent house to spend the rest of Christmas Eve alone. But Neve didn't want that.

And that was what it all boiled down to. She didn't want what he could give. He couldn't give what she wanted. It was a hundred per cent or nothing, and even his craving for what might be didn't make any difference. If there was any chance that he couldn't make her dreams come true, he had to hit the road.

The quickest route from the station to his car, parked outside his cottage, was along a footpath that skirted the back of Leminster High Street. She'd begun to drop back a little, unable to keep up the pace, and Joe stopped to wait for her. 'Okay?'

'Yeah.' She was too breathless to furnish any further detail.

The almost magnetic effect that being close to Neve exerted on him threatened to pull him closer to her. It took physical effort to maintain a safe distance. As they trudged towards his car he noticed that it was a perfect Christmas Eve, the sky above them clear and full of stars, and that somehow even that meant absolutely nothing to him.

'Get in while I clear the windscreen.' He called to her and she ignored him. Being ignored by Neve was better than making love to any other woman he'd known before.

Together, they cleared the fresh snow from the car.

Even that wasn't easy. Working silently together, alone in the empty street, he still felt as if these moments were golden, because Neve was there. It was a final, slightly unlikely confirmation of his resolve. He was leaving, and the sooner he went, the better.

Walking alone up the path of her house and slipping the key into her front door had been the final straw. After everything they'd been through today, Joe had stayed resolutely in the driver's seat, not even moving to help her with her bag.

The house was cold and dark. Neve and Joe had fallen apart before he'd had the chance to pick her up that Christmas tree he mentioned, and since she hadn't planned to be here, she'd given the rest of the festive decorations a miss too. She dropped her bag in the hallway, texted her parents to tell them what had happened and not to expect her, and went upstairs, leaving her coat on the floor in the hallway outside the bathroom door. Sighing, she began to run a hot bath in the hope that it might dispel the chill in her bones and the ache in her limbs.

The hot water was soothing but did nothing for the ache in her heart. If Joe couldn't relent on Christmas Eve, he wasn't going to. That was that. End of story.

She was just beginning to relax when her phone rang. Neve scattered water everywhere, getting out of the bath by the third ring and extracting the phone from her coat pocket by the fifth. 'Yes…?' She was shivering and naked in the hall, hoping against shattered hope…

'Neve…? Where are you?' Maisie's voice on the line dashed that hope.

'I was in the bath. Hold on, Maisie.' Neve hurried back

into the warm bathroom, wrapped a towel around her and made for her bedroom. 'I'm back. Sorry about that.'

'Ted said that you were going home tonight. What happened?'

'I decided it was too late.' Too late for a lot of things. Much too late to expect that every time the phone rang it was going to be Joe.

'I wish you'd said. He could have brought you over here tonight.' Reproof sounded in Maisie's voice. 'He'll come over and pick you up…'

'No, thanks, Maisie, I just want an early night.'

'In that case, you're coming to us tomorrow. No arguments.'

'I appreciate the offer but—'

'We'll pick you up tomorrow morning. I'll give you a call around ten to see what time suits you.'

It was time to give it up. Joe wasn't going to call or drop by, and there was no point in staying here, wishing he would. It was time to get on with her life.

'Maisie, I don't know what to say…' Suddenly Maisie's kindness made Neve want to cry.

'It's easy. Just say yes. And that you'll be awake by ten, when I call you.'

'That'll be great, Maisie. Thanks so much.'

Neve ended the call and put the phone down next to her on the bed. It was Christmas after all. Maybe not the one she wanted, but she had friends and she was going to make the best she could of it.

CHAPTER SIXTEEN

CHRISTMAS MORNING. YOU couldn't stay in bed on Christmas morning, even if there weren't presents or family waiting for you. Neve got up early, slipping on a pair of socks and a thick cardigan over her pyjamas, and padded downstairs to the kitchen. Two shots of espresso, with a small spoon of grated chocolate, fluffed milk and nutmeg. That would start the day right.

She sat down at the kitchen table, making herself comfortable, for the first sip of coffee. Closed her eyes and tried to believe that it tasted like heaven when all it really tasted of was pain. Perhaps some carols. She reached for the radio and fiddled with the dial.

A quiet scrape at the front door. She wouldn't have heard it if she hadn't failed to find anything that sounded festive enough on the radio, had set it to retune and was waiting while it searched all available stations. She wouldn't have wandered out into the hall to peer through the letterbox and see what was going on out there.

Her view was obscured by a branch. It didn't look like any of the shrubs in her small front garden and it was unlikely that any of the trees in the lane had blown over. She fiddled with the latch and opened the door.

The first thing she saw was a large Christmas tree,

almost filling the small porch. The next was Joe, sitting in his car, the engine running and ready to go. When he caught sight of her, the look on his face would have done credit to a six-year-old caught feeding the goldfish to next-door's cat.

'I've left you a few things.' He gestured towards the tree. Neve took a step forward and almost fell over a couple of cardboard boxes, which were blocking her exit from the house.

'What? Joe…?'

He waved, in an uncharacteristic show of Christmas jocularity. 'Got to get on. Happy Christmas.' With that, the car window slid upwards and Joe started to drive away slowly.

That must be the way he wanted it. The sudden pain in her chest, the feeling that she couldn't breathe, made her choke.

'Joe!' She didn't stop to think. There was no point, the sudden jolt of sheer emotion made thought impossible. Shoving the boxes out of the way, Neve took the front path at a run. She was in the lane, calling his name, before she even felt the bite of the cold.

The car skidded to a halt. Joe was out of the driver's seat and powering towards her, and all she could feel was happiness.

'What the hell do you think you're doing?' He scooped her up in his arms, striding back towards the house. This was all that mattered. This moment. Everything else could go hang. She was where she wanted to be.

She was beginning to shiver as Joe kicked the front door closed behind him and carried her through to the kitchen. He was bristling with anger and somehow even that was bliss. Dumping her on the sofa, he knelt down in front of her, stripping off her wet socks and glaring at her feet.

'Well? What *did* you think you were doing? Don't you know that you can get frostbite in your toes even after a couple of minutes' exposure?' It appeared that his earlier question hadn't been purely rhetorical.

Shame, because she didn't have an answer, and the feeling that she'd just made a complete idiot of herself was tearing the fleeting happiness she'd felt to shreds.

'I could ask you the same thing. What's the idea of leaving stuff on my doorstep and then just driving away?' Neve snatched her foot away from him, tucking it up under her.

He looked up, his face clouded with doubt. 'I knew you didn't have a tree. I thought you might be pleased.'

'Oh, really. So you think it's okay to sleep with me then walk out on me and then just keep popping up again, offering me lifts, bringing me Christmas trees. It really is too much, Joe.'

'You were the one who called *me* yesterday morning, if I remember correctly.'

'I had an emergency on my hands. What was I supposed to do? And I didn't call you this morning.'

His brow darkened. 'Well, you'll just have to forgive me for caring about you.'

They glared at each other and finally Joe broke eye contact. 'You're right. I shouldn't have done it. You told me that if I left I wasn't to come back and I should have respected your wishes. I'm sorry.'

He picked up his gloves from the floor and got to his feet. She'd done it again. Said her piece and Joe had listened and was doing exactly as she'd told him and walking away. It was time to forget about pride, forget about making a point or being right. It was time to ask for what she wanted, however much it cost her.

Neve stumbled to her feet and took a few unsteady steps, grabbing hold of the kitchen table to support her. 'Joe, please stay a while.'

'I can't.'

'Dammit, Joe. I need you to stay. I'm begging you.'

He turned, the look on his face mirroring Neve's own shock at her outburst. A pulse beat at the side of his brow. 'Neve, you said it yourself. We can both see that this isn't going to work.'

'How can I see anything when you won't talk to me? Just talk to me Joe. Please.'

Talking wasn't going to do any good. It would just rip the wounds open, and change nothing in the process. But he'd already managed to prove that he couldn't stay away from her, even when she'd told him not to come back. Now that she'd begged him to stay, there was no way that he could leave.

'Sit down. Please, Joe.'

He'd never really been able to refuse her anything. Joe dropped his gloves on a chair and took his coat off. 'Here, finish your...' He caught the scent from the mug sitting on the table and recoiled. 'What on earth is that?'

'Chocolate, coffee and nutmeg. With frothed milk.' She sat down on the chair nearest the stove, holding her hands and feet towards its warmth. 'It's nice.'

'I'll take your word for that.' He handed her the concoction and she took a sip. 'What do you want to talk about?'

'I want you to tell me what happened to you, Joe. You

won't practise as a doctor any more, you won't even try to make a commitment to me. I want to know why.'

'And if I tell you that I don't want to talk about it?' Joe knew that it wouldn't change anything.

'I'll say that you've taken my life and turned it upside down. I think I've got a right to know what it is that's keeping you from me.'

'It's best this way...' Joe repeated the words that he'd hung onto for the last week.

'How can I understand that? Don't you respect me enough to at least tell me why? I deserve that, at least, don't I?'

She was honest and brave. At that moment Joe admired her more than anyone he knew. 'Yeah. You deserve that.'

He got up from his seat, walking over to the sink to get himself a glass of water. Something to relieve the parched feeling in his throat. Neve waited, still and silent.

'I was attached to a peacekeeping force, working as a surgeon in a field hospital. We saw all kinds of injuries, and we treated civilians who were caught up in the fighting, as well as our own troops. We'd been working for twenty-four hours straight when a new set of casualties were brought in. There was a local woman among them. She'd been sedated and had shrapnel in her leg.'

Neve nodded. Joe took another sip of water.

'I examined her quickly myself and read the notes. Then I made a decision that I would take another of the casualties into Theatre first. His wounds were potentially life-threatening and the woman seemed stable. I was wrong. She had internal injuries that had been missed on the first examination. She died on my operating table.'

Neve was blinking back tears. 'Joe, that's desperately

sad. But it wasn't your fault, you had to rely on the information that you were given by the other people in your team. We all do.'

'It was my unit. My decision not to take her into surgery immediately. How would you have felt?'

Neve pursed her lips in thought. She had to be honest with him. 'Yes, I guess I would have felt responsible, too. It doesn't mean that you were. Was there any kind of inquiry?'

'I was exonerated of any blame.'

'Then don't you think that's something you should take into account?'

Joe knew just what she was thinking. His own words came back to haunt him, echoing in his head. 'You mean that I should listen to my own words of wisdom—that it can take time for emotions to catch up with facts?'

'It's a thought. I know this is hard, Joe, and I won't for one minute pretend it's not a tragedy, but...well, losing patients does come with the territory.'

'This time it was different.'

'I don't understand...' She broke off suddenly, as if something had just occurred to her. 'What did this have to do with you being injured?'

'A couple of days later I went to see the family. I went alone, which was against regulations but I wanted to explain...somehow. Her father and mother agreed to meet me, and they listened to what I had to say. When I left the house I was surrounded by a crowd of people. Later I was told that the woman's brothers had found out that I was there and had come to demand justice.'

'What...what kind of justice?' Joe saw that Neve's hand was shaking.

'The kind that...' He shrugged. 'There were some

punches thrown and I tried to get back to my vehicle. Some pushing and shoving, and I stumbled. Someone swung a baseball bat and I heard…felt…a crack…'

Her hand flew to her mouth. 'Your leg.'

'Yeah. At first I thought I'd just fallen and that I couldn't get up again…' Joe felt the panic rise in his chest.

'Okay.' Her hands were in his now and he held them tightly. 'It's okay, Joe. I'll help you.'

He hung onto her, trying desperately to regain control. Trying to forget the dark images that had plagued his dreams.

'They must have kicked you to rupture your spleen.' He heard her voice, quiet and soft, bringing him back to the here and now.

'Yeah.'

'And the kidney failure. That was a result of a blow?'

'More than one.'

She nodded. 'The scars around your shoulders look like wounds from a sharp knife that's been used to slash, not stab.' Her hands were shaking almost as much as his were, and they were both hanging onto each other, trying to get through this.

'Yeah. That's right.' He made an attempt at a joke. 'You're pretty good at this. Ever thought about forensics?'

'One day maybe *you'll* tell me everything. From beginning to end.'

He'd wanted to spare her that but she already knew most of it from the scars. One day maybe he would be able to tell it all. That day wasn't going to be soon, and when it came he'd be back in Canada.

'Have you considered that maybe the symptoms of PTSD have fed your guilt over this woman's death? That the two together have caught you in a trap, unable to move on?'

It had taken Joe a while to work that one out, and Neve had thought it through almost immediately. 'Yeah. But it doesn't make any difference, Neve. Whatever the reasons, I still can't make any promises to you. I'm still not someone that you should be involved with.'

Neve had planned everything out so well. Find someone, fall in love. Make a home, have children. It had seemed like a smooth progression, one leading seamlessly on to the next. But that might never happen with Joe, and if she wanted him she was going to have to take the biggest risk of her life.

'Joe, if you don't want me, then you should tell me…'

He tightened his grip on her hands. 'It's never been a matter of not wanting you, Neve.'

'Then I'll tell you what *I* want. I want a family, a career, a nice home. Most of all I want someone to love…'

'It's not me, Neve…' Pain brimmed in his eyes.

'Let me be the judge of that. I want you, Joe. Maybe things won't work out between us. I'm going into this with my eyes open and I can take that risk. What I can't live with is not even giving it a try.'

There. She'd said it. It seemed as if a great weight had been lifted off her shoulders.

'But…all that you went through with your ex-husband. I can't do that again to you, Neve.'

'Let me tell you what I went through with Matthew. I lost touch with who I was, and what I really wanted, because everything was all about what he wanted. I'm not going to let that happen again. This is what *I* want, and whatever you say isn't going to change my mind.'

'Neve…' He was lost for words. Seemed only to be able to say her name. It was like the sweet aftermath of their lovemaking. 'Neve.'

'What do you say? It's not going to be easy.'

'No. I guess it's not.'

She grinned at him. 'It'll be sweet…'

Joe's sudden smile. The one that came out of nowhere and hit you like a cannonball. 'I have absolutely no doubt of that.'

'Then can't we just try?'

He thought for long moments. Neve knew Joe well enough to know that if he said yes he meant it and he'd committed himself. This was going to be hard, for both of them, and he had to think it through.

'I think…if we decide to do it, we should go slowly.'

'Yes. I think we should.' Their first two weeks had been a whirlwind of emotion, neither of them stopping to really think about the consequences of their actions. Maybe that was why it had all fallen apart.

'I mean…' He grinned. 'I'm going to hate myself for saying this but…I think we should just concentrate on sharing some of the practical things at first. If that works then maybe sleeping together might come later…'

'You think you're going to hate yourself? *I* hate you for saying it.' She loved him for saying it. Sex had never been the problem. It was the sharing, the trust, the everyday intimacies they needed to work on.

He chuckled. 'Am I right, though?'

'Yeah. You're right.' Neve leaned towards him. 'I guess for the time being we can pass the time on these long winter nights by talking, eh?'

'There's a lot we still have left to say.' His dark gaze

searched her face. 'Are you really okay with this, Neve? I have to know.'

Joe was nothing if not a gentleman. She liked that about him. Liked that he wanted to wait a little, until they'd both absorbed everything that had happened this morning.

'Yes, I am. As long as I don't have to wait too long.' She gave him her sweetest smile.

He chuckled. 'What have I let myself in for?'

'Well, someone's left a tree on my doorstep. You could get some exercise by carrying it through for me.'

'Can't manage by yourself?' He was teasing now.

'Yes, of course I can. But I've got to go upstairs and get dressed, and I don't want you to get bored while I'm gone. So if you could set it up just there…' She indicated a spot by the sofa, next to the old fireplace.

'Yes, ma'am.' His lips curled into a smile.

CHAPTER SEVENTEEN

JOE ROLLED UP his sleeves and got to work. Today hadn't exactly gone to plan so far, but he felt freer than he had in a long time. As if the world had opened up, and the possibilities that he had refused to acknowledge were… just that. Possibilities. Untested, but shining and new, like the fragile Christmas ornaments on a tree.

By the time Neve reappeared, pink and glowing from the shower and sporting a red sweater with holly motifs in honour of the day, he'd got the tree set up by the hearth and was carefully winding the lights around it, making sure that they were spaced evenly.

'Wow! It's a beautiful tree!'

Joe stood back and admired the thick, green branches. He'd taken a while that morning, tramping across the frozen ground to choose the best tree in the dim morning light, before he'd got to work with the chainsaw. Now that the tree was inside, he was satisfied with his choice.

'Glad you like it.'

'How did you know I didn't have one already?' She narrowed her eyes. She'd obviously been working through the practicalities in her head.

'You really want to know?' Of course she did. 'All right, I stopped the car last night and walked back.

Looked through your sitting-room window.' Joe tried to make it sound like something that anyone would do, on any night of the year.

Her hand flew to her mouth. 'You did not! What would you have done if I'd had one in here?'

'I looked through the kitchen window as well.'

'Oh. So you've been sneaking around my house, peering through the windows...' Her blue eyes were teasing him. 'Then you went out this morning and chopped down a tree?'

'I called Frank Somersby last night and asked if I could have one of the conifers he grows for the Christmas market. Then I went out this morning and chopped it down.'

'And you left it on my doorstep. What was I supposed to think, that Father Christmas had been in the night?'

'I was going to text you.'

She laughed. 'Ah. Well, that's okay, then.' She bent to examine the boxes that he'd brought in from the doorstep. 'Decorations as well. You are so organised.'

'I had them in the cupboard. I was going to get a tree but, to tell you the truth, I didn't feel much like celebrating anything this last week.'

For a moment he thought she was going to kiss him. But instead she straightened, looking around as if something was missing. 'I'll put the kettle on.'

'Yeah? What do we need hot water for?'

She rolled her eyes. 'We have coffee and mince pies while we're decorating. Don't you know anything? Only we'll have to make do with biscuits, I haven't got any mince pies...'

That he could arrange. Joe opened the second box, and reached inside. 'Here.'

It was only a packet of shop-bought mince pies, but she received them as if they were the crown jewels.

'You think of everything! I'll put them into the oven for ten minutes to warm.' She bustled over to the stove and started to arrange the mince pies on a baking tray. 'Don't just stand there. Start laying the decorations out...'

Their first tree together. And the faint possibility of a repetition next year, sparkling insistently in his future. Suddenly it was all that Joe wanted, and getting this right was all-important. 'Okay, and then?'

'We start with the largest baubles, and work our way down to the smaller ones.'

'There's a procedure, then.' Joe had reckoned on just hanging them all on the tree, in whichever order they presented themselves.

'Of course there is. So don't just stand there...'

Decorating the tree had always been one of those enjoyable Christmas traditions that Joe's parents had demanded he and his four brothers attend. But it had never been delightful. Magical. Full of joy, with a final burst of euphoria, as Joe lifted Neve up to place the sparkling, golden star at the top of the tree.

'It's beautiful!' He'd been loath to let her go, and when he set her back down again Joe had absent-mindedly left his arm wrapped around her waist.

He nodded with approval. 'Not so bad.'

Her elbow found his ribs. 'Not so bad? It's wonderful. Now the lights...'

He was torn between keeping her close and seeing her face when he switched the lights on. But she was practically running on the spot with excitement, and this was everything he'd wanted for her this Christmas. Joe plugged in the lights and flipped the switch, and she did a little dance of pleasure, clapping her hands with glee.

'It's beautiful. Isn't it beautiful?'

He was all done with understatement. 'Yeah. Beautiful.' Joe wondered if she knew that the observation was intended to describe her, as well as the tree.

She hugged him, her face tipped up towards his. Unbearably beautiful. 'Thank you so much, Joe.'

He couldn't think of anything in this world that he needed to do right now other than kiss her. There was nothing else…

The clock on the mantelpiece chimed. Ten o'clock.

'Maisie will be calling soon.' He broke free, and walked over to the table, stacking the empty cartons back into the box.

'Yes, I suppose… How did you know?'

He knew, because he'd called Maisie and let her know that Neve hadn't gone down to London as expected. He'd planned today like a military operation—the surprise left on her doorstep, the friends who would invite her to lunch. The one thing he hadn't planned on was being a part of all that.

'I…um…spoke to Maisie yesterday.'

She stared at him. Keeping anything from those canny blue eyes was nigh on impossible. 'Then you're coming too.'

'Maisie mentioned it. I wasn't going to but…' Things were different, now. 'Yeah, I'm coming too. I'll have to pop back home to feed Almond afterwards, though.'

She nodded. 'We can go to your place before we go. Pick Almond up and bring her here with some food and her basket. She'll be fine. The stove keeps the kitchen warm.'

One more step. One more thing that twined their lives

together. 'So you're holding my cat hostage, are you? To make sure I'll come back here after lunch.'

She grinned. 'Yeah. Pay up or the cat gets it.'

'Get's what?'

'Don't you know an empty threat when you hear it?'

Joe shook his head. She was delightful, irrepressible, and more joyful than he'd ever seen her. He could deny her nothing.

'You have a problem with that?' Her eyes were questioning.

'No. No problem.'

It was dark by the time Joe drew up in front of Neve's house. They'd had a great time at Maisie's. There had been sixteen around her table, and although it had been a little crowded the good cheer had made a virtue of that. Joe had seemed more relaxed than Neve had ever seen him.

Almond raised her head sleepily when Neve opened the kitchen door, and padded up to Joe, nuzzling at his legs until he picked her up and stroked her. Glancing at the baubles from the lower limbs of the tree, which were now scattered across the floor, he grinned. 'What have you been up to, then? You're in big trouble...'

Almond looked up at him and gave a meow, almost as if she was answering the question.

'Okay. So if you didn't do it, who did?' Joe raised one eyebrow and Almond ignored him, settling onto his chest and starting to purr.

'Hey! She said she didn't do it.' Neve grinned at him.

'Oh, so you're on her side, are you?' Joe set Almond back on her feet and went to gather up the baubles from the floor. Almond trotted after him, trying to bat the sparkling playthings out of his reach.

Neve couldn't help but laugh. Joe didn't compromise for anyone, but the tiny creature had him wound around her little finger. Neve picked up the empty food bowl and tore open one of the packets of cat food that lay on the counter.

Almond galloped across the room as if she hadn't been fed in months, nuzzling at Neve's legs and purring. Joe straightened up from replacing the decorations on the tree and chuckled. 'That's right. Show a guy where your heart really lies.'

Today had been such a lovely day. The thought that he might still take Almond and go home tonight was… unthinkable. 'Would you like something to eat?'

He grinned, throwing himself down on the sofa. So far so good. 'Food is the one thing I don't want right now. I don't think I'll be eating again for another week.'

Neve flipped open one of the kitchen cupboards and retrieved the emergency brandy from behind the biscuit tin. Collected a couple of glasses and walked over to the sofa, sitting down next to him.

'You can have a drink, though?'

He'd waved away offers of wine with his lunch and passed on the after-dinner port because he was driving. Perhaps he could be persuaded not to do any more driving today. Diffidently, Neve held out one of the glasses.

'I really shouldn't.'

'Joe, I know we said we were going to take this slowly. And I appreciate that, I really do. But there's nothing to say we can't take it slowly together, is there? I want you to stay here, and the sofa bed's comfortable enough…'

Maybe she'd gone too far. Maybe she was going to spoil everything. She shrank back from him.

'Hey…hey, don't do that.' He reached out for her, catching her hand. 'We said we'd be honest with each other, and that means asking for what we want. I thought you might want me to go, to give you a little time to think things over, that's all… I guess I should stop trying to second-guess you, eh?'

'Shall we try that one again?'

'Yeah, I think so.'

Neve sat down next to him. 'I'd like you to stay tonight. We could think things over together.'

He grinned. 'I'd like that, too.'

'So…' She proffered the glass again. 'Would you like a brandy?'

'Love one.'

She and Joe had talked until well past midnight, curled up on the sofa together. Stories about his time in the army, about her training down in London. His childhood in Canada, the trips up to the cabin in the north, when his grandfather had taught Joe and his brothers how to fish and his grandmother had told them the Inupiat stories that every boy should take careful note of before he reached manhood.

Finally, Joe brushed a kiss on her forehead, tipping her gently out of his arms. 'We really should get some sleep. It's been a long day.'

'Can't I hold you? Just a little longer.'

He grinned. 'Yeah. As long as you like.'

Downstairs, with the smell of the Christmas tree and the sparkling lights, seemed the right place. Joe pulled the sofa bed open and Neve fetched a duvet and some blankets to keep them warm. She went upstairs to change into her pyjamas, and found Joe under the duvet when she returned.

'Right here.' He patted the space next to him, and she lay down.

'Comfortable?'

'Yes.' She was lying on her back, staring at the ceiling. This wasn't quite what she'd had in mind.

'Hmm.' Joe seemed to be engaged in a complex rearrangement of the bedclothes. Blankets were pulled this way and the duvet pushed that. Then he gently rolled her onto her side, wrapping the duvet around her and pulling her into a soft layer of down between his body and hers. One arm wound around her waist, held her tight and firm against the shapeless, reassuring bulk of his body. 'Is that okay?'

'That's nice.' She stared into the darkness for a moment. 'The lease on your cottage. You said you'd given it up.'

'I'll call the agent when the office reopens and say that I've changed my mind. I doubt that they'll have re-let it at this time of the year.'

'I...don't want...'

'Are you going to chicken out on me now? I was going to go because of you. And now I'm staying for you. I can't promise to stay for good, but I will promise to see this through.' She felt his chest rise and fall. 'Canada will wait for me. Maybe I'll get to show it to you one day.'

'Maybe you will. I think I'd like that.'

'Yeah. I'd like it too.' His hand found hers and held it loosely. 'It's late. Want a bedtime story?'

'One of your gran's?' Neve doubted whether she'd be able to sleep like this, but she didn't want to move.

'Of course. The one about the boy who went fishing…'

The story turned out to be a long one, and Neve never did get to hear the moral of the tale. Before he'd finished she was fast asleep.

CHAPTER EIGHTEEN

'OH, NO!' THE SOFA bed rocked alarmingly, propelling Neve into grudging wakefulness. A startled yowl as Almond decided that getting out of the way was probably the best course of action, and Joe's running footsteps.

'What?' Neve pulled the duvet over her head. If the house was on fire, perhaps he'd put it out without any need for intervention on her part.

'We're late.'

'What for?' She opened one eye. Joe had his back to her and was pulling on his jeans. 'It's Boxing Day. What's so important?'

He turned. Three-sixty-degree view. Nice.

'It's the Boxing Day soccer match. Starts at eleven.'

'It's a Boxing Day *football* match. And it's only nine o'clock.'

'We need to be there early to help clear the snow off the pitch. And I've got to get back home to pick up my kit then back here to pick you up.'

'You're playing?'

He gave her a broad grin. Neve would walk a hundred miles in the snow for that grin. In her pyjamas. 'You want to be my girl? Then you've got to watch

me play soccer.' He bent to grab his boots. 'I'll be back
to get you in half an hour.'

It turned out that hard work in the freezing air was
just what she needed and the traditional Leminster vs
Cryersbridge Boxing Day football match afforded plenty
of both. Muffled in coats and scarves, the whole community turned up at the local school, which had opened
its changing rooms for the occasion, and was helping
clear the snow from the pitch that the tractor had missed.

Joe disappeared with the rest of the team to get
changed. The local Guides were out, doing a roaring
trade in hot drinks, and the teams decided that taking off
their sweatpants and shirts would be a little beyond the
call of duty. With their team shirts covered up, it wasn't
too easy to tell who was on which side, but everyone
seemed disposed to cheer both sides anyway, just for
turning out in the sub-zero temperatures.

'I still reckon you could have taken that shot...' Both
teams and most of the spectators had made a beeline for
The Bleeding Hart, which had opened its doors in honour
of the occasion, as soon as the final whistle had sounded.

'Everyone's an expert.' Joe grinned down at her.

'Just taking an interest. And that goal was yours for
the taking.'

He shrugged amiably. 'Adrian was in a better position.'

And Joe was the stronger player. Adrian was only
sixteen and the youngest member of the team. No one
had expected him to score and when he had, he'd run the
whole length of the pitch, arms outstretched in an impromptu victory dance, while everyone on the touchline
had cheered. Neve supposed that that was what Joe had
intended all along.

'You took a bit of a tumble in the first half. Are you all right?'

'Yeah, fine.' He displayed a length of sticking plaster wrapped around his wrist. 'I think our beloved team coach overdid the strapping a bit. It's just a graze.'

'Did he clean it?'

Joe rolled his eyes. 'No, we thought we'd see whether we could set up a culture so we left all the dirt in there.'

'Right. Just as long as I know.' Neve caught hold of the front of his jacket, looking up into his face. 'Not going to add to your collection of scars, is it?'

His arm around her waist, he pulled her close. 'If it does, I'll have something to remember you by.'

'Me? It wasn't me who tackled you.'

'Yours was the face that flashed in front of my eyes when I hit the ground.' His lips were about an inch from her ear.

'You didn't go down that hard. And if you were hallucinating, you should have come off the pitch.' She was tingling with pleasure. Joe seemed so... He wasn't different. Just more the man he ought to be.

It looked as if the party wasn't going to break up any time soon. But Joe downed a half-pint of beer with astonishing alacrity, was slapped on the back by his teammates and stopped to congratulate Adrian on the winning goal. Then he was back at her side.

'Ready to go?'

Neve had reckoned on being here a while and had been pacing herself, sipping her orange juice slowly. She downed the remainder of the glass in one go. 'Yes. I'm ready.'

He grinned. 'Let's go, then.'

Outside, in the car park, she caught his hand. 'Do you think you could…?'

'What?'

'I want you to kiss me.'

One look at his face told Neve that was exactly what he wanted too. Winding his arms around her waist, he brushed a gentle kiss against her lips.

'Not like that, you idiot.'

'Like this?' His kiss was warm and giving. Crushing her against him, he almost lifted her off her feet.

'Much better.' Neve looked around as a wolf-whistle sounded behind her. One of the Leminster team waved at them cheerily and disappeared through the doors of the pub.

'How long do you think it'll be before Maisie hears about this?' His grin was intoxicating.

'I reckon…' Neve checked her watch '…about six o'clock. It's got a fair way to go.'

'You did this on purpose, didn't you?'

'Do you mind?'

'Mind?' He dropped another kiss onto her lips. 'I was thinking about taking you back inside and doing this all over again. That way everyone'll notice.'

'Nah. Once is enough to start the rumour. You can take me home and do it again.'

Joe attacked the snow-filled roads with unusual recklessness, even spinning the wheels once or twice. No need to ask what all the hurry was about.

They shed their coats on the way to the kitchen. When they got there, Joe lifted her up onto the table, pulling her boots off. Then, suddenly, he straightened up. 'We said that we'd wait yesterday…'

'A lot can happen in a day.'

'Yes, but…' He was looking at her intently. 'I won't rush you into anything, Neve. This is much too important to me.'

She put her finger over his lips. 'I know what I want, Joe. Just promise me that you won't lie to me. Not about anything.'

'You already have that promise. I'll make it again…'

No need. She pulled him towards her, kissing him, revelling in the softness of his lips. 'I don't want to wait any longer, Joe.'

'Good.' He hugged her tight. 'Because you've been driving me crazy…'

'How crazy?'

He chuckled. 'That's going to take some time to answer.'

By the time they made it to the bedroom she'd already stripped off his sweater and shirt, his skin warm against her cheek as he carried her up the stairs. He laid her on the bed and she pulled him down next to her.

His dark gaze found hers. 'There's something I want to ask you.'

'Anything you want, Joe…'

He shook his head. 'Don't say that until you've heard what it is. You might not like it.'

'Then I'll say so. That's the whole point of trust, isn't it?'

He nodded, kissing her. 'Don't take this the wrong way, Neve, but I want to be the one that you rely on and who cares for you. I don't want to tell you what to think or what to do but…'

She put her finger to his lips, silencing him. 'I know. I want that too.'

That sudden grin of his. He didn't need to break

through the barriers she'd shielded herself with, Joe's smile made her want to rip them down herself with her bare hands.

Slowly. Slowly. He stripped her naked then pulled off his own jeans. They traded caresses, taking their time over each one. Each touch of his fingers on her skin felt like a bright, new beginning.

'Look at me, Neve.'

The unbearable intimacy of looking straight into his eyes while he made love to her. Knowing that he was watching her, too. Joe rolled her onto her back, settling his hips between her legs. Slid slowly inside her, his gaze never leaving hers.

'I see you, Joe.'

'And I see you. Can you do this?' The connection between them was almost tangible. Frightening in its intensity.

'Yes.'

He took her hand in his, guiding her arm up over her head, and wrapping her fingers around one of the brass rails of the bedstead. Then the other. The feeling of being stretched out beneath him was glorious, and Neve hung on tight as he started to move.

She could see her own pleasure reflected in his face. He was reading her like a book, finding infinite variations of each caress, long and slow, or hard and demanding. Breaking her in his embrace. Making her strong.

They came together. By this time one powerful movement from him was all it took to plunge them both into a release that should have blocked out everything else. But he was there still, with her. Joe. From this moment on, it would only be Joe.

* * *

She was clinging to him. All he wanted to do was to please her, keep her safe. Keep her here, with him. Suddenly *safe* and *with him* didn't seem like so much of a contradiction in terms.

'Okay, honey?' He smoothed a strand of golden hair from her forehead.

'Joe…' Her fingers were digging uncomfortably into the flesh of his arms but he didn't care. Just wanted her to hang on tight to him. 'What did you do?'

She was there with him, in that warm, after-sex place where there was no thought. No consideration of what you were going to say before you opened your mouth. No tact and no caution, just the unvarnished, beautiful truth.

'I…' What the hell *had* he done? The unthinkable was jangling insistently in his head, demanding to be heard. 'I just loved you, sweetheart.'

It was more than that, and they both knew it. She'd given herself up to him. He wondered if, now that the moment had passed, she'd try to deny it.

'Hmm. You're a thief, Joe Lamont. You've stolen my heart.'

'Thieves don't generally give you their own in return.' He rolled her over, pulling her with him, letting her sprawl across his chest. Soft, pale skin with a delicious flush of pink. He ran his fingers slowly down her spine, counting each vertebral disc.

'Same number as yours.' She snuggled against him. Joe could get seriously used to this.

'Just checking.'

She chuckled, her lips forming a little air-kiss, as if she wasn't quite done with kissing yet, but his lips were too far away. 'You can do a thorough inventory. In a while.' She stretched across his chest.

'Take as long as you like.' If she thought that she was going to get out of this bed any time soon, she was wrong. He knew now that he had the power to keep her here, and he was shamelessly unafraid to use it.

She grinned. Reached lazily for his hand and pulled it to her lips. 'You have great hands. You know that?'

They were her faithful, dedicated servants, ready to do whatever she wanted. 'I love you, Neve.'

She raised her head, focussing on his face. 'You do?'

'Afraid so.' He wondered whether she'd say it back. Whether he deserved her love. And then she said it, and his heart practically burst from his chest.

'I love you too, Joe.'

CHAPTER NINETEEN

THE LAST FIVE MONTHS had been…pretty much every emotion that Neve could imagine. It had taken time, some professional help and a lot of love before Joe had been able to tell her everything, and when he had the nightmares had returned with a vengeance. But he'd stuck with it, showing a stubborn courage that wrung her heart. She'd shared those dark nights with him and as he'd healed his passion for medicine had returned.

He told her that he loved her every day. Proved it, with a constancy that was impossible to doubt. Neve had feared repeating the patterns of the past with Joe, but he had shown her a different future.

Now it was time to celebrate. Joe had completed his six-week clinical attachment at the hospital with flying colours and was now eligible to apply for a job in the NHS. His parents and youngest brother had flown over from Canada for a holiday, and Joe and Neve were spending a week with them in London. There would be seven for dinner tonight, as Neve's parents were joining them.

'You look stunning.' Joe had booked them into a nice hotel as a treat, and was lounging in an easy chair, watching her get dressed.

'You like my dress?' Neve twirled around to give him the full effect.

'The dress is great. *You* are stunning.'

Joe had a way with a compliment. She walked across to him, standing between his outstretched legs. 'So I wasted all that time I spent choosing it?'

'No. If you hadn't spent all morning on it, I'd be inclined to rip it off your back and make love to you.' He grinned. 'Again.'

'But you know that if you tore one stitch of this, you'd been in deep trouble.'

'Exactly. So we'll be on time for dinner.'

Neve chuckled, perching herself on his knee. 'Well, you're looking particularly handsome tonight, too.' He was wearing a crisp white shirt, still open at the neck, and dark trousers. The matching jacket was slung over the back of the chair.

'Thank you. I have a particular reason...'

'What, because of the parents? My mum and dad think you're wonderful already, and your parents don't seem all that stuck on formality.' Neve had only met Joe's parents the day before, but she felt she already knew them well from long conversations via the internet.

'No. There's something else. Two things, in fact. The first is that I have a job.'

'Another one? What is it this time?' Joe seemed to be in constant demand, helping with various projects in the village. On a couple of occasions Neve had worried that he'd taken on too much, but Joe always would thrive on a challenge.

'Guess.' His eyes were gleaming with suppressed excitement.

'I can see it's something a bit special.'

'Yes. Something very special…'

'Something…' Neve hardly dared to ask. She knew how much this meant to Joe. 'Something to do with medicine?'

'You're getting warm.'

'At the hospital?'

'Warmer.'

'Ow! Tell me, Joe, I can't bear it.'

'When I was doing my clinical attachment, a post in surgery came up. It's pretty senior, but I asked if I could apply anyway, and they said they'd welcome it. I got an email with a formal offer this afternoon.'

'Joe!' Neve leaned forward and kissed him. 'Why didn't you say something?'

'Because I wanted this moment.'

She dug her fingers into his ribs. 'I'm going to get you back for this, Joe Lamont. You wait and see, I'm going to find something to surprise *you* with and make you as happy as I am right now…'

'You surprise me every day, honey.' He kissed her and she melted into his arms. 'Do you think your father will be pleased?'

'I expect so. What's he got to do with it?'

'I wouldn't want him to think that his daughter's associating with a guy with no prospects…'

'He doesn't. He's a very good judge of character.'

'Good. Because I told you there were *two* things…' He shifted her gently off his knee and got to his feet. 'Come here.'

Joe took her hand and led her over to the high French windows, which opened onto a stone balcony. Below them were the gardens at the back of the hotel, where they'd taken tea that afternoon.

'What are you doing? You've got an air of mystery about you.'

'Really?'

Neve slid her arms around his waist. 'Don't give me that innocent look. Now I know there's something going on.'

'Yeah, okay. There's something going on.'

He reached behind him, unclasping her fingers, and suddenly he dropped to one knee. Neve's hand flew to her mouth. It couldn't be… 'Joe. What is this?'

'Marry me.'

A tear ran down her cheek and she brushed it away. It was typical of Joe, no long speeches or declarations. Everything else had already been talked about, they knew each other's dreams, and these two words sealed his promise to fulfil them.

'Yes.'

'I'll be a good husband and a good father.'

'I know.'

'I'll love you always…'

'Yes! Do you hear me?'

He grinned, and her poor heart flipped another somersault. If he kept going like this, she was going to die of happiness. 'Yeah, I heard you. Just wanted you to say it again.'

'Yes.' She bent down and kissed him. 'Yes. I'll cook your dinner…'

'I'd prefer it if we took turns.'

'Wash your clothes…'

'We have a washing machine.'

'Warm your bed…'

'Yeah. That I'm going to insist on.'

'Make babies with you.'

'Now you're talking. Give me your hand.' He rolled his eyes. 'No, not that one.' He reached for her left hand.

'You've got a ring?' Neve could have jumped for joy. Would have done if she hadn't been wearing such high heels.

'I've got a ring.' He felt in his pocket and something sparkled in his hand. 'Now, it was far too good the first time not to repeat. Let's take it from the top. Will you marry me?'

'Yes, Joe. I want to tell you *yes* for every day of my life. Starting now.'

He bent to kiss her hand then slipped the ring onto her finger. Neve stared at it.

'Say something…' A note of uncertainty sounded in his voice.

'I love it. I love you. I'm so happy…' She pulled him to his feet and kissed him.

'Me too. You're everything to me, Neve.'

A loud swoosh from below, and then a bang, and the sky was suddenly full of coloured stars.

'Must be a celebration.' Her gaze didn't leave his face.

'Yeah. My kid brother's down there with a couple of the hotel staff.'

Another two rockets shot up into the air, exploding into the night sky.

'He knew about this?'

Joe kissed her again. Long and loving and warm. 'All I told him was that he was to set off the rockets when he saw me kiss you.'

All she could see was Joe. All she knew was his kiss. 'Seems like he's missed his cue. The only fireworks I can see are up here.'

Joe chuckled. 'Perhaps we should give him a break

and just keep going until he gets it right.' He kissed her again. Stars exploded into the sky, and the world lurched under her feet.

Neve wrapped her arms around his neck. 'Yes. Let's just keep going…'

* * * * *

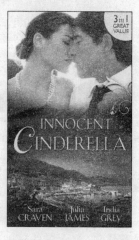